Praise for
EMPRESS OF A THOUSAND SKIES

"*Empress of a Thousand Skies* is packed full of star wars, betrayal, royal intrigue…" —*USA TODAY*

"Fans of Marissa Meyer's Lunar Chronicles and especially readers of Lewis' *Stitching Snow* will find much to like in this thrilling yet thoughtful intergalactic ride." —*BCCB*

"Belleza's ambitious debut lays the groundwork for what is sure to be a rich sci-fi series full of political plots and worlds on the brink of war, futuristic biotechnologies reminiscent of M. T. Anderson's *Feed* (2002), and startling plot twists." —*BOOKLIST*

"*Empress of a Thousand Skies* will compel fans of series such as Marissa Meyer's *The Lunar Chronicles*; Victoria Aveyard's *The Red Queen*; Beth Revis's *Across the Universe*; and George Lucas's *Star Wars*. Belleza's exciting novel debut will make readers desperate for the next book to complete this duology." —*VOYA*

"An epic space opera with all the elements of an addictive read— danger, deception, unlikely allies, and the fate of worlds hanging in the balance. A stunning debut." —*KAMI GARCIA*, #1 *New York Times* bestselling coauthor of *BEAUTIFUL CREATURES* and author of *THE LOVELY RECKLESS*

"This book glitters like stars. With a heart-pounding plot, twisty secrets, and characters you can't help but root for, *Empress of a Thousand Skies* had me turning pages well into the night!" —*BETH REVIS*, *New York Times* bestselling author of the *ACROSS THE UNIVERSE* series

"Belleza's debut is dazzling—an adventure as sweeping in scope as the galaxies it spans!" —*KIERSTEN WHITE*, *New York Times* bestselling author of *AND I DARKEN*

EMPRESS

OF A

THOUSAND

SKIES

EMPRESS

OF A

THOUSAND

SKIES

RHODA BELLEZA

RAZORBILL

An Imprint of Penguin Random House

RAZORBILL®

An Imprint of Penguin Random House LLC
Penguin.com

RAZORBILL & colophon is a registered trademark of Penguin Random House LLC.

First published in the United States of America by Razorbill, an imprint of Penguin Random House LLC, 2017

LIBRARY OF CONGRESS CATALOGING-IN-PUBLICATION DATA:

Belleza, Rhoda, author.
Empress of a Thousand Skies / Rhoda Belleza.
Summary: Two fugitives, a princess-in-exile and her accused killer, cross the galaxy as they fight to reclaim her family dynasty and save the universe from a deadly threat.
LCCN 2016053016 | ISBN 9781101999103 (hardcover)
CYAC: Science fiction.
LCC PZ7.1.B4524 Em 2017 | DDC [Fic]—dc23 2016053016

ISBN: 9781101999110

Printed in the United States of America

1 3 5 7 9 10 8 6 4 2

Interior design by Eric Ford

For Ate.

Everything I've achieved
is because you believed I could.

Desuco Quadrant

Nau Fruma

KALU

HOUL

Rhesto

Tinoppa

NAIDOZ

Navrum

CHRAM

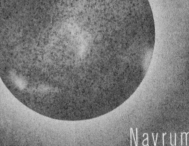

Erawae

DERKATZ

PORTIIS

Heryl Quadrant

RELLIA QUADRANT

DEMBOS

WRAETA

FONTIS

BAZORL QUADRANT

MAJOR CHARACTERS

KALUSIAN

Rhiannon Ta'an: Crown Princess, sole surviving heir to the ruling Ta'an dynasty

Vincent Limam: UniForce soldier, DroneVision star of *The Revolutionary Boys*

Andrés Seotra: Former adviser to the late Emperor Ta'an and current Crown Regent

Tai Simone Reyanna: Governess to Crown Princess Rhiannon

Nero Cimna: Kalusian ambassador to the Crown Regent's office

WRAETAN

Alyosha Myraz: UniForce soldier, DroneVision star of *The Revolutionary Boys*

UNKNOWN

The Fisherman: Outlaw in the galaxy's Outer Belt

PLANETS

KALU: Most populated planet in the galaxy and ancestral home of the ruling Ta'an dynasty

KALUSIAN TERRITORIES

Navrum: Terraformed asteroid

Rhesto: Larger moon of Kalu, the site of a nuclear plant before the Great War

Tinoppa: Tiny asteroid equidistant from Kalu and Nau Fruma, home to the sacred crystals

Chram: Dwarf planet allied to Kalu

FONTIS: Largest planet in the galaxy

FONTISIAN TERRITORIES

Wraeta: Decimated planet, destroyed by a Kalusian attack ten years ago during the Great War

NEUTRAL TERRITORIES

Nau Fruma: Smaller moon of Kalu

Portiis: Outlying planet

Erawae: Domed city on an asteroid in the Bazorl Quadrant

Part One:

THE BETRAYED

"After a series of tragedies befell them, it was believed that the Ta'an family was cursed. This made the sole survivor of that legacy, the young Princess Rhiannon, even more precious in the eyes of the public. When a reporter dubbed her 'the Rose of the Galaxy,' the moniker stuck. She was seen as something delicate, a thing to be preserved and protected until she came of age to rule. But Rhiannon had other plans."

—*Excerpt from* **The Iron Star: A History of the Ta'an Dynasty**

ONE

RHIANNON

RHEE tore a path through the bustling marketplace, kicking up dust that fell slowly in Nau Fruma's low gravity. The foreign tourists coughed and complained as she passed, but Rhee ignored them, scanning the fairgrounds for Julian as she clutched his miniature telescope to her chest. She wasn't accustomed to being *in* a crowd; so much of her life had been spent looking down at one from a balcony, urged to wave and smile and look as ladylike as possible. But now, among the people, there was a jostle and roughness to it that Rhee found thrilling.

It was the golden hour, and the sun dipped just below the horizon. Risking a quick glance behind her, Rhee spotted one of the Tasinn plowing through the ebb and flow of bodies, headed in her direction. His khaki fitted uniform and polished badges stood out amid the sea of vibrant linen robes. His skin was ashen and pale, unlike the men who'd grown up on this desert moon and knew the heat of the sun by its true distance—not through the refracted beams and domed cities on Kalu. From here she could see that his hand hovered above the stunner strapped to his belt.

The Tasinn were the royal guard—*her* royal guards, technically, but they felt like a relic of her father's era, wholly separate from the life she'd led here on Nau Fruma. They were an elite group of fighters plucked from the ranks of UniForce soldiers and trained in personal security. This guard was one of many men sent to find her so she could return home to Kalu, to the planet of her birth.

Rhee had been six when she left, just after her entire family had died in a crash—"an accident," the authorities called it, a tragedy Rhee had supposedly been lucky to avoid. But she knew better. There were two things for certain: that her family had been murdered, and that she was supposed to have died at their side.

A homemade firework screeched into the darkening sky, its high-pitched fury petering out into a low whistle. It exploded in the distance. She wondered if her family's ending had been that instantaneous and merciful.

Rhee slipped the telescope in her pocket and pulled her hood lower to hide her mismatched eyes, one brown and one hazel. She tucked back her jet-black braid and cut left between two rows of tents, squeezing past two laughing men. Dodging a tall woman carrying a cage, she flinched when the white bird inside flapped its wings—then felt silly.

"Stay at the ready," Veyron had always said as he'd held up two calloused hands for her to box and kick. She'd cycle through combos until all she could hear was her heartbeat drumming in her ears. In the dojo she wasn't a girl or a princess. She was simply a series of intentions: dodge, strike, block, kill.

Kill.

Now her stomach felt twisted, like the cactus trunks she and Julian would find when they snuck past the palace walls. The smell of smoke and charred meat from a nearby market stall nearly made her gag. A Derkatzian girl with yellow eyes sat perched on a stool, fanning herself with one hand and holding out a root vegetable with the other. "Grown from real soil," she called to those who passed.

Everyone was out: travelers and dealers from the fringes of the universe, local families, wealthy tourists. Tonight marked the eve of the Kamreial meteor shower, which came every 149 years. "Once in a lifetime," the holos had said. "Never to be seen again."

Which was precisely why the Crown Regent had arranged this night for Rhiannon to travel back to the capital of Sibu. The beloved Rose of the Galaxy, returning to Kalu in a shower of stars. It was all image and spin: a big fat lie wrapped up in a pretty bow. There was no love lost between Rhee and the Regent Seotra, who'd taken control of the throne until Rhee came of age. He'd been her father's childhood friend, and a decorated war hero before he'd entered politics to become one of the Emperor's closest advisers.

Until Regent Seotra had betrayed her family.

The Ta'an was an old bloodline. The throne had been in her family for twelve generations, and you could trace the Ta'an back nearly three centuries. They were among the first settlers in the east. The dark soil of Kalu was part of Rhee's skin, the ocean in her veins, the roots of the trees her own. She'd spent weeks replaying her memories of her childhood in the capital, so that when she finally returned, it would feel like home.

Seotra had rallied the support to send Rhee to Nau Fruma in the first place. "For her safety," he'd claimed. And while it was a politically neutral moon according to the Urnew Treaty, it also kept Rhee as far as possible from her true birthright—the throne. It was a power move to remain Crown Regent and block her ascension to power. Seotra was worried.

As he should be. Rhee would see to it that he pay for what he'd done to her family. She'd trained for years for the very moment when she would end his reign, and his life.

She only wished she could kill him more than once.

"Honor, bravery, loyalty," she whispered.

Rhee looked back toward the palace where she had spent most of her childhood. It was high up on the hill, just a short distance from the town, though it felt like a world away—a prison meant to keep her from the real world, and her destiny. It had once been the second home of her family. To the east of it she could just make out the throat of an old volcano, isolated, rising up from the flat desert plains around it. *Crown's Rock*. Tai Reyanna, Rhee's longtime governess, had remarked on how fitting it was for Rhee to be so close to a crown.

"Eweg nich!" boomed a deep voice, and she was nearly knocked off her feet by a Modrussel. Its tentacle left a sticky residue on her clothing. Looking over her shoulder, she could only make out antennae protruding from a high-collared outfit, its

clothes soaked with a slimelike secretion—as their temperatures ran high, Modrussels were known to sweat profusely.

She hurried on. A message came through her cube just as she reached the square, and Tai Reyanna's call sign flashed across her vision. Rhee's blood leapt.

The Tai was a sect of teachers and caretakers, and Simone Reyanna was a Tai of the highest order. She served the royal family and had been Rhee's exclusive governess ever since her family died. Rhee wasn't used to ignoring her calls. But she wasn't used to running off in the first place.

Rhee knew what she had to do. Sucking in a deep breath, she brought her finger to the spot behind her right ear and pressed to power down. Immediately she felt dizzy, disoriented, like something essential had drained out of her. It was the security of being online, the comfort of never getting lost, the knowledge that every thought and experience would be recorded to play again and again.

But it was freeing too. Nothing would be recorded, and nothing could be accessed either. At least not the specific memories she'd programmed to recall immediately and in full, memories that seemed to absorb her. With her cube down, the chatter of the crowd instantly shifted from her native Kalusian language to different dialects from across the solar system. She forgot that her translator had been connected to her cube, and now the foreign words, tongue clicks, whistles, and beeps shattered the air around her. Her great-ancestors had managed without cubes, and Rhee wondered how they could have possibly learned so many languages just by studying.

"They're auctioning off droids too. Decommissioned models . . ." a boy ahead of her said. His Nauie caught her ear, a local accent with a singsong cadence.

Julian. He turned around even as she picked him out of the crowd. His blue eyes widened. They'd been the same height for as long as they'd known each other, until he shot up a couple of years ago. She had to look up into his eyes now, which annoyed her to no end—it was a competition she would never win.

"Shhhh!" she insisted just before he called out her name. "You have to power down your cube. Quickly," she added, when it seemed like he might argue.

"You're being paranoid," he said. It was supposedly impossible to hack into someone's cube, but there were rumors that Seotra and his lackeys monitored the citizens this way, by invading their memories and observations through their cubes, and Rhee couldn't risk it. "Besides, my mom told me if you do it too much you'll go mad."

So they said. Most people went their whole lives without going offline, but there were entire communities—hundreds of thousands of people in the Outer Belt—that hadn't had native cubes installed. And what were a few minutes here and there offline? Rhee wouldn't say she *liked* the feeling, but she liked the discomfort of it. With every minute she managed to endure, she felt stronger.

"Just do it," Rhee said.

"I hate the way it feels . . ." But Julian put his finger to his neck and made a face like he'd been pricked with a giant needle, and Rhee relaxed. "And what are you even *doing* here?"

"Well, *ma'tan sarili* to you too," she said, muttering the Kalusian greeting under her breath. Had she wanted him to be pleased? Rhee wasn't sure.

She shoved her hand deep into her pocket and felt the cool telescope in her palm. It belonged to Julian—it always would. They'd known each other ever since Andrés Seotra had banished her—or *practically* banished her—to Nau Fruma nine years ago when he became regent. "My flight's been delayed," she added. It wasn't exactly a lie, since the craft wouldn't leave without her.

He glanced behind him at the boys he'd been speaking to, then turned away from them again, nudging her farther into the crowd. There was a layer of dust on his skin and matting his dark blond hair. Veyron, his father, was part Wraetan—but Julian looked Nauie through and through; his great-great-grandfather on his mother's side was one of the original settlers on Nau Fruma.

"You know the *Eliedio* is one of the safest crafts out there," he said, reaching for his cube out of habit. "There's only a two percent malfunction rate, and there's never been any kind of accident that—"

"That's not why I left," she said, grabbing his hand so he wouldn't power up. She dropped it quickly. Ever since their last spar, it felt strange when they touched. "I'm not scared, if that's what you think."

"Okay." He tilted his head and squinted, a thing she'd seen him do a million times before. Rhee stiffened at the way he sized her up, the way he seemed so certain he was right. "I just thought, because of what happened to your family . . ."

"Come on," she said, grabbing a handful of fabric at the edge of his sleeve. "The Tasinn are looking for me." Rhee led the way as they threaded through another row of vendors, glad that Julian couldn't see her face. She didn't want to talk about her family. Instead she quickly described how she'd slipped away, evaded a Tasinn, and ignored her Tai's call.

She gripped Julian's shirt like it was a lifeline. He was her best friend—her only friend, really—and he was the son of her trainer, Veyron, who'd taught them side by side the past nine years. Julian didn't like being offline for even a moment. He had to know everything, always—and loved using his cube to pull up some memory in order to prove a point, or to prove Rhee wrong. It was maddening. But now she wondered if she'd miss it.

It was getting darker. Hundreds of sparklers burned brightly. Night was falling quickly, and the sense of urgency felt big and real in Rhee's chest. The sun was a massive, burning star—leaving, just like she was. But she didn't know if she'd ever be back. Not after what she had planned.

They passed a crowd that had formed around a small make-shift ring, watching as two scorpions circled each other in the center. More of the insects were trapped in glass jars, trying to crawl their way out. A skinny bookie with sharp elbows hollered the odds and took bets on the side.

"So how much longer do you have?" Julian asked. "When does the craft launch?"

An hour ago. "Keep walking," she said over her shoulder by way of an answer.

"*Zuilie*," Julian said in a huff. "Are you going to be this bossy when you're empress?"

He was joking. She was *always* this bossy, whether they were competing in archery, stealing moonplums, or playing pranks on the staff who tended to Rhee day and night. But that word—*empress*—was like a thick black smoke filling her lungs. An entire valley of Kalusian flowers would be cut down to decorate the capital city on her sixteenth birthday, the day of her coronation. In just one week's time, she'd come face-to-face with Seotra. Then, she'd finally have her revenge.

She took a breath, stopped, and turned to him. "Listen. I came to tell you . . ." *I don't deserve this.* "I don't want this," she said instead. Rhee held up the telescope that Julian must have slipped in her bag before they said goodbye. She guessed it had cost months of his wages from working in the greenhouses. It was made of silver—a metal so rare that it could be mined only in the Outer Belt, and it came at a steep price.

"That was your birthday gift," Julian said softly. "You weren't supposed to find it 'til you were on your way." Rhee shook her head. He was hurt; she could tell. But it was too generous. "You hate it," he said flatly.

"Don't be stupid," Rhee said as she shoved the telescope into his hand. There was dirt from the greenhouse under his nails. "I don't hate it." As if anyone could hate something so beautiful. "It's just . . ."

She didn't know how to explain it in a way he'd understand. In truth, she loved it. She'd loved everything he'd ever given her—found things, mostly. A tiny sun-bleached skull of a bat, or a jagged crystal that reflected the light in a rainbow if she held it just so. Rhee would be leaving those behind too. It felt wrong to accept anything from him. It felt like by taking something so special from Julian, she'd have to have a heart as pure as his.

Julian slid the telescope open. Each compartment was smaller than the last, tapering toward the eyepiece. At full extension, it was the whole length of his arm.

Just then a kid tore past them, the sparkler in his hand illuminating Julian's face briefly in the darkness. From this angle, she could see the scar from where he'd split his chin open years ago, scaling the south wall of the palace to see her. He'd just returned from the old ruins, looking for moonsnakes—and that night he'd brought the castoffs of their milk-white skin to show her.

"Look up there." Julian pointed to the constellation of Terecot. Up in the sky, the maiden's hair unraveled into a spiral that ended with a tiny orange light. He handed her back the telescope. "Don't lose that spot."

But Rhee struggled to find the light when she brought it to her eye. There was only a blue-black sky in the viewfinder, and as she searched left and right she grew anxious. She levered onto the balls of her feet, as if an extra two inches would bring her closer.

Julian guided the telescope higher. She could feel his calloused palm cupping her hand. Her hood fell back as she tilted her head up, and she felt his breath on her neck. A memory surfaced without her calling for it, surfacing *organically*, making her skin prickle: the moment just a week ago when he'd pinned her in the dojo. If she'd turned her head just a fraction of an inch . . .

She gasped when Kalu came into sight. Swirls of orange and white cascaded across the planet's surface. It looked just like the birthday sweet Julian's mom had made Rhee when she'd turned twelve—whipped cream smeared on a warm piece of tenkang—simple and delicate and almost too beautiful to eat. She'd loved it more than the elaborate cake imported from Kalu. "Oh, holy *ancestors*. That. Is. Awesome."

"You know the atmosphere on Kalu is so thick that they don't get yellows in their sunsets?"

"I didn't know that," she said absently, still looking up at the brilliant planet. She remembered the sky and sunrise and sunset, though, especially her last dawn on Kalu—blues and purples peeking over the horizon and scattering across the sky.

The moment she learned of her family's deaths, she'd fumbled through all the memories on her cube, searching to recall their last moment together—only to wish she hadn't. Her mother's hair, gray and frizzy; the dark circles under her father's eyes; her sister purposefully ignoring her. All of them angry, disappointed, colder-looking in recall somehow than they had seemed in the flesh. As if they'd already been dead for years.

No one told you that about the way recall worked: how easily you could ruin the things you loved. Rhee chose to rely on her organic memory to remember only the good moments: Joss sneaking dried myrah candies to her in bed when she was sick; insisting the tailor make them both a set of pants like their father's; and flinging aside her parasol to cartwheel in the sun, over and over, in the buckwheat fields outside the palace. Her father, a tall man, lifting Rhee easily onto his shoulders for a daily walk along the palace perimeter. And her mother, undoing Rhee's tight braids every evening—something a servant could've easily done—and rubbing her aching head with lavendula oil.

"Be a good girl" was the last thing she'd said to Rhee. And Rhee remembered nodding, as if she'd been saying *I will.*

But she'd lied.

Their father had given the sisters special coins once, souvenirs from a trip he'd taken in the Bazorl Quadrant—one for Joss and one for her. When her father ushered her family on the craft the night of the accident, Joss and Rhee had been fighting about whose turn it was to press the thruster deploy.

"*Stars* you're stupid. *Soil* you're still stupid," Joss had told Rhee, flipping her coin to show Rhee it didn't matter which side landed first. Rhee had been six years old, and furious. She'd snuck off while her parents were distracted. She'd wanted to go get her own coin—and prove Joss was *even stupider.* Acting like a baby, just like Joss always said.

She'd been gravity-bound when the craft launched, when it tore off into the atmosphere and disappeared. She hadn't known, of course, that it would never return, that exactly four minutes after takeoff it would burn up in the outer rings of Rylier and crash, killing everyone on board, instantly.

All because her father had wanted peace. In signing the Urnew Treaty that ended the Great War between the planets, he'd signed his own life away. Seotra had warned him. *Half the beings in the galaxy will want you dead,* he'd practically snarled. His hands clutching onto the collar of her father's shirt. *Your own people will make you pay.* Rhee had burst in at that moment, interrupting their standoff. No one had ever spoken to her father that way, or handled him so roughly. Rhee clenched her fists as she remembered the threat laced in the Crown Regent's words, the menace she felt when she went through her cube playback, searching for all the memories she had of her father just before he died.

Your own people will make you pay.

As in, *Seotra* would make him pay. He'd made her father believe that he had to take their family and flee from some imminent danger on Kalu. But the only danger was Seotra himself.

Once her family boarded the ship, isolated from all of their friends and allies out of a need for secrecy, it would have been easy enough for Seotra to orchestrate the explosion that ended their lives. He'd had connections from the war. And there was no doubt in Rhee's mind he'd killed plenty of men before he'd killed her family that day.

She'd never shared the memory with anyone. No one would've believed a child. And now that she was grown, mere hours from becoming empress, there was no need to tell anyone, ever. She'd have her revenge on her own terms.

"Just take it," Julian said now, motioning to the telescope in her hand. "Pretend it isn't a birthday gift. Let's say I'm just letting you borrow it 'til I see you next."

'Til I see you next, she repeated in her head. By then, everything would be different.

She'd learned that there was no guarantee of anything, or anyone, ever.

Streaks of orange and red cut across the black sky. Shining, burning, bubbling. Edges chipped away as the meteors moved at impossible speeds. Cheers erupted all around them as everyone burst into applause. Rhee couldn't record it; she'd just have to remember how she felt at this moment, looking up into the void, every joy and fear inside her boiling, as if she were the same temperature as the supercharged rocks hurtling across the sky. With each flare the question she'd asked herself for years burned brighter and brighter inside of her: Why *her*? Why did *she* survive?

"Do you think I'm good?" she asked him suddenly. There was a prickling sensation in her throat.

"Rhiannon . . ." He trailed off. After all these years, she wasn't sure if she'd ever heard him say her whole name, and she didn't like it—didn't like the formality of it, the way it made her feel as though she'd already floated far away from him, and from this life. But wasn't that what she wanted? Wasn't that better for everyone? He seemed as if he was going to say something serious, but finally he shook his head and took her hand. "No. I think you're weird."

They'd held hands a million times before. To help each other over the crest of the sand dunes, or to pull the other up off the dojo mat. But now, he laced his fingers through hers and squeezed. She held her breath, wondering if she should squeeze back, if it even meant anything, if she was overthinking it completely.

The crowd to the left began to murmur. People parted like water cleaved by the prow of a boat, revealing a tall, white-haired man. He was too old to be a Tasinn. He had a slightly uneven gait and a funny rhythm to his walk, as if one leg was longer than the other. Veyron. She and Julian wrenched their hands apart.

His expression was illuminated in the light of a nearby torch: sad, knowing, stern. He barely looked at his son. Instead, Veyron touched the back of his neck and spoke something into his cube. She could read his mouth: *I found her.*

With every step Rhiannon took, the long, white corridor of the *Eliedio* seemed to narrow—as if the royal ship were slowly closing in on her.

It was done. They'd left Nau Fruma, and it would be years before she'd see Julian again. There was no sadness to draw from, only a static numbness. She'd opted to keep her cube off; she didn't want to remember any of this.

Rhee focused on Veyron's coat, which trailed behind him like a flag at half-mast. Because she was meant to be empress, the rules of decorum stated that no one should walk in front of her. Yet Veyron did, evidently still angry with her for running off. She could tell Tai Reyanna was irritated by this transgression; she made a point of standing behind Rhee, though they'd often walked side by side.

"There are a variety of festivities planned upon your arrival," Tai Reyanna said, delivering the words in the breathy, high-society accent she'd urged Rhee to adopt. She walked slowly and deliberately, just as she did everything—and Rhee could hear the many fine layers of her formal silk robes *swishing* as she moved.

"How exciting," Rhee responded. She hadn't meant it to sound so sarcastic. Her footfalls were heavy, and though she knew it was the craft's artificial gravity, there was a heavy feeling in her chest, too, as if her heart were pumping liquid metal to every part of her body. Her hair had been rebraided so tightly that her head ached. She looked down at her hands. Her palm still tingled where Julian had touched her.

"It *is*," Tai Reyanna agreed, and Rhee could hear the chastisement in her voice. She was native Kalusian, like Rhee, and they shared the same broad cheekbones and tan skin. "Our Empress, coming home at last. Have you seen the holos today?"

When Rhee shook her head, the Tai took a handheld device and projected a three-dimensional image into the air as they walked. A *Countdown to the Coronation* logo appeared, the swirly script curling around an image of Rhee taken last year—digitally enhanced to bring out the green specks in her one hazel eye. She wasn't smiling in the image, which Kalusian focus groups reported made her look older and more determined. There'd been a big media push as of late to convince the public that a teenage girl could rule the galaxy.

"We're less than twelve hours away from making history, when Princess Rhiannon Ta'an will take the blood oath and swear her fealty to the people of Kalu," Nero Cimna announced. Appearing as a holo that seemingly walked alongside Rhee in the corridor, the *Countdown* host wore a black short-sleeved shirt with a high, rounded collar, as was custom in diplomacy positions. As ambassador to the office of the regent, he'd interviewed Rhee several times in the past few months. Asking her a series of frivolous questions about her upcoming coronation, he'd smiled in a way that showed off his perfectly square jaw and made Rhee flush. He had that effect on millions of viewers.

"Last-minute preparations are still under way," Nero continued. Rhee had seen in the studio how the cameras filmed him from every angle; the holo feed adjusted to suit and integrate the viewer best. The footage cut to a live feed of Lenys Valley on Kalu, just outside the capital. The sloping hills of the valley, green and lush, created a natural amphitheater where the coronation ceremony would take place. Rhee would be front and center as she went through the ritual of slicing open her palm to symbolically spill her blood for Kalu. A crowd of thousands had already collected and would wait there through the night. Flower arrangements were still arriving, and a small army of people seemed to be moving things back and forth for no apparent reason other than to fuss. The whole event looked extravagant, cloyingly beautiful, and like yet another careful orchestration from Seotra.

"We'll see it in person soon enough," Rhee said, gently lowering Tai Reyanna's hand. Her Tai turned off the feed so that the hologram zipped closed and disappeared. "I'm eager to speak with Regent Seotra. Will he be available when we arrive?" His name in Rhee's mouth tasted bitter, acidic, but she needed to keep track of his every move.

"Of course." Tai Reyanna raised her eyebrow, giving Rhee a questioning look. "He's been preparing for your arrival for months."

And I've been preparing for years, Rhee almost said.

Veyron didn't even acknowledge their conversation. Tonight he seemed even quieter than usual—and she felt that familiar shame she'd often felt from her trainer: that she'd somehow disappointed him.

"We'll need to discuss the logistics of your arrival," Tai Reyanna continued as they reached a fork in the corridor. "Shall we head to the bridge? The captain is ready to meet with us."

Rhee stood between two paths, her mind racing with invented excuses to avoid whatever Tai had planned. She'd have to pass the entire onboard staff en route, who were no doubt furious with her for running off earlier.

"Perhaps the girl needs to rest first," Veyron said, his back still to them.

"I'd like that. Veyron could escort me to my chambers," Rhee said quickly. He was not a man of many words, but he was perceptive. He'd given her an out. "It's been a long day."

Other than a slight thinning of her lips, Tai Reyanna concealed her displeasure well. Rhee knew she'd never admit how distasteful she found it that Veyron was half Wraetan. There were old wounds from the Great War that Rhee feared would never be healed.

"Yes, it has been a long day, hasn't it?" Tai Reyanna said after a moment passed. There was blame threaded into her tone; it had been a long day because Rhee had delayed their flight. "We'll be sure to reconvene after you've gotten some rest."

The closer they got to the coronation, the more Rhee had dared to defy her Tai, though it didn't change the mixture of terror and respect she had for the woman. She bowed her head before Tai Reyanna could change her mind, essentially dismissing her. The ceremonial Kalu headdress that sat upon Rhee's head shifted slightly, and she had to steady it with her hand. It had a colorful plume that gathered at the top of her head. She'd been forced to wear it, just like she'd been forced to change into a red dress embroidered with gold thread. The grit had been scrubbed from her tan arms, which now prickled with goose bumps.

Veyron and Rhee continued on after Tai Reyanna excused herself. It felt strange to be walking in silence—especially after the long procession of Tasinn and security sweeps. Whenever Rhee had complained about the escort, since the time she was a child, Tai Reyanna always replied with the same answer: "They're for your protection." And Rhee had always bit back the same answer: *All the security in the galaxy didn't protect my family.*

At the end of the corridor, Veyron tapped a code into a silver keypad. Just as Rhee caught up to him, the door slid up with a quiet hiss and opened to a large room with floor-to-ceiling windows. Her ancestors were projected via holo onto the only solid wall in the room. Clustered along a small ledge were offerings— grain, fruit, myrah candies. Not her quarters, but a room of worship. She nodded to Veyron in respect and thanks. He'd been raised on Wraeta; honoring the ancestors was not part of his religion, but he knew that the practice always calmed her.

Rhee walked toward the windows, bowing before every ancestor and lighting incense as she passed, until she reached the portraits of her own family: her father, her mother, and Joss. If their bodies had been discovered, their cubes intact, she might have been willed certain memories they'd put aside. But even those had disappeared the day they died.

Through the glass, Kamreial fire rained against the darkness of space. In the distance, Rhee saw a pulsing orange light.

Kalu no longer seemed like a fixed point in the enormous sky, but a future she knew would be hers. Another chill ran over her arms. She'd be meeting with various dignitaries, and she'd been prepped by Tai Reyanna in the customs of every planet, until she could curtsy, bow, and sign in her sleep. But there was still much to learn.

She touched her neck instinctively to recall the well-worn memory of a family breakfast, startled to forget she'd powered off. On the cube, her memories weren't arranged chronologically but by how often she'd revisited them—and this particular memory was always stacked at the top of her queue. But now, without the cube, Rhee had to search for this memory, closing her eyes and climbing down her memories as if feeling along the roots of a tree.

Her father at the head of the long table, teaching, always. "As empress, you must be fair, but decisive," he'd said, smearing his toast with one stroke of butter, as if to demonstrate his point. He'd been talking to Josselyn, of course. Her older sister had known all her life that she would rule.

Funny. Without the cube, parts of the memory receded into the background while others rose to the surface. How Josselyn had fed a piece of meat to their hounds under the table, winking at Rhee as if they were in on a secret. While on her cube, she had never replayed the memory that far.

She opened her eyes just as a particularly dazzling display of flares burst across the sky. Orange marks clawed against the darkness and faded just as quickly. The silence made it feel like a sacred act. Or an omen.

She looked over at her trainer, who threaded his fingers behind his back. He faced the window, shoulders squared and chest out. Like the soldier he was. He'd barely said anything since they boarded.

"Are you angry with me?" she asked him.

"No," Veyron said, though he wouldn't meet her eye. "But they do things differently in the capital. Running away from your duties would not have been tolerated there."

"They'll think whatever they please." Her habit of wearing pants, her martial arts training—it would all strike them as odd. But Rhee feared something worse than popular opinion. She feared that after all this time, all this preparation, she would freeze when the time came to avenge her family and kill Seotra.

But she could not allow Seotra to live. He'd masqueraded as her father's friend, but it was *Seotra* who'd arranged for their departure and seen them off that very night. How many times had she replayed the memory of the fight she'd interrupted?

Half the beings in the galaxy will want you dead. Seotra's bared teeth. The certainty, the hatred, in his voice. Surely this was why her father had gathered them in the darkness of night. Seotra made the Emperor believe they had to flee for their lives, and then he destroyed their craft.

"The Crown Princess has always been so obstinate," Veyron said now.

Crown Princess. She scowled at her trainer. "You know I don't go by that title." It was Joss's claim. She'd been next in line to inherit the throne, and only because of her death would Rhee be empress.

"I do." He nodded again as he gazed back at the door behind them. The lights of the flares made red slashes across the side of his face. "But as we grow older, we must also accept the people we've become."

"What do you mean?" Something in his tone made prickles of anxiety spiderwalk up her back.

Veyron turned, and she saw for the first time the look on his face. He had dark skin from his Wraetan side and blue eyes common in second-wave Kalusians—an unusual pairing, and evidence of his mixed heritage. It was strange to see him upset; he was always so good at concealing his true feelings. At that moment, his resemblance to Julian was striking. "I'm sorry, Rhee. I hope the ancestors forgive me."

"Sorry for—?"

Before she could say *what*, Veyron grabbed her throat and pushed her hard against the window. Her headdress fell from the force of the impact, and Veyron stepped on it, crushing the feathers under the tread of his boot. From his thumb to his index finger, the length of his hand fit cleanly around Rhee's neck. He lifted her off the ground and squeezed. She felt her windpipe closing. She gasped for air as she tried to claw his fingers off one by one.

It was impossible. His familiar face—the face of her best friend's father, of the trainer she'd known for years—seemed to warp before her eyes. Everything was slowing. Her tongue felt thick and dry, and she fought for breath. White bursts of light softened the corners of her vision. The ancestors peered at her from their portraits, holos frozen in time, waiting to see how it ended. Would she would join them?

"I'm sorry, Rhee," he repeated. Even as Veyron brought his other hand up to her throat, tears were welling in his eyes. "They gave me no choice. I had no *choice*."

TWO

ALYOSHA

THE ship cut a hard left. Alyosha slammed against the boiler. The metal hull groaned and flexed. Tools flew off his belt and floated away; they landed just out of reach. His cube buzzed faintly on his neck. He tapped to answer.

"What's your status?" Vincent asked.

"I lost my favorite wrench," Aly said, squatting down to see where it had fallen.

"And the grav beam?"

"I'm ten minutes out from fixing it." *If* he could find his socket wrench.

"Work your magic and shave off some time, yeah? Just tried hailing this crazy-looking ship in a routine stop, but now the pilot is acting feisty." Vincent sent a view of his dash, which played on the back of Aly's eyelids, so that it briefly doubled his vision. The ship in question was shaped like a beetle, too small to be a cargo ship, too big to be a standard civilian pod, and about thirty klicks northeast. It wasn't slowing down, even as they pursued it. The UniForce had a term for ships like this: *noncompliant*. They'd need the grav beam up and running to lock on to the target and reel it in.

Annoying for Aly. Fantastic for ratings.

"Seven minutes out," Vincent said.

"I'd work faster if I wasn't trying to hang on for my life," Aly told him, blinking out the image. "Where'd you learn to fly?"

"Your mom's bedroom—she taught me this move." The *Revolutionary* barrel-rolled, and Aly scrambled for a handhold while the world somersaulted around him. What a showboat.

"If I throw up in the reactor, it'll be your fault."

"But we'll all be dead, so who'll blame me?"

A freaking philosopher, this one.

For the past sixteen months, they'd been aboard the *Revolutionary* together: a two-man sweeper staffed with a droid named Pavel that Aly had programmed himself. Pavel was a fan favorite—more famous than either Aly or Vin, which was saying something, because they were pretty popular. After all, they were the two stars of *The Revolutionary Boys*.

Neither Aly nor Vin had set out to be famous. Far from it. As members of the UniForce, Kalu's military, their assignment had originally been seen as a punishment for two slackers who'd barely survived basic. They'd been banished to the perimeter of the Outer Belt, policing renegade poachers and investigating claims of stolen or illegally modified ships when someone put a bulletin out, that sort of thing. When the producers had decided to bring the cameras on board for a short, feel-good pro-UniForce documentary, no one had expected the show to blow up.

Well, almost no one. Jethezar, the Chram kid they'd come up with in basic, had called it from about a million miles away. Whenever Aly pulled up the memory of Jeth on his cube, Jeth would shake his head and exhale a plume of smoke through the gills on either side of his neck. "Y'all don't forget me when you're famous and stuff," he'd said in that Chram twang, in a way that was so solemn Aly hadn't known if he'd been serious or just had a really solid deadpan going on.

Now *The Revolutionary Boys* was the most popular show on DroneVision. The cameras had stayed, and the whole thing became a production. They were on their second season, and Aly couldn't scratch his butt without a camera beaming it to the worlds at all hours of the day. The single glorious exception was the hour in the morning when the two Kalusian moons, Nau Fruma and Rhesto, crossed orbits. Then, the DroneVision network was completely disabled—and there was no way any satellite signals could come in or out.

It wasn't exactly the life of a soldier. It was *better*. Sure, maybe Aly wasn't a natural in front of the camera. Not like Vincent, who was game to smile for the daisies whenever and wherever; those little cameras brought out the best in him—the one-liners, the perfectly timed expressions, the mouthful of perfectly white teeth. But it was sure as hell better than being stuck in some Wray Town, coughing up dust.

Plus, there were benefits to the *The Revolutionary Boys* attention. Like the girls. Rubbing elbows with celebrities (rubbing *something,* Vin had joked) at the occasional fund-raiser. All the fan messages that made him feel like he mattered.

Of course, there were bad things too. There'd been a few signs at the last season-premiere party, on all the fan holo-forums, pasted over the show's advertisements: GO HOME, DUSTIES. It didn't matter that Aly was always on his best behavior—he wanted to rep his planet right—but to a certain kind of person he'd always be the enemy. A lot of folks couldn't get over the memories they had of the Wraetan uprisings, and the way Wraeta had sided with Fontis against Kalu during the Great War. That was why Aly had originally lied about having Wraetan blood. He'd heard stories about how Wraetans were treated in the UniForce, since there was still bad blood and the whole refugee situation—so he'd checked a different box and told a little white lie. No one would've known if it weren't for the show, which sent a bunch of journalists digging into his past.

At least the show had Aly's back, so long as the ratings were good. When it was finally revealed that Aly had Wraetan blood, the producers ignored the protesters—the loud contingent of Kalusians who ran around calling Wraetans animals and savages, or worse: *dusties.*

The *Revolutionary* angled left again. Vin cursed into his cube. "Aly! Target is taking evasive measures. Hurry up on the grav beam already."

"I'll finish what *I* started—don't worry about me. You focus on flying and try not to get us killed."

"Deal. You have six minutes now. Out." It was probably the longest conversation they'd ever had over their cubes. Vin never kept his cube on when he didn't have to. His parents were funny like that. Vin was forced to *meditate* and *use visualizations* and mnemonics, which kind of cracked Aly up, since a whole chunk of the universe had to do all that anyway. No fancy names required—it was just called being born poor. Only certain governments could afford to subsidize cube installations for their citizens.

Aly wasn't a native cube user, and he'd gotten his installed pretty late in the game. He knew there were all kinds of folks in the wider galaxy addicted to their memories. There were public campaigns to "stay healthy and in the moment," which mostly meant not to waste away like those sad sacks who kept on revisiting their glory days when they had a full head of hair and a girl on their arm.

Aly didn't get that—why you'd want to live inside the past. He liked recording his new life. Maybe eventually he'd accumulate enough good memories to crowd out the bad ones, so that they never showed up again in his feed.

A DroneVision camera zoomed into his line of vision, and Aly swatted it away. "At least do something useful if you're gonna get up in my face," he told the daisy. That's what they called the DroneVision cameras—a linguistic evolution that started with the casual term *day-sees*, based on the cameras' ability to provide bright lighting, and quickly became *daisies*—even though they looked more like giant spiders than any flower *he'd* ever seen, on any planet. "Light."

A light from its underside flicked on, illuminating the small room. The daisy was compact, the size of his palm, and it fluttered up to the low ceiling. Aly got on his hands and knees, staying close to the ground as the ship veered wildly from left to right. What the hell was going on up there?

Finally, he spotted the wrench in the far dark corner, wedged in the middle of a network of pipes and wires. Two years ago he could've crawled over to it easily enough. But at seventeen, he was just shy of twenty hands tall and still going. His growth spurt had come late and with a vengeance—even his *bones* hurt, like he'd been strapped to an old-school torture device and stretched every which way. He wondered, now, how much taller than his dad he was.

He knew for damn sure he was too big to fit through anything constructed by a Kalusian. They had leaner builds, and everything they made was, like, 25 percent too small for Aly to ever use comfortably—but their engineering was top-notch.

His arms were long, too, which meant that: one, he could take Vin down in a slap-boxing match, and two, he could *just* brush the metal wrench with the tips of his fingers.

He eased it into his palm, sprang up, and went to work on the grav beam core—ratcheting, tightening, realigning. His hands moved carefully; the trick was to focus on all the things he could control. Vin's insane flying, the rusty ship two seconds away from falling apart, the cameras that crept up on him everywhere he went—all of that fell squarely into the realm of the things he *couldn't* control.

The *Revolutionary* jerked left again. Steadying himself, Aly planted his feet and worked quickly, ignoring the daisy that lowered to get a look at his face. It was always waiting to zoom in on "thoughtful" moments that the producers could use as B-roll and insert anywhere. Aly almost swatted it away again, but he caught his reflection in the lens—and the nick in his eyebrow that girls were always asking about on the holoforums. Even into the second season, he was still not used to the fame. He'd been the kind of kid who studied physics diagrams for hours, not the guy pulling pretty girls. It didn't help that Aly was so dark. But now, for some reason, folks seemed to think he looked all right—describing his skin like it was kape or chocolate or an expensive type of wood. If he was being honest, it annoyed Aly—you never heard Kalusians compared to food. But it was better than catching *taejis* about it.

He reached for the daisy. "Sorry, little guy. I need to borrow something," he said. It tried to flutter out of his grasp, but his reach was long, and he snatched it up effortlessly. "Easy, *easy* . . ."

He unscrewed its lens while the mini propellers still spun. When he got the lens free, the daisy shot up and fled toward the doorway. Aly jammed the lens into the core, adjusted the angle, and powered it on. There was a high-pitched whirl as the grav beam charged up. The sweetest sound, like a chorus of loyal subjects chanting his name.

"I am the god of grav beams!" he called into his cube.

"Great. Now come be the god of copilots and help me lock down this *choirtoi* of a target."

"On it!" Aly ducked through the short doorway and scrambled up the access ladder. Across the catwalk and down the corridor, he ran toward the bridge as fast as he could in point-three gravity. He'd never gotten used to the buoyancy. He'd been shuffled between refugee camps from one Wray Town to the next—his past was mostly a blurry series of evacuations—and even though he'd never had a home to call his own, he'd always had gravity.

But up here, he half ran, half swam. At the next corner, Aly grabbed a makeshift handhold, swinging around the turn and launching himself forward. He'd set up dozens of shortcuts in the same way: broken poles and useless metal components all soldered to the inner hull. He and Vin scaled them like monkey bars.

The door to the bridge slid open, and there was Vincent, standing over the ship's console as he bore down on the throttle. He flew the *Revolutionary* like he was playing a video game, which was to say: recklessly. But he was a good pilot. A dozen cameras hovered around him in a semicircle, positioned at different angles and distances. He was a second-wave Kalusian and looked it, with light eyes and fair skin that turned golden when he tanned.

"Just in time!" he called over his shoulder. "I've never seen this model. It's unscannable, but the navigation equipment must be top-notch. I've lost it twice already." Half the daisies turned in Aly's direction, like a flock of ugly birds.

He took his seat at the helm. "What do you mean, 'unscannable'?"

"I can't get a read on it." Vin tapped the screen on his console. "It's invisible on all the nav equipment."

Aly touched his finger to his cube and magnified his vision. "It almost looks like it's made of . . . wood?" It wasn't impossible. Modified organic material could be used for all kinds of things in deep space. But not a lot of people had the tech. The UniForce definitely didn't. "It's kind of weird."

"*Weird*," Vin agreed, with an edge in his voice.

"Did it respond to your hail?"

"Yeah, with some sort of code. I got your boy working on it now." Vin gestured to Pavel. The droid's eyelights pulsed—or rather the two soft blue lights where his eyes would be if he were human pulsed.

"Twenty percent through my language database," Pavel announced.

Vin wiped his forehead on the sleeve of his shirt—the only indication that he was stressed. "See if you can lock the grav beam on at this distance?" he said.

A chase scene, Aly realized. High-speed chases weren't as common as people thought, since 90 percent of ships would stop when hailed by the UniForce. But the producers had told them that the viewers loved chase scenes, which was a way of saying *make them happen*. Sometimes they even hired merchant crafts to go rogue, just to fill in footage of the *Revolutionary* wheeling through space in hot pursuit.

Aly slid his chair toward the console and locked on the first try, but the pilot pulled up hard and shook them off.

"You're losing your edge, Alyosha. Whatever it takes," Vin said. His blue eyes were wide and clear, and Aly expected him to cock his eyebrow at the daisies like he always did when he was hamming it up. But he didn't.

"Keep her still and I'll take care of my end." But they tried a dozen more times, and the ship outmaneuvered them every time. In the distance they saw the planet Fontis, known for its lushness, with the ocean that supposedly glowed at night. From where they were, the planet was swirls of blues and greens.

Vin cursed. "You gotta be kidding me."

Pavel piped up. "Treaties dictate no military personnel—"

"We know the treaty, P," Aly said. Everyone did. The Great War had started off as a beef between Kalu and Fontis thousands of years old, but eventually it engulfed all of their colonies and allies, including Wraeta. It had officially ended nine years ago when the late Emperor Ta'an had signed the Urnew Treaty, when Aly was eight or nine. Each side was supposed to play nice now, try not to invade each other, that sort of thing. Once that ship broke Fontis's atmosphere, it would be essentially claiming sanctuary. And since they were in a military craft, they wouldn't be allowed to follow.

"Aly, what are our odds?"

He eyed the daisies that hovered nearby. "We'd need to boost our velocity, so if I turned on the thrusters and we burned like hell 'til we closed in, we might be able to grav beam them back."

"Do it, then." Vin's in-it-to-win-it vibe was convincing. Was he making a show for the daisies, or did he really want that vessel? Aly guessed it didn't really matter either way. He tried not to argue with him in front of the cameras. People already thought Wraetans were loud and picked fights. He wasn't going to add fuel to that fire.

"Roger that." With the press of a button, the thrusters blazed, and they jumped forward. They were gaining on the beetle craft, but the beetle was gaining on the planet. Aly ran the calculations. They would lock on in five, four, three, two . . .

But the beetle surged forward, just out of their beam's reach.

"What the hell?" Vin slammed a fist on the console.

Yeah—*what the hell?* Aly hadn't expected that kind of power surge from a ship so small. His console recalculated. They'd lost it. "It's gone, Vin."

"It's not gone." Vin leaned into the throttle, gunning straight for it.

"Drop it, Vin. It'll be in Fontis airspace by now." Three daisies zoomed up close from different angles. He swept his arm out and ended up swatting one away. "Pavel! Redirect these damn cameras! Get 'em all out of here!"

"It's hauling something important," Vin said through gritted teeth.

"What are you talking about?" When the ship broke Fontis's atmosphere, Vin didn't deviate their course. Aly felt a flash of anger. He didn't understand—whatever "important" thing the ship might be hauling couldn't be worth a suspension. But Vin was like that. A golden boy. A high-society Kalusian. He did whatever he wanted because people had always let him.

"Priority transmission from headquarters," Pavel said.

"*Taejis*," Aly cursed. Why was the UniForce HQ calling? "Vin—*stop*. Pavel, hold the call."

"Not possible," Pavel said. "There's a security override. Level five priority."

"Level *what?*" But even as Aly said it, autopilot took over, and the *Revolutionary* pulled up abruptly. The tail of the ship skimmed the surface of the Fontisian atmosphere and burned up a pocket of air. Vin cursed. Aly realized his hands were still gripping the throttle. He'd never even heard of a security override, or level five priority.

"Transmitting," Pavel said. From its chest, the droid projected a holo of Nero himself—the public face of the Crown Regent's office. He wore a crisp black shirt with little silver badges lined across his collarbone like a row of sharp teeth. Behind him hung the Kalusian flag, with wide red and gold stripes and seven blue stars arranged in a semicircle, each representing one of Kalu's continents.

"Brave soldiers of the UniForce, I regret to inform you that at approximately eighteen hundred hours today, in the Rellia Quadrant, there was an apparent assassination of Crown Princess Rhiannon Ta'an of Kalu." Nero seemed to hesitate. Or perhaps it was just a lag in the holo feed. "Our sources have confirmed that she is dead."

THREE

RHIANNON

WHY? Rhiannon tried to scream as Veyron tightened his grasp around her throat. But no sound came out. She could no longer move her legs. She would join the rest of her family—just as it should've been, all along. But the thought of it made her struggle harder, even as she caught sight of Josselyn's holo portrait in her blurring vision. Joss had been younger than she was now when she was killed. Rhee could let herself slip away and finally see her, and their parents, again. But she was a coward. She wanted to live.

Focus. She tried to still herself; she willed her mind that was desperate for air to calm. Veyron always said to play to her strengths, which were speed—and surprise.

With the last of her energy, she released a hard kick to Veyron's groin. He dropped her, and she collapsed to the ground, gasping for air. She could feel oxygen flood the ends of

41

her fingers and tips of her toes. Her ears were ringing. Her neck burned with pain.

When Veyron looked up, she saw him withdraw a switch-blade. He'd used it for everything—to cut his meals, to trim his garden, and now to end her life.

"Please," she croaked out. "Stop." Her throat felt as if someone had taken a grater to it. Veyron—the man who had taught her everything she knew about combat—had turned against her. Veyron. *Her Veyron.*

"I told you," he said. "I have no choice." He lunged for her.

She jumped backward, away from the slicing arc of the knife. Her heart thundered. They both ducked low, circling each other like the scorpions in the ring—just as they had hundreds of times before.

Of course, this was different. This wasn't training. He was trying to kill her. He *would* kill her. Her head throbbed. She wouldn't make it out alive. But she wouldn't lie down and die either.

Veyron lunged with the knife once more. She sidestepped him, but just barely. When he was off balance, she rushed him, just like he'd always taught her: *Catch your enemies off guard.* Planting her left foot on his thigh, she launched herself into the air. She grabbed his extended arm and slammed it down across her right knee. The knife went clanging to the floor, and Veyron cried out. But with his other hand he grabbed her by her braid and flung her to the ground.

"How many times have I told you? You need to be three steps ahead of your opponent," he said, panting. Even as he was trying to kill her, he still could not forget that he'd been her teacher all these years. It was true; she was cornered now. "You never *think* before you move."

Coming toward her now, he had no knife, but he seemed even more terrifying with his uneven gait and his arm bent at an impossible angle. She *couldn't* think—the anger was a vise, clamping down, cold and hard.

She crawled backward, slipping on the yards of fabric that pooled under her from her elaborate red dress. Veyron found the knife and retrieved it. His face was freckled and leathered by the sun. He'd fought and lived through a war. She saw in that instant how pathetic she was, how weak, despite all her years of training. She'd never face Seotra; she would never have a chance to avenge her family.

Finally, the wall was at her back. She had nowhere left to go. But Rhee struggled to get to her feet. She was the last Ta'an—twelve generations of emperors and empresses, all warriors in their own right. She wouldn't die sitting down. Her ancestors were watching—their faces hovered in holo on the walls this very moment.

"Why?" she panted out.

"For my family," Veyron said.

Silently, a ceiling hatch opened just behind him, and a boy descended from it, like some kind of upside-down bird. Tattoos all along his neck. Skin so fair it was translucent. His pointed ears poked through his light hair. *A Fontisian.* He caught Rhee's eye and held a finger to his lips. She froze, paralyzed by the sight of him.

"Veyron, don't."

But her trainer raised the knife. She thought of Julian. She could still feel the small silver telescope tucked into her robes, lying against her heart. "Honor, bravery, loyalty," she whispered.

But a second later, the Fontisian tackled, taking her trainer by surprise. The boy flipped Veyron over and hit him in the face, splattering the curious ring he wore with blood. Veyron didn't wince, but the thud of bone was proof enough of pain. Still, he was a skilled fighter and soon managed to throw off the Fontisian. They rolled together, like a single body with two heads, until the Fontisian reared back, kicked a leg under Veyron's chest, and heaved. He launched him over and backward. Rhee had to scramble out of the way as Veyron hit the window and collapsed on the floor, groaning. Instinctively, Rhee swooped down and snatched his abandoned switchblade.

The Fontisian stood, his chest heaving. He was probably only a few years older than Rhee, but easily a head taller than Veyron.

"Who are you?" she demanded. She brandished the knife, willing herself not to shake. The bones of his face were sharp in a way that couldn't ever appear friendly.

"Not even a thank-you, then?" he asked in accented Kalu.

"Who are you?" Rhee repeated. Apart from their missionaries, Fontisians did not travel freely through the universe. She'd known only of high-level diplomats visiting their planet. They practiced an unusual religion that worshipped only one god, Vodhan. They didn't venerate their ancestors, or leave offerings, or seek counsel from dead relatives in times of need. Rather than honor the family from which they were born, they drank sacred plant elixirs and prayed to this god.

"We've no time for introductions." He motioned to Veyron. "His reinforcements aren't more than two minutes away."

She'd never met anyone from Fontis, but she'd heard that this was their way: speaking in negatives, gauging things by how far they fell short.

"Go, Rhiannon." Veyron stirred. His voice was pained. "They're coming for me. I'm dead either way."

"Do not speak." The Fontisian drove the heel of his boot into Veyron's stomach. She looked away. Veyron had just tried to kill her. But still she could hardly believe it was real, that her trainer, the man who had carefully wrapped her knuckles when they were bloodied and taught her to move on her toes, could have done such a thing. "I've readied an escape pod. If we do not move now, we will die."

His matter-of-factness scared her. As if he was used to violence. As if it didn't frighten him at all. "I'm not going anywhere with you," she said.

"You've no alternative."

"What about him?" Rhee asked, gesturing to Veyron.

The Fontisian took a step toward Veyron. But Rhee grabbed his arm, and the boy turned to her stiffly, examining her hand as if it were an insect on his skin—but he did not advance. Rhee stepped in front of him and kneeled next to Veyron, gripping the switchblade.

"Why were you trying to kill me?" she asked Veyron in a whisper.

"Because I had no choice."

"Don't make excuses!" She tried to steady her breathing—to

find focus, clarity, answers. "*You* had a choice. *You* tried to kill me. Why?"

"Are you really so young?" He opened his eyes, but they took a second to focus on her face. "You think we live in a universe where men like me have choices? You think Julian will grow up to have a choice?"

"Don't you *dare* say his name." She couldn't think of Julian. Not with his father's betrayal, and not after she'd almost died.

"He would have starved."

Behind her, the Fontisian shifted. "This man is wasting your time," he said, and she could feel his impatience, the energy coiled deep in his words. But she ignored him.

"It was Seotra, wasn't it?" she asked Veyron. With only a day before the coronation, it must have been a last desperate attempt to quiet Rhee forever before she could take back the throne. He'd have her killed so he could remain regent. She was the last of her line; perhaps he was even hoping to become emperor.

Veyron wiped the blood from his lip where the Fontisian had split it open. "You think you have all the answers?" He began to cough. Her face burned, and she turned away. She knew what others said—that she was spoiled, entitled, for merely asking questions and expecting answers. But she didn't think Veyron had ever thought of her that way. Never him. "Don't lower your eyes, child." He said the word with more tenderness than he'd shown in all the years he'd trained her. She wished it had been venom so she could feel a sting. "You've been blind. Blind and willful. You worship your ancestors for their bravery on the battlefield but never for how they ruled.

With wisdom. Restraint. What would your ancestors think of you now?" he asked.

Rhee was all the Ta'an had left. She couldn't bear the thought of failing her legacy.

At that moment she hated Veyron. She hated the truth that spilled from his bleeding mouth. She was blind, and naïve, and not worthy to rule. She'd underestimated Seotra, the depth of his hatred for her family, his ruthlessness.

Then: a slight movement she nearly missed. Veyron reaching into his pocket.

But she was quicker. Without thinking, she drove the knife into his chest. She heard a high scream, and it took her several moments to realize that the sound was coming from *her* chest, tearing through her throat, as if it would split her in two.

Julian's dad. She had just killed her best friend's father.

She was filled with a sudden blind panic. She had to stop the bleeding. She had to fix this. She pulled the knife from his body and tossed it aside, but the blood came fast—it poured out of him. With both hands she tried to stanch it, but as she pressed into his chest, its warmth seeped between her fingers.

He blinked up at her. His pale blue eyes were the shade of a frozen river.

"I'm sorry," she whispered.

He put his hand over hers and squeezed. All their fingers were slick with his blood.

"The man tried to kill you, and you apologize?" The Fontisian's voice was flat. If it were another boy Rhee would've confused his tone as caring, soft.

"Shut up," she muttered.

Veyron coughed. A gurgling sound emerged from his throat. A moment passed. His muscles seized once, and then he was still.

Rhee couldn't breathe. This is what it felt like to kill a man: like heartbreak.

She stood, her fingers dripping with blood. "SHUT UP!" she yelled again at the Fontisian, although he hadn't said anything more. The boy only looked away as Rhee tried to pick up the switchblade; its handle was red and slippery now. It seemed cruel and strange that such a little thing could *take* so much. She'd lost Veyron and Julian forever.

"We've not long," the Fontisian said.

"Where are we going?" Rhee asked. Her thoughts were spinning: a sandstorm raging through her head. Could she leave without Tai Reyanna? Had even Tai Reyanna known what Veyron was planning? Impossible. Then again, she never would have thought it possible that Veyron would try to kill her, or that she would kill Veyron. The impossible had suddenly become all too real. The Fontisian bent to hook Veyron beneath the armpits, and Rhee could only watch. "What are you doing?"

With a grunt, the Fontisian began to backtrack, hauling Veyron's body, leaving a trail of blood. "This room isn't far from the escape pod. If we send off his body in place of yours, his collaborators may think he was successful in killing you—which will buy us more time."

Rhee had no more strength to argue. She looked to the holos of her ancestors, and thought to press her hands together—to bow and say a prayer—but her palms were wet and shiny and red.

The hands of a killer. It was selfish to ask for a prayer now. She hadn't honored them. At the escape pod, the boy tossed Veyron's body in carelessly. It landed with a thud that made Rhee flinch.

"Wait," she said just before he closed the door. She brought the weapon up to her braid and sawed it off—one, two, three pulls of the knife before it came free in her hand. Her hair fell to her shoulders, and all the tension released. With the braid still intact, she squeezed inside the pod and laid it across Veyron's chest, gently, as if he might awaken. "*Ma'tan sarili*," she told him solemnly. It was an everyday Kalusian greeting, but it meant much more than hello or goodbye. It translated to "highest self," and to say it was a pledge to be the best person you could be. And for Rhee, that meant to be honorable, brave, and loyal to his memory, to the man she'd known, to Julian's father.

"Surely this man isn't worthy of such an act?" the Fontisian asked. Rhee nodded, surprised that he knew what it meant. It was an ancient tradition among Kalusian warriors. Her first kill deserved a personal sacrifice—usually a lock of hair, or the shedding of blood. *The Act of Attrition*, it was called.

And Rhiannon hated her braid. She always had.

"So he'll know I did this," she said. Veyron might've been the one who tried to kill her, but it was Seotra who'd forced his hand. If he could do that, what couldn't he do? "So Andrés Seotra will know I'm coming." Then she slammed her hand on the ejector button. The door slid shut behind her, and the pod sailed silently into space.

FOUR

ALYOSHA

ALY felt like he'd just been punched. It had to be a joke. A sick joke. But Nero kept talking as they played B-roll footage of Princess Rhiannon boarding the *Eliedio*, right before the royal spacecraft exploded.

"As many of you know, Princess Rhiannon was en route from Nau Fruma to Kalu for her coronation tomorrow." Vincent kicked his chair, which was bolted to the floor and didn't give. Aly bet that had hurt. "While we do not yet know who is responsible for this heinous act, several teams have been deployed to the scene. Unless otherwise directed, all personnel are to report to the nearest base."

Nero disappeared abruptly. The holo screen beamed off.

"Vodhan," Aly said. He knew he shouldn't take the god's name in vain. He wasn't sure if he even *believed* in Vodhan anymore, but it was his first instinct to call on him in prayer. Blame it on all those years being preached at by Fontisian missionaries.

The princess with her two different-colored eyes was gone. Lately she'd been plastered all over the holos nonstop in the coronation coverage that Nero Cimna hosted. He was ambassador to the Crown Regent Seotra, which didn't actually mean he was an ambassador—just the public face of the office, and more like a glorified press secretary. Charming as hell, the guy was next-level dreamboat status as far as the boys and girls were concerned. Everyone called him Nero, just Nero, like he was so cool he didn't even need a last name. But Aly had heard somewhere his real name was Nerol anyway. He'd invited Vin and Aly to a gala once, with a mix of rich politicians and their DroneVision star friends. It was the first time he'd ever felt famous.

Lately, Nero had been doing feature pieces on the *Countdown to the Coronation* show, and even though it was girlie as hell, Aly had still watched. It was funny how every time they showed footage of the Princess, she'd been scowling at the camera. He thought *he* had it rough, but what were a couple of million viewers on some obscure DroneVision channel versus however many billion viewers across the galaxy watching your every move?

Some people were bothered by the idea of a sixteen-year-old running the whole operation. But there were loyalists who were adamant that a Ta'an—*any* Ta'an—needed to be on the throne, and that with the right advisers she'd manage just fine. Either way, no one thought she was ready, not really.

Still. Didn't mean she deserved to die.

He suddenly remembered one of the kids who'd died on the road during the evacuation almost ten years ago. He'd been a little boy, just a couple of years younger than Aly, six or seven, and he must've been sick. His ma had cried up a flood and dragged him along like a rag doll, thinking he'd still wake up. And that's when Aly's dad had let go of his hand to carry the dead boy for miles . . .

Aly shook his head as though to clear it. He hated when memories crept up on him. *Organic memory* was what they called it. The organic ones hit harder, too, when you weren't expecting them. He'd gotten his cube after his family had left Wraeta and moved to their first Wray Town; the Fontisian missionaries sponsored their installments. Any memories of his life before then weren't stored—they just came exactly when Aly didn't want them to, and they never left soon enough.

On the console, he saw that the autopilot had set a course for the closest base: Dembos Station. It was rare to dock at the enormous station—its own city in space—one of the largest, and most infamous, of its kind. Kalusian contractors had been hired to mine the nearby asteroid, and they ported at this station, too—which meant plenty of mining money and tons of stupid *taejis* to spend it on.

"We're going to Dembos," Aly said, dropping the Kalusian accent. He'd never seen Vin this pissed off and was careful not to meet his eyes. It was like when he was a kid, and a friend's mom was yelling at the friend, and he didn't know where to look while it happened.

"I'm beat. I'm staying on board." Vin was staring out the window, his back to the bridge. "You should go down to base without me."

"I was planning on it," Aly said, maybe a little too quickly. He could get down with some alone time. That memory had him rattled, but there was something else, too—a feeling he couldn't quite loosen, like a bolt he'd screwed on way too tight.

Vin raised his eyebrows. "You mind leaving Pavel here?" he asked.

Aly shrugged and looked to the droid.

"Cool with me," Pavel said. It never got old, hearing him talk slang in his robovoice. He was mirroring language. It was how his vocabulary evolved. He blinked his two blue eyelights. "I'm scheduled for an update, and I'd also be interested in calculating the velocity with which—"

"Right, P. Sounds like a party." Aly stood up, eager to get off the ship, away from Vin. "*Ma'tan*," he said with a wave as he headed out.

Vin didn't bother responding. He'd never seemed to care about politics, and Aly was suddenly annoyed that Vin was taking the news about the Princess so hard. The cameras were off. Vin didn't need to keep up the act. He stopped at the doors off the bridge, working up the nerve to say what he wanted to say. Then finally: "What the hell was that back there?"

"What?" Vin turned around then, all those pretty-boy features hazed over with confusion—that playing-dumb expression Aly hated.

"What do you think? The stunt you pulled back there with the stealth ship," Aly said, pointing out the dash. "You know how serious it could've been if we broke Fontisian atmosphere?"

"You're pissed about *that*?" Vin asked. "That was . . ." He trailed off as Aly waited. "That was nothing," he said finally.

"It's not *nothing* to me," Aly said. "I could get deported." Not even the producers could protect him from that *taejis* storm. There were people foaming at the mouth to get the Wraetan refugees off Kalu.

"Sorry, man," Vin said. "I wasn't thinking."

That was the problem: Vin never thought. He never had to. He was protected. Immune. All he had to do was *visualize* a problem, and it went away with a great big smile and a can-do attitude. Yeah, right. Kalusians didn't know how the rest of the galaxy worked.

Meanwhile, Aly was constantly stressed about what to say or how to stand, always trying to look polite and friendly and not even a little bit angry—so that maybe for one second people could forget about the uprisings. It was easier than trying to educate them, to explain how the Wraetans were just trying to defend their own land. It was like everyone on Kalu had amnesia. And sure, he knew Vin hadn't meant it. But that didn't change the fact that Vin didn't get it. He never would.

On the far side of the *Revolutionary*, Aly stripped off his black uniform until he was down to his military-issued ribbed tank and boxer briefs. He suited up and slipped into the Tin Soldier, the *Revolutionary*'s exploratory pod. Dembos was the Wraetan moon, which meant that in a way, he was headed home—or near it. Near enough to get a look, anyway. He plotted a course for the station that would allow him a decent view of northern Wraeta, his birthplace.

Or what was left of it, at least.

About an hour out, following a slightly curved trajectory, he was able to make out little specks emerging from the black space to his right. Wraeta.

Way back when, Wraeta was just the fourth rock from the sun—not particularly pretty, not especially powerful, and only a little bit useful because of the elements mined from there. For centuries, Wraeta had maintained political neutrality. When Aly's great-grandfather was still alive, Wraeta had even hosted the G-1K summit—which stood for the "Galaxy's One Thousand." It was a meeting at which one thousand of the galaxy's most brilliant scientific minds spent months tinkering and negotiating. The scientists of the G-1K had produced the universe's first cube right on his home planet. On a school trip when he was little, Aly had even gone to see a monument dedicated to the first successful cube installation.

Fast-forward another sixty years, and the thing that *actually* put Wraeta on the map was the fact that Kalu had bombed its capital to hell a year before the Urnew Treaty was signed. The damage radius was as far as it was wide. Not to mention all the dust and debris sent into the atmosphere, the lowered temperatures . . .

Aly had survived, obviously—they'd started the evacuation months ahead of time. But Wraeta was destroyed, uninhabitable, and seeing the rubble of the former planet gave him a weird, floaty feeling in his chest, like someone was messing with his personal gravity.

He slowed down the Tin Soldier so he could stare. The last time he'd been here he'd thought the same thing: crazy there'd been a bright, shining planet a decade ago. Now it was half a planet with a massive bombed-out crater on the north side. A lot of people thought Wraeta had it coming because they'd thrown in with Fontis instead of staying neutral. But with Fontisian missionaries running around the planet, Fontisian money infusing its economy, it didn't seem to Aly like they'd had a choice.

There were free-floating rocks that used to be pieces of the planet, naturally charged. It made them easy to corral within a fixed space, inside a massive electromagnetic net that prevented them from floating light-years apart. Thousands of tiny steel plaques reflected the lights of his pod. They'd been brought by mourners and released within the net, as mementos of the ones who were lost on the battlefields when Kalu invaded, or during the passage, or when they had refused to evacuate their homes.

Aly had released his own plaque two years ago, during his first visit. He scanned for the moment on his cube now, down in the knotted architecture of his memory. He knew many folks kept their cube spick-and-span and were able to find anything anytime—and he wished he were that guy. But too much time had gone by, too many memories accumulated, none of them sorted.

It took him a couple of minutes. His vision clouded and his eyes ached during the search: It was like trying to find one single grain in a great big silo. But finally he located the memory file:

two years ago, thinking of his mom and his sister as he ejected the plaque into space.

Now the great mass of rocks swayed, like a phantom hand was moving them.

And in the corner of his eye: a ghost, hurtling past the rocks of Wraeta. Aly followed it, or tried to, but he was still learning how to drive the Tin Soldier. The thing he'd seen—whatever it was—wove in and out of his vision, and there on the side he swore he saw it: the royal seal.

Impossible.

His heartbeat quickened. It *was* the royal seal, he was sure of it, which meant it was an escape pod from the royal ship. The Princess had been confirmed dead, but what if she had survived? What if she escaped?

What if she had survived? What if she had escaped?

"Dembos, do you read me?" Aly said, tapping his cube. "Dembos, this is Private Alyosha Myraz. I have a visual on an escape pod with the *Eliedio* call sign. Over." But there was silence. He tried the station three more times, the *Revolutionary* twice, and a handful of satellites in southern Wraeta. No dice. The electromagnetic net that kept the various fragments of rock together was probably also messing with his signal.

He hesitated. He should go back, or at least loop around to get a signal and call it in—but he might lose the pod. This was his chance to do something big, his chance to be a soldier. He'd be a real hero, not just play one on DroneVision. And then they'd never send him away, no matter what.

The pod was disk-shaped and spun wildly, end over end. If the

Princess was in there, she didn't know how to drive the thing. Even watching it made Aly want to throw up. The Tin Soldier had about zero thrust and was more of a steering machine, but Aly found a current alongside the electromagnetic net and rode it hard.

Without thinking, there it was—the organic memory, the worst one. He was suddenly eight years old all over again, watching his mom and his big sister, Alina, pull away in the back of a truck loaded with a bunch of women from the Wray during the evac.

"Now or never," the driver said. He was more like a savior, since he'd been there to take the ready and willing to work in the factories in the south of Fontis. Aly still remembered the look on his mom's face when she saw there were only two seats . . .

So Aly had pushed Alina toward his mom and turned away. His ma started crying, grabbing Alina with one hand while she tried to reach out for Aly with the other. The Fontisian watched on like he was bored, and Aly's dad had to step up, calm her down, be the wall that separated a mother from her son. "I'll watch out for Aly. Take our baby girl," he'd whispered.

And his ma went, crying her eyes out as she picked a thrashing Alina clean off the ground. In his memory, Aly stood behind his dad, clutching his dad's shirt and willing himself not to break, not to make this harder on his ma. But as soon as the truck started, Aly was running, small and worthless, as gravel kicked out from behind the truck's wheels and his family receded into the distance. His mother and Alina had looked like copies of each other, their smooth faces like dark pearls, big hair blown back as the truck picked up speed.

Aly didn't want to think about that sad little kid who'd cried his eyes out, sprinting after a life and a family that wasn't ever going to be. Aly knew the score now, and right in front of him he could see that he was closing the gap between his pod and the *Eliedio*'s. He locked on to it with his grav beam and slowly stabilized its spin. *It'll stop*, he told himself. *It has to.*

And when it did, he clicked the air locks into place and shouted—a wild, primal scream. He grabbed the medbag from under his seat and waited for their air locks to depressurize.

The hatch hissed open, and the metallic smell hit him first. He stepped through and nearly slipped on the slickness underneath his feet. There was blood, lots of it. His heart shot up through his throat.

"Princess Rhiannon?" he called. His voice had cracked. *Stupid*, he thought. A dead girl couldn't respond.

Do it, he urged himself—but waited until he thought his heart would burst before he finally went any farther. The first thing he saw was a boot. A guy's boot. It wasn't the Princess, but an old black man—maybe Wraetan, like him. He looked like the grizzled old veterans of the Great War who were so common at interstellar refueling station bars. Aly looked away and pressed his index and middle fingers lightly to each eye—as if he were asking Vodhan for mercy. His heart still beat rapidly. Relief and disappointment stirred in his blood.

He'd seen dead bodies before—he'd grown up in the Wray, after all, where it'd been crammed with refugees and a lot of *taejis* went down—but he'd never seen an old man who was murdered like this. His bloodied shirt was soaked through, and red hand-prints ran up his stomach and neck. Aly was so dizzy, so over-whelmed by the smell of blood, he almost missed the long, black braid laid across the man's chest. It looked like a snake. The stupid part of him was scared, like it might come to life and snap at his feet.

But then he recognized it: The braid belonged to the Princess. Back in boot camp, Vin would freak him and Jethezar out with wild stories about the ancient traditions on Kalu, and how their warriors left locks of hair on the first person they ever slayed. As creepy as it sounded, he had a feeling that Princess Rhiannon had made her first kill.

FIVE

RHIANNON

RHEE had replayed at least a dozen times the hologram of the *Eliedio* exploding. Even more souls lost. Another explosion she'd escaped. She should've been among them . . .

"Don't you get tired of watching the same thing?" asked the Fontisian. She'd recently learned his name was Dahlen, and that he was insufferable.

"No," Rhee said. She pulled the handheld back, just out of his grasp, and the projected image distorted across the pod's ceiling. "Not even close."

Only a few passengers had managed to escape, Tai Reyanna among them. Rhee was relieved to hear of her Tai's survival—her caretaker, who'd lived with her family even before the accident, and her only remaining tie to that life in the palace. Even now, Tai Reyanna was organizing a public vigil at the base of the sacred crystals in Tinoppa—a tiny asteroid currently equidistant from

Kalu and Nau Fruma. It was famous for its ancient monument of crystals, impossibly large and arranged in a half circle. It was thought to be a sacred site, and it was there the galaxy would mourn Rhee's passing.

Would Julian go? Could his mother afford it, now that Veyron was gone?

Rhee pushed the thought aside. Her skin felt itchy. The wool Fontisian-style tunic she'd been given to wear aggravated her skin, though anything was better than the red embroidered coronation dress.

Dahlen shook his head and placed a red pill on the console in front of her. After they'd jettisoned Veyron's body in the *Eliedio* escape pod, she'd boarded the Fontisian's craft; it was made of some kind of organic matter that must have belonged to his native planet. It smelled strongly of oak and cloves, and it looked like it was carved from the inside of a tree. It was bursting with plants, like a rain forest in the sky, and the green foliage seemed to angle toward Dahlen wherever he went. The console itself was a stump, with rings that Rhee could trace with a finger.

"You're out of options," he said. "Take this." He couldn't have been older than eighteen, but he acted like all adults did: bossy, distracted, annoyed to have to repeat himself.

"I *told* you already," she said. "I won't take it." She picked it up to examine it.

The pill was the size of her pinky nail, and filled with a gel-like substance. It was a scrambler—it would rearrange her DNA so that the scans wouldn't detect any trace of Rhee. Not in her eyes, her fingerprints, her blood, or her saliva. If she took the red pill, Rhiannon Ta'an, the last empress of the Ta'an dynasty, would be gone.

Only for a time, he'd claimed. But how could she trust him? If he was lying, twelve generations of Ta'an would end with her.

"I can't tell if you enjoy being this difficult, or if you've not been raised properly." Dahlen had high cheekbones and thin lips that made his expression hard to read. Disinterested, like the sleek, wild desert cats that wandered the sands of Nau Fruma.

But cats pounced. She had to remember this. She cleared her throat. "My apologies," she said, with deep sarcasm. "Was this supposed to be an easy kidnapping?"

"I'm *not* kidnapping you. If it weren't for me, you'd be dead."

"And yet you haven't told me why the order sent you," she said. Her hair fell in front of her face, and she tucked it back behind both her ears. It was short now—too short. She'd been growing her hair out for the royal braid since she was in diapers.

He claimed his mission was on behalf of a Fontisian order, the Order of the Light. Rhee had heard of them in passing—children ordained as religious warriors to defend their mountain-top monasteries. Half priests, half military elite, the Order of the Light had been established during the Great War. Rhee had always known them as a cult of sorts, elaborately tattooed to let the world know of their commitment to Vodhan. She'd heard of even stranger practices too. Animal sacrifices. Plant elixirs with psychotropic properties . . .

Dahlen didn't seem like a religious fanatic, though. He wasn't savage or intense so much as deeply composed—a calculated coolness that in some ways scared her even more.

In the hours since leaving Nau Fruma, they'd almost been caught by a UniForce ship and had nearly burned up while breaking into Fontis's atmosphere. Dahlen had fired commands at her: *Be quiet, stay down, stop asking questions.*

"Is it not obvious?" he asked. "Our planet benefits from a Ta'an on the throne." The Urnew Treaty dictated as much, if there was to be lasting peace between Kalu and Fontis.

Rhee refused to back down. "You say so, but what *isn't* obvious is how you knew of the assassination attempt before it happened. How you infiltrated a Kalusian network and knew of a secret plan ordered by the Crown Regent himself."

"You seem smart enough, and yet you speak like a child."

"And you're so much more worldly for all your years," she fired back. Was this boy, who goaded and insulted, her best shot at staying alive?

A vine sprung up from the console and coiled around Dahlen's wrist, as if urging him to stay calm. His eyes flickered slightly. "My order obeys no man-made boundaries, and has spies everywhere. We didn't know for sure that you were in danger, only that it was extremely likely."

She was desperate to replay every single memory of Veyron, to track his betrayal, to see if and when a change occurred. But her cube had to stay off or she risked being tracked. Rhee had to rely solely on organic memory: Slippery and uncertain, it was like trying to hold on to mist with her bare hands.

"I'm not in the mood for a lecture." She squeezed Julian's telescope, still safe in her pocket. It was cold and heavy, but it felt good to hold on to something solid, something to tether her to the life she'd known—to a best friend she'd trust with her life.

To a best friend she'd betrayed.

"What you're in the mood for is not my concern. Your life is no longer dictated by what you want. At this moment, your survival is dependent on anticipating your enemy's next move." Rhee looked up at him. He reminded her of Veyron in that moment, the way he demanded discipline and restraint in the dojo. "When Seotra learns you escaped, and he will, he will send another assassin. And another, and another—and he won't stop until the job is done."

"But at least I will die a Ta'an." Rhee tossed the pill back onto the console. She wouldn't die as Veyron had—a traitor.

Dahlen turned away from her, obviously disgusted. "What do you know about death?" he muttered.

"Plenty," she said sharply.

"Because you've lost your family?" Dahlen asked. She pictured the still holograms of her family among her ancestors lined up in a row, gazing down at her from above the religious offerings. "Because you've killed one man?"

"That makes me more qualified than most," she said, lifting her chin. Veyron's words echoed in her head then: *You've been blind. Blind and willful.* Had he been right? She felt blind now. Her coronation had been highly publicized, the dates and details planned with care. She was overwhelmed by how many people might have been involved in her assassination attempt. Could she trust anyone, in any corner of the universe? Her own Tasinn?

Had anyone who'd resisted Seotra's influence remained loyal to the dynasty? She second-guessed everything—even Tai Reyanna.

"You haven't a clue. That makes you *just* as qualified as most, which means not qualified at all." The leaf tendril around Dahlen's wrist uncoiled toward her, and she shooed it away. Many plant varieties on Fontis were sentient. It was well-known and scientifically documented, but it still made her uneasy.

"What's that supposed to mean?" She felt insulted, and swatted away the dark hair that had fallen into her face again.

"No fewer than a billion souls perished during the Great War," he said. "There were massacres, famines, clouds of chemical gas that scorched whole cities to dust. Everyone loses something or someone when planets go to war. To think your loss sets you apart is childish."

"I don't need a lesson from a Fontisian in my own history, thank you." She lifted her chin. It was her own father who'd signed the treaty that had ended the war, after all. "And who are you to talk?" Rhee asked. "What is it you've lost?"

"Everything." He said it without scorn, in a way that embarrassed her because it seemed so honest.

"Your family?" Rhee asked.

"Everything," he repeated. After a pause he added: "A sister who would've been your age, though not nearly as foolish."

Rhee regretted she'd asked. She felt a rush of resentment for him, her own curiosity, and for the way war had somehow made them the same. The two of them, broken. Violent. Adrift.

"Are you not still the Princess, no matter what your DNA

says?" Dahlen continued, motioning to the scrambler. "Once we reach our contact on Portiis, there's a procedure to reinstate—"

"To reinstate my identity. I heard you the first time." He wore her patience thin. "How is it that you benefit from having a Ta'an on the throne?"

"Your father was the one who brought the Great War to an end," he said. "He ensured we did not become a race of slaves, that our planet was not ravaged and burned, like so many others. We intend to repay the favor."

Kalu had been well on the path to victory when her father had signed the treaty. History painted him as merciful, and he was. But he hadn't done it just to spare the Fontisians and the Wraetans. He'd signed the treaty to spare his own people, too—the hundreds of thousands of Kalusians who would still lose their lives before Kalu could triumph. Those who had opposed the treaty, like Seotra, hadn't understood that. They thought the truce had been a form of surrender, just when their victory was in reach.

But Rhee knew there must be more to Dahlen's motive than just repayment. His order had gathered intelligence on her, had been observing her, had anticipated Seotra would make a play for Rhee's life on the day she left Nau Fruma.

She picked up the pill with her thumb and forefinger and held it inches away from her face. Had it been served on a plate atop a doily, it would've looked like a fancy dinner digestive. A meal in pill form. They had been common during the union strikes, when produce wouldn't come for weeks and the greenhouses on Nau Fruma couldn't grow enough to feed everyone on the moon.

But it wasn't a synthetic meal. It was a dangerous little pill that would shake out her insides and put them back together, different than before. Even her face would change, Dahlen had warned.

"Have you seen anyone take a scrambler before?" she asked.

His expression remained neutral. "If you're worried about the pain—"

Rhee nearly snorted. "I'm not afraid of pain." She thought of Veyron slamming her to the ground. How her heart broke when he'd died. The sharpness in her chest when she thought of Julian's smile. None of these moments had been recorded, but still they returned to her again and again, as though on a loop. Organic memories were somehow more visceral, more real; experiencing them through the cube was more like watching them through a screen. "I don't know you. Why should I trust you? This could be poison, for all I know."

"Wouldn't I have killed you earlier if I wanted you dead?" Dahlen asked bluntly. The wall of vines shifted behind him, as if in agreement.

Rhee had always appreciated people who spoke plainly, but the Fontisian talked about murder with the same tone as he might his lunch. Even if the pill didn't kill her, it would be a clever way to strip her of her title, especially if it turned out the scrambler wasn't reversible. With a different DNA sequence and no recognizable features, she would no longer be the last Ta'an, the final heir to the throne.

"I could announce my survival instead." She thought of Nero and his coronation coverage. Thanks to his pretty words and even prettier mouth, the universe hung on his every word. Should Rhee choose to come forward, she could reach out to Nero in a moment's notice. "Not hide—not take some pill that will change my DNA."

"You have no following." Dahlen shook his head. "To the public, you're merely the Rose of the Galaxy. Even if you could prove Seotra was behind your assassination attempt, you're not a leader. You're a sheltered girl. What does one have to do to earn your trust, apart from saving your life? Princess, listen to me: You'll have little luck finding anyone you *can* trust."

She turned away. The truth rubbed her raw. He was right, again. She didn't know her people, and she wasn't sure they would rise up for her. She'd been busy training, plotting her revenge. And Seotra's reach was long. The people liked him. Under his rule, the planet had become wealthier. Now not a child was born in Kalu who couldn't afford the cube. Some critics said this was deliberate, so that Seotra and the UniForce could spy through the network. But most people thought only of their own comfort and convenience.

"With Seotra on the throne, the stability of the galaxy is at stake. Surely even you can understand that." He picked up the pill, holding it out to her. "The order can protect you—long enough to gather public support, to rout out the traitors and return you to the throne. To do all that, you have to stay alive."

Rhee took the pill from Dahlen's hand once again. Her own palms felt sweaty. She knew he was right. If the Ta'an bloodline died out, so did the validity of the Urnew Treaty. There would be nothing to stop Kalu and Fontis from going to war again, and from dragging the rest of the universe into the conflict. "I'll take this on one condition."

Dahlen's expression remained flat. "Which is?"

"I want to go after Seotra first." A flower bloomed within seconds off the side of the stump she sat upon, and angled itself up to her.

"Go after the Regent himself? The celebrated war veteran who wants you dead?" he asked. Rhee couldn't tell if he was mocking her or if he was simply intrigued by the idea. "Isn't it enough that he is trying to kill you? Why seek him out; why give him the chance?"

"If he's trying to kill me," Rhiannon said, "he won't expect me to come looking for him."

Dahlen squinted at her, and for a moment he looked almost impressed. "He's not without his own contingent of Tasinn. I understand that all the important Kalusian officials have escorts."

"We'll have to figure out a way around them," Rhiannon said, hoping she sounded more confident than she felt.

He tapped his fingers across the wooden console. It was practically the first human gesture she'd seen from him. In the hours she'd known him, he'd been all straight lines and sharp movements. She saw in detail the ring she'd noticed when he was fighting Veyron: The outline of a horned animal was etched into its black metal. She wondered if it was another religious relic.

Dahlen started to speak—but just then, a red light began to blink on the screen of his console.

"What's that?" she asked. Rhee saw they were approaching

the Outer Belt, near Dembos and the remains of Wraeta. "What's happening?" A red blinking light was never good.

"It's a checkpoint," he said tersely.

Their pod shuddered violently, and the pill fell from Rhee's hand and through the grating. She dropped to her knees and peered through the metal slats to see where it had rolled.

A low beep sounded through the bridge. The unfurled leaves and open flowers closed up into tight buds and retreated toward the walls.

"They've locked a grav beam on us." Dahlen was losing his cool. "We're being hailed."

"I thought you said we were undetectable." Panic was drilling through Rhiannon's blood, like a secondary pulse.

"We were," he said. "At least we used to be." He shook his head. "The UniForce must've upgraded their systems."

Dahlen held a finger to his lips, indicating silence. He pressed the comm link on the console. "This is the *Genoma* answering hail 2787 from Dembos. Over," he said. He spoke in Kalu, the official language of the UniForce.

"*Genoma*, this is Dembos," a male voice said. He had a twang that Rhee would've placed from the southern hemisphere of her planet. "You're flying in Kalusian airspace. We've instituted a mandatory checkpoint across the southern belt. Your vessel is unscannable—looks like organic matter? Either way, we're going to have to board. Over."

"I regret to tell you that's not possible. This is actually a Fontisian vessel, composed of organic matter from the sacred forest of Dena," Dahlen said, sounding light and self-assured, as if he weren't harboring an escaped princess. "According to the Urnew Treaty, article nine, these vessels are under religious protection. Over."

"*Genoma*, please be advised that Kalu has declared martial law. Boarding your vessel in three minutes. Cooperation mandatory. Over."

The transmission went static, and the ship shuddered once more. The Dembos grav beam was pulling them in.

"Martial law?" Rhee repeated.

Dahlen's blond eyebrows angled down toward his nose. His complexion was ashen. "It means your military can use force—"

"'—use force and suspend certain civil liberties in periods of war or civil unrest,'" she said impatiently. "I know what it means." Everyone always expected princesses to know nothing except how to bow and smile and curtsy. "Martial law hasn't been declared since the start of the Great War . . ."

She trailed off. Because suddenly, she understood.

Martial law meant that Kalu was preparing for war.

SIX

ALYOSHA

"COME on come on come *on*!" Alyosha muttered. Air whipped up through the overhead vent as soon as the bay door sealed behind him. He needed to get to Vincent, but the *Revolutionary* was as old as dirt—the air lock took forever to stabilize. His suit was a one-man sauna. Sweat stung his eyes. His tank top was plastered to his chest and back. The visor of his helmet had fogged up so that he could barely see.

Even after all these years, the air lock freaked him out. He'd never gotten used to the change in pressure, never could shake the feeling that a giant with a vacuum was up there sticking it to him. But what was worse was the suctioning *sound*—loud, vicious—like something had crawled into his ear and was pulling out his soul.

Soul. A word hardly anyone on Kalu used. The truth was he still thought about his soul a lot. Blame it on all those years of prayer.

They were all the same: dark, drooping tents with a Fontisian preacher front and center while he riled up the Wraetan folks to praise Vodhan. An impossible, stifling heat that left Aly feeling like he'd spent the entire service three inches from a bonfire. But if Aly stayed very still, if he behaved, if he didn't fidget, maybe he'd have a cushy afterlife. That's what he had been told, at least. He'd believed it for a long time, too, back when he still prayed, and back when he believed in a lot of things.

He looked up at the thought of heaven—a force of habit he didn't think he'd ever shake. Instead of the divine, all he saw was a vent working overtime. He willed himself to forget the noise, but in that muted space his thoughts became crowded. The image of the old Nau Fruman came to mind. It wasn't so much the blood that bothered him. Aly could handle that. No, it had been the little red handprints on the Nauie's wrinkled shirt, and that long, black braid placed across his chest.

The lightmount on the wall switched from red to green, and the inner door of the chamber finally creaked open. He pushed the helmet off and threw up in a trash can. Relief was short-lived. He gulped at a breath of recycled air, his stomach clenched a second time, and he purged himself again. He looked up, suddenly self-conscious that the daisies would zoom in and catch him puking his guts out—way worse than getting caught with his pants down, which had happened plenty of times. But then he remembered they'd stopped broadcasting.

"Vin," Aly said into his cube. He caught the pitch of his own voice, rusty, like it needed oiling. "Get out here. Suit up. Over."

Pavel rolled toward him. A panel opened at the top of

his domed figure, and dozens of magnetized pieces emerged. Stacking and clicking into place, the droid extended to his full height, just short of Aly's waist. Aly nodded at him distractedly. He'd programmed the droid to detect subtle motions—greetings like nods and waves, disappointment like a head shake or crossed arms. Pavel blinked his blue eyelights in response.

"Did you get my hail?" Aly asked.

"I went into sleep mode during the upgrade." His eyelights went red. "I did not see any incoming messages."

"VINCENT!" Aly said again, touching the spot just below his ear. Silence. He wondered if Vin still felt weird about how they'd left it earlier. "Where is he?"

"Heat signature reads his bedroom," said Pavel. "Pulse is low, delta waves have slowed."

"Are you telling me he's asleep?" So much for mourning.

"He's likely in NREM, stage three of the sleep cycle. Humans often—"

"Hold that thought, P," Aly interrupted. "Vin, WAKE. UP." He yelled a string of what he thought were particularly colorful insults into his cube, and threw in some Wraetan ones for good measure. He could say whatever he wanted with the daisies off, but his whole rant was met with more silence.

Aly found his rhythm despite the bulk of his suit. Pavel enabled his density mode and rolled closely behind him. Slipping and sliding, Aly finally reached Vincent's threshold and burst through his door. His cramped room was a disaster zone. Vin was still in bed.

He kicked his way through the piles of clothes. "Get up,

taejis face." Aly hopped over a gadget he didn't recognize—one of Vin's new projects, probably. "I found an escape pod from the royal ship."

"Alyosha—" Pavel started.

"Look, I'm sorry for being kind of pissed earlier, but we gotta *go*. Rise and shine, you lazy son of a *choirtoi*." Vin had made Aly teach him a bunch of Wraetan curse words, and that one was his favorite. He flung the sheet off him, but Vincent wasn't there. All he found was a pillow and some balled-up clothes. What the hell was going on?

"Pavel," he called back to the droid. "You said you read a heat source?"

From under his base, Pavel switched out the wide treadmill wheel to two large all-terrain ones, then climbed the stacks of clothes to stand in the center of the tiny room. His dome rotated in a circle as he scanned. Then he extended an arm and picked up a gray cylinder—the gadget Aly had stepped over to get to the bed.

"It's some kind of external heat device," the droid said.

The pressure felt like too much, like everything was bearing down on him. He didn't know what to do. He looked around the room—really looked—for the first time. Vin had always been messy, but this was different. All of his drawers had been pulled out and emptied on the floor. Tiny machine parts were scattered everywhere. Everything that had been up on his bulletin board was torn down. Someone had searched Vincent's room, it seemed. But who? And what had happened to Vincent?

Aly felt cold. Vin had disappeared just after Aly had found

the royal escape pod and sent out a hail across an open cube channel. It couldn't be a coincidence.

"Who else is on board?" he asked Pavel.

Pavel looked distressed—for a droid, at least. "I detect no additional heat signatures." So Vincent had left—or had been taken.

Aly felt a quake starting inside his chest. With a sweep of his arm, he sent everything on the desk flying. A familiar hammer landed on the floor. It was his. Vin was always stealing his tools. He could never keep track of his own. They'd gotten into a fist-fight over it once. He suddenly regretted how stupid he'd been; he should've just given it to him.

"Cube transmissions are scrambled," Pavel said flatly. "Something is wrong."

"No *taejis* something is wrong."

But at that moment he saw a shadow eclipse the doorway: a humanoid droid—tall and shiny, made of a high-grade alloy. *Military*-grade alloy. It was the NX series, but from a model that hadn't yet been released. Aly didn't know why or how it had boarded the *Revolutionary*, but it stood at least eight feet tall and had to duck through the doorway.

Technically he and the NX droid were both soldiers for the UniForce. They were on the same side.

So why did Aly suddenly want to piss his pants?

"Private Alyosha Myraz," it said, scanning his vitals. Its eyes flashed once and then turned red. "Mark identified."

Alyosha's knees buckled. Definitely *not* on the same side. No wonder Pavel had detected no additional heat signatures on board. UniForce—it had to be UniForce—had sent a droid to do their dirty work.

As the droid went for him, Aly grabbed a drawer off the floor and flung it at the NX as hard as he could, but the metal behemoth swatted it away. It smashed against the wall and splintered in two. Alyosha scrambled for more things to throw. The droid was on him quickly, and kicked its heel into Aly's chest. Even with the giant suit Aly was wearing, the impact was like getting shot. He flew backward against the wall and took down the bulletin board, collapsing on the desk, gasping.

The military droid took hold of Aly's leg and yanked him off the desk. Aly landed on his back on a pile of clothes, and he thanked god that Vin was such a slob. He might have broken his neck on the bare floor otherwise. And then he remembered that Vincent had taken off. A feeling wormed itself in, right there up between the pit of his stomach and the back of his heart—not just anger or sadness, but both, a sense of the unfairness of it all.

To his left he saw the hammer, and he grabbed it before the droid could kick it away. He knew it was no use. This model of droid couldn't even die, really; it would just reboot. Still, he whacked it blindly in the direction of the droid's control panel, roaring with sudden rage, unwilling to die in a heap of Vincent's dirty laundry.

Then the droid ripped the hammer from his hand. It grabbed his neck, and Alyosha's brain blinked out. He was going to die . . .

The droid went suddenly still. Its eyes went black. Its whole body began to spark. The terrible steel hands around Alyosha's neck released, and he sat up, coughing and gasping, massaging his throat. The droid was on its back now, twitching like a dying insect. Aly turned to Pavel, who was humming loudly in overdrive.

"What . . . what did you do?" Aly asked, through the pain in his throat.

"I uploaded a virus to its operating system." The way he said it had a lilt. Aly could almost hear the shrug in his voice.

"What virus?" Whatever Pavel had done, he was glad for it.

"A virus I just invented. I coded it now."

Aly could've hugged him. He staggered to his feet, his head still dizzy and his chest like a bombed-out crater. But he was alive.

He knew the droid was being tracked, though—all military droids were—and shorting it had made them more high-profile than ever. Military droids didn't travel solo, and reinforcements must be getting ready to storm the *Revolutionary* now. Aly ripped out Pavel's comm unit, an external cube he had installed so the droid was wired to the network. Then he powered down his own cube, and stumbled. It felt like a fist had wrapped around his brain to wring out all the juice, the connectivity. He was offline. He couldn't record anything. He couldn't look anything up. But at least their GPS would go dark. Still, they had Aly's heat signature to take care of.

"Let's go," Aly said, taking one last glance at Vin's empty bed. He grabbed the hammer off the floor, praying Vin had bolted before some titanium beast had crushed his head like a grape.

Please let Vin be okay.

Then they ran—rather, he ran and Pavel rolled.

"How much of the medical bible do you have downloaded?" he called over his shoulder.

"Approximately thirty percent. First aid and basic surgery."

"Anything on anesthesiology?"

"No. I'd need to go back online."

"We can't go back online." Not until they were out of danger. *If* they were ever out of danger. Why had Kalu's UniForce gone on the attack? Aly knew it must be because he'd found evidence the Princess might still be alive, but he was too jacked up to untangle any more of the puzzle.

They entered the medbay, and Aly barred the door behind them. He tore down medicine bottles and smashed salves onto the floor until he found what he was looking for: gel nitrogen compound. He shrugged out of the suit, then pulled off his shirt and pants and began covering his body to insulate the heat. "I need to lower my body temperature. What's the baseline so I lose my heat signature?"

"Below twenty-two degrees Celsius, you become undetectable by standard scanning techniques. But every computable attempt carries an eighty percent chance of fatality by hypothermia."

"Not if you resuscitate me first." Aly started to cover his face and smeared a thick layer across the crown of his head, gooping it into his coarse hair.

Pavel was clearly flustered. Metal attachments extended and retracted as he scanned med labels and did calculations on the fly. His movements were jerky, like the old-school service droids that worked in the Wray. Pavel held up a newly filled syringe. "If I inject cathariiuum into your blood, your temperature will lower down to twenty-five degrees, and I can resuscitate you with any of the illium ions within seven minutes to prevent death."

"You said I had to get it down to twenty-two degrees."

"True," Pavel said. He held up a second syringe. "But the heat sensors have a margin of error. There's a seventy-seven percent chance you will remain undetected."

"Not good enough."

"Then our only alternative is the tauri-based compound. You'll drop down to twenty degrees. But after three minutes you'll suffer painful paralysis, and after four minutes you will be dead. Also, the sucra serum meant to reverse it is highly unstable."

"What I'm hearing is: We use the tauri. You inject me with the juice, and we make a run for the escape pod." Aly picked up the sucra serum. It was purple, like the dawn. Last time he saw the sunrise he'd been on leave and went to Jeth's on Chram.

"I strongly recommend against it," Pavel insisted now.

"P, there's no other choice." He grabbed for the second syringe and plunged it into his heart before Pavel could stop him. A black hole rose up to meet him, and he fell into it—through the air, through the floor, into the dark space that crushed all matter.

He was both trapped in the body and floating above it, his soul split in two. Then all the matter of his body re-collected at this point in space and time, bouncing back in a fraction of a second. He shot up. Everything felt numb and powerful at once. He wanted to crush something with his hands, and he was suddenly angry. Really. Angry. He'd mow all the capital sons of *choirtois* down now.

But when he tried to take a step, his legs wouldn't work. He would've fallen again if Pavel hadn't rolled over and buffered his fall.

"Paralysis set in early. Three minutes and twenty seconds out."

He was draped over Pavel now, his feet dragging behind them. He walked, or tried to, which meant that he kicked his feet out weakly and focused on the hum of Pavel's wheels. They had exited the medbay, and he was cold. Shivering, teeth-chattering cold.

"Aly? Your heat signature is now undetectable. Answer if you can hear me."

He let out a groan.

"Two minutes and forty-five seconds out. Irreversible damage will set in soon. On your order, I will inject the serum."

"The serum?" It sounded familiar, urgent even—like a very important part of a very important plan they'd discussed. But what plan, Aly couldn't quite recall . . .

"I believe you are experiencing temporary memory loss. It may mean your brain is being deprived of oxygen."

But no. He could remember. He was back in school, with the Fontisian missionary, trying to pronounce Vodhan's name for the first time—and how weird the word felt in his mouth, all the sharp syllables rolling off his tongue in exactly the wrong way. Still, he'd liked the idea of one god, one master plan. Sometimes it still felt like Vodhan talked to him in whispers, and he felt just a little bit lighter and a little bit less alone.

"Do you see a light, Aly? If so, be aware it is an electrical surge in your brain, and it means you will likely die."

"You're a bummer, Pavel." Aly's jaw felt heavy, his tongue swollen to three times its size. "I can't bring you anywhere."

"Good, Alyosha. Attempts at humor mean the frontal cortex is still intact. Two minutes and fifteen seconds out." But just then Pavel came to an abrupt halt. "I detect movement."

Pavel backtracked through the hallway toward the access ladder that led down to the engine room. "A temporary solution," the droid said in a low voice. "Based on your bone density and the height of the fall, you should not sustain serious injuries."

"Fall?" he asked, even as Pavel laid him down and rolled around behind his shoulders. "What fall?"

The droid pushed.

Aly dropped. When he slammed against the ground, his head hit the grating and he saw stars—but it didn't hurt. Nothing hurt. It was only cold. He thought of the day they'd gotten the news that his mom and Alina had died. He saw his dad standing over him all over again. *Be a man*, he was saying. *Be a man . . .*

"Two minutes out," Pavel called down to him. His voice at the top of the ladder sounded tinny. Aly realized where he was—steps away from the engine room. Then Pavel disappeared.

"No," he tried to yell, but his mouth wasn't working anymore. He was alone, shivering, his head busted open. How, exactly, did he get here? He'd never seen snow, but this was what it must feel like to be buried in it. Even his brain was freezing over. Memories flashed from his life: walking alongside his dad, water dripping off a corrugated metal roof. Someone was coming toward them, but he couldn't remember who or why. They were on their way to fly a kite . . .

Aly slipped out of consciousness and then woke again. How long had it been? A second? An hour? He heard the NX marching.

The hiss and zip of expensive hydraulics boiled the blood in his heart.

He was seven. His dad's enormous hand pawed at his shirt and pulled him close.

"Don't speak unless spoken to. And don't say anything *smart*." His dad had whispered the last word like it was something foul, shameful. A Fontisian was passing, but he wasn't like the missionaries who taught Vodhan's word in the droopy makeshift prayer tents. The Fontisians were generally larger, with pale skin and pointy ears the kids would whisper about. It was rumored they could hear anything, anywhere. But this particular man had dark tattoos all along his neck that looked like they were clawing their way out from under his shift.

"What's this?" the Fontisian had asked, as he grabbed roughly for their kite. Aly was too scared to speak—and the man had repeated himself, this time in Wraetan. He'd accented it in all the wrong places. And when his dad told him it was a kite they'd made together, the Fontisian's answer was cold.

There is only one way to get to heaven, and it is not by flying.

Now Aly felt the cool grate against his face. How much time had passed? More than two minutes, he was sure.

He was going to die. Maybe he was dead already.

He could still feel the rain from when he'd been tossed outside all those years ago. In his mouth, on his eyelids, sliding down around his ears. It was like the water had been gathering all these years, between then and now, rising. Then it swallowed him up and everything was quiet.

SEVEN

RHIANNON

THE UniForce soldiers would board any second, and Rhee could no longer trust that they would protect her.

"Take the pill. The scrambler takes up to a minute to work," Dahlen said. There was a new sense of urgency in his voice.

"I've lost it!" Rhee peered through the grate into the darkness. She'd made a mess of everything. "Help me get the grate up!"

He cursed in Fontisian. "There's no time," he said. He went to the wall and slid his fingers along its gnarled surface. He found what he was looking for: the opening of a hatch that had been invisible. He motioned for Rhee to crawl inside. When the hatch closed behind her, everything went dark.

But it didn't go still.

The bark shifted under Rhee's weight, poking and prodding her as she tried to get comfortable. She knew the ship was alive—it was organic matter, after all—but she hadn't expected it to squirm and wiggle. She felt sick, like she'd digested something rotten. No, like she was *being* digested.

Outside, the ship had settled into a grav beam, and she heard the bay doors open. Dahlen offered strained greetings, and Rhee felt the weight of the craft tip as though several soldiers had come on board at once.

"Sergeant Niture," a man said, introducing himself. "Just a routine sweep. Interesting vessel . . ."

"I've never seen this kind of droid before," Dahlen said. Rhee heard the zip and hiss of a machine sweeping across the small pod. Something cracked. "It's pretty, certainly. But can it be more careful?"

"I'm sorry, sir," the sergeant said in a tone that suggested he was not sorry at all. "These NX combat droids haven't been programmed for a soft touch. Sooner we're done, sooner it's off."

"Of course," Dahlen answered. "Can you tell me, Sergeant, when martial law was declared?"

A tense silence followed. Rhee figured this Niture character must not like being questioned, even if the question itself was a reasonable one.

"Since riots broke out across all of Kalu, that's when," the man said roughly. "Lots of people devastated by the Princess's death, and lots of people wondering exactly who's responsible. Like the allies don't have enough problems. Enough dusties to choke off whatever resources they have left . . ."

Rhee heard a long pause, and she wondered what had been

communicated in that silence. She was worried about the riots. She'd have to check the holos next time she got the chance.

As the droid moved closer, Rhee hugged herself and, as if in response, the wooden walls of the ship enfolded her even more tightly. As she waited in the darkness, Rhee thought of when she'd explored the sand caves with Julian, his crooked smile when he looked at her, the rough stone walls against the skin of her palm—it was the first time they'd ever done a cube-to-cube trans-fer. She'd felt goosebumps, seeing and feeling his life through his memory.

Now, without her cube, even this memory was gone. Distorted, like all organic memories were. The cave walls closed in and all she felt was terror.

Rhee urged her mind to somewhere calm, and a new mem-ory emerged: a game of hide-and-seek with Josselyn, the time she'd gotten lost in the cellars.

Her parents had thought it was filthy down there and never uploaded the layout to her cube to prevent her from exploring the tunnels. She'd been down there for hours, blinded by the torch-light when Joss had finally found her—relief and shame clutch-ing at her insides as she hid her face so her big sister wouldn't see her tears . . .

"Hmm. The material makes heat signatures impossible to detect," the sergeant continued. Rhee placed her hand against the wood as if to thank it. She knew so little about Fontisian tech. "You'll have to enable your cube playback for us."

"I'm from a Fontisian order," Dahlen said. "I turned off my

cube once I took my vows. It's against our practices." She could tell, now, that the calmer he sounded, the more annoyed he really was.

The sergeant grunted. "Fontisians, sure, the great Vodhan, I've heard. Freedom to practice and all that is fine and good, but since you don't have playback, we'll need to ask you some questions. NX-101, enable interrogation."

"Interrogation mode enabled. Level six."

"Dahlen of Fontis," the sergeant said. "What is your directive?"

"Missionary work," Dahlen said evenly.

"Affirmative," the droid said.

"My brother fought in the war. He was stationed on Yarazu and said you lot don't feel pain. Should we test his theory?" the man asked casually. Then after a silence: "Break his finger anyway."

Rhee brought a fist to her mouth as she heard a terrible *snap*, and wondered if the droid had done what it was asked: Dahlen had not cried out in pain. The walls around her shifted and contorted her into a new position, pushing her leg at an awkward angle.

"In hindsight, we should've avoided the ring finger. It will prove difficult to remove . . ." Niture said without emotion. "Next question: Are you sympathetic to the royal family of Kalu?"

"Of course," Dahlen said. She thought she could hear a slight strain in his voice. "The last Ta'an girl has just died."

She shivered, despite herself. It was strange to hear him talk about her like she was already a ghost.

"Let me rephrase. Do you support the Urnew Treaty?"

"I'm not a political man."

"Let me guess. You're a man of *god*," the sergeant said, his voice dripping sarcasm. "Next question . . ." But his voice trailed off, and a terrible silence hung for a minute. When the sergeant spoke again, his voice was very soft. "Interesting piece. Is it silver?"

Rhee's heart seized. Julian's telescope—she'd left it on the console.

The sergeant continued in that soft, falsely courteous voice. "I thought your kind was too good to mine sacred metals. Where did you get this?"

After a short pause, Dahlen said, "It was a gift."

The soldier droid whirred in the silence. "Negative."

"Ah." The instructor paused, a sneer in his voice. "Why lie about a telescope? Robot, second finger." Another sound like the harsh crack of a whip. Rhee flinched as nausea rose in her throat. Dahlen only exhaled, a small sigh. How long could this go on? How long could she let it?

The walls and floor around her shifted again angrily, clamping down her leg. It seemed to be pulsing, as if in response to Dahlen's pain—and the other man's hatred. This was all her fault. It was her telescope. And if she'd just taken the scrambler, then she could've saved them both.

She heard her dad's voice. "*Ma'tan sarili*" was the last thing he'd told her when he'd kissed her forehead. Such a simple phrase but such a tall demand—to pledge your highest self to someone else, to ask someone else to do the same.

Rhee felt for the knife and moved into a crouch. The wood

released her as if it knew her intention. She'd fled her family's ship and left them to burn up without her. Killed a man she loved like a father. She could not allow someone to die for her.

Get up, Joss had said the day she found Rhee alone and sniveling in the cellars. She hadn't teased her or called her a baby, but Rhee had never forgotten the look on her face, as if Joss had expected more. *Get up*.

Now Rhee pounded on the hatch. Outside, Dahlen cried out for the first time. But she knew she had to save him.

"What the—?"

Rhee squeezed the knife in one hand. She breathed in through her nose, out through her mouth. She imagined her muscles expanding. Focus. That was what Veyron—dead Veyron, traitor Veyron—had always taught her. Too many fighters fell because they lost focus.

Then there was an explosion of splintered wood as the droid burst open the compartment. Air and light flooded in. She saw Dahlen restrained, staring straight at her—terrified, or perhaps angry with her. It didn't matter.

The droid was a newer model, made to look like a shiny, metal man. It looked her up and down with its glass eyes. "Rhiannon Ta'an," it announced, after its program had finished scanning.

"Empress . . . ?" The sergeant nearly choked. "You're—you're alive?"

Then the droid picked her up from the back of her tunic, like a mama dog picking up her pup by the scruff of the neck, and deposited her neatly in front of the sergeant. He was entirely ordinary—a paunchy Miseu with a pear-shaped body and deep yellow skin. Antennae came out the side of his head where a human's ears would be, and the high gravity of Kalu had taken its toll: His face looked like a deflated balloon. Rhee had seen his kind countless times before—little men who squeezed into double-breasted suits, following around some adviser or another, oozing with compliments in hopes of being welcomed into the political entourage. He was like every low-level diplomat she'd been forced to shake hands with, who were quick to point out how articulate she was for her age, or how lovely her light complexion was—as if she were incapable of detecting a backhanded compliment. Essentially, he was an idiot. He was an embarrassment to their military.

"Isn't this a pleasure?" he said with a traditional bow. "The Regent's council will be thrilled to know you're alive."

He'd no doubt be thrilled to receive his reward.

"The pleasure is mine," she said sweetly. "But I won't be joining you."

In one smooth motion, she threw her arms up, slipping out of the oversized tunic. Still clutching the switchblade, she landed on her knees and drove the knife into the sergeant's foot with both hands. He screamed in pain. The droid grabbed her head and slammed it down to the ground, and for a split second her vision went black. With her face against the grate, she saw a flash of red as her vision cleared: the DNA scrambler.

The droid picked her up again. For a half second she was staring up into the cool indifference of its metal face. Then she saw a flash of green—a snake?—wind around its neck and yank the droid backward, forcing it to release her.

She scrambled to her feet. She saw now that Dahlen had managed to wrap a vine around its steel throat. For a second the Fontisian and the droid staggered together in a terrible dance, and the droid was squeezing Dahlen's neck. Rhee was temporarily mesmerized by the sight of dozens of thick vines slithering from the wall, slowly winding their way up the droid's legs, punching through its steel plates, tightening around its thick metal waist. Protecting Dahlen.

The scrambler. She dropped to her knees again, threading her fingers through the grate, fumbling for the pill.

"Rhee," Dahlen managed to gasp. "Look out."

She turned. The sergeant had freed the knife from his foot. Now he didn't look so ordinary; she could believe he'd fought in the Great War. His eyes were cloudy with rage. He looked like a monster. How would she escape?

You never think *before you move*, Veyron had said.

Her fingertips grazed the pill. One more inch . . . At last she managed to get it into her palm.

And before the sergeant could attack, she whipped around and kicked at his shins, cutting his legs out from under him. He slammed backward. Before he could recover, she was on top of him, disgusted by the spongy feel of his skin.

When he opened his mouth to call for the droid, Rhee shoved the scrambler down his throat. She clamped his jaw shut so he couldn't spit it out.

His rounded eyes went wide and he began to choke. Rhee realized in horror that the scrambler was designed for *human* DNA, and she didn't know what would happen. She watched as his chubby face began to lengthen, so that the tip of his chin and the top of his forehead stretched out like a piece of dough. Then it thinned out further, worn through in places, nearly transparent in others: She saw down to the bone and blood.

"Stop! Stop!" he screamed. Even his voice was becoming distorted, as if it, too, was being stretched to the breaking point. "Please stop!"

True to its programming, the droid stopped struggling immediately and darkened to standby mode. The vines began to withdraw. Dahlen, still breathing hard, ripped out the external comm unit mounted onto the droid's neck. It was a droid's equivalent to a cube, except the droid couldn't function without one.

Dahlen limped up to Rhee, cradling his broken hand. He held out the tunic she'd shed. She wrapped it around herself, and together they watched as the Miseu's eyes went milky and his cries began to change, higher and then lower like he was testing out a frequency. It was as if he were melting before her eyes, and she turned away, feeling as if she might vomit.

"It was a clever move," Dahlen said.

"I didn't do it to impress you," she fired back. "I did to save your life."

"My life is not your concern." He reset his fingers, taking in a sharp inhale that was barely audible over the cracking of his bones. He pulled the black ring off and slipped it on the opposite finger of his good hand. "I'm grateful to you, but you're meant to be empress. To unify the galaxy. Your survival takes precedence over my life. It takes precedence, too, over your need to be honorable."

"I don't believe that." Honor, bravery, loyalty—these made up her *ma'tan sarili*, the three values.

"You're not old enough to know what to believe," Dahlen answered as he kneeled down next to Niture. As if he were that much older. Dahlen began searching the sergeant's neck with one thin hand. For a confused second, Rhee thought he was checking for a pulse. Then she saw he was holding the knife.

"That's my knife," she said. Her surprise morphed into dread.

He ignored her. "Do you know where they implant cubes on the Miseu?" He grabbed the sergeant—now horribly deformed— and jerked him up to a sitting position. "Here, at the top of the spine."

"What are you—?" she began to ask, but had to look away, as Dahlen plunged the tip of the blade into the sergeant's neck and gouged out the microchip.

"He might know something of value," Dahlen said simply.

Dahlen cleaned the cube of a sticky white substance she assumed was Miseu blood. "Can't you just enable playback?" she asked, knowing full well it was impossible. There were mechanisms and fail-safes that prevented forced playback, and in any event the holder had to be conscious.

"There's a driver embedded in the dashboard just under the console. See what you can find."

Rhee was glad for the opportunity to turn away from the mangled body of the sergeant. Whatever memories he'd willed would be lost; his family would be devastated. Rhee knew the feeling all too well, and wouldn't wish it on anyone. She located the driver and inserted the chip into it, angry, hopeless. Rhee wasn't sure what Dahlen was trying to do. Sergeant Niture's death would have triggered an automatic wipe of his memory system. Maybe the cube was outfitted with an identification number, so they could access the sergeant's files—like his military history, or who he might've been reporting to.

The console lit up. The prompts and instructions were in Fontisian characters. She tried her best to navigate through the foreign characters using the touchscreen, not sure what she was looking for. She pressed a word that made the whole ship go dark, with hundreds of holograms creating a circle before her. Most of them looked like photographs, moments frozen in time, and she found herself drawn to an image of a smiling Miseu. Rhee lifted her hand up as if to touch her face, and her hand activated something on the hologram—because the woman threw her head back and her laughter filled the ship. Then she reached her arms out toward Rhee as if to hug her before the file cut out. *The sergeant's mother*, Rhee realized, feeling sick. There were hundreds of memories in hologram form, piled on top of one another. It was like being in the man's mind. It *was* being in his mind.

Which was impossible. Unless . . .

"He's—he's still alive?" she asked, horrified. She turned to see Niture, sitting up, his back propped against the wall of vines, his features so horribly melted and disfigured he was unrecognizable.

"I'll take over from here," Dahlen said, temporarily distorting the hologram as he walked through it.

"How is this possible?" Rhee asked. She was using technology that wasn't supposed to exist. It was a crime to look into someone's cube without permission—it was more than a crime. Cubes stored not just information but memories, feelings, sensations, thought-impressions. "This is wrong. This is illegal. At the G-1K summit—I can't remember if it was the third or the fourth—but it was clearly forbidden by law—"

"'Forbidden by law'?" Dahlen tilted his head and looked at her. *Through* her. "Have you seen what terrible things the laws of men enable?"

No. She believed in the law. She believed in the laws that came out of those summits, certainly. Over the past sixty years, ever since the cube had been invented, the universe's greatest scientists had gathered at the G-1K to review and regulate the interplanetary laws around its use. They were high-profile individuals, and every planet or territory inevitably plastered their names on a landmark or their faces on a digital credit.

Dahlen sorted through the holograms with his hands, flicking away the ones that didn't interest him. There was a pattern to it, and Rhee did her best to follow, but couldn't make sense of another man's mind. She was curious, ashamed, but most of all, furious.

"Stop this."

Dahlen ignored her, working in a way that was methodical and mechanical—but with every image he slid away, a seismic shudder moved through her. She was watching an entire life collapsed, and felt the weight not just of bringing the Miseu to near death, but of something much worse.

"It seems I'm not wrong." Dahlen said. "Here. Look." Buried under so many layers of memories, some fragmented and some crystalline, was a recent memory of a priority message sent to all

Kalu government personnel. The hologram showed a man, his skinny lips pursed, his expression serious.

Rhee's breath caught in her throat. It was Crown Regent Seotra. Her father's best friend, grim-faced and power hungry, who'd stood in the hangar and sent her family off to their deaths. Rhee had seen Seotra as she snuck off the craft, had seen the way he smiled—how many times had she replayed that memory?— and a look of glee, as if he were only inches from the thing he wanted most in the world.

Only *hours* from what he wanted most.

Dahlen touched the image of Seotra, and like water disturbed by a stone, it began to ripple and move.

"I won't mince words. This is a dark, dark day for the galaxy." Seotra paused and brought a closed fist to his mouth like he was desperately trying to contain emotion. "Since she was the last living member of the Ta'an dynasty, Rhiannon's death places the hard-won treaty between Fontis and Kalu at risk. But I must emphasize that *even if the treaty no longer has legal validity*, we still have a moral responsibility to honor its provisions."

Rhiannon's heart sank. Seotra was smart—too smart. On the face of it, he was encouraging the Kalu to keep the peace. Between the lines, he was reminding them that with her death, the treaty that had ended the universe's bloodiest war was all but broken.

"I would like to reiterate that for those of you who are so selfishly using the Princess's death as an excuse to sow violence and chaos in the capital, and in order to justify your despicable acts of civil disobedience, punishment will be swift and severe."

So the sergeant had spoken the truth: There was rioting in Kalu. Her heart swelled at the thought that some people, at least, were furious about her death, but she clamped any bit of joy down quickly. What did it matter? All it meant was that there were only more deaths, this time in her name.

Revealing herself now would legally reinstate the treaty, but could she wrest power away from Seotra successfully? Would her people welcome or denounce her? Would she be killed before she could get her revenge?

"As of eleven hundred hours, martial law will be in effect across the planet, all Kalusian colonies and territories, and Kalusian designated airspace." Seotra brought a hand to his forehead, the first sign he'd shown of discomfort. "I'll be traveling to Tinoppa to honor the Princess's life, and her death, at a ceremony three days from now, conducted by Tai Reyanna, Princess Rhiannon's personal adviser." His fingers tightened on the podium. Even in holo, Rhee could see his knuckles whiten. "I ask you as a planet to pray for us that we will see our way out of these dark times."

Rhee balled her hands so that Dahlen wouldn't see they were shaking. "That hypocrite, 'paying respects' with the Tai to win points with the interplanetary community even as he mobilizes for a war in *my* name," she said. She wondered, secretly, if it was more than just an act. Could Tai Reyanna have conspired with him? Rhee shook the thought loose, angry for even thinking it. "We need to go to Tinoppa. We need to stop him."

Dahlen continued to sort through more messages. Reports of a hyperloop hijacked in Uryra, an electromagnetic pulse detonated in Erisha, an occupied embassy in Sibu—Kalusian cities wrecked by havoc.

Rhee's anger was going to suffocate her. She reached out and pounded on the console. Dahlen turned to her finally, a look on his face that bordered on boredom. "Are you listening to me?" she hissed, and drew herself up a little taller. "I demand we go to Seotra."

Dahlen walked through the circle of the holograms and fiddled with the navigational controls. With a graceful dip, the ship began to wheel in the sky. They were no longer heading toward Portiis.

"As you wish, Empress" was all he said.

EIGHT

ALYOSHA

ALYOSHA awoke to an explosion that rocked the ship and rolled him halfway to the engine room.

Pavel was back. He extended a zipline down the ladder and clamped on to the leg of Aly's suit.

"Fifty-three seconds out," Pavel said, as he lifted Aly with metal hooks and dragged him down the corridor. Aly's mind was fracturing. He couldn't keep his eyes open.

"Save yourself," he wanted to say, but he couldn't make the words form.

"P, what did he say?" someone asked. That voice. He knew it. He recognized it. But the name, and the image of the guy's face, came and went like something that passed in a rushing river.

"Undecipherable. His vocal cords have seized," Pavel answered. "He has thirty seconds left to live."

"What are you waiting for?" Vincent. His friend. His *best* friend. Vin was back.

"Positioning myself for maximum velocity," Pavel answered. "I'll have to puncture the chestplate—"

Vin grabbed the syringe from Pavel and drove it down into Aly's chest, through layers of muscle and bone.

Suddenly, his heart flooded with the color purple, and the rising dawn. Every muscle spasmed, and he gasped for air. His body burned; heat came back to him in the form of a fire, coursing through his veins. Memories came back, a whole universe exploding inside of him, everything he had ever known and thought.

"Sorry, man," Vin said. When he pulled back, his smile was rough around the edges. Aly didn't know if Vin was about to laugh or cry.

Vin helped Aly sit up. "Where the hell did you go?"

"Hiding in the engine room."

Aly realized it'd been too hot for Pavel to detect Vin's heat signature down there. Why the hell hadn't Aly thought of that? Vin stood and yanked Aly up to his feet, while Aly gripped on to Vin's palm to make sure he was real. "I'm gone for five minutes and you inject yourself with tauri? Don't explain," he said, when Aly opened his mouth. "Let's get going already, before any more of those metalheads come looking. No offense," he added to Pavel.

"'More of those'?" Aly repeated. His head still felt like it had been stuffed with cotton balls.

Vin and Pavel had to support him to the Tin Soldier; then

Pavel picked Aly up and strapped him in. Back again, but in the passenger's seat. It was a tight fit.

"The droids aren't the directive. They're just following orders," Vin said.

"The *directive*? What are you talking about? *Who's* the directive?"

"The Regent is. Seotra killed the Princess," Vin said. Simply. Just like that.

Aly thought of the dead Nauie, the Princess's braid. He felt like he'd been let out of an air lock. He'd been on Kalu's side, served in their army, been the poster child for their little TV piece of propaganda. Vin was on UniForce enlistment posters, for *taejis* sake. And Aly couldn't keep his thoughts straight anyway. Everything was gumming together, and then breaking apart.

"Why would Seotra want her dead?" he asked Vincent slowly.

"Why do you think?" Vin was breathing hard, scanning left and right, as if he expected another droid to spring on them. "He wanted to *stay* regent. Once she took the throne, he'd lose all his power."

"But what does that have to do with us?"

Vin made a face. "I was compromised."

Aly stared at him. *"Compromised?"*

The *Revolutionary* and the Tin Soldier had both been taken offline so that they couldn't fly. But almost immediately Vin started working in commands to restore the system. Aly felt a creeping sense of anxiety. Where had Vin learned to override UniForce commands?

"Back in business," Vin said when the dash lights came on. He punched in coordinates for the Outer Belt.

Feeling was creeping back into Aly's body, like pins and needles along his fingers and toes—and with it, a new suspicion, even a dread. Vincent was his best friend. They could talk all night or spend the whole day in silence, and either way it usually felt pretty all right, natural in a way he'd never felt with even his own family. Sometimes Vin acted differently when the cameras were on, but he knew that was just for show. He knew the difference between the real Vin and the fake Vin. At least he thought he did.

"Vincent." He swallowed. "Who are you?"

Vin got that squinty look on his face he'd get sometimes if he had a beer too many, just before he launched into some philosophical theory. Aly waited for him to explain. But then the look melted away, his face a slate wiped clean.

Vin only said: "I'm the guy who's going to save your sorry ass." Then he lifted the transparent casing and pressed the red ejector button.

They jettisoned into space, and the g-force bore down on Aly's chest. Pavel had suctioned himself low to the floor. Vin gripped the throttle and had the nerve to grin.

"Answer my question." Blood was dripping from Aly's forehead into his eye, and when he caught his reflection on the dash, he realized he'd split his eyebrow open again. He wiped the blood away and tried to pinch the wound shut.

"Eyes on the heat sensors!" But as soon as Vin said it, he

swerved right and just missed a laser beam. A white royal cruiser was at their rear and gaining speed. It fired a second laser, but Vin ducked their pod beneath it effortlessly—the only pilot Aly knew who could pull that off. Vin shot him an irritated look, as if to say *told you.*

The cruiser was on their tail, and soon a second one joined it. But Vin didn't seem afraid. He actually seemed kind of calm about the whole thing.

"Answer me, *choirtoi.*" Aly was losing it. "Or—"

"Or what?" Vin had to shout over the noise of the engine from the sentience systems. They went into a nosedive, then a barrel roll, avoiding the rapid fire that shot out from behind them. "Look, I've been working for the United Planets, okay?"

"The *United Planets*?" Aly asked. It wasn't the answer he'd expected—not that he knew what to expect. The United Planets was a neutral organization that played peacemaker between all the planets. As far as Aly knew, members of the United Planets sat around in a circle and asked nicely for favors and spent most of their time voting on things. As in, they didn't get *taejis* done.

"I was placed on the *Revolutionary* to gather intel on Kalu's UniForce," Vin said. "I wasn't gaining any traction. Sometimes I forgot I was even a spy. But the United Planets made contact a few weeks back and said to keep an eye out, and that there might be an attempt on the Princess's life. That pod we were chasing earlier—I had a bad feeling. So I tried to hail my contact. I was careful. But maybe someone got wise. Heard the message . . ."

"You chased down that pod like a *maniac*. You think that didn't put us on someone's radar?" Aly shouted. "Then you hail someone, and you want me to think you were being careful? You don't even answer your cube—"

"I turned it off! They're spying on us, Aly. I've been telling you for years to turn yours off too."

"I thought you were just one of those naturalistic freaks!"

"It was a cover. I couldn't be on DroneVision and start talking about conspiracy theories."

Aly shook his head. "Are you for real?"

"Don't even give me that look." Vin pulled them into another nosedive. "Kalu has had the tech for decades. All those G-1K summits? You wouldn't believe some of the shit they tried to do. You wouldn't believe what they can do already. They can *pull* memories . . ."

"You're talking straight-up crazy," Aly said, but he was shaken. He remembered what the missionaries had warned: the horrible rumors about soul-sucking, mind-pulling, the evil that would destroy you. The Ravaging. "How long have you been working this side hustle?" Vin wouldn't look at him, so he leaned forward and got in his face. "How long have you been playing spy for the United Planets? And don't lie."

"Since before boot camp," Vin said after a pause. "Before I even knew you or Jeth or anyone else we trained with."

He didn't realize he'd bit down on his tongue until he could taste blood in his mouth. He thought they had come after him because he'd found the royal pod. But Vin figured it was because his message had been intercepted. Aly didn't know which one was true. The timing might've been a coincidence.

Which meant there was a chance no one knew Princess Rhiannon might be alive. He'd keep that in his pocket for now. He wasn't about to tell Vin, not when he'd held back so much for so long.

Vin was still talking, trying to tell him how it wasn't all that big of a deal and everything was the same and that they were going to look out for each other. He was still spinning and dodging artillery like it was cake, notching up toward dangerous levels of interstellar speed like it wasn't any kind of thing. "We have to get to Portiis. The Lancer will meet us to debrief, and until then we'll be safe."

"The Lancer?"

He shrugged. "I don't know his real name. Safer that way."

"In what universe is *this* safer?" They were headed toward a cluster of asteroids. Vin tilted the throttle so they squeezed, just barely, through a gap between two giant pieces of floating rock, and they zoomed in at an insane speed. Pieces of rock chipped off as their wings kissed the surface of the asteroids. One of the cruisers tried to follow, but the angle was off and it clipped its wing. Aly watched as it spun wildly, stark white against a sheet of black, before it receded and disappeared. Aly felt a brief burst of regret. He wondered if that pilot would survive. And if he didn't, what would that make the body count today? Three? Four souls?

"I know it's a lot to take in," Vin said—but with irritation, as if *Aly* were the one being unreasonable. "You gotta trust me."

"Oh yeah? And why should I do that?"

"I needed to keep my cover. I was doing recon!"

"Right. *Recon.*"

"I saved your life."

"*After* you nearly got me killed," Aly pointed out. "So what? You show up, to the rescue, with all this specialized training I never knew about. You tell me I gotta cut and run and leave everything behind. But you know what? I *like* my life. So just drop me off at the nearest station, and I'll run over to the UniForce base and explain that I had nothing to do with your little spy game. I can just pretend this whole thing never happened."

"No, Alyosha. You can't." For the first time, he actually sounded sad. Vin pulled his handheld device out of his pocket and slammed it on the dash. "Enable newsfeed."

From a tiny opening in the front, it projected a hologram newsfeed between them showing footage of the *Eliedio*, the royal ship, exploding. Even in holographic form, the fire and the choking smoke were horrible to watch.

A familiar voice, patched in over images of the gruesome explosion, reached out like a cold finger and moved all the way down his spine.

His voice.

"I'll finish what *I* started," he heard himself say. He looked up and saw dark, grainy footage of his face. His face was covered in shadow, his skin darker than it was in real life. You could only see the whites of his eyes. "Get 'em all. Get 'em all."

"I never said that," Aly croaked. The sound of his voice, so soon after the edited version, seemed like a strange doubling. "They must have taken that audio from the show, messed with it somehow."

"I know," Vin said. He looked sorry. "But it doesn't matter what I think."

Under the footage a caption read, "Private Alyosha Myraz and Popular *Revolutionary Boys* Star Wanted for the Assassination of Princess Rhiannon."

Part Two:

THE MARKED

In the year 918, Kalusian forces bombed the planet of Wraeta.

"I was on one of the last crafts to make it out of the blast radius. I was six. I didn't see the bomb drop, but I saw the Kalusian vessel break the atmosphere. At first the side of the planet rippled. There was a huge explosion. Pieces broke off. I thought it would be loud, but it was quiet. All I heard were the people in my cabin, sobbing. Everything we'd ever known. Our homes. Taken away, destroyed."

—Wraetan refugee account

NINE

RHIANNON

THEY'D arrived in Tinoppa early that morning and headed straight to one of Dahlen's contacts. Since she had refused to take the DNA scrambler, Dahlen pointed out that she would need another disguise to get close to Seotra.

The Fisherman's workroom was dank, lined with dark tanks—empty but for stagnant and scummy water. A single cot and balled-up blanket had been shoved in the corner. Rhiannon couldn't imagine living here, but supposed that the Fisherman was comfortable in wet, dark places. Judging from his stretched-out anatomy, he hadn't grown up in a high-grav environment. Combined with his bizarre speech patterns, which made it sound like his vocal cords were full of liquid, Rhee guessed he was far from his native planet.

She knew the feeling. They'd been traveling for three days

and had barely gotten here on time; the ceremony Seotra was to attend was scheduled for this afternoon.

And this afternoon, she would kill him, at last. At last, it would all be over.

Then what? a little voice whispered. That was the problem with being without the cube. Not just the organic memories. The whispers, the doubts, the fears that crowded her like faceless spectators moving in the shadows.

She forced the thought from her mind. *Honor, loyalty, bravery.* Revenge.

"How long will the procedure take?" she asked.

"As long as I want it to," the Fisherman replied. He lifted his enormous hand to Rhee's face, opening her hazel eye so wide she thought he'd rip her skin open at the corners. She flinched away but he grabbed her chin. He was pale blue with a long face—all his features crowded down onto the bottom half. He had human-like eyes, tilted down at a forty-five-degree angle, which gave the impression that his entire face had slid down over time. His thin mouth made a suction sound as he chewed his tobacco. The smell made her insides twist in disgust.

But strangest of all: He had no cube. She'd never met a soul without one, though she'd heard of cultures in the Outer Belt that had refused to adopt them. The second G-1K summit had established interplanetary availability on every single world in the universe, to eliminate the technology gap. They'd even drafted a wide-ranging resolution so planets could modify their cubes according to local customs and traditions.

That was decades ago now, and an interconnected universe was only a reality for the wealthier territories.

Rhee wondered what it was like to live a whole life without a cube, or simply to turn hers off like Dahlen. She'd been without hers for just a few days and felt as if she were walking through a murk of uncertainty, with impressions that struck and then disappeared, a past unraveling behind her like a string. It was terrifying—but electrifying, too, as if she hardly existed at all.

"Hold *still*," the Fisherman said with a grunt. The tiny light he shined on her was impossibly bright, and Rhee felt her eye well up with tears. When she could no longer take it, she wrenched herself free.

"Just as well, then," he said, shrugging. "Before we get started we'll need to discuss the matter of payment."

"Name your price."

"Credits amounting to five million," he said smugly.

"We don't have it," Dahlen answered. "On the honor of my order, I can assure you when she is empress—"

"There is no guarantee that she'll become empress." He glanced over at her—it was hard to tell if he was smiling or not. She knew, and he knew, that it was a risk to come here and reveal her identity, but they had no choice. "Oh *please*, don't glare at me, Princess. It's not that I *want* you to fail. I just don't care enough to have an opinion."

"You have no opinion on an intergalactic war?" she asked.

"War was my father's cause—not mine. Whichever planet rules supreme will do so for another twenty years, and then the power will flip, then flip again. Let all the planets who want to play raze each other to ash so the rest of us don't have to deal with petty struggles."

Petty. Sheltered. Young. Blind. Rhee had been insulted more in the past three days than she ever had before. Rhee forced herself to reach into the folds of her tunic and pull out Julian's telescope. She felt her heart splinter as she handed it over. "Here," she said. "It's pure silver."

"Must've cost something fierce." The Fisherman brought the telescope close to his eye, not to look through it but to inspect it. She knew he'd never use it the way it was intended—to look up at the sky, to know you weren't alone.

Did Julian know he wasn't alone?

Did he think of her as often as she thought of him? She'd stayed up every night, terrified Julian would discover what she'd done.

The Fisherman tossed the telescope up in the air and caught the other end, seemingly happy with the trade. He stood up, and she expected him to rummage through his cabinets for chemicals and salves. Instead, he tore the tarp off a nearby tank and stuck his arm in the cloudy water, all the way to his shoulder.

"What are you doing?" she asked.

"Most people reckon these here tanks are empty," he said, by way of response. Then, with a grunt, he extracted his hand.

Rhee gulped in a breath. In his palm was a creature with long tentacles frantically coiling and whipping through the air in all directions. She jumped back. Its bulbous head barely fit in the palm of his hand.

"It's what's called an octoerces," he said, looking at it with a sort of respect and affection.

"Where—where did it come from?" Rhee licked her lips, regretting her decision to trust Dahlen.

"The same place this silver of yours was mined." Of course. It was from the Outer Belt in deep space, a free strip of interconnected planets that Kalu had wanted to colonize for years. She'd heard of locals who fished it with nothing but a suit and an alloy harpoon gun, snatching up creatures that could survive without light and atmosphere, creatures that defied everything anyone knew about life. "It's a bit angry now. It doesn't like air, see, doesn't breathe it . . ."

"But what are you going to *do* with it?"

The Fisherman squinted at her. "For the mark. Your Fontisian didn't tell you how the procedure works?"

Dahlen shrugged at her, with not the least bit of sympathy.

As Rhee seethed, the Fisherman made a clucking sound. "The Vodheads can't be trusted—the freaky potions they drink do something to their *brains*," he said. *Vodhead* was a slur, one Rhee knew but had never heard anyone actually use. "How'd you end up in the company of a madman like him?"

"Same way I ended up in the company of a bully like you." Rhee shifted in her seat as she eyed the creature. "The universe just has a way of bringing unlikely people together."

The Fisherman squinted at her, sizing her up. "The bully, the madman, and the empress," he said, stretching his mouth out into a smile that took up all the space on his pointy chin. "I *like* the sound of that. Now let's get down to business!" He held up his free hand so that the octoerces wrapped a single tentacle around his palm. "It's going to sucker itself to your face and bring the blood up to the surface in a random pattern," he continued. His eyes narrowed in pain as the octoerces squeezed around his wrist and fingers. After a few seconds he yanked its head away and the whole thing loosened, leaving a series of faint, red circles. "Like this, but much darker. You'll need five minutes, though." The Fisherman reached into a drawer and pulled out a white rag. He tossed it to her. "Might want to put this in your mouth," he said. He must've seen the confused look on her face. "So that you don't bite your tongue off. Hurts, this one does."

Rhee numbly put the rag in her mouth. It smelled fresh and was newly starched, seeming at odds with the dank place. Rhee's breathing became shallow. She willed herself to stay calm. There wasn't even her cube to distract her, some peaceful memory, some sensory program she could employ.

Just five minutes. She'd killed a man in less than five minutes.

The creature came closer and closer until she could feel its sticky tentacles exploring the left side of her face. *You will not scream*, she told herself—but she *did* want to scream. She wanted to run, too, but it was too late.

Then the slick, strange thing attached itself to her with a sucking sound, and pain exploded in her head. Stars burst in her eyes, though she wondered if they were blood vessels. It felt like it was slurping up her brain to the surface of her skull; she couldn't think clearly. She could feel it suck on her eyeballs, too, through the flimsy flesh of her eyelids.

The Fisherman gave his hand to her then, strong, dry, scaly—but at the very least, familiar. "Just a little longer . . ." he said, in a surprisingly gentle voice. "Be strong."

A tentacle fell across her neck, and she saw Veyron choking, gasping on his own blood . . . Her cry was muffled in her throat. She couldn't breathe.

Then the Fisherman's voice reached her, so quiet at first it seemed to be coming from inside her blood, from the murmurings of her own pain.

"The Outer Belt is home to many things that science says should not exist," he whispered. "Strange creatures. Magic creatures. They shouldn't be alive and yet they *are*, they stay alive, simply because their will to live is so strong. Do you understand what I'm telling you, Princess?"

She did. His hand in hers, the pain, the clouds of color. It all made sense, it all resolved into a single message she knew by heart: She would find Seotra and make him pay.

She tried to focus on her revenge, on how it would feel to sink the knife into him. But instead, she called up not her deep hatred but the moment with Julian in the dojo when they'd been inches apart—the feelings she didn't know how to define, and the *almost* kiss they'd shared.

Starbursts continued behind her eyes. Pain sang through her veins. She should not have survived. Twice, she should not have survived. But she had.

Rhee wrapped her robes around her tightly as they walked toward the Crystal Monument, where the mourning ceremony would take place. She could see the vapor of her breath. The icy air on Tinoppa exhilarated her; on Nau Fruma Rhee had only ever felt the sun burn her skin or watched as the heat made things in the distance appear blurry and strange. But there was something certain about the crisp weather here, like time had been frozen and she, only she, would be responsible for setting it in motion again.

"The *Revolutionary Boys* star Alyosha Myraz is still at large," said Nero on the public holo screen. It cut to footage of Aly scowling, then to the *Eliedio* exploding. The image always made her flinch. How many people had been on board the royal cruiser? How many crew members did the *Eliedio* require? She had never thought to ask, and now she regretted it. "The Kalusians have upped the reward to five hundred thousand credits." Nero put his hand over his heart. He looked exhausted from the around-the-clock coverage.

Rhee had seen Nero with that same weary look on his face, just weeks after her family died. He'd been younger then and even more fresh-faced, without the tiny wrinkles across his forehead that he had now. It was her first interview since the accident—one she hadn't wanted to give—but she had been urged by her advisers to restore the public's faith. She'd felt numb as the cameras rotated around her. When Nero saw her face, he'd called them off. In private, he'd leaned over and squeezed her little shoulder. "The ancestors saw it was an honorable death," he'd said. "Through them we ensure a new, worthy leader will rise." Rhee remembered looking up at Nero, surprised and grateful. It had been the first time anyone had spoken to her like an adult.

"Don't gape," Dahlen said, pulling her from her memory as he nudged her along.

"I'll finish what *I* started. Get 'em all." Alyosha's voice, amplified, boomed out over the space, as on the holo screen the *Eliedio* combusted into stardust.

The *Revolutionary Boys* star had been blamed for her murder, and Rhee had no idea why. She knew Seotra had opposed the measure to accept Wraetan refugees years ago, but would he really stoop so low as to frame the most high-profile Wraetan on DroneVision? Why was he so eager for war?

Rhee wondered how and why Seotra had chosen *him*. She'd seen his reality show—it was a little bit cheesy, which was exactly why she liked it. Vincent was the more popular star, with his blue eyes and easy smile, but she'd always preferred Aly, the black guy with the habit of shying away from the camera. She'd admired him for refusing to quit, too, after it came out he was Wraetan.

You've been blind, Veyron had said. *Blind and willful.*

"We haven't discussed the plan should you fail," Dahlen said.

"Your faith in me is heartwarming." The plan was simple: She must get close enough to Seotra that she could sink Veyron's blade deep into his heart. It was elegant, Rhee thought, that Seotra would die at a ceremony meant to mourn the princess he had tried to murder.

Dahlen was silent for a moment. "Hand me your knife."

He produced a whetstone and wielded it lightly along the edge. She watched him impatiently. He moved with painstaking slowness, as if they had all the time in the world, as if there wouldn't soon be a man on the other side of the knife.

Unexpectedly, he began to speak. "You can't apply too much pressure to the blade," he said. "You move the steel in the arc—one fluid motion, like so—so that the entire length of the edge sharpens equally. The angles must be precise."

"It'll work fine for my purposes either way," Rhee said.

"A knife is not only for killing," he replied. "A knife might be used a dozen different ways, all of them subtle, some of them unexpected. And you'll be glad you planned ahead, worked all the angles, sharpened it to perfection . . ."

Dahlen was talking about the day she would become empress. Hadn't Veyron said something similar—that Rhee needed to think, to plan?

"I was ready when Veyron came for me." Rhee's voice was without pride. It was laced instead with guilt, and anger, and the memory of the man's blood-slicked hand reaching for hers as he died.

"It won't be the same as it was with your trainer." He remained focused on the blade. "Every death by your hand is different than the one that came before. You'll be changed."

"I'm counting on it." She *wanted* to be changed. It was revenge that directed her focus and gave her purpose. The hole in her heart would finally be filled.

He held up the newly sharpened knife and examined its edge. The silence stretched. "Don't say you weren't warned," he said eventually. "Every time it's for the worst."

He handed it back to her. In the reflection of the blade she saw the damage done by the octoerces: a plum-colored scar that covered half her face, and burst blood vessels that made her entire right eye red. It gave her speckled, hazel iris a dark brown color.

"Do you think of those moments?" she asked. "The moments that changed you?"

"The order does not encourage recall. It's the reason we turn off our cubes, as part of our vows. Even our fellow Fontisians don't seem to understand that memories cloud judgment. They make one . . . weak."

Rhee wondered what he could possibly mean. Memories were the foundations for people's lives. Who would she be without her memories? Without the crystal clear moments with her family, preserved forever in her cube?

"What was it like? Growing up the way you did?"

"You're not asking what it was like. You're asking what made me this way." Dahlen almost smiled; his mouth moved as if it had been touched by something bitter. "Erawae was a territory to which we did not belong. But there was no place for fear or sadness when Vodhan walked beside you. He knew every move, every intention of my heart."

"How do you know he exists?" Rhee asked. "How can you be sure?"

"You do not doubt your ancestors. I do not doubt my god." Rhee could tell by the way Dahlen's eyes went cold that there would be no more conversation. "We should not delay any longer," he said.

They gathered along the chain-link fence that surrounded the site: dozens of large, jagged crystals arranged in a semicircle atop a grass knoll. They were easily three times Dahlen's height, some of them even taller—but all of them had a beautiful cloudy quality to them, and reflected the light in such a way that all the colors of the spectrum were trapped in the crystal formations. No one knew how they'd got here; early civilizations couldn't have had the technology to move something so impossibly heavy. It was thought to be a religious site for an ancient species, perhaps one that had retreated to another planet.

Rhee saw the image of her own face projected above the crystals. Hundreds of people had gathered, possibly to mourn Rhiannon, possibly just because they hoped to tell future generations that they had been there. *So many witnesses*, she thought, as the gates swung open, and from here she could see the crowd surge. The smell of incense hung in the air.

She moved to join them, but Dahlen stopped her. "You won't be dissuaded."

He spoke flatly, but she knew it was a question. She shook her head.

Something moved behind his eyes, an expression gone too quickly for her to decipher. It was as if a sigh had moved through him in the form of a shadow. "Grip the knife in your hand and drive the blade up, here, into his kidney," he said, taking her hand and pressing it against the spot just under his rib cage. His stomach was hard; he was breathing heavily. "He won't survive. Do not wait to check."

Rhee pulled back. Stunned. Confused. The same hand that was close to Dahlen's vibrant body was about to take a man's life.

A life for a life. For *all* the lives, of her mother and sister and father.

"Let's go," he said, then led her toward the entrance. The crowd made a path as it caught on that she was Marked, not knowing the disfigurement was on account of the octoerces. Some were polite in trying to conceal their horror, but others turned or shrank away from her. During the Great War, Fontis had dropped its biological weapon first, though Kalu retaliated—and the result was a mass die-off from radiation and cancer near all the drop sites. Those who survived were changed, and they passed the mutations down through their lineage. And their children, if they had children, would be Marked—scars, boils, health problems—each generation worse off than the last. They saw the ugliness of war when they saw her.

She didn't miss the way they looked at Dahlen, and how their eyes lingered over his tattoos.

At the entrance, the stream of people narrowed, but she moved freely after the crowd gave her a wide berth. A Tasinn, his face wide and the shape of a mooncake, nodded at her to enter. Dahlen forked to the right, around to the other side of the wrought iron fence where the rest of the crowd stood. She was pushed forward by the force of people behind her, but she kept her eyes on Dahlen until he was swallowed by the masses.

Around her, people were chattering in languages she couldn't understand. Now she was too hot; it was so crowded she could almost imagine that she was back on Nau Fruma pushing her way toward the marketplace. But the mood wasn't happy or carefree. There was nothing to celebrate.

Instead of families and merchants, the crowd was made up of children, many younger than her, all of them pushing forward like a single living organism. Hundreds of people were weeping, and Rhee felt as moved as she was disturbed. Did they truly mourn her? Or were they here to partake in spectacle, to say they had been at the vigil for the Rose of the Galaxy?

These were her people—the ones she would serve, dedicate her life to, just like her father had—but she didn't know them, didn't know what they were thinking or what they feared. When this was all behind her, she would think of them, always. But not a moment sooner. Not until Andrés Seotra took his last breath.

In the distance, Rhee could see Seotra standing at the edge of the crystal formation, his face turned down as if he were deep in thought. Rhee could kill him just for the false grief on his face.

She was also, unexpectedly, overcome by a desperate wish to see Tai Reyanna. She was convinced that if she could just look the woman in the eyes, Rhee would know once and for all if her caretaker had betrayed her. But the crowd had begun to snake up the hill, and her view of Tai Reyanna was blocked. Before the vigil started, people had forced their way up to the crystal formation so Tai Reyanna could lay her hands on their heads, touching them for a brief moment as she mumbled a prayer.

Closer, closer, closer Rhee moved. Step by step. Person by person.

Fear began to beat a rhythm in her chest, and she kept wiping her hands on her tunic, terrified that when she grabbed for her knife, her palms would be too slick to hold it. As she approached, the crowd became less generous despite her mark and shoved back, though the look of disgust was plain on their faces. Rhee knew that even if it had been manufactured, she'd been marked in her own way: the last Ta'an, a bad omen of sorts, as if the family history of tragedy were contagious. She'd never felt more anonymous, or more alone. Instinctively she sought Dahlen out in the crowd. It was telling, the way he killed with confidence. It meant he'd had practice, and had done it many times before.

A wave of momentum traveled through the crowd and pushed her forward, knocking her to her knees. Something was wrong. Rhee had never been superstitious, but she knew immediately—the thought of one bad omen had triggered another. Suddenly she had to break free, to kill Seotra now—before it was too late.

Rhee plunged through the crowd, ignoring the children's moans and complaints. The harder she pushed, the more ashamed she felt.

"Think you're special?" someone growled in her ear as she passed.

Did she think she was special?

You think you have all the answers? Veyron had said.

Someone grabbed the back of her hood, another one her arm. She wrenched away from a boy with a shock of red hair, his face covered with plague scars.

"Wait your turn," a little girl cried, but she couldn't wait. Seotra had to die, now, before she lost her chance.

She was close now, a short sprint. She could see Seotra and the Tasinn guards behind him, hands ostentatiously resting on their holsters. He was smiling. That smile—it was the same smile that had moved across his face as he watched her parents' craft embark.

It *was* a smile, wasn't it? A smile of knowing, of triumph?

Not simply a look of relief because they were escaping? Now that she couldn't call up the memory on her cube, she couldn't be sure.

Time slowed. It was the final stretch. She pushed and shoved her way forward. Blood thundered in her ears, and it almost drowned out the children behind her, jeering, calling her names. So close now that she could almost, almost reach out a hand to touch him . . .

She froze.

At that second, Tai Reyanna, bending over a toddler to murmur a blessing to him, looked up and saw her. And Rhiannon nearly died. She nearly turned to liquid and melted into the ground, because she knew—she *knew*—that Tai Reyanna had seen right past the mark on her face, had seen and known exactly who she was.

Tai Reyanna's mouth dropped open in surprise. Seotra, puzzled, began to turn in Rhee's direction.

Now.

And then, just as she reached for her knife, a hood fell over her face, and two arms encircled her so tightly the air left her body in a rush. Rhee inhaled the raw fiber of wool as she opened her mouth to scream and found that there was no air in her lungs.

TEN

ALYOSHA

DERKATZ, Aly decided, was the armpit of the universe.

And after three days on the run from the UniForce and staying offline, hopscotching with Vin between the shadiest of intergalactic safe houses, he could say he was the definitive expert on the topic. Kalu had just declared martial law across all their planets and airspace—which meant that border restrictions were tighter than Regent Seotra's you-know-what. Just getting out of the core territories had taken balls of steel.

When stopping to refuel, they'd stuck to sad little asteroids that didn't bother scanning anyone coming or going.

Here on the Outer Belt, they could move more freely. In theory. And Aly knew why: Nobody wanted to come this far to patrol a pile of sand-dust settlements, and the patrols that did come left as soon as possible.

A dwarf planet, Derkatz was a distant planetary oxygen pit

stop infamous for its black market. So far, however, Aly and Vincent hadn't had any luck finding oxygen. Or to get technical, they hadn't had any luck *buying* it in any form. They'd just been chucked out of their third greenhouse by an enraged Derkatzian merchant who vowed to bite off Alyosha's mouth and eat it, the kind of threat that would be common only in the Outer Belt.

As soon as they were outside, Aly pulled his goggles back onto his forehead and pawed his face mask off. He squinted toward the darkening horizon. Grains of sand whipped into his eyes.

"Pretty slick back there," he said.

"Don't even start." Vin shook the sand out of his hair.

"No, for real. I'm impressed." Aly slipped into his Kalusian accent and made a show of straightening out the front of his jumpsuit. It was the same as Vin's and the same as every other humanoid on this rock, since it was the only thing that did a halfway decent job of keeping the sand out of your junk. It had a utility loop on the hip, where Vin had hung Aly's hammer just to taunt him. "Tell me, Vincent, what's your secret negotiation technique? To piss off literally every carbon-based life-form in the known universe?"

"Ten thousand is a rip-off and you know it."

"We were negotiating. He *would've* gone lower if—"

"If what, Aly? If you stepped in and tickled his balls? I had it in there until you started talking. Maybe if you weren't always trying to get people to like you—"

"Oh, so it's like *that*?" Anger knifed its way up Aly's spine. "So I was the one who screwed it up back there?"

"Calm down. I didn't mean it like that." Vin raised his palms in surrender. That was his game. Vin never *meant it like that.* "You're supposed to be lying low, remember? You're one flimsy particle mask and some murky-ass goggles away from being recognized as the universe's most wanted murderer."

But deep down, he wondered if it was possible the robodroids had swarmed because he'd found the royal escape pod. What if they'd arrived because someone heard Aly broadcasting his distress signal, and not because Vin had sent out a call? But he'd used his cube to send out the signal, and cube communications were supposed to be secure. Foolproof. Unhackable. And if that was the case, then Vin might be right—what if Seotra and his lackeys really could drop in and pay an unexpected visit to anyone's cube? The question was too messed up to contemplate.

All he knew was that he had somehow become the fall guy. The UniForce had even raised the price on his head—claiming not only that he'd murdered the Princess but that he'd also kidnapped his beloved costar, Vincent Limam, *for the probable purposes of extortion and negotiation.*

Which was funny, because Aly would for sure *negotiate* to kick Vin to the other side of the universe right about now.

"Of all people, you should care about what's at stake," Vin said, sounding like one of the old missionaries in the church tents, all pucker-faced, like the taste of their words was sour. "Don't you want to know why they picked *you* for the universe's toilet paper?"

Aly's mouth flooded with a bitter taste; wind whipped sand onto his tongue and between his teeth. Because he already knew. Of course he knew, deep down, even if he didn't want to believe it.

Because he was Wraetan.

Because he'd tried to be something else.

"Don't tell me what to care about." Aly was shaking.

"You're the one living in a fantasy land. Not me," Vin said. His eyes flashed. "You're so busy trying to be a Kalusian poster boy, you get on your *knees* for the people who robbed you—"

"I dare you to keep running your mouth . . ." It was bad enough that the UniForce had screwed him over, even though he'd smiled for the cameras and played their little game. But he couldn't stand for Vin to say it, to know that Vin saw what Aly had tried for so long to conceal.

"Or what? Aly, I'm giving you the chance now to do something about it, to join a revolution—"

"*Fuck* your revolution," Aly exploded. He leaned forward so his face was just inches apart from Vin's. Alina and his ma were dead; everyone would die. Maybe they were looking down on him now, the way the Kalusians believed—shaking their heads about the mess down here. Or maybe it was like the Fontisians said, and it was Vodhan who'd built the world, and now he was pissed they'd ruined it. He imagined Vodhan throwing his hands up, peacing out, just disappearing to try again somewhere else.

"Don't act like you know me. I sure as hell don't know *you*. Liar." Aly felt toxic. "You play revolutionary because you think it's fun. Or maybe you just think you're a hero. Why not? Everyone's always told you that you're a hero, right?" Shame and anger edged each other for space deep down in his gut. "It's easy to be a hero when you've never faced anything, never fought anything, always had everything handed to you. It's easy to fight when you've never tasted blood in your mouth—"

Vin hit him. Aly staggered backward, and his goggles flew off his face and spun on their strap halfway around his neck. For a second, Aly just stood there, stunned, while Vin watched him with no expression on his face—vague, almost curious, flexing and unflexing his fingers.

Then Aly tackled him. They went down into the sand, and plumes of grit came up in their eyes and mouths. Aly landed a punch directly on Vin's nose and heard the crack. Blood was streaming into Vin's mouth, and Vin was choking, and suddenly Aly pulled away, horrified and ashamed.

Then he realized Vin wasn't choking. He was laughing.

"See?" he said, propping himself up on his elbow. His voice sounded thick. "Blood in my mouth. Happy now?"

Before Aly could apologize, the greenhouse door opened behind him. Instinctively, he turned around. He saw his mask and goggles scattered across the floor. On instinct, Aly's hands flew up to try and cover his bare face.

"Because I'm feeling generous, I've decided to do half a crate for four thousand—" The Derkatzian merchant froze, both arms full of plants. He looked at Aly with his round black eyes and stuck his flat snout in the air. Pointy ears that had laid back flat, hidden in his fur, perked up. "Well, well, well," he said. "If it isn't the most wanted *dusty* in the universe."

He lifted his hand toward his neck to access his cube, but Aly tackled him before he could transmit. The Derkatzian let out a garbled yell as they fell back and landed with a thud on the ground. He was wrapped in a filthy tunic like all the other locals, and his exposed fur was matted with sand. Aly gagged from the smell as he pinned the man down, grabbing hold of his wrists. Plants were scattered everywhere.

But the Derkatzian was a big guy, at least a foot on Aly and another seventy pounds. Vicious as hell, too—his kind was an evolution of the desert foxes that walked on their hind legs. He snapped and growled, managing to plant his foot and throw Aly off. Aly scrambled back toward him, kicking up sand as he lunged. He grabbed the furry ear and yanked it back so hard the Derkatzian yelped.

Meanwhile, Vin dived, and drove his elbow down on the guy's stomach.

"*Uhhhfff*," the Derkatzian groaned, crumpling on himself. Aly got him in a wrestling hold, and Vin pinned his arms to his side. But it wasn't just his cube they needed to worry about; the Derkatzian threw his head back, called out a series of quick barks into the wind, and then began to howl.

"*Taejis!*" Vin said, and kicked him a second time. He yelped once and went quiet.

Vin's eyes were wide as he scrambled to pick up the plants by his feet. In the distance, more Derkatzian howls rose up and intermingled with the shrieking winds. Aly had forgotten how much they could communicate with the tone and frequency of their barks. "We have to go!"

They ran for the village; there was no other way to get back to the docks. They cut left at an alley to move toward an inner circle, where the shrieking of the wind died down. The central village in Derkatz was plotted as a series of concentric structures that kept each inner courtyard more protected from the sand and howling winds than the last.

They hurtled left, and right, and left again. The principal village had been a fort during the Great War—one way in, one way out. Finally, they ducked into the shelter of an alcove so that Aly could knot a handkerchief around his nose and mouth. Anywhere else he would've looked like he was going to rob someone. But here everyone wore bright fabric, the color of prayer flags, around their faces to keep out the sand.

"Take these," Vin said, shoving the crate of plants in his direction. Aly hugged it to his chest, trying to orient himself, without a cube, to the look of the unfamiliar streets. "We need to split up. The Derkatzian probably said there were two of us."

Aly nodded, hoping he'd be able to find his way back to the docks. *Taejis.* He had hardly been paying any attention when they'd walked the village earlier. He was always using his cube for things like this, on the fly. But how hard could it be?

"We'll meet each other west of the docks, near the customs bureau. Stay calm, and don't run unless you have to."

They emerged from the alley.

"And remember, the Derkatzians can smell fear," he added as he went left. "Be cool."

Perfect parting advice. Aly went right, his heart thudding like an engine working double time. He dodged a man who barreled through, holding a chicken by the neck. Aly took his next left, backtracked when he hit a dead end, and almost mowed down a group of kids—humanoid and Derkatzian alike—who'd made a game of floating a ball on the wind. He swatted it as he passed, and it bounced against a wall, pinballing between surfaces as the children screamed happily. As he cleared the group, he saw two Derkatzians sniffing their way toward him. They'd gotten down on all fours, a position used only for hunting, and Aly could see the fox resemblance now more than ever. Except for their size, of course.

He shot down an alley, hoping they wouldn't pick up his scent, then kept threading through: half circle, alley, back out again, up a staircase three steps at a time. He didn't know if he was going the right way; he wasn't used to navigating without his cube to tell him exactly where to go. A woman crouched low over a basket, and he pivoted around her. Gravity was slowing him down. He wasn't used to it anymore; he felt like he was moving through soup.

He couldn't be far from the docks now. But at his next turn, he caught a glimpse of black uniforms and shiny badges, and his heart nearly stopped. *Tasinn.* They were coming up the stairs. He ducked into an open doorway and pressed his back against the wall. What the hell were they doing here? Derkatz was neutral territory, and way too far for Kalusian guards to travel.

Get it together, he told himself.

Inside, there were rolled-up sleeping mats and a low table in the center of a sparse room. There was one window, and it was dark. Quiet. He could hear himself breathing. His legs burned. He was out of shape.

"Snatch-yah uptu?"

The voice was quiet, but Aly knew it was a question by the way the whole sentence tipped up like a seesaw. He looked around him. A little boy was squatting in a corner. It was as if he'd just formed out of the shadows.

Aly shook his head, not understanding. They spoke Kalusian here, but it had its own water-like quality, all the words fluid and rushed.

"Snatch-yah uptu?" the boy tried again, speaking very slowly as he mimed grabbing something with his hands.

Aly stared. "Snatch me up?" Something about the kid's expression made his stomach drop. "Who would snatch me up?"

The boy shrugged. "Men they started coming last year. Used to give us candies, but no more." Aly could tell the boy was making an effort to speak slowly, in a way he'd understand. "The dahkta," he started. *Doctor.* "He come to put up the solah panels and ended up stayin' . . ."

Outside was a swell of voices—the Tasinn were close. The boy stood up and went toward the door. Aly nearly reached out a hand to stop him, but didn't want to frighten the kid into yelling. He disappeared through the door and out of sight.

And now, outside, there was the sound of boots scuffling against the ground. The flimsy mask over Aly's mouth was damp with his sweat. He could hear the Tasinn demand to know whether the boy had seen anyone running this direction. Aly held his breath. But the boy only responded with one word.

"Nyah." *Not here.*

And then the sound of the boots retreated.

The boy returned and gestured for Aly to follow him to the window. He scrabbled up onto a crate and shoved the window open with his shoulder. "Shortcut."

Aly stuck his head out and looked down. There was a wooden plank that stretched between the window a story below and the balcony across the way. There must've been a market under this level. It was more crowded than the other circles, and a few Derkatzians stalked the ground below. But Aly decided to take his chances with them rather than the Tasinn.

"Thank you," he said, and moved the plants to the crook of his arm. Then Aly touched his own giant thumb to the center of the boy's palm. It was a Wraetan tradition among family. It communicated too many big emotions that were impossible to translate—but it was a show of love and gratitude, and the closest phrase in Kalu might be something like *my life in your hands*. He, Vin, and Jeth had exchanged that same gesture the day they graduated boot camp. He'd had no other family apart from those two.

Vin was waiting for him now.

Whether or not the boy understood the meaning of Aly's gesture, he nodded. *One of those kids with an old soul*, Aly thought. He lowered himself through the window, feet first, and landed lightly on the balcony.

When he turned back around, the boy had disappeared.

He went east and flew down the stairs, only to see it too late: a Tasinn arriving at the base of the staircase. Aly grabbed the banister and launched his weight over it. He landed on both his feet and stumbled forward on one knee, but he scrambled up and kept running, still keeping a tight hold on the crate of plants. A Derkatzian came out of nowhere, and with a low growl, he lunged. Aly sidestepped, and the fox flew past him. He heard the warning bark he let out.

The crowd split. People abandoned handcarts and baskets and went screaming for the streets. The Tasinn were made clumsy by their weaponry, but the Derkatzians were gaining ground, bounding across the market.

He was getting closer to where the crafts were docked. If he could just make it to the Tin Soldier . . .

Someone grabbed for him, yanked him into an alley, and slammed him against the wall. Vincent. He kept a hand on Aly's chest, pinning him to the wall at arm's length. The doorway was narrow and almost entirely concealed by a well-placed moonfruit cart. Two foxes flew past them. And after a couple of seconds, Aly swatted Vin's hand down. Neither of them had been breathing.

"Where the hell have you been?" Vin asked.

"Had to take a detour," he said, breathing hard. "In case you hadn't noticed, there were Tasinn *and* foxes on my ass."

"Right. You're a badass," Vin said. "Let's move."

They were no more than a quick sprint from the docks. Nearly a thousand souls, half of them humans in jumpsuits, worked the port—importing and exporting goods across moons and planets and asteroid colonies. Apparently traffic had tripled in the black market when Seotra had shut down Sibu's ports after the assassination. Aly could see the Tin Soldier in the distance—docked between a flotsam of bigger and more expensive craft—small and battered and so familiar it pulled at Aly's chest.

"We gotta make a run for it," Vin said.

"Aren't we *already* making a run for it?"

They had to lean into the wind as they tore across the playa—their jumpsuits flapping, handkerchiefs to their mouths. Aly zipped his jumpsuit higher so that the plants would be safe. Without his goggles, he couldn't keep the grit out of his eyes, and he focused on watching Vin trek in front of him in the sea of jumpsuits. They threaded through the crowd of Kalusians and Miseu, hoping they'd lost the Tasinn and Derkatzians behind them. As they gained on the docks, where they'd parked his pod, they also left behind the shelter from the wind. Every step that closed the gap felt harder than the last—like the world had tilted and now they were walking up a vertical line.

At the last second, Vin turned and seized Aly's hand, dragging him for their last few steps. Together they fell out of the howling wind. By the time the Tasinn had enough sense to comb the port, they were already gone, vanished back into the darkness of deep space.

ELEVEN

RHIANNON

AN hour had passed, maybe two, since Rhee had been captured at her own memorial service. She had been just moments away from plunging the knife into Seotra. She recalled the surprised look on his face as he turned to see what the commotion was about. Rhee wondered if Seotra had recognized her.

Now she was being led by two silent guards down a pitch-dark corridor. She wanted to fight her way, but the adrenaline had drained her body, and her knees buckled as she walked. Rhee guessed she was underground by the damp smell, and by the muffled sound her voice made as she asked question after question—*Who are you? Where are you taking me? How does it feel to serve a traitor?*

As the guards brought Rhee to Seotra, they probably thought *they* had the advantage—simply because she was their prisoner.

But she was the one who'd spent half her life preparing for this moment.

Rhee stopped counting the turns, but squinted as light began to permeate the woven threads of the cloth covering her face. Natural light. They'd brought her above ground. Finally, they stopped, and a door opened before her. Rhee was pushed through a threshold as someone yanked off her hood.

She was blinded by the sunlight that reflected off every surface. The room was all white, full of white furniture and white tasseled pillows and white curtains that blew in the breeze. Someone in the center of the room came for her now, a dark silhouette moving swiftly. Rhee fumbled toward a nearby table and snatched up the first thing she could get her hands on.

"Stay back!" she yelled.

"Ancestors, *ahn ouck*, what do you plan to do with that?" A woman's voice, deep and familiar. Tai Reyanna. It had always sounded to Rhee as if her voice were full of smoke. It lingered in a room even after she was done speaking.

Only then did Rhee realize she was holding a hairbrush.

"You," Rhee said, face-to-face with Tai Reyanna. She had hated being called *ahn ouck*. It meant *child*, and felt especially patronizing since she no longer was one. It was a tactic—a way to remind Rhee of the girl she'd been when her family died. "*You* had me kidnapped?"

"It was that or have you imprisoned," she said. Rhee realized it was the first time she'd ever seen her Tai's hair. Rather than tucked up under an elaborately arranged scarf, it fell around her face in black waves, threaded with streaks of silver. "I feared you were moving toward the latter option by shoving your way through the crowd like a maniac. I told the guards you were merely a young girl, and you might need some guidance. Which you *do*."

"Why did you blindfold me?"

Tai Reyanna shook her head. "So you couldn't run away before we spoke."

Her adviser had been lettering—Rhee could see the uniform lines of cursive across a scroll of brown paper behind her. Watching her Tai practice the ancient art used to relax her. It required a certain stillness and patience that reminded her of Veyron. He and Tai Reyanna had never seemed friendly, but the two had been alike in so many ways.

Rhee studied Tai Reyanna's face. She was her adviser, her mentor, her teacher, and her guide. Could the woman who'd taught her history and languages, fled with her to the safety of the desert moon, watched over her for the past nine years, have conspired to have her killed? Rhee didn't want to believe that was possible.

But Veyron had looked after her too.

"Where are we?" Rhee asked cautiously. But one look out the window and she already knew; the Tinoppa crystals in the distance. That meant Dahlen was close by.

"*I* will ask the questions," Tai Reyanna said in a raised voice. Her face had turned stony, rough—like the hard-packed sand that was left once the foam of a wave receded. "Where have you been?"

Rhee looked down. It was unusual for Tai Reyanna to show emotion; she'd been rigid and focused during those years on Nau Fruma. But now organic memories bubbled to the surface of

Rhee's mind. Tai Reyanna, younger, helping her dress and teaching her to read. Her laugh—how forceful it was, a loud exhale. *HA!* just once before she began to snicker. How could Rhee have forgotten those moments? But she knew the answer: because she hadn't saved them, replayed them. They'd been archived from disuse so long ago.

"Answer me!" Tai Reyanna demanded.

Now Rhee's tongue felt fat and clumsy, and she couldn't find the words. It was as if they'd been transported back to Nau Fruma, to the dusty palace and the daily lessons. What could she say?

Tai Reyanna strode across the room, back straight, with purpose. Rhee tensed. She glanced outside and quickly counted three stories down; there was a small tree to break her fall if she needed to jump.

But Tai Reyanna only swept her into an unexpected hug. Rhee was not used to their touching; in fact, the last time the Tai had held her, she was six and had just learned of her parents' death—another memory she'd archived, hidden deep within her cube so she wouldn't ever have to remember it again.

Rhee felt herself succumbing, becoming that little girl all over again. The Tai was skin and bones—had she always been this tiny?—but the familiar smell of incense that clung to her robes was bold and fragrant. Rhee inhaled deeply, feeling her eyes well, feeling at last that she was holding on to a piece of home.

For a second, she forgot all of it: Veyron, the *Eliedio* exploding, the riots and the martial law, Seotra here on this very asteroid.

"How did you escape?" Tai Reyanna said into Rhee's hair. "How did you survive?"

The question brought Rhee back to herself. She pushed out of the Tai's embrace.

"How did *you* survive?" Rhee asked, not unkindly—but she took a step back just the same. "I saw the *Eliedio* explode."

"We were evacuated. I went to find you, but the Tasinn forced us onto the escape pods, and I trusted Veyron would . . ." She trailed off at the mention of his name, as if it deserved the respect of their ancestors.

"Did everyone manage to escape?"

"No," Tai Reyanna said, straightening the folds at the front of her robes. She'd always demanded perfection, though Rhee couldn't help but wonder if it was an excuse to look away. "There weren't enough pods for everyone." Rhee felt a twist of new guilt: They'd used a pod for Veyron's body. "It wasn't until I was grounded that I realized you hadn't made it out. I heard that Veyron died trying to save you from an attacker—a Wraetan boy," Tai Reyanna said, and even she, who was supposed to be neutral, couldn't help but show her distaste.

"That's a lie," Rhee said. "I've never seen that boy."

"All of the holos are reporting it."

Rhee knew that. She'd been watching. They'd claimed Alyosha Myraz had enlisted in the UniForce under false credentials in a long-term plot to assassinate her. Rumor had it he'd planted that explosive device in case his attempt on her life had failed.

"Have they caught him?" Rhee asked. When Tai Reyanna shook her head, she exhaled with relief. But with his image beamed everywhere across the universe, it couldn't be long. So many people, dead in her place.

"What's going on, Rhiannon? What have you done to your face? What *happened* to you?" Tai Reyanna asked. There were dark half-moons under her eyes.

Rhee brought her hand up to touch her face, which was still swollen. "You know what happened," she said without bitterness. She'd lost the will to play games, trying to outmaneuver and outsmart at every turn. The mounting deaths weighed on her, and the memory of Seotra waving from the knoll burned inside of her. "Seotra sent Veyron to kill me."

There was a question buried deep inside, clawing its way out of her throat and onto the tip of her tongue: *Did* you *conspire with him?* But she couldn't bring herself to ask it.

"*Veyron?*" Tai Reyanna repeated. The woman turned away, gripping the windowsill as though to stay on her feet. "No. He wouldn't."

Tai Reyanna looked back to her. "Whoever sent him, it wasn't Andrés Seotra. He was your father's closest and oldest friend," she said, her voice a low current that shocked Rhee. "They were as close as brothers. Andrés Seotra fought to be Crown Regent so he could protect the Ta'an's interests."

"I know that. It makes his betrayal ten times worse," Rhee said.

"There was no betrayal," Tai Reyanna said sharply. "Not by him. He has been loyal to your bloodline."

"He opposed the Urnew Treaty—"

"—because it did not go far enough," Tai Reyanna cut her off. "He wanted a peace that endured even if there was no Ta'an on the throne. Don't you see? He worried that otherwise there was incentive to kill you—to kill *all* of you. Ancestors, help me,"

Tai Reyanna murmured, pinching the bridge of her nose. "Is this what you've believed the whole time? Is this why you refused to see him all these years?"

"You knew that he—that he wanted to see me?" Rhee felt the knowledge bleed through her, staining every bit of her silly, petty soul.

"Of course. He'd consulted me on the matter. He thought he must remind you of your grief, and we'd agreed we had to give you time."

Every hair stood on end. *Half the beings in the galaxy will want you dead*, he'd said in her memory. Is this what he'd been speaking of? That the treaty did not provide strong enough protections?

Had she even ever bothered to find out?

No. She was getting confused. Seotra was responsible. Rhee was sure of it—she'd always been sure of it. The goal she'd worked toward was so tantalizingly close, and she couldn't afford to be distracted by any doubts.

"Take me to Seotra. I want to talk to him," Rhee said. "I want to know everything that he'd meant to tell me. From the beginning."

It was a half-truth. She *did* want to talk to Seotra, to face him, to call him a liar—and to kill him, still. Despite what Tai Reyanna said, or perhaps because of it. Rhee still wasn't certain she could trust her entirely.

"You should've reached out earlier." Tai Reyanna turned away from her and moved to the door. "I mourned you. I prayed to you. And this whole time you were still alive."

Rhee didn't answer. She imagined her heart as a stone—something impenetrable, unmoved. Someone had to pay for her grief.

No—*Seotra* had to pay. Because the terrifying truth had come to her: She wanted him to be guilty. She *needed* him to be guilty, so she could finally atone.

Rhee should have died with her family.

This was the only way to say she was sorry.

The Tinoppa palace library was nothing like the libraries she'd known. Her mother had maintained the palace library back in Sibu, but its smell had been worn and musty, and comforting, too—like a soft blanket slipped around your shoulders. Sunlight would filter in, slanting slowly across the room.

This library was cold, dim, and without windows. As they moved through the enormous towers of books, goose bumps formed on Rhee's arms and shoulders. The room must have been climate-controlled to preserve the paper, but her body was reacting to something apart from the temperature. Half the books were wrapped in plastic, sheathed like dead bodies, or tucked behind glass. Their footsteps barely made a sound on the carpet.

"Where is he?" Rhee whispered. The library appeared to be deserted.

Tai Reyanna just frowned and shook her head. Rhee heard light footsteps and turned just in time to see the shadow of a man pass quickly between shelves. Electricity danced on her skin. A trap. It had to be a trap.

She looked at Tai Reyanna. "You lied to me." Her governess

was short, like her; they stood face-to-face, and Tai Reyanna looked terrified. "Where is he?"

Tai Reyanna shook her head. "Seotra?" she croaked, and then cleared her throat. "Seotra?"

"No!" Seotra's voice came from somewhere in the stacks. "It's a trap. Get her out of here!"

Just then a high-pitched whine sounded throughout the room, a noise that reminded Rhee of charge, of current, of electricity humming to life. Before she could wonder what it was, they were thrown backward by the force of a blinding white explosion.

Debris was flung everywhere, and charred paper and ash fell among them like snow. Rhee could barely hear anything; it was like the world had been muted and replaced by a low hum. She pushed herself up on her elbows and saw Tai Reyanna, a few feet away but unmoving. Rhee tried to call to her but could barely hear her own voice. She crawled through pieces of splintered bookshelf, through fluttering paper, feeling as if her body, too, had been blown apart, as if it were taking forever for her brain to send commands to her arms and legs.

Tai Reyanna opened her eyes when Rhee shook her. But immediately the hazy look fell away, her eyes wide, as she pulled Rhee close and said something in urgent tones. Rhee couldn't make out her words over the hum in her ears.

"I can't hear you," she said, then tried to repeat louder. "Stay here!" Tai Reyanna's eyes were wide. She looked like she was on the verge of tears. Rhee had never seen her cry.

Fear filled up every atom of Rhee's body. She felt like it would overflow out of her eyes, but she pushed herself forward. She slipped between two bookcases that had miraculously remained upright. She squeezed the hilt of the knife so tightly her knuckles went white.

She sidestepped down the row, still trying to clear the buzzing from her ears. She used to hide in her mother's library, too, back on Kalu. Those floors were covered with tasseled rugs, woven through with red and orange hues, so thick it felt like a forest floor. She'd crawl along those very rugs, through a maze of table legs and chairs in a game of hide-and-seek—and she remembered now how Josselyn had surprised her once, poking her head out upside down from the table above, her thick braid swinging like a pendulum as she said: "BOO!"

Another explosion. This time Rhee dropped and clamped her hands to her ears, and when the dust and paper mist cleared, she found she hadn't lost full use of her hearing: From somewhere nearby, she could hear Seotra moaning.

Someone *else* was after Seotra too.

Maybe someone who didn't want her to have answers?

There was no more time to think. She spun around the bookshelf and had a quick view of a bloodied Seotra on the ground, and a tall figure in a hooded cape standing above him.

When the man began to turn, she spun her leg out in a low roundhouse. As he collapsed, she jumped, driving him to the ground and then mounting his back. She stuck her knee in a pressure point at the base of his spine and sunk the point of her knife in his neck so that it barely broke skin. It happened so quickly that only when she was positioned did she see his neck was covered in tattoos, and that he had dirty blond hair and wore a black ring on his right hand.

"Dahlen?" She moved off of him and stumbled backward, horrified. "What—what are you doing?"

"This is what you wanted, isn't it?" Dahlen extended his right hand toward Seotra as if he were commanding him to stop, and Rhee watched in horror and fascination as electricity gathered in the base of his palm. It was the ring, Fontisian technology at work. Tiny surges flared outward like the veins in a leaf, seemingly grabbing energy in the air and burning it, converting the air to forks of blue and white flame.

"Stop," Rhee said. The stream of smokeless fire wrapped Seotra up and lifted him off the ground, folding him nearly in two, as he moaned in pain. "STOP!" She sprang to tackle Dahlen. But she crashed into a wall of air, clear but firm—and it wouldn't let her get to him.

"He is a war criminal," Dahlen said. "He deserves what he gets."

"Stop! Stop! Stop!" Rhee was screaming so hard her voice was raw. She ran again and again for Seotra, trying to break the invisible barrier, but it was impossible. She was bruised, thrown backward off her feet as if she were running into a solid wall. And finally, mercifully, Dahlen did stop. The Regent collapsed backward, his mouth dark with blood, his clothing smoking.

"Why?" Rhee couldn't help it. She was crying now. "Why?"

"He does not deserve your tears," Dahlen said coldly. "He betrayed the order, and he betrayed you."

Seotra struggled to sit up. "I've made peace with your Elder, boy!"

"And what of all the souls you took?" Dahlen asked. "You can't make peace with the dead."

Seotra shook his head and looked at Rhee. "I never betrayed you."

"You betrayed my family," she said, but as the words came out she felt uncertainty gripping her. Her skin felt tight. That smile she'd seen . . . the words she'd overheard . . . fragments, really. What did they mean?

"That's what you think?" He was consumed by a hacking cough that brought up more black blood. "I swear on my life, Rhiannon. I loved your family like my own. I've wanted to speak with you for so long. So many memories I wanted you to see. I've been trying to protect you. I've been—"

The words died in his throat. Dahlen held up a hand again, and the Regent began to seize. Sparks danced from his body. Fire flowed like a ribbon tying Dahlen and Seotra together. Then Seotra's body burst into sudden flame. He mumbled, but Rhee couldn't hear, couldn't understand. Only one phrase reached her:

"*Ma'tan sarili!*" he yelled.

In a single second, Seotra's body began to crumble, the fire eating away at his edges until his face and eyes and shock-white hair disappeared into black. He dropped like sands of an hourglass, into a tiny mountain of ash on the gray floor.

He hadn't even screamed.

Rhee looked at Dahlen. "How *dare* you." She tasted ash on her tongue.

"He was not a good man," Dahlen said, his tone flat and expressionless as always. He opened his palm, and the ring gave off blue sparks before it turned black again. Dahlen's hand was badly burned. "He held my Elder hostage for years, but not before he commanded the slaughter of one monastery in the order. The very home of my family . . ."

"You know this boy?" Tai Reyanna's voice was practically a whisper, but it still startled Rhee. She turned and saw her adviser limping toward them through the wreckage. "This fanatic?"

Rhee felt as if she were the one who'd been incinerated. All of her beliefs were smoke. They'd all blown apart. For the last nine years she *knew* Seotra had been responsible for her family's deaths. And now she couldn't even trust herself to tell left from right or up from down. "Dahlen saved my life."

"He killed the Regent. An ally to your family. The one man trying to keep peace—"

"This man did not believe in peace," Dahlen said. His eyes were dark and unreadable. "He's a murderer who has never atoned for his sins. But Vodhan will be his judge."

"Your precious Vodhan," Tai Reyanna said with so much hatred that it transformed her features to someone Rhee didn't recognize. "There is no god that could help a soul as rotten as yours."

A crash sounded above them. Footsteps rattled the lights in their glass casing.

"Tasinn." Dahlen turned to Tai Reyanna. "You called them."

"You called them yourself," Tai Reyanna snapped. "Or did you imagine that you could burn half the library without anyone remarking on it?" Rhee's heart felt as if it might jump straight out of her chest—the footsteps were closer now, and if they were caught here, with the remains of Seotra . . . "If your god exists, I hope your punishment is slow and vengeful."

Rhee took a step backward. Panic welled inside of her. "I can't be caught," she said.

"No, Rhee, you're safe now." Tai Reyanna's voice was gentler this time. "Your guard is coming."

"Veyron was part of my guard, and he betrayed me," Rhee said. "I must go."

Tai Reyanna caught her arm. "Go? With this *murderer*?"

"She has no other choice," Dahlen said. "I can better serve her than you can."

Both were true: He was a murderer, and she had no choice.

If Seotra hadn't been responsible for her family's deaths, her would-be assassin was still out in the universe, roaming free.

Tai Reyanna pulled Rhee into a fierce hug, whispering an old blessing into her hair. "May the ancestors be with you."

Rhee bowed her head and let the blessing wash over her; she felt the warmth of a thousand perfectly sunny days on her skin. Tai Reyanna pulled away.

"There's a secret passageway there," she continued. "Behind the second column. It leads underground and out near the ruins. You'll be in darkness, but there is only one path. Follow it."

It had been Tai Reyanna watching over her the whole time she was in Nau Fruma. She'd taken that time for granted. "I'll come back for you," Rhee said.

"You can't. It won't be safe," Dahlen interjected from behind her.

Rhee ripped the hem of her tunic, and a long scrap of it came free. "I'll have to tie your hands. They can't think you had anything to do with what happened here," she said. Rhee's fingers were shaking as she wound the fabric around the Tai's wrists. Her adviser's hands were limp. She looked at Rhee as if she'd never seen her before.

Maybe she hadn't—not the real Rhee.

"Princess," Dahlen said from behind them. "We're out of time." His voice made her insides curdle now. He had robbed her of her one chance to know the truth. He was a murderer. *You'll be changed*, he'd said. Dahlen knew this more than anyone, because he was too far gone.

"I'm sorry," Rhee said. "For everything."

Tai Reyanna leaned in and put her mouth close to her ear. "I will be loyal to you until the day I die."

Dahlen grabbed Rhee's arm and pulled her into the tunnel entrance. Rhee feared it would be the last she ever saw of the Tai: the woman who had been like family to her, crouched at the remains of a dead Regent. What's worse: She feared her Tai's words were an omen, a prophecy.

"*Ma'tan sarili*," Rhee pledged over her shoulder. *Honor, bravery, loyalty*.

"I hope you mean it, child," Tai Reyanna called out as Rhee walked into the darkness.

TWELVE

ALYOSHA

ALY watched through the monitors as Derkatz receded in the distance. They'd easily slid past the first customs checkpoint and would soon be in Portiis, where they would meet Vin's contact. So close. Alyosha finally felt like he could breathe.

Literally.

"Oxygen levels have already improved by twelve percent," Pavel announced. "The specimen is a shangdi variety indigenous to the western hemisphere of Fontis. Very unusual, known to bloom during the monsoon season."

"Oh yeah?" Aly said distractedly. Pavel was particularly chipper; he'd stayed back and updated all his software. But Aly wasn't in the mood for chipper.

He eyed the hammer on Vin's hip for a second, then leaned forward in his chair. He watched Vin plot the coordinates— they'd been hopscotching their way toward the outer planet of

Portiis. If they flew in a straight line it would take three days, tops—but it was hard to tell which routes were being patrolled at any given time. It was safer to stay in random orbits. Fly around, blend with the intergalactic traffic, get lost in the shuffle, which would add *another* ten days at least.

The Tin Soldier had been modified from the inside out, practically gutted so that it barely looked like the pod Alyosha knew. That was the point—to be unrecognizable. And Aly had made a few adjustments of his own, in secret. He typed in a ten-digit code on his side of the console. "So you gonna apologize?" Aly asked finally as their pod slowed to a halt.

"For what?" Vin wouldn't look at him. "What the hell did you just do?" He jabbed the keys of the console. Still, they hung motionless, suspended in space.

"For getting us into that mess back there." He leaned back again, enjoying himself. For once, he was in the right.

"You got us into this mess," Vin countered evenly.

"How do you figure? *You* knocked my mask off."

Vin still wouldn't look at him as he tried punching in code after code to unfreeze the console. "Fine, Aly. Everything is my fault. You're always right." He slammed the dash with a fist: "Now unlock the nav system!"

"Say it like you mean it."

Vincent suddenly unclipped and lunged—but Aly blocked him with his free hand and held him at arm's length. Vin's legs started to lift up in the air, and he floated nearly upside down. "Unlock it," he said. "We don't have time for your bullshit."

"Look who's talking." Aly unstrapped, and they both floated

up toward the ceiling—but he levered off the walls, kicking away from Vin. It had started as a joke, kind of, but he could feel his anger bubbling up from all the hidden places. "My face is plastered on every telepod across the entire known universe. I've been framed for murder, and all you've done is give me *taejis*."

"Stop playing the victim." Vin's blue eyes were as big and intense as ever. "This is war, Aly. Massive-scale, insane, galactic war. So maybe instead of sucking your thumb and feeling sorry for yourself, you should stop and ask yourself: *Why?*"

"Gentlemen, please." Pavel stretched out two claw attachments and tugged at their pant sleeves, trying to wrestle them back into their seats. They both kicked out of his grip, and Pavel gave off an engine whirl that sounded like a sigh.

"Why did they frame you?" Vin's voice had dropped. "*I'm* the spy. *I'm* the one who sent out the hail."

Something thick and sticky was working its way through Aly's brain. The silence stretched out around them as if it, too, were free of gravity, and diffusing through the ship.

"Because I'm Wraetan," he said finally. It would always come back to his nation, his second-citizen status. He remembered what Vin had said earlier. *If you weren't always trying to get people to like you* . . . Was that true? Probably. He was mostly just trying to get people to like *Wraetans*. To show everyone that Wraetans were more than the rabid guerrilla fighters they'd seen on the holos during the Great War. But he was trying to show the Wraetans, too, what they could be, what he wanted them to be. "It was easy for the public to swallow. They want to get back at us for allying with Fontis . . ."

"Yeah, all of that." Vin looked at him. "You were convenient. You were the perfect spur-of-the-moment scapegoat to stoke the flames of war. But you were a *diversion*. The question is: What were they trying to *hide*?" The fire had seemed to drain out of him. He gripped his way to the dash and looked out into the darkness. "They needed to distract the public from rumors that the Princess is still alive."

"You know?" Aly asked. He hadn't told him about the braid he found in the escape pod.

"We suspected as much." He leaned back like he was trying to get a better look at Aly, trying to take him all in. "How long have *you* known?"

"Since I found the dead Nau Fruman in the royal escape pod . . ."

"Wait." Vin stared at him. "What escape pod?"

Aly told him, finally, about catching up to the royal escape pod, and the dead man with a braid coiled on his chest.

Vin just stared. "You're talking about Princess *Rhiannon*?"

"No, the *other* assassinated princess," Aly said, but when he saw Vin's face, he knew to drop the sarcasm.

"Holy *taejis*. Do you know what this means?" Vin asked. "You knew this whole time, and you didn't say anything?"

"Don't try to lecture me about keeping secrets," Aly said. Vin made a face. "And anyway, who the hell are *you* talking about?"

Vin hesitated. "Princess Josselyn," he said, after a pause. Aly nearly laughed—would have laughed, if Vin didn't look so serious. Sure, there were always rumors that she'd survived the crash—conspiracy theories, that kind of thing. You could find anything if you went deep enough on the holos. "I've been tracking her. When I was back in Sibu—"

Aly could barely process what he was saying. "When were you in *Sibu*?"

"During leave a few months back . . ."

The last time they were all on leave, Alyosha went to Jethezar's house. Vincent had said he was going to the coast to meet up with a fan. Aly figured he was off doing who knows what, with one of the thousands of girls who proposed to him on the holos or cried when he came on screen. For some reason this lie hit him harder than the others.

"Can I believe *anything* you tell me?" Aly hated how he sounded, like a desperate younger brother shut out of a game.

"You can believe this," Vin said softly. "I think she's alive. The United Planets thinks she's alive. It's even more important now that we find her." Aly could see him chewing the inside of his mouth, like he did sometimes when he was thinking. "Listen, we have to risk taking the direct route to Portiis, even if there are patrols. We need to get there as fast as—"

Just then a loud pop made the whole hull shudder. The craft tilted noticeably, and the metal shell around them groaned.

"What the—?" But Aly knew right away what it was. Someone had locked on to the craft.

"A grav beam?" Vin swam back down into his seat, kicking off the walls and strapping in. Aly did the same and unlocked the nav system from his screen.

"It's not a grav beam," Aly said. The velocity was too slight. "It feels almost . . . magnetic." As he said the last word he swung to the window. He had a visual on a body thirty astro units in the distance. What quadrant were they in again? *Bazorl.* Bazorl Quadrant. He scanned the nav stats and his blood went cold.

"*Choirtoi,*" he swore. "We're being pulled into Naidoz."

"Naidoz," Vin repeated. He said it like a death sentence. He frantically began pressing buttons and pulling at the console. But Aly knew it was too late.

Naidoz was another dwarf planet, with an enormous valley of magnetic lava that had cooled and hardened centuries ago. Equipment failed constantly and crashes were common because everyone was pulled into its magnetic field. Every pilot knew to avoid it. But they'd drifted—they'd stopped paying attention all because of a stupid fight that Aly had started.

The pull got stronger, and they picked up speed as they were drawn helplessly toward the planet. It felt like the pod was made of glass, like it might shatter.

"P!" Aly had to shout. "What are our chances of pulling out?"

The droid's lights went red and blinked blue again. "Our mass is too small and our thrust insufficient, even with recent upgrades."

Translation: *No chance. We're all screwed.*

A sudden jolt pushed them against the hull of the ship, and he could feel the g-force building. Everything was vibrating. He could hear them cutting through space—as loud as a bolt of thunder that never stopped. The shaking became intense and rattled its way into his brain. Metal seams shifted and flexed like tectonic plates.

Lights flickered on and off, the console a staticky red until it was total darkness apart from the red glow from Pavel's eyelights. Outside, pieces of the Tin Soldier detached and burned through the atmosphere alongside the main pod, a trail of red-orange fire behind them.

"We have to make it to Portiis. We have to get to the United Planets!" Vin shouted. "But if one of us doesn't make it . . ."

"We're going to make it!" Aly yelled. "We'll get there!"

A wing detached and darted away into the void. They barrel-rolled, end over end, so many times he lost count. He felt sick—an ocean in his stomach ready to come up and drown them all. It was just like how Vin used to turn the *Revolutionary* over for fun to mess with him, except this wasn't for fun, and Vin wasn't going to pull them out. They were going to die.

"Look, Aly. I'm sorry for what I said. I meant to tell you—"

But his voice was drowned out by an urgent mechanical beeping. The Tin Soldier, his old friend, was coming apart.

Down they plunged, burning through atmosphere, hurtling toward the surface of the planet's ocean.

Faster. More pressure. He could barely breathe.

Then, a thunderous boom. A violent jolt. Metal groaning. He grabbed for Vin. His best friend. The two of them going down, after all they'd been through.

"You can have my hammer," Aly told him.

Or maybe he thought it?

A wave of water slammed them backward. Then a current of white water poured in from the metal cracks and tore them apart.

Part Three:

THE DEPARTED

"In the last G-1K summit, Kalusian neurobiologist Diac Zofim surprised the scientific world when she introduced what she called *a reader*. It could override security measures and read the contents of a person's cube. Impressive enough, but think about this: For what purpose would you use it? What gave anyone the right to access someone's cube without their express consent? It would be useful for interplanetary security, the supporters argued, but it sounded like a slippery slope to me. There were a lot of living rights activists who agreed, and it sparked a series of protests that would've been front and center, but they were overshadowed by the twin bombings of Rhesto and Wraeta. Eventually the tech was quietly deemed illegal, but they'd announced it at a time when the public had other things on their mind . . ."

—Living rights activist and reporter, identity unknown
Archives provided by the United Planets

THIRTEEN

RHIANNON

RHEE and Josselyn had always fought for the window seat. They'd traveled often as a family, her father urging diplomacy, to take turns and to share. That didn't always work. Josselyn and Rhee would pinch each other's thighs and whisper insults, until finally—boiling with rage, screeching and hissing like vultures—the two would be separated, neither of them with the window seat to show for it.

She hadn't thought of that in ages. Not when there'd been so many *good* memories to replay, moments where it felt like they were a team. Rhee had willfully forgotten how lonely it was sometimes to have a sister. How sometimes, you could be sitting alone even if she was right next to you.

After five days offline, the sense of liberation had rapidly worn off. Rhee had thought that without her cube, her mind would remain clear and focused—and that the temptation of revisiting memories would be removed. But all it did was open up a path for the more painful ones to surface—her last fight with Joss, the goodbye with Julian as comets burned overhead, Veyron's tears as he tried to end her life . . .

"You're not still upset?" Dahlen asked her. It had been two days since parting ways with Tai Reyanna and traversing the dark tunnel that had allowed them to escape from Tinoppa, and these were the first words he had spoken to her.

Rhee angled her body to the zeppelin window so as not to have to look at him. Every time she did, her eyes zeroed in on the ring he wore. She knew it was Fontisian technology—he'd explained that he'd pulled electromagnetic currents from the air and focused them with his ring into heat energy—but Rhee swore instead that it was charged with hatred and vengeance and all the other dark feelings she knew too well.

And what did it mean, that he no longer scared her? She understood him. He'd killed Seotra for the same reason Rhee had planned her own revenge for so many years. He'd lost people he loved on Seotra's order, watched them die on his word. Rhee had been right about the bigger picture but wrong about the details. The man was a killer, certainly. But he hadn't killed her family.

He'd killed Dahlen's.

What made up Dahlen's *ma'tan sarili*? She'd thought it was about following orders, about obeying the word of his god without question. But she wasn't sure now, and it irked her—how interchangeable their anger was, their bloodlust. He'd killed Seotra after she'd pleaded for him not to, when he knew the man had invaluable information about the death of her family. Was this part of his plan all along?

Rhee was the one who'd brought him there. She felt stupid and young, so singularly focused, unable to think ahead or see the bigger picture. She ached for her cube now, to replay that conversation with Veyron just before his death. Hadn't he confirmed it was Seotra who had sent Veyron after Rhee? Or had she only assumed?

You've been blind—blind and willful, he'd said.

"I may have miscalculated your response," Dahlen added in the wake of her silence, "but your consent to join me in Portiis is the right choice."

She turned to him and found his expression remorseless. By now Rhiannon spoke "Dahlen" fluently. He'd meant *sorry* and *thanks for coming*, in his own way. She disagreed though. It wasn't the right choice. And while Dahlen *believed* she'd at last agreed to receive the protection of the United Planets in Portiis—or at least his order's mysterious contact *at* the council—she had other plans. Dahlen had proved he cared only about his vengeance, that he'd put it above all else.

Which meant: She was free to care only for hers.

She would find a way to sneak off at the next stop, where Nero would be meeting with the governments of Kalusian allies to discuss the political climate. The Urnew Treaty was in turmoil, and the public was becoming restless. The news of Seotra's death—or rather, disappearance, since his body had been incinerated—was everywhere. Nero had been covering all of it and had been on air for twelve hours straight. He'd arranged to make an emergency appearance on Navrum to try to rally support for Kalu's interests.

"The brave and honorable people of Kalu don't just need answers; they demand action," Nero's holographic image said sternly. The man a row in front tried to adjust the size and volume of his holo projection, and Rhee leaned forward—straining to see and hear. "The people who killed our Princess Ta'an and took our Regent Seotra think we'll bow down, run scared. But it's *they* who are the cowards, jealous of our freedoms, trying to destroy our Kalusian values—"

Dahlen kicked the man's seat, and he lurched forward, dropping his handheld. The holo disappeared.

"Apologies," Dahlen said, barely audible. The man scowled back but said nothing.

Nero was misguided at best, and Rhee knew it would likely only further notch the galaxy toward war. But it was a rallying cry, a call for revenge against those who'd killed the family he served. He'd loved her father, and the brilliant speech he'd given after his death—praising his accomplishments as emperor, urging continued loyalty and patience as the last Ta'an learned to rule—had inspired a galaxy.

An idea opened up in her mind, like a fist unclenching: The sooner she got to him, the sooner she could unveil herself on his broadcast. Too many people had already died, and now her priority was to take back the throne and restore the terms of the truce. It was only as empress that she could root out the true traitor.

Stepping into her role as empress would make her untouchable, and with that impunity she would find her family's real killer.

The speaker system came online with a single crackle of interference. "Approaching a patch of solar wind. Cubes will go temporarily offline," a mechanized voice said.

The announcement triggered unease in the cabin; people were uncomfortable offline, even for a few minutes. On the zeppelin this close to the sun, electromagnetic waves had caused signal losses throughout the trip. The passengers were so distressed about it, no one had noticed Rhee and Dahlen had been moving from one passenger car to another. Now he motioned for her to gather her things.

It was perfect timing. As they slid out of their seats, a service droid was just entering their car, tall and lean, its metal dull with age. "Tickets, please," it announced in a low monotone.

The droid offered the screen on its chest to a squat Chram woman with tiny iridescent scales that looked gray from Rhee's angle. In the first row, the woman touched her finger to her cube and simultaneously pressed a finger to the droid's screen with her other hand. It blinked blue and beeped an approval when the woman's data was accepted.

The overhead speakers crackled to life again. "Approaching a patch of solar wind. Cubes will temporarily go offline in two minutes."

Dahlen leaned forward to whisper to Rhee as she pushed past him into the aisle. "Whatever happens, don't touch the droid's screen."

"I know that already," she snapped back. Once her finger-print was in the database, they'd match it to her DNA. With any luck, however, while the droid was offline they could sneak past it and return to a car that had already been checked.

Rhee counted seconds in her head as she dodged a tentacle and brushed up against the fur of a Yersian, which generated a charge on her bare skin. Several passengers shrank away from her, obviously unhappy to be sharing the train car with a Marked girl. Dahlen's presence didn't offer them any reassurance, the tattoos crawling along his neck, his cheekbones sharp like cut glass, his dirty blond hair matted like an animal's against moon-white skin. It was almost as if pheromones radiated from his skin and warned everyone of danger.

"Please remain in your seat," the droid said, as Dahlen tried to pass.

"Won't you kindly move?" Dahlen asked, with such exaggerated politeness Rhee couldn't believe the droid didn't register the sarcasm. Before she could prevent him, he grabbed her hand. "My sister isn't feeling well."

Julian was the last person who had taken Rhee's hand.

Rhee wrenched her hand away from Dahlen, annoyed by the obvious lie. And yet why not? With her face still purpled with the mark, and her non-pointed ears hidden beneath a hood, she might have been Fontisian. In that split second, she realized: The boy she disliked most in the world could have been the brother she'd never had—both orphans, rigid in their beliefs, born for strife and loss and revenge.

The droid pivoted its base so it blocked as much of the aisle as

EMPRESS OF A THOUSAND SKIES

possible. "Please provide your ticket information before proceeding." It sprayed its screen with a pine-scented sanitizer, angling it down toward Rhee. She felt the skin on her neck tingle.

"Approaching a patch of atmospheric solar wind. Cubes will temporarily go offline in one minute," the speaker voice announced.

"Here, let me," Dahlen said, feigning irritation. He touched the space on his neck two inches above his cube and moved to touch the screen. Just before he did, a small charge shot from his ring to the screen. It was so subtle that no one would've seen it apart from Rhee. The droid rolled back an inch, and light shuddered across its touchscreen, as if it had flinched.

"Unreadable," it said.

"Perhaps your reader is defective," Dahlen suggested, still with that tone of politeness that to Rhee's ears sounded obviously false. "Let me try again."

"Can I assist?" a second droid said. Turning, Rhiannon saw that they'd failed to notice an additional ticket collector had entered the car.

The speaker crackled. "Approaching a patch of atmospheric solar wind. Cubes will temporarily go offline in ten, nine, eight . . ." Now they'd attracted attention. She heard the sucking sound of someone's tentacle: a Nilapas, babbling in his native tongue, no doubt trying to shush them. Rhee could feel herself sweating under her tunic. Still she tried to move slowly and with grace—a quality Tai Reyanna had urged again and again.

"Excuse me, can you give her some room? She's not feeling well . . ." Dahlen said.

The second droid ignored him. It angled its screen down toward Rhee. "Please provide ticket information." When Rhee hesitated, a red light began blinking on its touchscreen, prompting her with use instructions. Now the first droid rolled over Dahlen's foot, closing in on the other side, and both droids began to speak at once.

"Please provide ticket infor—"

They were interrupted by a thunderous boom that shook their cabin. Rhee's ears popped. A girl to the side yelped, her light blue skin turning a dark shade of purple in alarm, and a Kalusian man in the front row flinched in his seat. Rhee remembered the sensation of her cube going dark, like her energy had been sapped all at once. Immediately, both droids powered down in the aisle, their armlike attachments hanging limp at their sides. A section of Yersians groomed one another's fur in agitation.

Rhee exhaled. Just in time.

"Let's move," Dahlen said in a low voice. The doors between compartments had come unlocked as well, and Dahlen cranked the handle and leaned heavily on the door to open it, gesturing Rhee inside. As they barreled through the door, Rhee crashed into someone. She reared back and then stifled a gasp. It was the royal guard.

Her royal guard.

She couldn't tear her eyes off the stunners on their belts. The broad-chested man she'd bumped into wiped the spot on his khaki uniform where they'd touched, making a big show of being disgusted. The mark on Rhee's face felt as if it were on fire. The other guard stood there, smiling. She noticed for the first time how cocky they seemed, like they owned every place they cared to set foot on. Had they been like that even under her charge? Under her father's charge?

Dahlen had gone perfectly still, and Rhee felt a pressure inside her mounting.

"Apologies," she said in a terrible Fontisian accent, then bowed out of nervousness—realizing too late that bowing was reserved for diplomats and Tais.

The taller Tasinn got a good laugh. He took a step forward to block the threshold, standing so close that Rhee had to tilt her head all the way back to see his face—a long chin and a sloped nose. He looked like a jackal. She suppressed the urge to bare her teeth. What were they even doing here, outside of Kalusian territory? Rhee felt Dahlen's hand squeeze her shoulder protectively. She swatted it off.

"Don't I get a bow too?" the taller Tasinn asked in his crisp capital accent, the one Tai Reyanna had preferred she spoke with.

Rhee balled her fists at her side. Suddenly, she remembered Julian flicking his hair out of his face, explaining how diamonds form under high temperature and pressure. How did beings in the Outer Belt deal with organic memories like this, flooding your brain without warning, at the worst possible moments?

She'd come all this way to find out the truth about her family. It wouldn't end here, at the mercy of two arrogant men heady with the tiniest bit of power. Rhee couldn't be caught, couldn't afford to have their cubes scanned. And so she bowed. It was a beat too late, though, and they must've noticed.

The big-chested one hooked his thumbs in his belt. "Where are you two headed?"

"Nau Fruma." She felt Dahlen stiffen. Too late, she realized she should have named somewhere on Fontis instead. She hadn't known why she said it—only that it was the first place that had formed on her tongue. It was home.

"The moon? I didn't know there were convents for the Marked there."

"There are likely a number of things you don't know," Rhee mumbled.

"What did you say?" he demanded. He tried to push her hood back, but Rhee dodged out of his reach.

"That there are a number of things to *see* if you *go*," she said, with a simpering smile.

The taller Tasinn to the right laughed. "It's best you didn't touch her," he said to his partner. "Marked *and* a Fontisian? If the little thing's not covered in germs, then she's certainly got the worst luck I've ever seen."

"Probably right," the round one said. He eyed Dahlen. "You don't talk much."

"Afternoon, sirs," Dahlen said, lowering his head. He was a looming presence at Rhee's back, but his voice remained passive.

"*Sirs!* I like that. This one's got the right idea."

The taller one nodded. "Perhaps you could teach this one a thing or two about manners."

As if she *needed the lesson in manners.* Her guards had acted as shadows in the quiet palace of Nau Fruma, receding into the background when she became focused on history lessons or lost herself in play. They rotated in and out, so she never became acquainted with one for long—though they hadn't seemed interested, standing like sentries at doorways, their faces neutral whenever she passed. Rhee wondered now if they'd been instructed to do that, and where their instructions came from today. Seotra's council?

Rhee's ears popped again. With a clap like a lightning bolt, they emerged from the atmospheric pressure patch. People sighed happily and even cheered. The Tasinn looked relieved too.

But Rhee felt panic moving down her body like sweat. The doors behind them opened with a hiss, and now the mechanical voices of both ticket collectors crested in unison, like a shout.

"Please provide your ticket information before proceeding. Please provide your ticket information before proceeding."

With no options left, Rhee broke into a run. She tried to push past the Tasinn, but a blow to her chest knocked her off her feet and drove the breath straight out of her lungs. Stars exploded in her head. Dimly, she could hear Dahlen shouting, and the droids announcing trouble. When she could finally take a breath, the oxygen shocked her into awareness again: The taller Tasinn had hit her with one of the steel batons the royal guard always carried.

"Jumpers," the guard said. "I'd bet Kalu on it." By the way he smiled, Rhee could tell he'd been baiting them, that he'd known the whole time. Turning to the droids, he gave them a dismissive flick of his wrist. "Leave. We'll handle it from here."

"Want me to get a read on them?" The big-chested man stepped forward, and Rhee saw he was holding a cube reader.

Time slowed. He was Veyron's build, and Rhee grasped for organic memories of her trainer—of all the sparring sessions she'd had with him over the past year. Every recollection was a pin shoved through her beating heart, but she pushed the pain aside, calculating all the ways she could break this man's arm should he try to access her cube. Assuming Dahlen didn't kill him first.

She tried to climb to her feet, but the taller Tasinn pinned her again with the end of his baton. "Don't bother," he said, with the pinched expression of someone confronting a particularly disgusting piece of garbage. "Like you said, these two probably carry diseases. Throw 'em straight into the pen instead."

FOURTEEN

ALYOSHA

ALY was on his way to Portiis because it was what Vin had wanted them to do, and because he had nowhere else to go. He thought of this one time he, Jeth, and Vin had been on leave there. They had spent their last night staying up way too late and drinking in Jeth's backyard, talking about nothing and everything—about the things they'd do, the places they'd see, how none of them were going to be anything like their fathers . . .

They were due back to duty the next day, and they nearly fell asleep in formation they were so damn tired. Sergeant Vedcu made them clean the squad bay for half a day—scrubbing floors that were already spotless, thinking that maybe they'd die on their hands and knees with a washrag as their only witness.

"Worth it," Vin had said.

Vin never had any regrets. Never let anything stop him. What was that expression, for the kind of guy who went big?

He knows how to live.

And now Vin was dead while Aly hid out in the cargo hold of an interquadrant zeppelin. It was as terrible as it sounded—hours trying to spot your own hands in the dark; a crinkly tarp on the cold ground for a bed; storage containers as bathrooms, placed all over like he had to mark his territory.

But the worst part? Having all the time to *think*. To wonder, a million times over, why *he* was the one who'd survived. Aly had never killed anyone before, and he'd thought that if it came down to it, it would be in a face-off against an enemy on the battlefield. Instead, Aly had killed his best friend to get a stupid apology he didn't even deserve.

The crash on Naidoz had left him weak. Sometimes, when he started to fall asleep, he felt himself tumbling toward icy dark water again and woke up with a start. Pavel had had a surprisingly effective floating mechanism, but Aly had had to drag Vin to the surface. By then he wasn't moving on his own, but his eyebrows remained arched in surprise, like maybe even in death he was thinking, *For real?*

Pavel had helped him bury Vin, there on that cold, rocky planet. Aly had left the hammer on his chest.

Now metal wire sparked at Aly's fingertips as he tried to rig the door open. He dropped it with a curse and looked at his throbbing hand. It wasn't the first time he'd electrocuted himself learning this system. His fingers were cold, clumsy. Distractions weren't helping him any either. *Stop thinking about Vin.*

"Soldering iron," Aly whispered to Pavel, who wordlessly passed him an attachment shaped like a stylus. You couldn't get the system open without a barcode—so this was Aly's only option. After a few more adjustments, the door slid open. The sound of compressed air had never been so sweet. The light-bulb outside in the hallway was unscrewed, just as he'd left it—which meant he would be invisible. He counted off a few seconds—enough so that anyone watching or listening would assume he'd slipped out into the hallway—then moved into a crouch again.

Time to catch the *choirtoi* who'd been stealing from him.

After the crash, Aly had walked for a whole day to the nearest town, where he stole a pod outside an oxygen bar and booked it to the neighboring planet of Fannah. He felt bad about the pod, but he had to get the hell out of the Kalusian territories, fast. Besides, he was sure it would be recovered prac-tically as soon as he ditched it. Then the holos would be on fire with all the *Revolutionary Boys* conspiracy theories. If and when they found Vincent's body, Aly would be on the hook for another murder.

From Fannah, he'd hitched a ride on a freighter headed for the Outer Belt. With a stolen ID, a head scarf, and a fake Chram accent, Aly had managed to sneak on board alongside thousands of refugees fleeing Kalu's newly declared "military zones"—code for places that would get wiped as soon as they started dropping em-stones that rendered anything that ran on electricity useless.

He was a refugee, twice over.

At least during the forced evac of Wraeta he hadn't been

alone. Even as they'd walked for seven days to the nearest port, there were entire families alongside them, babies they all took turns holding, other kids to make up games with. It had been the most arid season in decades during that exodus. They'd arrive at each stop covered in a layer of dust so thick, people joked they couldn't be told apart. It's why they'd called them *dusties*.

Now Aly had nowhere to go and no one to walk beside him. He thought about calling Jeth, but if he powered on his cube, he might as well surrender: Half the Kalu army would be on both of them like white on rice. A part of him wanted to hustle to a far-off planet and just disappear, but Vincent's voice kept coming back to him. *But if one of us doesn't make it*, he'd yelled as they burned through the atmosphere. His dying wish was for Aly to go to the United Planets; he'd been sure that they would help. Then again, he'd also believed Princess Josselyn might still be alive, so he was probably out of his mind.

Still, with no money, no plan, and no other options, Aly was headed to Portiis, to find Vin's contact. Aly had no idea how he was supposed to find Lancer, or where he would even start, but he'd have to figure it out on the fly.

It had been almost a week since the *Elieido* exploded, though he'd been hoping that Princess Rhiannon might resurface at any point, miraculously alive. He'd had daydreams of official pardons, of receiving an apology from the Regent himself and the DroneVision producers of that damned awful show.

But if Rhiannon Ta'an were alive, she would've showed up at the party by now, if only to fend off the war that with every day looked more inevitable.

Now they'd been holed up in cargo for a whole day. It was always pitch-black, so much darkness it was like a physical force, a mouth ready to swallow him. But he knew his way around well enough; there were a lot of broken machines that looked like old medical equipment that would probably sell for scrap on the Outer Belt. He'd taken some apart to distract himself, without tools, unscrewing bolts for hours until his fingers bled.

He'd managed to sneak some food off the service cart between shift changes once, when it was parked for five minutes, unmanned, just outside of the cargo hold. A small window of time, but enough to stuff his pockets with meal pills, fancy dehydrated nuts and fruit, and a bottle of water. It wasn't much—barely enough to survive on, in fact—which was exactly why he'd figured out someone *else* was stealing too.

Stealing from Aly this time.

He'd thought he was alone with Pavel and the lady who made the annoying announcements about approaching solar wind and cubes going offline, and she wasn't even a lady so much as a digitized voice that sounded vaguely feminine. No. There was someone else in the cargo hold with him. Last night when he'd left his stash out, they'd lifted a portion of it.

He wasn't risking everything just to feed some stranger. He still had another ten days before the loop hit the Heryl Quadrant, where Portiis was.

As big as he was, Aly was decent at staying quiet. Geared up in camo, a slow advance crawling across terrain on his belly—*that* had been his idea of a good time when he was in boot camp.

He didn't have to wait long before he saw a figure, a silhouette, moving toward his camp, weaving around the crates and the old pieces of equipment. He hoped to god the guy didn't have a weapon on him. He held his breath. Just a little closer. A little closer . . .

When he was in striking distance, Aly launched to his feet, grabbed a handful of the guy's jacket, and threw him up against the wall. "You little *taejis*," he said, covering the kid's mouth. "Don't even think about yelling. If some poor conductor comes running, it'll be the end of both of us."

The kid struggled, swatting at Aly's hands. Whatever excuse the little punk was trying to make came out in a muffled plea. Finally, he calmed down.

"I'm going to take my hand away, and if you—*GAHHH!*" Aly yelled out in pain, pulling his hand back.

The kid had sunk his teeth into the pinky edge of Aly's hand.

"Don't threaten me," the voice said. A little soft, and a little high. A girl. He stumbled back, releasing her. He almost felt bad. Almost. His hand stung where she'd bit him.

"Or what?" he asked, his anger still sparking. He heard Pavel approaching. "Light, Pavel." Pavel flipped his beam on just as Aly yanked the scarf off the girl's head.

She flinched and put her hand up to block her face. "You got another setting on that thing?" she asked Pavel.

"Apologies! Dimming by forty percent," Pavel said as the light softened. "Is this acceptable?"

She dropped her hand. "Yes, thank you."

"Turn it up, P." Aly didn't want her to see his face. His head scarf was tangled up somewhere with his belongings. And if she knew she was talking to the most wanted criminal in the universe, he doubted he could keep her from screaming. "And don't apologize either. She's *fine*."

Pavel let out what sounded suspiciously like a sigh—damn learning technology—but the light intensified again.

She had long black hair and bangs that covered her eyes.

The girl pawed her hair away from her face like she'd read his mind. She was kind of a mess, in the way that pretty girls looked messy, like she'd just washed up from the ocean, raw—open up a clamshell and there she'd be. She had dark gray eyes and sharp features, but her skin was tan and her cheeks were broad. It gave her a mixed look, maybe a blend of native and second-wave Kalusian blood. She was swimming in an expensive-looking jacket, two rows of buttons down the front, like the kind he'd seen diplomats wearing on the holos. It obviously wasn't hers.

"If you're willing to live with the guilt of burning my retinas off, then that's on you." She had a full mouth pulled into a straight line—like she was born to argue.

"A thief trying to lecture me on manners?"

"Says the guy who was stealing to begin with." She jerked a thumb toward the service cart.

This piece of work. Ballsy as hell. Turns out when she wasn't biting people, she was running her mouth. "You owe me," he said.

"I've got nothing to give." But Aly saw her bring a hand to one pocket and skim it, as if for reassurance. A tell. It was the same way folks gave themselves away in the Wray, absentmindedly tapping the pockets where all their important stuff was.

"Then what's in your pocket?"

"I *said* I have nothing to give," she repeated. "And anyway, what would you want with a rusty old coin?" She held it out in the palm of her hand, and when he reached for it she grabbed his wrist and pulled him into the light.

Aly froze. But it was too late. He'd been recognized.

"You," she whispered. She dropped his wrist and pushed him away, but she didn't run or scream out like he thought she would. Instead she pressed herself against the wall, so he backed up to give her some room. Her expression—the way her mouth parted, her eyes squinting like her brain was locking into that *aha* moment this very second—it reminded him of someone he knew. He just couldn't think who.

"Kill the light, P," he said quickly, and Pavel did. They'd plunged from bright light to total darkness. "I'm not going to hurt you," he told her. "Don't be scared."

"Who says I'm scared?" She didn't sound too confident, but she wasn't screaming her head off either. "Maybe *you* should be scared."

"I am," he said honestly. For a lot of reasons. That it would all end here. That Vincent had died for nothing. That the Ta'an had been wiped out and the planets would go to war.

"It really is you," she said. "I can't believe it. You're Alyosha, from *The Revolutionary Boys*." Then: "Where's the other one? Where's Vincent?"

"Dead," Aly said shortly. Maybe Aly *was* a murderer. Anyone who rolled with him ended up dead. "I buried him." Aly could feel the back of his throat closing off, his eyes watering, a deep blue filling up his chest.

She was quiet for a bit. "They said you kidnapped him."

"Is that what you think?" he asked bitterly. "That I'm a murderer? Some sort of terrorist?"

"Is that what you are?" she replied evenly.

Aly couldn't read her tone. "It's what everyone believes, isn't it?" Even if she couldn't see him, he could still feel her eyes searching his face. It reminded him of the first time they'd brought a camera on board the *Revolutionary*, and how he didn't know what to do with his hands.

"If all we are is what people think we are, then we're all screwed." There was a knife's edge to her voice. She sounded pissed. Or scared. Or both.

"Well, we're all screwed anyway," Aly said, but her words bothered him. He knew as well as anyone that it was other people's rules that mattered. In the real world they told you who to be, not the other way around. It's why he pretended to be Kalusian when he first joined the UniForce—it just made life easier. "You're crazy, you know that?" Aly told her. "I could be dangerous."

"Let's say I *am* crazy and you *are* dangerous, and we call it a draw? Besides," she added, "you haven't hurt me yet, and you could've. That's a gold star in my book."

"That's a pretty low bar . . ." Aly said.

Just then there was a faint hiss as the doors opened at the northern end of the hold. Aly snapped back to the present just as the beam of a flashlight shifted across the floor. The girl grabbed his wrist and pulled him down to crouch behind what looked like an old MRI machine nearby. Pavel had enough sense to go still and keep his lights dark. No one had come in here for a full twenty-four hours.

"Entering carriage 95," a man said, speaking into his cube.

Aly poked his head up and saw he was wearing the uniform of a Tasinn. He couldn't believe it. The Tasinn were showing up more and more now, in places they weren't meant to be—like on Derkatz, and now here on the zeppelin. He'd been worried a droid would find them, but this was way worse.

As the girl yanked him back down, he accidentally nudged a piece of equipment. It made a sound as it scratched across the floor.

"Who's there?" the man called out.

Aly's body tensed, and for whatever reason he and the girl reached for each other at the same time. Could he trust her? *She'd* grabbed *him* to hide, hadn't she? They were so close, her tangled hair had somehow made it into his mouth. Thank god she didn't smell like fake flowers or extinct fruits or else he'd be sneezing his face off. Her head just smelled like a head.

Could she hear his heart beating? Her breath was hot on his neck. The guard's bootsteps came closer.

Aly had slung one arm protectively around her and wished to god he still had his hammer. He scanned the floor for anything he could use. What were they going to do? Crouch here spooning each other until the guard found them? Because at this rate he *would* find them.

Crunch. Aly heard the Tasinn curse softly as something crackled underfoot. Aly's blood froze. He'd left his supplies out, just scattered across the blanket for anyone to see, hoping to tempt the thief—the girl—into revealing herself. He heard the rustle of fabric as the Tasinn moved into a crouch, saw the beam of a light sweep across a sad collection of spare parts he'd stripped from the machines. The guard was less than five feet away, separated from them by only a thin arrangement of extra sheet metal.

They would have to fight. There was no other choice. Slowly, as quietly as he could, he crept forward . . .

Then, suddenly, the guard touched his cube. "Hold on, 401, let me transfer you to a holo." He pulled a small handheld holo from his pocket. "Go ahead, 401."

The device projected a hologram of another guard wearing the same army outfit with the red sash. "They've found the freight jumper. Male, six foot, medium build, a Vodhead—crazy tattoos and all. Traveling with a Marked girl."

"I'm in cargo," he said, poking through Aly's stuff with the tip of his baton. "Looks like they've been living down here too."

"Leave it. We're landing in fifteen, and we'll need all hands on deck. Just heard Nero's skipping town early and he's got a whole party with him."

"Yeah, there were about nine million staff requests to be put on his security detail . . . everyone is trying to meet him."

The Tasinn stood up and retreated, moving back through cargo the way he'd come. Aly didn't realize he'd stopped breathing until the hiss of the mechanized doors told him he was safe— didn't realize, either, how tightly he'd been holding the girl until she moved away from him.

"Whoa," the girl muttered. She stood up, and Aly did too. Pavel lit up tentatively, as if afraid to fully power on, so she was cast in low blue light.

"They'll be back," he said. He'd have to disembark earlier than he wanted and find some other way to Portiis. He asked himself for the thousandth time what Vin had expected him to do with his crappy half-information, about a maybe-lost princess and some random contact in the United Planets.

Then again, he couldn't stay on the zeppelin, especially if Nero was sharing his airspace. Since his cube was off, Aly'd been missing most of the news—he wasn't all that interested in seeing a MURDERER or WANTED label slapped over a bad picture of his face—but he'd picked up that Regent Seotra had up and disappeared. "Vanished," the holos said. More like *assassinated*, Aly figured.

Now Nero was practically in charge, making a big show about how Kalusians—the good guys they were—had tried diplomacy. Now it was time to take action.

Take back what's ours had become the rallying cry of Nero's rabid supporters.

It was a veiled call for blood. Aly's blood, specifically, as well as the blood of anyone who supported Fontisian or Wraetian calls for peace. Aly guessed people were fed up and didn't need a whole lot of convincing. All Nero had to do was just remind them how horrible their lives were and point a finger on the sly. See who they blamed then. It helped Nero's case that he looked the way he did. A jaw that cut glass, a slick-looking haircut, a permanent smile on his face that made people go weak in the knees.

Aly had felt off that time Nero invited him and Vin to the gala. He was easygoing and seemed to take a liking to Vin; they were both second-wave Kalusians and Nero could've been his cool, younger uncle. Nero was nice enough to Aly, too, and introduced him with the minimum level of pleasantries—but there was something about the way his eyes flickered over him, like Aly was a roach in a tux. When Aly brought it up to Vin, he said what he always did: "It's in your head." Apparently not.

"I gotta keep moving," the girl said. She stared at him for a long time. Her gray-blue eyes were intense, like the choppy parts of the ocean where you weren't supposed to swim, but he willed himself not to look away. He realized she was half asking for permission and half trying to say goodbye. "Don't worry. I won't tell anyone about you."

Aly nodded. What else could he do? He wasn't going to hold her against her will. He wasn't going to become the monster that Nero and his council were trying to claim he was.

As the girl passed Pavel, she touched the top of his dome. His blue eyelights blinked softly. Maybe he was surprised by the gesture too. When she got far enough away she turned, breaking into a sprint as she wove her way toward the same door the Tasinn had used. She stopped suddenly before she reached it.

"Where will you go?" she asked.

"To find help."

She spun around to face him then, and for a split second Aly thought she might charge him. But instead she blurted out: "Do you want to come with me?"

Yes.

"Why?" he asked instead. "Why trust me?"

"I don't." She shrugged. "But if you're still alive when half the universe wants you dead, you can't be an idiot. And there's safety in numbers."

"Not when one of us is plastered all over the holos," Aly said. Besides, he wouldn't be anyone's charity case.

"I'm going to a safe house," she said finally. "There's one on Rhesto."

"A *safe house*? On Rhesto?" Was everyone in the galaxy some kind of spy? "But that whole place is poisonous."

Rhesto was a small moon and the site of a nuclear plant before the Great War, but it had a meltdown when Fontis bombed it. Anyone who hadn't died had abandoned it: Supposedly, the radiation would last in the soil for something like twenty thousand years.

"Nothing radiation pills can't fix." She spoke matter-of-factly, and he wondered if she was being serious or if she had a sense of humor to rival Jeth's. Why the hell would she help *him*? "It's still not as toxic as staying in Kalu." She frowned, and he waited her out, banking on the fact she'd say more eventually. Thankfully it worked. "It's my mom, okay? She's a scientist and was part of the G-1K summits. A bunch of them have been targeted, hunted down. But they're smart, obviously, and they organized themselves. This safe house is *theirs*. And they set up a massive universe-wide broadcast to beam a DO NOT ENTER signal across all the holos. They have to manually disable it every day. If there was trouble, we would know."

By then Aly's heart had started beating very fast. An idea flashed in his brain like a starburst. "You said they can broadcast . . . *out*?"

She nodded.

Rhesto was one of the Kalusian moons, the other one being Nau Fruma. For an hour a day, the two crossed orbits; it blocked any DroneVision broadcasts.

For the first time in days, some of the bleak grip of hopelessness eased. He'd had no idea Rhesto had its own tower, or capabilities to broadcast out. If the planet could send that kind of distress call, then it could send out his cube playback, easy, for the whole universe to see. He'd broadcast his own version of events. He'd show them, once and for all, that he didn't kill the Princess. And maybe then they'd stop chasing him. Aly could finally stop running. Vin had told him to go to Portiis, which was all the way in the Heryl Quadrant and nearly a week's ride away, and ask for the United Planets' help—but *this* was the immediate solution, and exactly what he needed to prove his innocence. He'd still see his promise through to Vin, but he'd do it afterward.

There was a dinging service announcement. The girl did that thing where she looked up, like the voice had come out of the sky—but Aly somehow got fixated on the tan skin on her neck, the way her shirt fell just so, and had to look away. He couldn't let himself be distracted. "Arriving in Navrum. This zeppelin will be making stops in the Bazorl and Desuco Quadrants," the captain announced, then repeated the message again in Fontisian, Wraetan, and Derkatzian. That meant, Aly knew, that the freighter must cut a path directly through Rhesto's orbit.

"Okay," he said. "I'm coming with you." Aly still didn't totally understand why she was helping him, but getting to the safe house in Rhesto felt like the most solid plan he'd had in days. But then it occurred to him: "Navrum City is at the edge of the Rellia Quadrant. Rhesto isn't a scheduled stop. How the hell are you planning to get off this thing mid-orbit?"

She raised an eyebrow. "You hitched a ride on a zeppelin," she said, "but have you ever hitched a ride *off*?"

FIFTEEN

RHIANNON

RHEE and Dahlen had been herded into a holding area by the two Tasinn who caught them, and now they stood among dozens of other loop jumpers waiting to be kicked off at the next stop. Fortunately, the *next stop* was exactly where Rhee wanted to go.

"Descending onto Navrum shortly. Please fasten your seat belt and ensure all belongings are secured," the overhead recording announced.

The zeppelin shuddered as it burned through the atmosphere. Rhee was hemmed in too tightly to lose her balance. She'd never believed in luck, but this was almost enough to convince her. It was her plan all along to sneak off onto this very planet, where Nero was meeting with governments of Kalusian allies and broadcasting interviews. She'd seen on the public holos how Kalu was being edged into war now that everyone believed her dead. Rhee desperately needed to reach Nero, to use his platform and fame, so she could reveal herself alive on his broadcast. Now that Rhee knew of Seotra's innocence, she could stalk the inner workings of the council and find out who'd really been behind her family's betrayal. It was a risk to expose herself, she knew that. But now was the time to be bold.

A sharp, sudden pressure at the base of her spine made her stumble forward, into a woman in front of her. "Is that *necessary*?" she asked, twisting around to glare at one of the Tasinn, who only laughed in response.

It was the third time a member of the royal guard had rammed her with the tip of a metal baton. There were too many people corralled in too small a space, and the Tasinn seemed to make a game of it, jabbing them forward at random, using specialized metal prongs to shock the ones who complained. She overheard two guards gossiping about one of their own losing his badge, but apart from that, Rhee barely understood all the languages and dialects piping up among the prisoners. She didn't need to speak to them, though, to pick up the fear and tension in their words. The whole thing made Rhee sick. Who was commanding them? Who would keep them in line? Her father would have never stood for such cruelty from his own royal guard.

A familiar shame snaked around her organs, as if the weight of every responsibility was hers to feel. Was that what being empress meant? And was it honorable to take the throne solely in order to take her revenge?

Dahlen tried to press closer to her to shield her with his body, but Rhee pushed him away. He'd betrayed her. As soon as the opportunity arose, she would lose him and find Nero.

"Are you all right?" he asked.

"I'm fine," she said, without looking at him. *He'd killed a man*, she reminded herself. Killed him horribly, without mercy, without giving him the chance to defend himself.

But would she have acted any better?

She refused to feel guilty for lying to Dahlen, for misleading him about her plans to abandon him—not when he had lied to her first, and ruined her chances of learning the truth from Seotra.

"Hey. You. Vodhead. No talking." One of the Tasinn reached out and shocked Dahlen with a Taser, *hard*. He seized, and Rhee grabbed for him, feeling the jolt that rang through her whole head, like biting down on a metal spoon.

She recoiled as Dahlen collapsed to the ground. The other jumpers shrieked. Her heart shot up through her throat. Rhee moved to help him, but he pushed her away as if *she* were the one who'd electrocuted him. It was all so traumatic that she almost didn't realize she had his ring in her hand. It had slipped off Dahlen's finger when she'd tried to grab him. When their eyes met, he shook his head, and she felt a rush of doubt. His face had hollowed out in the last week since he had saved her life, and he looked even paler than usual.

Before he could stand, he was shocked again, by a different guard—a man who'd pushed his way through the crowd, dedicated to enacting this torture. That was twice now and counting. Rhee suspected they kept choosing Dahlen because they knew he wouldn't cry out. She squeezed her hand around his ring and breathed deeply, in and out, focusing only on her next move, on what was coming. Dahlen would be slower, now, after the electric shocks. Rhee would simply lose him in the crowd. Easy.

Her stomach was coiled tightly, guilt gripping her insides. She'd taken advantage of his torture.

The zeppelin touched down with a jolt. Everyone stumbled together. When the doors slid open, the sunlight stung her eyes, and the loop jumpers began pouring out. Rhee leapt down off the zeppelin, hearing the laughter of the guards at her back, taunting the jumpers and threatening worse punishments if they tried to get a free ride again.

"What's *your* problem?" A man's voice, deep and angry, sounded out behind her. Dahlen must've accidentally jostled him, because just two meters to her right she saw a big Derkatzian clutching the front of Dahlen's tunic, obviously spoiling for a fight. "You forget how to use your eyes, buddy?"

In the space between one heartbeat and the next, Rhee knew: This was her chance.

You must be fair, but decisive, her father had said.

At that very instant, as Dahlen tried to wrench out of the man's grip, his eyes locked on to Rhee's. In that moment, *she* knew *he* knew—Rhee would abandon him.

Dahlen tried to lunge for her despite the man holding him. But the man yanked him back, and in a split second, she was free. Elbowing her way out, she heard more yelling erupt behind her, but she didn't dare glance back.

She was free. Alone.

Rhee quickly made her way through the other disoriented jumpers who'd been shoved out of the holding car. The glass roof of the hub's freestanding grand pavilion had ribbed arches like that of an ancient cathedral. Her hood fell away as she ran, and Rhee quickly yanked it back over her head.

"Wait," she heard someone shout, maybe Dahlen, but she kept her head down and pushed forward. Her heart was pounding.

Honor, loyalty, and bravery, she repeated. Never mind the questions that came after: Who must she be honorable and loyal *to*? Who must she be brave *for*?

The central holo projected a clock high in the pavilion. There were three large archways marking the hub exits, and various holos flashing unfamiliar street signs, advertising specials, news, music. It was a madhouse: Even the central station in Sibu during the Harvest Festival was never this crowded. There must've been ten thousand souls, maybe more, from every corner of the galaxy packed into the hub. The walls were made of glass and metal beams, and a dizzying light from the sun shone through them.

Rhee knew that Dahlen's size wouldn't do him any favors in the crowded terminal. She squeezed through a current of people, like a salvion fish going upstream, dodging a family with three slobbering vitus hounds on leashes. The dogs barreled forward, dragging the children who tried to hold them back.

"It's Nero," someone nearby exclaimed, and Rhee's body reacted before even her mind could, stopping so quickly she nearly fell. Was Nero really here, in the station? The ancestors were on her side.

She stood on her tiptoes and had her answer—had the answer, too, for why the station was so crowded.

Nero hustled through the crowd, surrounded by Tasinn, so

Rhee could see him only in glimpses—broad shoulders, the forward stride, light hair trimmed and slicked back. He'd always seemed so easygoing, a generous smile trained right at the camera, but today his mouth was set in a grim line as he pushed his way through the crowd. Reporters were practically crawling on top of him as they shouted out questions and jostled to get closer.

"Is Kalu going to war?"

"Did they confirm there are UniForce troops on Wraeta?"

"Can the allies renew the accords of the Urnew Treaty without an empress or regent to sign?"

Nero must've been overwhelmed; Rhee knew the feeling. Still, he carved a path toward the departure platforms. Rhee remembered hearing he wasn't to leave for another three days; something must have happened to make him change his plans. Something bad.

For once, she was grateful to be less than twenty hands tall. She slipped through the roiling crowd to follow him, finding the smallest gaps like water flowing into sand.

"Any response to the Fontisian czar's accusation?"

"Has Rhiannon Ta'an's body been recovered?"

"Nero has no comment," a Tasinn called out. Strange, seeing as he always had a comment. Nero loved the cameras and yet he hadn't said a word or so much as looked at the reporters. As he hurried up the steps toward the first-class car of a waiting craft, Rhee was again struck by how much older he looked. And while he'd always been confident, he even *moved* differently, with more precision and command.

A line of Tasinn closed in after him and blocked the reporters desperate to pass. Rhee was caught up in the tide of journalists and pundits and hangers-on as they foamed down toward the very zeppelin she'd disembarked—toward a different entrance altogether, reserved for the first-class passengers.

There, another Tasinn was checking credentials before ushering the journalists—from all over the galaxy, Rhee noted, if the pair of long-limbed Ngisll sparring with the squid-like Ottos about who had been first in line were any indication—into the press car. With a handheld scanner he reviewed ID cards and admitted or rejected them with a nod or shake of his head. Two muscular brutes in the uniforms of UniForce rookies were on hand to hustle away anyone who didn't pass muster.

Rhee's mouth was dry. She licked her lips. She *had* to get back on board this zeppelin and speak to Nero before it was too late. This Tasinn was as tall as he was thick, with cool blue eyes that reminded her of Veyron's. A man you'd go out of your way to avoid. And Rhee was prepared to walk straight up to him and plead for her life. She made a split-second decision: She would power up her cube. She would let him scan it, if she had to, just so she could reach Nero. She wasn't in danger here, not with Nero so close—they'd had a personal connection all those years ago, and Rhee knew he couldn't resist the kind of ratings boost she'd give him. He could announce that Princess Rhiannon lived, and stop a war.

But before she could step up to the Tasinn, one of the UniForce rookies grabbed the back of her tunic.

"Nice try, girlie." His breath was hot and foul. "Press only."

"Wait!" She struggled to free herself from his grip, but his hands were like steel clamps. "Please—you don't understand."

Even as the UniForce soldier tried to steer her out of the line, however, the Tasinn checking credentials looked up and met her eyes. A quick change of expression skated across his face—had he recognized her? Rhee was hopeful and terrified all at once.

He lowered his scanner.

"Hold on," he said. His voice, she wasn't surprised, was just like his eyes: all ice. "Bring that one here."

Rhee was shoved over to him. For some reason, everyone had quieted: Maybe it was the effect of the Tasinn's voice, as if the very air had frozen. The man took one of his long, white fingers and flicked back her hood to better see her face. She looked into his blue eyes and again registered the change in his expression. He *did* know her.

She'd finally be the princess once again.

But before she could speak to explain, the Tasinn returned his gaze to his scanner and gestured the next journalist forward.

"Go on, let her in," he said casually.

"You sure, boss? Look at her tunic. You really want a Vodhead in there?" Rhee flinched at the slur; she wasn't Fontisian but the hate in his voice was meant for her nonetheless. The UniForce rookie obviously meant that because the tunic she wore was Fontisian, *she* was Fontisian. "Could be a spy or something."

The Tasinn sighed exaggeratedly. "This is why you're paid to shoot and shove things. Do her ears look pointed to you? She isn't Fontisian. Besides, she's *Marked*. Call Fiona and tell her this kid is going in. We'll want the holos to get a good shot of her with Nero, and the public will eat it up."

Rhee finally understood. She looked dirty and exposed, the vermillion mark burning halfway down her face. She hadn't been recognized. In her excitement to be so close to her announcement, she'd forgotten all about the mark that still disfigured her. But at least the UniForce guard released her and allowed her to pass through the press entrance.

Rhee entered and saw that they were being funneled back into the first-class cabin, through an ancillary entrance equipped with subtle weapon-detectors. The first-class cabin had been rearranged to look like a press room—there was a raised podium on a velvet dais at one end of the carriage—and the space was already packed. Her cube was offline, and she had no translator to make sense of the dozens of different languages filling the air with a confused chatter, but she picked up bits of conversation here and there—talk of war, the ongoing manhunt for her supposed killer, the finer points of the Urnew Treaty. She yanked her hood back up and picked her way through the aisle, finding a spot against the back wall. All the chairs were filled and neatly divided into sections, arranged in a semicircle around a podium. She scanned the room, eager to have a private moment with Nero before he spoke to the crowd. But he came in abruptly, aides on either side, and marched straight for the podium.

The room went almost immediately quiet. Rhee could tell which journalists were recording the press conference through their cubes because of the way their eyes dimmed and went unfocused. A camera droid on wheels rolled forward for a tight shot.

Rhee would have to wait it out and hope that she could get close to Nero to reveal herself and plan her announcement.

"Thank you, everyone, for your presence at such a crucial time in the history of our planets. We pray to the ancestors that Regent Seotra will be returned to us safely." His eyes seemed to flicker in and out of attention as he read prepared comments off his cube. Up close, Nero looked exhausted and overworked, but there was an intensity in his eyes.

"As you may know, I've been vocal about my concerns." He nodded at several people in the front row and then at the cameras. Rhee only now realized how he wasn't in his regular diplomacy uniform and instead wore a military-style double-breasted blazer that accentuated his broad shoulders. "I came to see our allies in the hopes that they would help Kalu in defending ourselves."

"You want their help to invade, not defend," a Kalusian woman called out from the back of the room. Heads and cameras swiveled in her direction.

"Part of defending Kalu means taking back what's ours," Nero countered. "Yet the United Planets have repeatedly denied our requests to increase sanctions on Wraeta and its allies. They call our pleas to protect ourselves, to protect our borders and our people, hasty."

The woman stepped forward and tried to speak up again, but Nero spoke over her.

"They have dragged their feet, claiming we don't yet have all the information we need . . ."

It was true. Nero didn't have all the information, but he was motivated by grief and fear. Rhee knew all too well what that was like. He wanted to send a message, and he wanted justice.

Don't confuse retaliation with fairness, her mother had said once, gripping Rhee and Joss by the ears. More forgotten memories. Her mother wrenching Joss and Rhee apart after they fought over who knows what. "You don't resort to violence just because you're sad or angry . . ."

Rhee wanted to tell Nero that now.

"For too long have we ignored the threat that these savages have posed," Nero continued. *Savages?* Rhee had never heard him use that kind of language before. "For too long have our immigration policies been lax. We let a Wraetan onto our planet, let him serve in our army and wear our uniform, gave him a place that could've belonged to one of your children instead. And he repays us by killing our princess!"

Rhee was surprised to hear murmurs of agreement. "Dusties," someone next to her muttered, and she felt a sharp twisting in her stomach. Was there really so much hatred in the universe, so much prejudice, even among people who claimed to be unbiased? Had this always been true? Or had something changed in the week since she was supposedly killed?

Where are they going? Rhee remembered asking as a kid when she'd seen footage of the Wraetan refugees traveling on the holos. It seemed like they'd walked forever, across an entire season when the flowers bloomed and died again. Yet another organic memory she had to shake away.

"They're looking for a new home," Joss had told her. Rhee picked up a stylus and began to draw all the houses they'd build for them on Kalu. At first, Joss's pout got a little bigger—like it did when she got sad and might cry—but then she'd just said: "Grow up."

The Kalusian woman who'd caused the outburst earlier let out a cry, and even though several people looked in her direction, the cameras didn't. She was being dragged out by two Tasinn, thrashing and kicking, and no one moved to help her. Not even Rhee. She stood perfectly still, shame burning her face, as the woman was taken.

"The Rose of the Galaxy is gone," Nero said once the woman had exited and he had everyone's focus once more. His face looked like it was carved from marble by a master sculptor. He'd never looked more handsome, or more ruthless. "As a planet, we should rally together and vow, once and for all: Wraeta, and any planet foolish enough to back them, will *pay*."

The energy in the car frightened her: It wasn't curious. It was charged, electric, angry.

"What's the status of the investigation of Alyosha Myraz?" a reporter now called out. "Was he receiving directions?"

"We think it is likely he was reporting to a larger terrorist organization, yes," Nero said, nodding his head.

"And his hostage? Vincent, from *The Revolutionary Boys*?"

"No word yet. We've been in touch with his family . . ."

"Any idea where the fugitive has gone?" someone interrupted.

"We've got every UniForce cruiser from here to the Outer Belt looking for him, and a bounty on his head that will make his captor rich for life. We're confident we'll find him."

A Toncdel whose camera was built right into the hardware

of his exoskeleton spoke up next. "Have you determined how he fled the scene? I have an anonymous source that says a royal escape pod is unaccounted for."

She straightened up. She'd assumed that the royal escape pod had been lost to the dark folds of the universe. Otherwise, someone would have found Veyron's body, and her braid. Someone would know she'd made it out alive. And the question had in fact caused a stir: Everyone was whispering, muttering, straining to catch a glimpse of the reporter.

"I'm afraid that's untrue," Nero said, and Rhee felt all the air go out of her chest. "All the pods were accounted for. The pods were used to ferry off the only survivors, an evacuation effort I and Regent Seotra were involved in."

Nero was lying. Not all the pods were accounted for . . .

The icy feeling spread to her head and built pressure behind her eyes. Tai Reyanna had said that Veyron must have planted an explosive device in case his attempt on Rhee's life failed. But how had they known to evacuate even *before* the initial blast?

Dahlen's ring burned a hole in her pocket; it gave her an uneasy feeling, as if its ability to capture energy meant it would capture the attention of others too. The world went mute as she looked around the room, really looked, for the first time. The press conference claimed itself haphazard and slapdash, but it had obviously been set up well in advance. Nero had never intended to sway the Kalusian allies. He'd shown up in a military-looking uniform, with every intention to position himself as a leader. One who could rule an entire planet.

The kindness he'd shown, the rousing speeches he'd given . . .

it was all an act, made more convincing by his good looks and those intense blue eyes she'd once thought of as soulful. Suddenly Rhee understood. It had been all for the cameras. Truly, it was Nero all along, not Seotra, who'd arranged to have her family killed—who'd tried to kill her. He'd plotted in the shadows and pressed for her early coronation so he could have her assassinated.

Rhee remembered what Nero had said after her family died, his words of consolation that had stayed with her for so many years.

The ancestors saw it was an honorable death, and through them we ensure a new, worthy leader will rise. He'd been speaking of himself.

It was Nero: the man who stood at the podium not ten feet away, the most powerful man in Kalu, who wanted to take their planet to war, who wanted her dead.

As if the realization were a literal bolt of lightning that struck at Rhee's feet, Nero turned and looked directly at her.

SIXTEEN

ALYOSHA

THE name of the game was to not get caught. Aly's only plan was to lie low, be inconspicuous, and maybe get to Rhesto in one piece. Kara—that was the girl's name—had moved them through four cars with a security badge she'd swiped from who knows where. She acted like she'd grown up on a zeppelin, which, she told him after yanking him into a bathroom to avoid a patrolling Tasinn, she basically had.

When he caught her eye in the mirror she quickly looked away. Her hair fell across her face, and when she blinked it got tangled in her eyelashes. How did that not drive her crazy?

"I spent a lot of time on zeppelin freighters like these," she said. She made a face in the mirror and tried to finger comb her tangled hair. It was no use trying to make it do anything else—it was too far gone—but he wasn't going to tell her that. Under the door he saw Pavel discreetly send a narrow attachment with a tiny camera at the end, and Aly nudged it back with the toe of his boot. "Kalu labs rent out space on zeppelins like this all the time, for experiments they can't get the government to approve. Since it travels between quadrants, then it isn't in violation of any one territory's laws. My mom's a scientist, remember? She used to work the Kalu–Navrum line that did four-day loops. She did neurobiology stuff and even helped develop cube-to-cube interaction."

Aly was impressed. "So you're some kind of genius like your mom, then?"

"I wish," she said to the mirror. She had this faraway look in her eyes, like she was actually seeing someone who'd disappeared from her reflection forever ago. "But I guess it got her in trouble, in the end. She was being watched by a bunch of different governments, all kinds of different planets . . ."

"Is she . . . ?"

Kara shook her head, so her bangs shook too. "I don't know. I don't think so. I hope not." Their eyes met in the mirror again. He got a sense of weird déjà vu when he looked at her. Maybe it was just the fluorescent lighting threatening to give him a seizure. "A dozen scientists she worked with at the summit had been disappearing over the last six months, one by one. She knew it wasn't coincidence. Someone was going after them."

"Who?"

Kara shrugged. "I don't know. But she left before they could take her. At least, I hope she did."

"*Zuilie*," he exhaled.

"That's what *I'm* saying. I heard it's always happened on the sly, ever since the Great War. People all over the galaxy rounded up, questioned about their involvement and their loyalties, all under the guise of preserving *peace*. But this is different . . ." Her face tightened. "It's targeted. Every one of them was at the last G-1K summit. Taken one day, maybe stopped for a routine traffic violation or called in to renew a federal license, and then just . . . gone."

Immediately, he remembered the little boy on Derkatz. *Snatch-yah uptu?*

Alyosha felt sick. This was what war was. It wasn't even the bombs or the cruisers loaded with bombs. It was girls like Kara in a zeppelin bathroom, suddenly, maybe, orphaned. It was boys like him, twelve-year-olds, running after a truck, choking on the smell of dust. People always measured war in terms of the numbers dead. Maybe they should measure it in terms of the people left behind.

"And your mom told you about the safe house on Rhesto before she ran?"

"She's gone on and on about it for years. A neurotechnologist from Derkatz turned up dead after the last summit. I never got details, but I got the feeling my mom was scared, like maybe it had been a deliberate attack." Kara turned to face him. A strand of dark hair came loose, and she tucked it behind her ear. "She made me memorize coordinates, take self-defense classes. I know, like, six languages because she crammed them down my throat." She looked down and started picking at her thumbnail. "I used to be ashamed of her. Thought she was a nutjob. A conspiracy theorist, you know? But when I came home that day, and our apartment was ransacked . . ."

Aly thought of Vincent's room on the *Revolutionary*, just before the robosoldier had come in and nearly split his skull open. Vincent had saved him. His best friend, messy as hell and a lazy *choirtoi*—but he was a spy, too, and he'd died trying to do the right thing. He'd died because Aly had picked that day of all days to start a fight. Now they'd never talk *taejis*, mess around. He was almost glad he was offline, so he wouldn't call up the memory over and over to torture himself.

"Hey." Aly reached out to take her hand, not sure what made him do it. It was warm, and he felt that same jolt of electricity where their hands touched. After a split second, she pulled away. There was a confused look on her face, like she'd been woken up from a spell.

"I'm fine. We should get moving."

Aly nodded, feeling stupid and embarrassed.

She slipped out of her jacket . . . and started to take off her shirt.

"What are you doing?" Aly asked, trying to turn away and cracking his elbow against the door.

She wore a loose tank top underneath her long-sleeved shirt. The tank top had a tiny pocket on the chest that had zero use except to draw his eye to it. He looked down at his shoes, at the ceiling, anywhere but at the tiny pocket. Her face was even worse—she was smirking.

"Calm down." She began tearing her shirt into long strips

of fabric, pulling out what looked like nail clippers to make the initial cuts. "See? Instant disguise."

"I don't think this is going to work," Aly said firmly, as she motioned for him to squat down. As she wrapped pieces of cloth around his head, Aly scrambled to distract himself, but the cloth was still warm and *smelled* like her.

"Trust and believe, friend," Kara said. Aly noticed Pavel trying to slide his camera under the door again, but he stomped on it—clamping it to the floor until Pavel eventually wiggled it back.

He'd always been nervous around girls, but keeping to himself had been an all right strategy—without fail, Vin would bring some pretty girls back to base and talk Aly up. Vincent was the ladies' man, saying charming things, laying on the compliments. Aly was cool enough by association.

When Kara was finished, Aly stood up and squinted at his reflection. "Okay, this is *definitely* not going to work." She'd wrapped cloth around his forehead and diagonally across his left eye and nose. "I look like a half-assed mummy."

"I should've bandaged your mouth too." She smiled at him in the mirror. "Look, it'll work because no one actually wants to look at a victim. Even if they *do* want to look, they'll steal a glance. They've been taught it's impolite to stare."

Aly wasn't sure about her logic but really didn't have any other options—she'd opened up a brand-new possibility for him, an out from his fugitive status, and a way to broadcast the truth. They just needed to survive long enough to get to Rhesto.

They slipped out of the bathroom, and he and Pavel followed

Kara as they moved through a series of passenger cars toward the front of the zeppelin. She either knew her way around or was picking a route at random. There was no hesitation as she turned one way or the other, doubled back, climbed up a flight of stairs and back down a different one.

"We need to get to the cars with the labs in them," she said over her shoulder. "We can hitch a ride on one of the vessels they use to transport supplies there."

The lower the numbered capsule, the more streamlined the zeppelin became—the prettier too. The hallways were quiet and flooded with a soft light. The seats were made not of patched synthetics but brushed velvet. Instead of dozens of passengers packed on bench seats, businessmen and businesswomen reclined in practically empty cabins.

Aly had taken zeppelins sometimes on leave, always in one of the high-numbered capsules. They were cheap and slow and not even a little bit fancy. He'd park his butt in one of the worn seats while a rusty droid rammed his elbow with the drink cart. The air was always stale and it took forever to get anywhere, but he'd still give his right arm to be one of these folks. He'd take a lumpy chair so long as it reclined, and a packet of calories delivered right to his hand.

There was no cruising now, no kicking back in one of the poky seats. They double-timed it down the aisle, without moving so fast they'd be suspicious. Kara's stolen badge did the trick again and again.

By some miracle they hadn't run into any guards, but he remembered Nero had boarded the zeppelin at Navrum City.

Probably the entire security team was guarding Nero's next fart. Aly never thought he'd thank god to be anywhere *near* a politician—but it was working in their favor now.

Or it was—until Kara swiped a door and they barreled through into a room *packed* with reporters. They were all facing a podium with none other than Nero standing behind it. And he looked pretty steamed. Everyone turned in their direction.

Alyosha was paralyzed. He was the most wanted criminal in the universe, and only a few flimsy pieces of fabric separated him from a room full of people who wanted his head. Literally.

"Oops," Kara whispered under her breath. Aly felt the weight of at least one hundred sets of eyes on him—one hundred sets of eyes attached to one hundred souls who believed he'd murdered the last princess of the Ta'an dynasty. He tensed up, ready to run. But his eyes landed on a girl, Fontisian by the look of her clothes, whose face was half-covered by an oversized hood. He could see her mouth, though, and the quicksilver flash of relief as she sighed.

An aide near the podium charged their way, and the girl lowered her hood and vanished into the crowd. The aide—public relations, you could somehow always tell—pushed them back out into the hallway. A big-ass Tasinn followed at her heels.

"What in the hell are you *doing*? Who let you in? This is a private event." Her voice had gotten so high she was practically screeching.

"We were looking for the medical wing," Kara said quickly. She'd shifted her accent seamlessly—now she sounded like she'd come straight from a high-society Kalusian country club. "The layout of this zeppelin is simply impossible to navigate! My apologies!"

"*Zuilie.*" The girl's yellow reptilian eyes flickered as she looked them up and down. "The patients are to be kept strictly quarantined," she said, flinging a hand in Aly's direction. Kara was right; the girl didn't want to look at him. When their eyes met for a split second, her blue skin flushed.

"Understood," Kara said evenly. "It won't happen again. They just needed to get his circulation going," she said. Aly did his best not to move, react.

"You're not even close to the medwing," the Tasinn said behind them. His eyes were narrow with suspicion.

Kara hesitated a beat too long, but Pavel piped in just in time. "That is entirely my fault," he said. "*I* led them out of the medwing. But my software must be outdated, and I lost the layout during the blackout."

Aly tried hard not to express surprise. *Look at my little man, learning how to lie.* He guessed there'd never been a reason to before.

"Unbelievable." The woman brought her hand to her face, her long fingers curling halfway around her head. "Okay, okay, what's done is done." She took a deep breath in and a long exhale out. Her eyes went cloudy as she checked her cube. "Take this hallway down until you hit a spiral set of stairs, up one flight and then two immediate lefts. There'll be signs from there, and it looks like the patient bay is up top, lab on the bottom. You got that?"

Pavel's eyelights flashed blue.

"Should I escort them, Fiona?" the Tasinn asked, and Aly's heart stopped.

"No, you idiot," the girl said, in a tone of deep condescension. "Your mandate is to protect Nero, not play escort. And *you*"—she pointed to Pavel—"tell those *choirtois* to update your software."

That was that: They were free to go. Alyosha nearly lost it. He wanted to roll around on the floor laughing until it hurt, until his sides split and he cried. But he was still shaking.

The woman and the guard both glared at them before turning and retreating into the conference room. They'd escaped an execution, practically, *and* gotten step-by-step directions to the place they wanted to go.

They moved in silence. He knew they were all too scared to speak—like they might break a spell and everything would shatter. Finally, they got to a door that was made of a thick, shiny metal that looked different from all the others. Kara swiped her security card, and they pushed their way inside.

They faced a long hallway lined with a row of shelves filled with scrubs neatly stacked and a wardrobe full of hanging lab coats. In the cabinets were boxes of latex gloves and hair caps. Kara ran her palm absently over them, as if she were petting an animal.

Aly shouldered through a set of swinging double doors. He expected to find a lab, but the capsule was flooded with light. It was made almost entirely of glass and reminded him, weirdly, of a tree house that he had played in when he was little. It was full of dark, scattered booths and benches.

Here people sketched, wrote, rearranged puzzles, or played instruments. Some even slept, resting their heads on propped-up elbows—and in one case, their tentacles. All the passengers were dressed in the same green patient scrubs.

A fragile man who looked to be in his seventies nodded to them as he strummed a small stringed instrument that reminded Aly of a vitola. Another man twisting a multicolored cube in his hands didn't acknowledge them as they passed, and neither did a Yersian woman with matted fur who wrote down music notes furiously across a grid of paper. Even the man who had his head down, cradled in his arms, looked like he was having a fitful sleep, like his mind was working through an important problem.

It was peaceful. Pretty, even.

So why were all the hairs on Aly's neck standing up?

He turned around and looked through the glass, to the medical cars visible beneath them. "What is this place?" he asked in a whisper.

It was the lab below them—a long one, at least five car lengths, with a narrow aisle down the middle. Men and women in identical white coats and green scrubs worked quietly along the high counters mounted on either wall. It seemed tense, like the pressure in the lab had been cranked up. Bent over petri dishes, peering through microscopes, the scientists were completely engrossed . . . Aly backed away from the glass. He knew that if one of them looked up, he was in trouble.

"I've never seen anything like it," Kara told him. She sounded uneasy, and he knew she was feeling that same bad juju, a dark undercurrent humming beneath the vision of peacefulness. Then she turned back around and surveyed the room they were in. "This doesn't look like any patient bay I've ever seen."

"You're new," an Optsirh woman said behind them, making Alyosha jump. When she blinked he could see her blue eyes under transparent eyelids. She was sketching a large triangle on a sheet of paper. "Come have a sit-down. Look at a drawing. This is my son." She pointed to the empty space of her triangle. "He has the most beautiful eyes, doesn't he?"

Aly tried to catch Kara's eye. But she was transfixed by the woman, or her drawing, or both.

"And this is my hometown of Anheles," the woman said, shifting her drawing to the side to reveal another paper underneath. Another wobbly drawing of a triangle. "The canals here freeze over in the winter, but it's so beautiful to sit and drink tarnitana tea."

"May I?" Kara asked the woman, and feigned a closer look.

Fine. He'd let Kara deal with the crazies while he and Pavel found a way off this thing—before they went too deep into Bazorl Quadrant and ended up a million astro units away.

At the end of the car was a locked metal door. He pressed his face to the window, but could make out nothing but darkness.

"P, take a look?" The droid extended his camera attachment two feet above him and angled it against the window, giving a decent impression of a human hand splayed against the glass. A flash went off and made Aly wince.

"It's a cargo bay." Pavel might have learned to lie, but he hadn't learned to whisper, and Aly shushed him hard. "There are two crafts. Series Aero and Gency."

The Aero was a mini freighter, probably for dropping off and picking up medical supplies. The other was a Gency ambulance, which meant it had good lines and lots of speed. A perfect get-away vehicle.

"Aly!" Kara whisper-shouted to him. She was still standing by the crazy lady and her stack of weird drawings. He thought the goal was to make an exit, not a friend.

He turned to tell her to hurry up, but when he saw the look on her face, the words died in his throat. All her color was gone. She looked horrified.

No. She looked terrified.

"Work on the door," he told Pavel, which seemed to have the most rudimentary security system of all: an ancient lock-and-key mechanism.

"I-I know her," Kara whispered after he'd rushed back to her side. "That's Mia Montenegro. She was at the G-1K, like my mom."

The woman was still babbling happily. "This one is a drawing of the sunset. Earlier today. So many brilliant colors."

"Look." Kara's voice cracked. She pointed at the woman's neck, and as he looked, nausea rolled like darkness into his throat.

There, in the place where her cube would've been, was a terrible wound, an ugly, gaping hole that seemed to have been sutured by burning. The charred skin was visible, and beneath it, a web of scar tissue in an exact triangle.

He felt like ice was creeping into his veins. He looked around at the other people in their baggy green gowns. He realized the man playing the instrument was in fact just strumming the same two chords again and again. They acted like they'd been lobotomized.

"I know all of them," Kara whispered. Her eyes were like two gashes in her face. "They're all scientists—that's Isaac Renaldioe, a biologist from Nau Fruma . . ." She bit her lip so hard he thought she'd draw blood.

"I've opened the door!" Pavel announced, so loudly Aly expected alarms to sound. But none did.

"Come on," Aly said, and went to take Kara's hand. But she yanked it away.

"We can't just . . . leave them," Kara said.

Aly looked at her and realized she was serious. "Kara, there's no way," he said gently. There were dozens of patients.

Still, she didn't move, and Aly fought a building desperation. The word *evil* kept drilling through his mind. He wanted out of here, as soon as possible. Could he leave Kara behind? He knew he couldn't. Not only was she his way into the safe house, but she was probably the only person left in the world who didn't think he was a murderer. He'd already lost Vin . . .

He reached for her hand again; she didn't pull away, but her hand was listless, flimsy.

"Look, we can help them better if we find your mom," he said, though he had no idea if this was true. "Kara?"

To his relief, she nodded, and shifted her grip to thread her fingers through his. He had her. They would leave together.

The cargo bay was dark, but Pavel lit the way down the ramp and up into the craft. Aly felt a thousand times better when they were strapped in and Pavel managed easily to override the security prompts.

"All right," he said a little too loudly to fill the silence. "Let's get the hell out of here, huh?" He peeled off his fake bandages, amazed by how good it felt to be back in the command seat. This was his home, now: running through the vast reaches of the universe. Maybe he'd been born to be a refugee.

Kara said nothing. She had turned away from him, and she was trembling like it was negative degrees.

"Hey." He reached out and put a hand on her thigh, then pulled away—scared it'd been too much. "Are you okay?"

"Don't you get it?" she said in a small voice. "Do you know what that was? Do you know what they're doing to those people?" Kara turned at last to look at him, and her eyes were dark and wet. "Someone is mining their cubes. Pirating them."

"That's impossible," Aly said automatically. The pod gave a sickening lurch as they jerked away from the main ship, but his stomach didn't settle, and the vertigo didn't go away. Stealing cubes . . . taking them by force . . . The idea went through him like a fire, turning everything inside to ash. It was the singular law across the universe: Cubes were protected. They contained people's impressions, memories, thoughts, dreams. You could transfer things cube-to-cube, easy. But hacking into someone else's cube, even stealing the hardware after they died, was indecent, evil—like a violent, twisted kind of murder. In any culture on any planet, everyone was in agreement. That was *the whole point* of the G-1K summits, to make sure that the laws were standard across the universe. And to make sure there was some *moral* standard too.

Aly was suddenly furious at Kara.

"How could you say that? How could you even *think* that?"

He was practically shouting, even as he was choking on the truth of what he'd seen: those vacant-eyed people, the horrible wound on the Optsirh's neck, freshly scarred over. It couldn't be true, it just couldn't be. "That would be . . ."

"Ravaging." Kara finished his sentence. He hadn't wanted to say it. He shuddered. It was a violation of all living things. Ravaging was a myth—at least, he'd always thought it was. A trump card that parents would whip out when they wanted their kids back in line—if you'd been bad, a man would come to *Ravage* your head in the middle of the night. You'd forget everything you ever knew, and you'd never form a new memory again. Stuck in a mind loop. An eternal hell.

They talked about it in church too. The Ravaging. They said it was when you were wicked, and Vodhan sent the wind down to lift your soul away, to save you from yourself . . .

"It's impossible," Aly repeated lamely.

Kara wiped the bottoms of her eyes, even though he hadn't seen her shed a tear, and sat up straighter—hands folded in her lap, blue-gray eyes straight ahead. "Right," she said, "impossible."

SEVENTEEN

RHIANNON

PEOPLE always said that time flowed, fled, sped by. Or that it slowed, stopped, and stretched.

They never talked about how time could grip and strangle. How everything good could fall away in your life and bring you to a fixed point, standing face-to-face with the man who'd killed your family.

Nero had stared back at her with a look of perplexity, as if on the verge of some grander realization. And he had been.

Time showed mercy too. Rhee had been pinned to a spot in time and space, breathless—and in the next instant, a ripple in the audience had swept the murderer's gaze away and allowed her to escape.

A boy with his face bandaged, and a girl with familiar eyes she could barely tear herself away from. Rhee and the boy had shared a look; something had passed between them she couldn't name. She knew only that he had a secret, just like her.

Nero had locked eyes with Rhee for a split second, and she wasn't sure if she'd been recognized. The interruption had bought Rhee just enough time to slip away.

Now she strapped into an escape pod and braced herself, placing her palms on the metal right in front of her face. She squeezed her eyes tightly, not knowing where to go—only that she needed to escape. Her finger hovered above the touchscreen, over the command that said DEPLOY. She pressed it.

The pod jettisoned off the first-class side of the zeppelin with a force so strong that her elbows gave in. She slammed into the casing, and the bitter taste of blood flooded her mouth. The seat belt hadn't been fitted for someone her size.

Blind and willful . . .

She'd been wrong, over and over again. First about Veyron, then about Seotra and now Nero. Rhee had actually thought he was kind—that he was loyal to her and her family's legacy. He'd only been biding his time, plotting her death for nine years as he earned the trust of the public. She'd been front and center as he reinvented himself, and no longer was Nero the charming ambassador to the regent's office—he was the new leader, spewing hate on a government platform that he now controlled.

Rhee plummeted into space, cocooned by a metal coffin that sliced through the air. Everything was vibrating. The temperature was rising. She pictured the pod cracking like an egg, disposing of her like a runny yolk into the unforgiving darkness of the universe.

She wanted to cry—from fear, from anger, from her own

stupidity. Rhee had sought Nero out. The very man who'd tried to have her killed, who'd killed her family. He'd orchestrated his own rise. *He* was the "new, worthy leader." Not Rhee. All her fantasies of revenge, the way she'd sharpened herself into a tool to best take down Seotra—all that effort had been misdirected, wasted, too little, too late.

Seotra. She'd been so certain; all signs had pointed to him. That fight with her father, the prescient threats, how he'd come off so cold and so proud. Nero had capitalized on their rift and positioned himself as favorable in supporting her early coronation . . .

Regent Seotra had trusted that there would be time to tell Rhee. He had taken for granted how naïve and stupid she'd been, how desperate she was to avenge her family and show the ancestors that she was worthy of their name. She'd refused to speak to him. Thought him rigid and unlikable and petty. And she'd brought Dahlen to Seotra's doorstep. She hadn't killed him, but she might as well have. He wouldn't have come face-to-face with the Fontisian if it weren't for her own foolish theories.

She was adrift, alone—for the very first time. There was nowhere to go, nowhere safe in the universe. If Nero knew Rhee was alive—and he'd be watching carefully—contacting Tai Reyanna would be impossible.

And Dahlen? He'd murdered a man to avenge his own family, and she understood that more than she cared to admit. He'd saved her, again and again. But he couldn't save her now.

Nowhere to go. Nowhere to go. An entire universe of stars and planets, and not a single one that would hold her.

There was Julian. He couldn't possibly know that she was

responsible for his father's death. But *she* knew. Could she ever face him again after what she'd done? She didn't think so. Besides, he wouldn't be able to help her.

Only when the automated system kicked on and gave time, speed, distance, and direction did Rhee realize something else: It was after midnight on the seventh night, after the seventh new moon of the year.

She was alone, friendless, and supposedly dead.

It was her sixteenth birthday.

Rhee began to cry, just as she had that night she got lost playing hide-and-seek in the cellars. She knew there was another exit, but in the darkness, full of fear, she couldn't remember how to make her way through the maze of slick corridors. When Josselyn came, Rhee'd been blinded by the torchlight, blinking away her tears.

Rhee had never forgotten the way Josselyn had looked at her.

"Get up," she'd said simply, and Rhee had scrambled to her feet, relieved and ashamed all at once. But Josselyn wouldn't point her in the right direction. "Which way, left or right?" she asked instead.

When she started to say she didn't know, Joss took Rhee's hand and brought it to her own neck. She pressed down Rhee's finger to turn her cube off, and it was like a whole universe rushed in to replace it: water dripping, the smell of wet, the fur of moss growing on the walls.

"Listen. Use your mind," Joss said.

Rhee had stood in the dark, still sniffling, and listened and thought. In the echoes she had begun to hear water running down from somewhere—faulty pipes, surely, the sound of leaking water. She went toward it. As she did, she touched the pattern of moss on the walls and found it thicker and more colorful in places, pigmented, because it was closer to the light. She had begun to make choices. Left, right, left. Josselyn had said nothing, never corrected her, just followed silently with the torch. They'd been down there for hours. Finally, Rhee found a set of worn stairs that led to one of the palace's pantries, and she had burst out into the light, exhilarated, exhausted.

Josselyn hadn't congratulated her. She had merely said, "Good." And then she'd bent down and taken Rhee's shoulders. "There's always a way in, always a way out. You just have to listen."

"What do I do, Joss?" Rhee whispered now. She closed her eyes. Her throat was the size of a fist: Her sister had said she would never be alone. But how could Rhee find her way without Josselyn there, without her torch? "Help me, please."

Listen. The word was the whisper of memory, and her sister's face, still and pointed and bright, like that of a flame. But she couldn't listen: Even with her cube off, she heard a clamor of memory, saw images pouring over her, threatening to overwhelm her. Seotra. Nero. Tai Reyanna, her eyes huge and full of grief.

And then she *heard*. The memory came rebounding like an echo and shocked her into opening her eyes.

Erawae. Dahlen had told her his order was there. She fumbled for Dahlen's ring in her pocket, and only now did it occur to her: Could his ring grant her refuge? Would the order be sympathetic to her cause, if it was she who could truly stop a seemingly imminent war? She felt a pulse of hope so faint it made her second-guess her own heart. The feeling reminded her of the afternoons on Nau Fruma—fine moon dust floating in the air, each particle catching the sun so that she saw brief shimmers that didn't seem real. But this was real. Erawae was real.

Josselyn had told her to listen, and Rhee knew, of all people in the galaxy she could trust, alive or dead, that she could trust her sister.

"Thank you, Joss," she whispered, and set a course for Erawae.

Part Four:

THE AVENGED

"It's no secret that among our vast universe, the enormous array of religious and philosophical convictions may always lead to tension and even dispute. Nothing that we can say or do here will change that fact. But I stand before this council in good faith, not in an effort to change Fontis or to be changed, but to live in peace. Let us work together. Let us respect those differences and not seek to eradicate them. Let us put the fear and distrust behind us. Let us establish cube technology standards to facilitate cooperation and communication. Let us end the war, so that future generations can know peace."

—Emperor Ta'an, upon signing the Urnew Treaty

EIGHTEEN

ALYOSHA

I F he'd thought Derkatz was the biggest pile of *taejis* in the universe, Rhesto was giving it a serious run for its money. Ten years after the bombing, and everything was still dead. Where Aly and Kara walked, branches cracked underfoot, and he didn't see a single speck of green.

Aly couldn't stop thinking about water. They'd passed two streams they were too scared to drink from, worried about contamination—even though they'd managed to pop some super-duper radiation pills, full of some hard-to-pronounce anti-oxidants that would heal their bodies as they went.

Still, Aly didn't feel too hot. His lips were chapped. There was a film on his tongue; he didn't think it would ever produce actual saliva again. Sweat dripped down his face, and not even big old eyebrows like his could keep it from stinging his eyes. He told himself he was too tired to care, but when Kara wasn't looking, he wiped down his face with the sleeve of his shirt.

They barely spoke as they walked, side by side when the rocky path allowed it. *One foot in front of the other.* That was all he'd let himself think when everything started to get too real in his head. Apart from Kara, there was all kinds of other stuff to worry about. Like the fact that he may or may not have seen the end result of a Ravaging—hollowed-out people who'd lost their souls, just like they'd described in the sermons. Their existence had a beginning and an end, and what was once a seed had grown and thrived and now withered on the vine, the roots rotted in the soil. Such was life. But he never imagined it would start with ladies babbling on about their sons and their favorite type of tea. And it sure as hell didn't say anything about the end of them all happening in a lab.

Kara said members of the G-1K summit were being taken— and Ravaged. Did someone want them to forget whatever they'd been working on? Or was someone trying to *use* their memories for another purpose? And who had that kind of power, to abduct these men and women from their homes, to Ravage them with impunity, to keep all of it secret?

Was it the Regent? Had he disappeared to engineer some master plan, or was he already dead?

As if *that* didn't already take up enough head space, there was the fact that when you came right down to it, Aly had traveled to Rhesto because *maybe* Kara's mom would be there, and *maybe* he'd be able to broadcast his cube playback to the universe so *maybe* he could avoid getting executed for a crime he didn't commit.

And then what? Even if the plan worked, it wasn't gonna

be this happy-ending-roll-credits. Best-case scenario: He got the
public on his side, proved his innocence to anyone with eyes and
ears and a heart—then there'd still be the Regent's council to
deal with. Those *choirtois*. They'd framed him, all because it dove-
tailed with their screwed-up plan to launch the galaxies into war
again. For what? Money? Wraetan minerals? Power, territory, silver? He didn't know.

What Aly did know, for sure: He'd been moved around like a
little action figure, like a worthless piece of plastic you could lose
and burn and replace.

Think you're a man? he'd heard his dad say. *Think you're a big
man, don't you?*

Aly could see him now, sweating moonshine, a crazy look in
his eyes. Aly had packed up his stuff, but his dad swatted it out
of his hand. *I own this*, he'd said. *I own you.*

So he'd left that day to join the UniForce with nothing but
the clothes he'd worn, as light as a feather, grin from here to there
thinking nobody owned him after all. Look at him now. It boiled
Aly's blood, picturing a bunch of old men sitting around a big
wooden table deciding his fate. They'd already decided Vin's.

The path was steep now, dirt and shale slipping under their
feet as they went single file.

"It's a forty-two percent grade," Pavel piped in behind them,
like they needed to be reminded why they were out of breath.
They were practically leaning into the mountain, scrambling up
with their hands when it got tough, grabbing dead roots on either
side of them for purchase. He could hear Pavel's motor struggling
as his wheels spun out in the trickier pockets.

It had taken two days to reach Rhesto once the Gency ambulance pod zoomed out of the zeppelin bay, and another half-day hike to reach the spikes of the refinery towers in the distance.

"Finally," Kara said as they reached the top of the slope. From here he could see it, a thing of beauty: the broadcasting tower. In front of that, smokestacks, huddled together and backlit by the dawn, looming over a squat mineral refinery building.

"Wraeta had thousands of refineries just like it," Aly said. "My dad used to work in one before the evacuation." He missed his cube for exactly this reason, because it was easy to make unwanted organic memories like this go away—just drown them out with some DroneVision channel, or set a memory of him and Vin and Jeth on constant loop.

But now, there wasn't one memory of that old rock that didn't lead back to his dad, to Wraeta, to his broken and crusted past. When he was younger, the refineries used to scare him. They'd looked like giant metal monsters turned inside out.

"We learned about your mineral refineries in second form," Kara said, and for some reason he flinched when she said *your*. Wraeta didn't feel like home anymore. How long had it been since he'd known what home was? "None of us would have cubes if it weren't for Wraeta. Imagine that."

"Imagine that," he repeated. All the first-generation cubes were Wraetan-made—all the materials mined there, all the cubes produced there. *Give the universe its greatest piece of tech, and then get yourself blown up.*

She looked back at the distant steel city. He imagined her in an art gallery, or whatever they did in the Kalusian capital, that same look on her face, trying to find some higher meaning out of nothing. It was funny. Sometimes she seemed just like a street kid; at other times, like some visiting ambassador from a rich planet. He wondered which one was the real Kara.

She started down the hill. They were halfway down the slope when Aly saw movement in the distance. Sun catching on metal. Hydraulic joints, perfectly calibrated to move as if it were a living, breathing soldier. Aly grabbed her arm and yanked her down behind a rubble pile of broken cinder block and stone. He got on his stomach and motioned for Kara to do the same. Pavel felt the urgency and compacted down so that his dome was low to the ground.

"What is it?"

"*Shhhhh*," he whispered.

His heart was thudding. He was clutching her arm too tightly, scared to look, like somehow it would make it more real. He counted to three, raised his head a fraction of an inch, and looked back toward the compound.

"It's an NX droid," Aly whispered. It was the same model that had come after him in Vin's room, and he remembered how easily the droid had chucked him across the room, like he was nothing but an empty tin can. "We must be out of his range. He would've charged us if he knew we were here. But that means the UniForce is here. They're *here*. How is that possible?"

"I can't believe it," Kara said. She looked shell-shocked. "The signal wasn't broadcasting . . . I checked it . . ."

"The UniForce probably got to it," Aly said quietly.

"*Taejis*," she said.

Taejis indeed. If the UniForce was here, it meant all the G-1K scientists or whoever else was in the safe house had definitely cleared out.

Or they'd been killed.

What next? Aly figured the manly thing to do would be to come up with some sort of plan to get them out of there. But Kara didn't look like she wanted to run. Her hair was pulled back in a braid, the bones of her face wide and strong—like she'd declared herself, refusing to hide.

"We need to find out whether the satellite dish is still operational . . ." she said. "We have to broadcast your playback so the galaxy knows you're innocent."

His stomach sank. "*We?* No. No way. This is my problem. You still have at least four hours of sunlight, and if you backtrack the way you came—"

"This is no time for chivalry, Aly."

"I'm trying to save your life."

"Don't you get it? It's not about my life, or your life, anymore. The stakes are too high."

She reminded him of Vin, of his conviction. Aly thought of the revolution he'd been so quick to make fun of. But unlike Vin's plan, this was really happening. "We'd have to go *through* the refinery to access the broadcasting tower," he said. "The UniForce will have every entrance covered, and we're sure as *taejis* not going to slip in unnoticed."

"Good thing I have an ex-UniForce soldier to tell me their protocol." She scanned the compound in the distance. "There's *always* another way in, Aly. Always a way in, always a way out."

He closed his eyes, pictured the old Wraetan refineries, the sky blackened with smoke, the constant hiss of steam . . . *Steam.* "The cooling tunnels," Aly said, opening his eyes. "There are tunnels running below the compound. They divert the current that runs through the refinery to cool the generators."

Kara nodded. "What are you waiting for?"

They made their way carefully and slowly through the rocky terrain, staying low in case any UniForce soldiers or NX droids were patrolling. He hadn't been too keen on signing up for this suicide mission, but it was his last chance to clear his name. Plus, he'd already lost Vin. He wouldn't lose Kara too.

Aly was banking that the sheer quantity of tunnels that must be running under a refinery this size would serve in their favor: There was no way the UniForce would have deployed forces to keep them all guarded, not when there was no convincing reason for them to be on Rhesto in the first place.

The tunnel's entrance was tucked into the slope, covered with moss. This one hadn't been used in a long time, but someone had artfully scrawled BALLS on the crusted walls. It was dark and coated in a slug trail of mud, so narrow they'd have to crawl.

"Right. Okay." Kara dropped her hand in her pocket and fished out a small bottle, emptying a pill onto the palm of her hand. She broke it in half and made a face as she swallowed.

"What's that?" he asked.

"I just have a headache." Even with her eyes all red and puffy, she had this elegant warrior look going on with the braid. He caught himself staring at her lips and quickly looked away.

"I detect traces of some sort of cholinesterase inhibitor," Pavel said, his eyelights red. "It enhances neurotransmitters and affects the basic chemical messengers associated with memory. What is your ailment?"

"Pavel," Aly said sharply, even if he was curious himself. He looked over at Kara with a pained smile, all teeth and a tight jaw. "Sorry. Not programmed with manners."

"It's okay." She pocketed the bottle once she put the remaining half of the pill away again. "It's just some neurological blip. Not a big deal." She shrugged. "There's just a lot I can't remember."

"Like you forget things sometimes?"

"Like I've forgotten everything from when I was little. There was some kind of problem with my cube. It was recalled when I was twelve, and I got a new one. They restored most of my old memories, but I have these bad dreams and . . . I don't know. It all feels made up. Like *I* made it up."

"My problem is the opposite," Aly blurted out. "All the memories from when I was a kid feel real. Too real. If I ever start to remember, I act like they're not mine—like they're fiction. Made-up."

He exhaled. Aly had never admitted that to anyone, and he was terrified she would make fun of him for playing make-believe. But she didn't.

"Well, let's not make up this moment then." Kara smiled. "Let's both agree to remember it happened this way."

"Deal."

Aly didn't know if they should shake on it or something else, but instead he did the whole "after you" gesture. They got on their hands and knees, crawling forward through a dark maze of twists and turns. Pavel rolled ahead in his most compacted shape, a dim beam of light shining the way.

But the silence seemed big in such a small space. There hadn't been a whole lot of chitchat since they got off the ambulance, and he guessed it wasn't going to start now. Aly was pissed at himself—he'd been stuck in his own head, while Kara had some brain condition and was probably worried sick about her mom. Had he even said thank you?

They snaked around a sharp turn and hit an offshoot of the tunnel. There was a rounded grate secured with an old-school padlock, and it opened just enough for the two of them to crawl out and crouch in front of it. It was so tight, Kara's knees brushed his, and it felt like the universe had narrowed down into the spot of skin where they touched.

Aly tried to ignore the heat and looked through the metal grating, where he could barely make out some sort of generator in the dark. "Pavel, can you scan for NX frequencies?"

"I detect one in proximity, but the diameter of my reach is only ten meters."

"Okay, not terrible," Aly lied, since being on the same *planet* as an NX was terrible. They had built-in heat sensors that detected subtle changes in temperature, but Pavel had his newly uploaded signal jammer on—meaning he could clone those temperature stats to report back "all normal." So long as no one saw them, they wouldn't be detected by temperature.

He waited for his eyes to adjust to the dark, straining to see past the generator. Kara shifted; a strand of light filtering in through the grate highlighted her eyes and lips, and cast a shadow over everything else. Her irises looked different, lighter. He'd never spent this much time with someone without some sort of memory trade, or a cube-to-cube transfer, so he could see and feel a piece of her life, and she could do the same.

He wanted to know something about her, anything, before this crazy suicide mission took hold. But every question he thought to ask, every way he thought to say it—it all sounded dumb in his head. He settled for: "Are you ready?"

When she nodded, Aly motioned for her and Pavel to follow. As soon as they were out, they made their way around the generator and down a labyrinth of alleyways, between machines the size of a small craft and conveyor belts the whole length of a football field. It was so tight they had to run single file. When they turned the corner he stopped so quickly he nearly went sprawling. There was an NX droid ahead of them, probably just outside of Pavel's detection diameter.

They ducked into the corner. Aly's brain was a blur of calculations and contingencies: the angle of its vision, how to move in and out of its blind spot as quietly as possible. A cold surge of terror worked its way through his body, like a block of ice was forming around him.

The droid kept coming. Aly pressed himself against the wall, like he could disappear into it. God, they were going to die. He'd willingly walked into a UniForce-occupied refinery and thought he could walk out with a neuroscientist and a girl on his arm. Chalk this up under worst idea ever.

As if Kara could read his mind, she grabbed his hand and

squeezed so hard he felt her nails dig into his skin. Aly's blood felt carbonated. It ran through his body and gave him a fizzy feeling—urgent, like his muscles would pop and spring.

Closer . . . closer . . .

"Hey!" Someone hailed the droid from the far end of the hall. He had a crisp capital accent. "You've new orders to patrol the south perimeter."

The droid turned immediately and walked out the other way, following the man. Aly dared a glance and saw the man disappear around the corner. He was wearing khaki—the color of the Tasinn uniform.

"Holy *taejis*," Kara said, and melted down onto the floor, exhaling.

Aly let out a deep breath. Kara started to laugh quietly—the nervous kind—and he did too. It was like exhaling all the tension stored up in his muscles, in the folds of his brain, and it felt deliriously good.

Too good, probably. Because no one noticed when a UniForce soldier turned the corner and stood right in the center, his jaw slack.

"You." He was looking straight at Aly with wide-set eyes that wrapped halfway around his head.

Aly could hardly believe it.

"Jeth?" The microscopic scales on his gray skin, shoulders as big as barn doors, gills that flared on either side of his neck when he laughed. "It's *you!*" He took a step toward him.

"Don't come any closer!" Jeth pulled his stunner out and aimed it at Aly, his huge eyes narrowing to slits and his skin turning a shade of crimson. Aly took a step back as Jeth panned it between him and Kara and then at Pavel, then back again. "Don't you *choirtoing* move, Alyosha."

"Are you serious?" Jeth, Vin, and Aly had come up together in boot camp. They'd been inseparable. *Three stars in the same constellation*, Jeth's mom had called them.

"Shut up. And you," he said to Pavel, who rolled alongside them, "you try anything and I'll run an EMP that will fry you beyond recognition. Now turn around," he said, and motioned for Aly to put his hands behind his back.

"You *are* serious," Aly said as Jeth snapped cuffs on Aly's wrists. He had tiny suction cups on his twelve fingertips, and they popped when they separated from the metal cuff. "You *choirtoi*."

"Shut up and start walking." Jeth cuffed Kara, too, and shoved Aly to get him to start moving.

"What happened to the safe house?" Kara asked, as Jeth frog-marched them down the hall. "What happened to everyone?"

Jeth didn't answer. He shoved them into what looked like an old office, with a holo projector so old you could call it vintage and sell it in the city. He turned and kicked the door closed behind him with his enormous boot. Jeth was a head shorter than Aly but three times as strong. "Of all the luck . . ." He shook his head, raked a hand over his bald head. "What the hell are you doing here?"

Aly looked at Kara. She nodded. "We came to find her mom," Aly said. "We thought she'd be here."

Jeth shook his head. "There were fifty squatters when we came," he said. "But the camp was cleared out days ago."

"Where?" Kara asked, and Jeth snorted through his gills.

"Think I'm going to tell you?"

"Don't be a dick," Aly said. "She didn't do anything."

"Well, where have my manners gone?" He bowed his head to Kara with a whole lot of flourish. "Begging your pardon, and your girlfriend's, except *I don't give two* taejis." Aly wished his hands were free so he could clock his old friend right in his stupid snout.

"If you've already cleared the place, what are you still doing here?" Aly asked.

"Great question. Because they needed a skeleton crew for this outpost assignment hellhole and I was their top candidate." He started to pace. "On a radioactive moon where I'm scared to even touch anything. Look at me, Mom! A shining *choirtoing* star . . ."

It was almost comical, hearing him cuss up a storm in that wholesome Chram accent. But Aly knew what kind of assignment this was. The UniForce had tons of old bases and "key strategic locations" where they posted a dozen soldiers, tops— far-flung locations that weren't all that relevant, and soldiers they were trying to punch. And Chrams were the bottom of the barrel when it came to the hierarchy of Kalusian allies. Of course Jeth would be one of the first ones on this *taejis* of an assignment.

Jeth kept eyeing Pavel, who was draining his battery over in the corner like a little dunce. Jeth knew the droid was sending out a signal jammer, and the fact that he hadn't powered him down meant Jeth was on the fence about reporting them.

"How long has your unit been here?" Aly asked. Maybe there was still a chance to get Jeth on their side.

"This isn't *my* unit, Alyosha." Jeth glared at him, and for a second he looked just like the skinny punk Vin and Aly had adopted on their first day in boot camp. "It's me, with a bunch of goddamned security guards on a power trip." He was talking about the Tasinn. "We've been here two days. And get this: Our orders are coming from a piece of *taejis* DroneVision host! Nero is dictating military strategy now. Dude has never even touched a uniform," Jeth spit. Aly thought of the big man on the train, squeezed into his expensive suit. Aly wasn't feeling too charitable seeing as his hands were cuffed, but he'd give Jeth this—he should be pissed. They all should.

"Nero?" Kara said under her breath.

"Where'd they send the squatters, Jeth?" Aly tried again for intel. It was worth a shot, since it looked like Jeth was feeling chatty.

Jeth stared at him. He never blinked—he didn't have eyelids—and he had a pretty serious evil eye when he put his mind to it. "Houl," he said finally. "There's an internment center there for political *agitators*. Fontisian agents, that sort of thing." Aly had to keep himself from rolling his eyes. "Brand-spanking-new and totally inescapable. You'll know all about it soon enough, you idiot *choirtoi*. Walking right into a UniForce base. What the hell are you even *doing* here? In case you hadn't noticed, you're wanted *for murder*." He yanked open the top button of his uniform and committed the worst of dress code violations as far as their Drill Sergeant Vedcu was concerned. If he were there he would've gone crazy, made them all drop down and give him fifty.

"I didn't murder anybody," Aly said, losing patience. He

struggled against his cuffs, though he knew it would do no good. "Let us go, Jeth. You know they lied! This is the biggest pile of *taejis*."

"Of course it's a lie, Aly. But you know what? You show up to an agitator safe house—"

"They're not agitators," Kara interjected. "They're scientists. They were running for their lives, and you sniffed them out like dogs. Sent them who knows where for whatever *experiments*—"

"Hey, talk all the *taejis* you want. I got the UniForce shoving Tasinn up where the sun don't shine!"

"Shut up, Jeth," Aly snapped.

"Look at you, so ready to jump to her defense." Jeth spit in disgust, a wad of saliva denting the plaster of the wall. Aly and Vin had always been jealous that Chrams could do that. "What about us? Your unit, your brothers? You know what we went through once you disappeared? They wanted to make damn sure no one else was working with you." Aly tried to interrupt, but Jeth held a finger up as he kept talking. "Bullseye, Einstein, Shrank," he said, listing call signs of all the pilots they came up with. "They're gone. Disappeared."

"*What?*" Aly felt like Jeth had lasered him straight in the stomach. "*Why?* I haven't even—I mean, I haven't talked to any of them for years."

"Yeah, well, tough tits for everyone. I only got sent out here as an errand boy. Rhesto's close enough to Fontis to refuel an armada, if it came to that. But we wound up stumbling on a bunch of squatters. It's just shitty coincidence *I'm* here."

So now Aly understood why Jethezar was still stuck on Rhesto.

It was punishment, for being even vaguely associated with him. "Everyone else got sent to Zubil, Yarazu, Hapecha . . ." He listed Fontisian territories. "I'm sitting on the sidelines up on this rock while the rest of the unit gets their balls handed to them."

"They've already deployed?" Aly looked from Jeth to Kara.

"We're at war," she deadpanned. And he'd known that, hadn't he? He'd seen announcements on the holos, martial law, armadas moving across space, Tasinn on even the farthest neutral rocks. But Kara's mom being taken, guys he knew being deployed—it felt more real than anything else had in the past few days. It wasn't just his life. It was everyone's.

"Right, exactly what she said." Jeth patted down the front pocket of his gear and pulled a face when he realized his tobacco was gone. "Swear to the ancestors, Aly, you have the worst timing." He paced some more.

"Let us go, Jeth. What are you going to do? Turn us in?" In the silence, Aly felt his eyes sting. "Man. All those nights we shot the *taejis*? All those times on leave with your family? We came up together. We came up with Vincent . . ."

Aly closed his eyes as he trailed off, remembering that Vincent was dead because of him, because of what he'd done.

"Hey," Jeth said, forcing Aly to look up. He took the cap off his funny-shaped head that narrowed toward the back like a wing. He scratched his head as he paced some more. Then he stopped suddenly, pulled out a thin metal baton, and reversed the charge on Aly's cuffs so they fell away. "Don't make me regret this," he said.

"Now that that's settled"—Kara rubbed her wrists after Jeth

freed her as well—"let's talk about how to get to the broadcast tower."

"Kara, no." Aly stared at her. "We need to get the hell out of here."

"What he said," Jeth said wryly, sounding more like the boy Aly knew.

"We didn't come all this way to have nothing to show for it. You're innocent!" Kara said so forcefully that Aly flinched. He hadn't heard anyone say it yet—that he was innocent. "And Nero has my mom. When everyone across eight galaxies finds out he's a liar and a fraud, they'll be foaming at the mouth to take him down. And when Nero goes down, then I get my mom back."

NINETEEN

RHIANNON

ERAWAE. She'd come here seeking Dahlen's order, though she had no idea what she'd do once she arrived. It was only a domed city, a little terraformed pocket that took up a quarter of the asteroid deep in the Bazorl Quadrant. And it was neutral territory, in theory.

In theory. Not in actual practice. Upon arriving, Rhee had seen the burnt remnants of the Fontisian embassy. The Kalusians had invaded, yet another sign of the utter disregard of the Urnew Treaty—and Nero's growing influence. Any remaining Fontisians were being rooted out and rounded up in all the corners of the city. She'd been quick to shed her tunic for a more appropriate scarf to cover her face—though the vermillion mark was still bright as ever, a disguise that had gotten her this far.

From the locals she'd learned that most of the Fontisians who hadn't managed to flee in time had been captured. Though it was easy enough to find sympathizers, and soon she'd learned that not *all* of them had scattered to the wind.

There was a monastery impossibly high in the mountains—the Order of the Light, it was whispered—that served as a sanctuary to any Fontisians who hadn't been caught and deported back to Fontis. But the future of the monastery was uncertain. The borders and ports were closely monitored, and transport off Erawae would not be arriving soon: Martial law prohibited enemy ships to dock.

Rhee was certain the monastery was where she would have to go. She felt it in her gut. She was no longer misguided by memories venerated as half-truths, but driven by something else—a need to regroup, regain her throne, and take her true revenge on the man who had killed her family.

Of course, she might be traveling toward her own death too.

She had heard that the hillside of switchbacks and hidden stairs that led to the temple was full of hidden archers, and Kalusian forces trying to climb it had been pushed back from every angle. Even though the temple itself was rumored to be impenetrable, anyone seeking the temple was said to have no care for his or her life.

After passing through the business district, Rhee rode along the canal on the sidecar of a simple madùcycle until the rows of modular architecture faded away and the structures became simpler, sparser. Their tires kicked up white moondust on unpaved roads, and it reminded her of Nau Fruma, and of Julian. Dust in his hair. The way he licked his lips before he spoke. How he'd almost kissed her, how he *would've* if she'd just looked up that day in the dojo.

She looked up now at the surface of the dome. It was too large for climate control to be consistent throughout, and as she headed toward the city's southern quadrant, it began to feel like monsoon season. Hot and wet, a fickle condensation that clung to the air like an indecisive rain.

Her guide was a droid, since no Kalusian who'd settled in the domed city was willing to take her. Its shiny exterior reflected her own image back at her as it pointed up to the mountain they approached. Huts were hemmed into the soil around the monastery, which was snug against the steep slopes as if it had grown out of the ground. The mountain itself made the shape of a tusked animal, reared up on its hind legs.

"This is where I leave you," the droid said, stopping at the base of the mountain. Just beyond it she could see the transparent barrier where the dome enclosing them ended and the bleak, exposed surface of Erawae began.

It let her off, then pivoted the madùcycle and drove away. The low *whizz* of its engine grew fainter, until it was just silence. A makeshift staircase had been carved into white moonrock, switchbacking up toward the crest. As landscapes went, she couldn't think of one more unfriendly or unwelcoming.

She pushed those thoughts aside as she scrambled up the mountain. The wet, white chalk crumbled below her feet, and wood cracked with every step. Everything could collapse under her—not just these stairs, but the entire known history of her family. She was the very last Ta'an, here on a bleak and forbidding planet, climbing toward a monastery for an order that might very well want her dead.

But it cleared her mind to focus on the landscape, where to put her foot next as she made her way toward the monastery. The blunt ends of her dark hair were plastered to her face with sweat. Rhee never thought she'd miss her neat braid, with all her thick hair tucked away, until now. It began to rain lightly—a condensation off the surface of the dome—but even this offered no relief from the heat. Glancing warily at the empty mountain plains to either side, Rhee knew someone was watching her. Like an electrical hum to the air, an energy generated by someone else's gaze.

When she'd nearly reached the top and the door was in sight, she was startled to hear a creaking, like a tree falling, as the massive door opened—imported bark, as there wasn't any true wood on this asteroid with the same deep color. She wondered if it was from the Dena forest on Fontis, made of the same wood as Dahlen's ship.

"We don't usually accept unannounced visitors." A man had appeared in the doorway. He looked to be at least eighty, but he was still fit even if a bit hunched—she wondered if it was the gravity or merely old age that curled his shoulders in just slightly. The tattoos along his neck were blurry, soft shapes that barely resembled the severe angles of Dahlen's markings. He wore a sash across his waist, which marked him as an Elder.

Rhee was struggling to breathe. What a climb. "You couldn't have put a sign at the bottom that said so?"

The man made a noise—somewhere between a laugh and a

snort—and with the slightest motion of his hands, six archers materialized around her. Rhee grabbed for her knife, but it was useless. They'd formed a semicircle around her, and she was outnumbered seven to one. Her instinct had been right all along—there *were* people watching her. From the roofs of the squat houses, in the bushes half-hidden, and on the steps below her. The monks of the Fontisian Order of the Light had been taking aim this whole time, and they were prepared to murder her if an order was given. She knew from her time with Dahlen that for members of the order, violence was an accepted part of life. They would not think twice before firing.

The man's eyes flickered, but he only stood there, his expression seemingly bored. "Who are you to climb our mountain?" he prodded.

Pulling her scarf off, Rhee hoped she'd be recognized before the arrows were loosed. She did her best to stand tall as the rain fell on her face.

"Rhiannon Ta'an," she said softly. Then forced herself to repeat it louder, and added: "Last princess of the Ta'an dynasty."

The archers murmured among themselves as she bowed her head, and she felt their recognition as they saw past the crimson mark that took up half her face. Even if she was considered an enemy, the empress to a hostile planet, the last of her slain kin, she wished to appear dignified. There was relief in not hiding. Her time spent slouched in shadow, hidden off to the side, hated for the disfiguring mark on her cheek—it had all taken its toll.

Only the Elder didn't react, although he motioned for the archers to lower their weapons.

"The boy isn't with you," he said.

With a start, Rhee realized the Elder meant Dahlen. "He's been detained," she lied smoothly, even as her mind desperately tried to untangle all the connections—had this man sent Dahlen to save her on the *Eliedio*? Did that mean he was on her side?

"You're either very brave or very foolish, to show up like this." It wasn't exactly reassuring, but when he motioned her to follow him inside the monastery, she did.

Rhee walked through the threshold, glancing back briefly to see the archers follow her in a single-file line. The monastery was dimly lit with candles; there were rounded pillars bolstering a ceiling lost to darkness.

The old man introduced himself as Elder Escov as they made their way inside. He wore the robes of a monk, but moved like a soldier, each step carefully placed and each movement perfectly contained. It occurred to her that he was old enough to have fought in the Great War.

He stopped to bow in front of an altar to Vodhan, and Rhee did the same, keenly aware that the six archers who'd followed her in were now joined by six more inside. The dozen of them were evenly distributed against all four walls. The sound of the rain was loud, angry, and the tiles near the open doors and windows were beaded with water. It was slowly seeping in from the outside world, as if it were beating its fists in anger.

The Elder finished his prayer and motioned for them to continue on into a courtyard, where fifty or sixty boys as young as eight and as old as Dahlen were doing two-three punch combination drills in perfect sync. They were soaked.

The Elder stopped to watch the boys train, his eyes scanning the lines in the same critical way Veyron would watch her and Julian spar. She wanted that again. Not just the challenge but the breathless focus. She'd never danced with a boy, but she knew—punching and kicking, weaving in and out—that it was a kind of dance. And most of all she missed Julian's touch. Even to bring up her knee and block one of his kicks. That jolt. The pressure.

Now, in the courtyard, there was a girl, her blonde hair worn in a tight braid, who executed a perfect flip throw—rolling backward onto the wet ground as she gripped her opponent. She catapulted him up and over, then stood and reset, wiping water from her eyes. Rhee raised herself onto the balls of her feet, feeling her calves flex, aching to spar now.

"I didn't think you'd survive this long, given how young you are and how many people want you dead," the Elder said. His feet were evenly planted and his hands were flexed open—all muscle memory, Rhee assumed, from when he himself was a soldier and had to be combat-ready at a split second's notice.

"You and everyone else," she said, already feeling defensive. Her youth was a deficit she'd have to make up for with cunning and strategy if she were to take back her throne.

The procession passed inside a vaulted chamber, this one elegantly tiled. The temple must be hewed directly into the center of the mountain. At last, the Elder gestured for her to sit. With the rustle of a snake in the grass, the archers fanned out around them. The hairs on the back of Rhee's neck lifted, but she knew she had to ask the Elder about Seotra. She hadn't come this far to be killed before she knew the truth about her family.

"Did you know Andrés Seotra?" she asked.

"*Did* I?" the Elder asked, and Rhee silently cursed: She'd given herself away. "Does that mean Seotra is . . . ?"

"Dead," she confirmed. She wanted some sort of reaction. A flinch. A smile, even. Yet the Elder gave her nothing.

After a long minute of silence, he asked, abruptly, "Do you know how many souls perished in the Great War?"

Rhee couldn't see what the Great War had to do anything, but she could tell the Elder expected an answer. "Estimates are at a hundred million," she said impatiently.

"Closer to three hundred million, but I'm not surprised that's what your history books tell you. They would hardly mention the faults of your planet . . ."

Rhee swallowed her frustration. "I've not come for a lecture on sins I didn't commit."

"And I haven't invited you inside my home to give one," he said, seemingly matching her own impatience. "Your father ended that war. He and Seotra both, in a way. It was Seotra himself who called off his unit after I'd refused to surrender. He told me Fontis was destined to lose the war. And I told him that we would take one hundred thousand more Kalusian lives before that happened." Elder Escov looked down at his palms, as if seeing an old story written on them. "I was a prisoner of war for a time, but then the Urnew Treaty was drafted and I was released. Seotra and I became . . ." He trailed off, searching for the right word.

"Friends?" Rhee asked.

"No," he said firmly, but there was some warmth in the

man's blue eyes. "Not friends. Allies, perhaps." Rhee wondered if Dahlen knew of their history. Surely Dahlen wouldn't have killed Seotra if he'd known the truth. "I met your father because of him—not a bad man by any standard. There was nothing he wouldn't sacrifice for peace. I was to receive him on Fontis the day your family crashed in the rings of Rylier."

"We were going to see *you*?" she asked. She knew they were going to Fontis, but not to visit an Elder of the order.

"Surprised?" he asked mildly. "Surprised your father was keeping the company of terrorist fanatics?"

"I don't think that," she said quickly. She'd first said it out of fear—the archers still hovered nearby, after all—but then realized that she meant it. She thought of Dahlen and how she was scared of him, but she admired him too. He was smart, calculating, cunning. She wondered about his coldness, and what atrocities he'd witnessed to make him that way.

"What is it you've lost?" she had asked Dahlen.

"Everything," he'd answered. And Rhee knew he'd spoken of his family.

Now she looked up to meet the Elder's eye. "Your father confided in Seotra that he sensed danger," he said. "Some of the people were angry about the terms of the Urnew Treaty. For some, peace was inconceivable because of the hatred they'd been taught to feel. And for others, peace was merely an inconvenience— it prevented them from mining freely on Wraeta, and profiting from a war."

Nero. His flowery language, his love of the camera . . . it was designed to make him seem trustworthy, competent, dynamic. *A new, worthy leader will rise . . .*

"The night your family died they were not going on vacation, as they had publicly claimed, but you already knew that."

Rhee could barely bring herself to nod.

"They hadn't made it to their final destination, but they were fleeing to Fontis with one of our escorts. To us, peace was very important." His voice softened. "To us, we owed him that."

And Rhee should have been with them. She should have died on that ship. She felt a wrench of pain in her gut, as if someone were turning a knife there.

"When did you come here to Erawae?" she asked, still unsure whether Elder Escov could be counted as a friend.

"Just after your family's death. It was a dangerous time, and neutral territory had seemed safer. I was wrong, of course . . ."

Rhee wondered what it must've been like to witness the raids here, and watch as his people were rounded up and imprisoned.

"I admired your father greatly," he continued. "I met him once, on the day he signed the Urnew Treaty. I met you and your sister too."

"I don't remember." Without accessing her cube, she couldn't pinpoint the moment they met. Now the memories from her childhood were faulty—just scraps, like ribbons fluttering on the wind. But she'd practically lived in those memories. She'd replayed that day enough times to know she'd worn a Kalusian formal dress, and waved at a crowd. There'd been confetti that she'd tried to snatch out of the air. That night she'd fallen asleep in Josselyn's lap, while Joss had fallen asleep on their mother's shoulder, the remnants of a celebration around them. It was a still image they showed on the holos every year, on the anniversary of her family's deaths.

Now she tugged at the memory like a lifeline that would pull her up into that moment, that feeling. And it helped her remember why she'd come all this way.

"You knew my father, and you admired him. He's dead now, just as Seotra is. And Nero, the man who's installed himself as a ruler, will bring war down on all of us. But I'm here now. Help *me*," she insisted. "Tell me what Seotra had planned to do."

"Help you?" he repeated, as if the idea had never occurred to him. "My people are being rounded up. Taken to some secret prison. Some rumors say they're being experimented on. Help you when I have to beat back your army every hour of every day?"

Rhee felt a flare of anger. She hadn't come all this way just to hit another dead end. "I'm the last remaining princess of the Ta'an dynasty. I'm the only person who can keep the universe from war. If you help me stay alive, if you give me shelter, I will find a way to win the throne back. I can still stop the war. I swear I will keep your people safe."

He was silent for a bit. "It isn't true," he said.

"What?" Rhee asked, confused. "That I can take the throne?"

He looked at her, finally. "No," he said. "That you're the last princess." His eyes were very blue, like chipped ice. "You aren't. Your sister, Josselyn . . . she's alive too."

TWENTY

ALYOSHA

JETH was right. The broadcast tower was unbreachable. A prewar structure made of brick with a narrow staircase winding to the top. Aly could see it through the tiny vertical windows that ran up the tower side. One way in and one way out—with an NX droid standing guard at the base. Pinched speaker grill and narrow infrared eyes, like their faces were designed to look constipated.

The actual satellite dish, though, that was a different story. It was two hundred meters across—and even though it was built in to a massive sinkhole, it still rose above the ground by another fifty meters, taller than a ten-story building. It was accessible via two service ladders, and these, too, were guarded.

But the UniForce hadn't bothered posting guards anywhere else around it, which was either careless or cocky or a little bit of both. Maybe the army didn't think it could serve any use to anyone. It was a strategic misstep that they hadn't just blown the thing up. It's what Aly would've done.

Then again, he felt like making a lot of things explode lately.

Now Aly, Kara, and Pavel crouched on the north side—the farthest point possible from the tower, hidden by the dish itself.

"Jeth's not coming," Aly said. He looked at Kara. She poked at one of the levers on the machine he'd built in the past couple of hours. He wondered if she thought he was some sort of nerd. Anything he made in the Wray got kicked around or stolen.

"Shut up already." She didn't sound mean, just distracted. Aly knew she was thinking about her mom. He'd asked if Kara was okay earlier, but she'd just pursed her mouth into a straight line and shook her head. "He's coming. Definitely. If he'd ratted us out they would've come for us by now." Just then, Jethezar came into view, glancing behind him casually. Kara gave Aly a *told you so* look.

Jethezar broke into a sprint as soon as the tower was out of view.

"Nice of you to show," Aly said when Jeth dropped to a knee beside him.

"Yeah, sorry I'm late, I was busy *trying not to die*." He pulled a shrink-wrapped plastic bag out of his waistband and threw it in front of Aly. "That touched my butt crack. I don't even feel bad about it."

"Gross," Kara said. Her face opened up into an almost-smile, which made Aly feel stupid amounts of happy—but annoyed him, too, because he hadn't been the one to make her smile.

"Holy *taejis*, we've been separated barely long enough for me to steal a supply or two and take a dump," Jeth said, pointing to the machine. "You built this from all the stuff I pulled out of your pockets?"

It was just a small platform with a stand and some other things. Aly was still trying to calculate how far back to pull the lever for it to force the spring.

"Pavel had to give up some pieces too. For the greater good," Kara said, raising an invisible glass.

The droid hinged open the front of his inner compartment and showed how half of his attachments were missing. "Worth it," Pavel said. Aly felt a twinge of pain. Pavel had learned that phrase from Vin.

Aly picked up the corner of the bag. He made a show of wiping it on the grass while giving Jeth the finger, then ripped it open. Immediately a twist of strings as thin as shoelaces expanded and grew quickly, until it looked like a massive, coiled snake. Compressed synthicone rope, courtesy of the UniForce.

"Good looking out, Jeth," Aly said.

"You can thank me after it works." Jeth looked up. From here the satellite dish blocked out half the sky. It was a monolith. It'd been built so people could talk across planets, maybe even understand each other. Depressing to think all it'd been used for in the past few years were some DroidVision reruns.

But today they'd see something worthwhile.

"It'll work." Kara ran her fingers alongside the metal edge. There were flecks of blue polish on her nails, and for some reason, he thought it made her cooler, out of his league. "And he's right, you know?" she said to Aly. "It's pretty incredible you built this."

Aly shrugged and ducked his head. He made himself busy by looping the rope through Pavel's claw attachment and setting it on the platform. He could barely spell, couldn't draw for *taejis* or hold a tune. But sometimes he *thought* in blueprints, like he'd get an idea and see everything fitting together, all the little pieces encased, the edges smoothed, the hinges oiled. It embarrassed him, sometimes, how his mind didn't work like anyone else's.

Jeth looked in both directions where the landscape disappeared around the base of the satellite dish. "I gotta get moving now." They shook hands. Aly was about to drop his hand when Jeth pulled him into a hug. "I'm sorry I doubted you," he said into his ear, "and about Vin." Then he patted him hard on the back. He and Kara nodded at each other as he stood up, adjusted his belt, and went on his way.

When Jeth was out of sight, Pavel helped Aly position the device according to the wind and the angle. Aly silently counted to three and released the lever; the claw catapulted into space, and the rope streamed behind it, whistling as it cut through the air. He held his breath until the claw cleared the edge and caught on the rim.

"It *worked*." Aly could barely believe it himself. He gave the rope a tug.

Kara buttoned up her big coat, and after Pavel compacted into a dome, she helped strap the droid to Aly's back. Then she grabbed hold of the rope. "Mind if I go first?" she said, already grabbing for it.

"Wait," he said. He looked up. It was a long climb. "How's your head?"

She shrugged. "Broken."

"I'm being serious. Are you going to be able to make it? What if—?"

"I get it, Aly. Chivalry is not dead and all." She gripped the rope with one hand and mounted it. "My head has lasted me this long. What's a ten-story rope climb?"

Aly watched as pieces of the silicone rope slid out at a forty-five-degree angle, spreading halfway down the sole of her foot to grip it. It peeled away like putty when she took her next step. It wouldn't bear their entire body weight for long, especially not his, but at least their biceps wouldn't be melting.

Aly decided he would take her word for it. He grabbed hold of the rope and climbed after her, trying to get used to Pavel's weight on his back—and it went all right until he felt himself slipping halfway up, the rope thinning out. It was slow to repair, and the texture started to change; it got stickier just as the wind picked up. They sailed a few feet over to the left, both of them clamping down with their feet, knees, elbows, and hands to stay on. The rope continued to stretch as they climbed, and every time he gained a foot he'd fall back down six inches. He was scrambling desperately—the rope gummy, like melted marshmallows coating his palms. He swore he was going to fall.

When Kara finally reached the top she heaved herself over the edge of the satellite dish and disappeared. Aly launched himself right behind her just as the rope fell away from under his feet. With nothing to anchor it, the claw attachment skittered down the slope toward the concave center of the surface. It was a long way down.

He landed next to Kara, the two of them on their stomachs holding on to the lip of the structure with both hands. He was shaking as he tried to catch his breath.

"Are you *laughing*?" he asked Kara. Her mouth was parted; her expression was somewhere between relief and terror, kind of like the girl on the zeppelin during Nero's press conference.

"It's just—doesn't it feel like we're in a giant cereal bowl?" she asked. His arms were outstretched, and he readjusted his grip to look behind him.

It kind of *did* look like a big bowl, with Rhesto's mountains just beyond the brim. He imagined a giant taking it to his lips and sucking up the last of the milk. "You're nuts, you know that?"

"You're not the first person to call me that."

Aly rolled onto his side and held on with one hand, the other unstrapping Pavel from his back. He set the droid's wheels on the surface but kept him attached to the strap, so they were tethered to one another, and he rolled down only a few feet below them.

"You sure you want to do this?" The claw had finally hit the port that jutted out of the center.

"You're asking *now*?" She looked below them. "Let's go on three."

Her hazel eyes—were they always hazel?—met his and never left as they counted together. "Three," they said in unison, and Kara flipped on her back and slid down, riding the surface of her massive jacket like it was a magic carpet. Aly flew down right with her. Somehow their hands found each other's.

Time moved fast and slow all at once. It didn't feel like it was stretching out so much as getting bigger, the big rim of the bowl shifting above him and framing the sky in its perfect center. It was an impossible moment of peace. He'd prove his innocence. He would show everyone.

Suddenly Pavel's leash whipped out of his hand, and they fell away as the droid stayed stuck on a ridge he and Kara had just barely missed.

"PAVEL!" Aly called, and tried to flip himself over to slow down. Kara tried, too, but they got tangled up, rushing down like a tide. They tumbled. Everything happened in near silence and small grunts. He'd given up trying to get Pavel back, but now they were coming in fast on the port below, right at the center of the bowl. It had looked far smaller from up top, but now he saw it was a raised cylinder in the middle. At this rate, if they didn't stop, they'd break their legs, best-case scenario. Worst-case scenario, maybe flip over it and break their necks.

Aly tore his sleeve open as he dragged his elbow into the surface; it was raw and bloody, and he could feel where the friction heat and metal were burning his skin. Kara's eyes went wide as she saw the port, and she clawed at the surface. Her hair in his mouth. His hand on her waist. He dug a heel in and could smell the rubber of his sole burning. Their bodies had found each other in the mad scramble, parallel now by the time they'd slowed—his foot just tapping the port. The curve of her hip brushed against him, and even now—filthy and exhausted, skinned to hell, and on the run for his life—Aly felt his face flush.

He was quick to push himself up to sit, and he looked behind him, up the slope. They were outside of Pavel's signal jammer, and any second some NX could pop up over the crest to find them.

Kara sat up and rubbed the heel of her palms against her eyes. He crawled toward her and pulled her into a hug. Her braid had come undone, and her crazy hair made a halo around her face. Or a lion's mane. "Holy *taejis*," she said breathlessly.

"You good?" he mumbled into her hair. His adrenaline was off the charts. He'd bloodied his knees and elbows, and he was sure that everything would hurt later, but it felt fantastic here—his arms around her, his face in her big mess of tangles.

"Don't worry about me, Aly." She looked up at him. Their faces were an inch apart. Only for a split second, though—Kara blinked and pushed him away. "Now or never."

Now or never.

He exhaled through his nose, then powered up his cube for the first time in weeks. It was lightning running through him, pain and pleasure, striking nerve after nerve. And with his other hand, he touched the metal conductor to transfer his playback. There was a jolt of electricity, and his limbs went numb.

Aly closed his eyes as he shuffled through recent memories. It was hard to get back into it. His mind felt closed off, rigid. He pictured sticking his hands into the big, dark knot of his memory, up to his elbows, feeling his way around. Then something hooked on—a moment, a feeling. He'd found it.

"Stream playback." His own voice sounded distant, but just saying it, dictating what he could and couldn't do with his cube and his memories—it made him feel like a god. The data transfer felt like his soul was pouring out from the point on his neck and funneling into the hologram that projected up into the sky, out into the worlds. Alongside millions of strangers, he rewatched the moment he found the dead body on the royal escape pod. There he was, slipping on the Nau Fruman's blood. The robo-droid, throwing him one-handed across the room.

With his memories transferred, Aly fell to his knees and tasted salt in his mouth, felt his face flood with tears. His hand fell away and he doubled over, one hand to support himself while the other one wiped his face.

"Aly!" Kara said. She kneeled before him and lowered his hand from his face and wrapped her arms around his neck. She squeezed him. He could smell her, feel all the warmth from under her coat. For a long time, there was quiet, except for the sound of Aly's heavy sobbing.

There was the rest of it, too, the stuff he couldn't show them because he'd gone offline. But he'd never forget any of it: stabbing himself with the syringe full of tauri. Vincent piloting the escape pod.

"Who are you?" Aly'd asked him.

"I'm the guy who's going to save your sorry ass," Vincent had said. At the time Aly had been pissed, taken for granted that Vin had a mission more important than ten Alys put together. Despite it all, Vin had saved Aly like he said he would. Vin had died to keep his word, because Aly hadn't been able to save *him* when the time came.

"They're coming, aren't they?" Aly asked now. His face was wet. He wiped it away and hoped he didn't have snot coming out of his nose.

"You did it, Aly." She'd ignored his question for a reason, and he knew he was right. "Everyone's gonna know the truth."

The guards rappelled down and approached slowly from all sides. Jethezar led the charge.

"Traitor!" Jeth said, grabbing Aly's shirt with his sticky fingertips. He was a big guy, and he heaved Aly up to his feet so they were face-to-face. For a split second, Aly saw regret pass over his old friend's features, just before he spit in Aly's eye. To a Chram, it was the deepest insult—but it was for show, and Jeth had gone easy on him. Aly's eye hurt like a *choirtoi* but at least he still had one. Jeth could've blinded him if he'd spit at full velocity.

Jeth pushed him to the ground and kicked him in the stomach. Kara cried for him to stop. The Tasinn watched in amusement. But Aly knew Jeth was doing what he had to do. They were all doing what they had to do. Aly crumpled up in a ball to protect himself from more kicks. His kidneys and ribs were getting pummeled.

Jeth pulled him up to sit, rough, and cuffed him. It was the second time today.

"Sorry," Jeth whispered, so quietly Aly wasn't even sure he'd heard it. And then loudly for everyone to hear, like an announcement he'd been dying to make: "Guess where we're taking you, *murderer*."

TWENTY-ONE

RHIANNON

RHEE felt as if she'd been catapulted out of her body, as if she were hovering somewhere in deep space, her lungs seizing—not here, with her feet firmly planted on the temple floor of the order.

"That's impossible," a voice that sounded like her voice was saying. "Josselyn died."

"We had to make a decision." The Elder folded his hand on his lap. "Your sister was gravely injured, but survived," said. "She was taken to Fontis for life-threatening wounds. Seo swore everyone to secrecy. It was important to protect the hei the throne under any circumstance, and she was safer if the a sin believed she'd died."

It was the same reason Rhee had chosen to stay hidden Nero tried to take her life too.

"My sister," Rhee repeated again, her mind a cloud—s with rain and rage and lightning. She had imagined J

death as if she'd been there alongside her when the craft exploded and tore apart in the air. The outside seeping in. Their breath snatched away. *It would've been painless*, Rhee had imagined. It would've been sound and fury and then just a dark, quiet end.

Memories assaulted her. She couldn't think straight. All Rhee could see was their hair, playfully bound together in one long braid so they sat like conjoined twins for nearly an hour. Changing her clothes to match Joss, only for Joss to change them again—a cycle of clothes and crying and copycatting that made Rhee furious. The way Joss loved sensaberries. The way she let Rhee share her bed during a thunderstorm. All along, Josselyn had been alive. It wasn't fair. This whole time they'd been apart.

"She was the only survivor, but when she stabilized she was sent away to a secret location. I never knew it. Seotra coordinated all of it. I had contact with her handler once or twice."

"Her *handler*?"

"You both had one. Yours, unfortunately, was convinced to work for the other side."

"Veyron." Her voice cracked; she could barely say his name out loud. The Elder nodded. "So where is she? Where are Josselyn and her handler now?"

"Unfortunately, we lost contact with her about a month ago. We have some reason to believe the handler is being detained in a prison camp."

"When were you going to tell me?" she asked.

"Perhaps never." The Elder said it so casually Rhee felt as if she'd been struck. "She had no memory herself of what had

happened, and as far as the public was concerned, *you* were the Crown Princess."

"But I'm not," she said, realizing that she was no longer the empress. Was she sad? Had she truly wanted the throne? There were those who were loyal to her, but their support was scattered, and those who doubted her ability to rule were countless.

The only thing she knew for certain was that she still wanted revenge. That gave her strength. It was her coil, her tether. Anger swept through her like a current. "Joss is my sister," Rhee said. "She's not just some—some *toy*." Then something occurred to her, and her insides soured. "Did Dahlen know?" Rhee asked. The Elder paused, as if considering how to answer. "Did he?" she demanded again.

"It's not as simple as *yes* or *no*. There are things he knows, and things he doesn't know that he knows . . ."

"What does that even *mean*?" She was shouting without meaning to. "How could you just . . . *hide* her all these years? How could you *lose* her?" Rage burned through her like a fire. "You and your holy order. You pretend to be a keeper of the universe's secrets. But you're just as horrible as all the rest of them—horrible and selfish—"

The Elder's face didn't change. "If the Princess won't watch her tongue . . ."

"You'll what?" She knew she was being reckless but she didn't care. "You'll kill me? And Fontis and Kalu will go to war again, and half the planets in the galaxy will be blasted into nonexistence?"

Only the swift rustling of arrows recalled to her that the

archers were watching. In an instant, their bows were all pointed in her direction again.

Then the cracking of wood echoed throughout the monastery, and glass came shattering down. Tasinn swarmed the monastery, exploding ancient relics, dropping the archers where they stood. They wore tactical gear of lightweight armor, and a gas bomb made her eyes and throat burn. In the struggle that ensued, the Tasinn threw monks against the altars—destroying statues, scattering offerings. She couldn't even hear herself think; the sound of coughing and choking was unbearable.

The Tasinn were worse than the droids that were made just for the purpose of destruction. They had hearts and minds and chose not to use them.

The Elder grabbed her hand and tried to run, but a stunner sent him flying forward, and Rhee let go of his hand out of reflex. Just a second too late. The electricity had passed through their hands and traveled up her arm. Then she felt two pricks in her back. An excruciating pain shot up her spine, a fire seizing all her muscles. All the order fell in the same way. The Tasinn had come prepared to use any means necessary.

"Princess," one of the Tasinn said. He came toward her, smiling. There was a patch over his left eye. "I can't thank you enough for your help today."

She was coughing too hard to reply. The gas had done something. It felt like there was glass in her lungs.

He squatted down and touched her cheek with long, oily fingers. "You were very brave, coming here on your own," he said. "Very brave, and very *useful*. We've been trying to find a way to get in past the Fontisian archers for a week now. It seems we should just have sent a princess to do our work."

Something had reached into her soul and tugged, made her unravel inside. Everything good in her life had been destroyed: Was it all her fault? The archers who had followed her inside had left the hillside vulnerable to attack.

The Tasinn had raided the monastery because of her—because she'd come, seeking answers. That organic memory bubbled up from deep within: that little girl in a new palace, sobbing away until there were no tears left, like a piece of dried fruit left out in the sun.

Rhee was shoved into the front of a small craft, surrounded by Tasinn with cruel faces that all seemed identical to her. Still, they seemed almost afraid to touch her. Through the window she saw a Fontisian girl get shoved and herded into the back of a craft—the same blonde one she'd watched in the courtyard. Rhee caught her eye, and the girl glared at her, made her feel like she'd tipped into a long fall.

Her thoughts quickly went back to Dahlen. Dahlen, who'd been by her side since the moment he'd saved her life—not that she'd ever admitted this to him, but he *had* saved her life. Rhee had never thanked him. Instead she left him at the mercy of the Tasinn, only proving that she *was* the spoiled girl he'd insinuated she was.

"Nero wants to see you," the Tasinn with the eye patch said.

As the hatch closed, she took in a deep breath, forcing down the noise rising in her throat—part sob, part battle cry. She was going to face the man who wanted her dead.

TWENTY-TWO

ALYOSHA

HE'D imagined it would go down differently. Sure, Aly figured he'd get taken in, be debriefed and whatnot—but instead the UniForce had manhandled Aly all the way here. He hadn't seen what happened to Kara when they took him; he didn't know where she was or if she was safe. Now he was locked away in a room barely bigger than the shack he and his dad had shared. All four walls made up of LED screens that played a twenty-four-hour DroneVision news channel that drowned out his thoughts, made him feel more crazy than he already was.

He'd been forced to watch dozens of "experts" paraded in front of the camera, each one a little puppet with Nero pulling the strings—just like Jeth had said. Each of them testified that Aly's cube playback had been forged, pointed to inconsistencies, minor technicalities that supposedly proved the footage had been manipulated with help from Fontisian scientists. They said the Fontisians had gotten hold of a dangerous technology suppressed and supposedly discarded after the G-1K summit: the overwriter. It was technology that allowed not just Ravaging but *rewriting* of old memories.

There had been rumors of this for years, though. Like there were rumors that Josselyn was alive, like there were rumors the government was hacking data from individual cubes without permission.

Aly couldn't write off any of it as conspiracy theories anymore.

He scratched the spot on his arm where the warden had injected him with . . . what? He wasn't sure. He noticed then that his knuckles were bloody from all the times he'd punched at the walls. It turned out these plasma screens were self-repairing. Every time he thought he'd shattered one, it would smooth out again—like a ripple in the water. When he closed his eyes, invisible soldiers cranked the volume to blasting.

He'd seen the segment on loop, counting 277 until the screens went dark and the outline of a door appeared in the static of the feed. When it opened, Kara walked through.

He knew it was a hallucination, or maybe a hologram. She was too calm, too clean, too graceful. That smile. That's always how they mentioned the Fontisian saints. Isn't this when they appeared too? At your darkest hours? Ready to take you to your eternal home?

Aly scrambled toward the corner, pressing himself hard against the plasma. He tried to flip that switch inside himself, when he'd crawl into the corner of his mind and block it all out. Every time his dad had called him all those names, every time those Fontisian preachers had told him he'd burn in hell, every time someone had said he was smart for a Wraetan—he flipped the switch, and an invisible armor went up over his dark skin. *Leave me alone. I'm innocent*, he repeated to himself. *I did nothing wrong.*

But the switch was *choirtoing* broken.

"It's me, Aly. Stop! Shhhhh. It's me, Kara." She grabbed his wrists. He tried pushing her away but he felt sluggish, like all his limbs belonged to someone else. "What's wrong with him?" Her hands felt cold. They felt real. But he knew they couldn't be real. He didn't even know if *he* was real anymore.

A woman had entered behind her, so skinny she seemed to be made entirely of muscle. She had light skin and hair, tiny wrinkles at the edges of her green eyes. "He's been drugged," she said.

"Help me," Kara said to her. Desperate. Begging. He'd never expected to hear her speak in that kind of tone.

The woman leaned down and pushed Aly's head against the wall, gripping him by his hair. With her free hand she pulled out a syringe and uncapped it with her mouth.

"No." He tried to free himself, but his body felt like it was filled with lead. Then the woman stuck the syringe into his neck and he felt a sudden release, like pressure let out of a balloon.

"That should reduce the effects. Now get up, Aly," she said. "We're saving your life."

I'm the guy who's going to save your sorry ass, Vincent had said. Everyone had seen him say it now in Aly's playback. But not a single person in the galaxy believed Aly.

He tried to shake himself out of this god-awful nightmare.

Bits of darkness still clung to his mind, but he felt them cracking, peeling, falling away like old paint.

"We're going home, Aly," Kara urged. *Easy for you to say*, Aly thought. He had the Wray Town, but it was only ever a place he'd lived once—and he was never going back. He didn't *have* a home.

"What's going on? Where are we?" he asked. He turned to the older woman. "Who are you?"

It was Kara who answered. "We're on Houl. This is my mom, Lydia. Can you believe it? She's been here all this time—she came and found me and broke me out."

Aly felt his eyebrows raise halfway up his forehead. Would've gone back all the way if it were anatomically possible. He was an expert at being in the wrong place at the wrong time, and here was Kara's mom, in the right place at the right time. A little too right.

Kara told him he'd been there only a few hours—but that was impossible. He was sure it had been weeks.

"It's the drugs," Kara's mom said. "They manipulate the temporal experience. You'll be dizzy too."

"'Temporal experience'?" Aly still didn't understand, and when Kara helped him up, he doubted his own legs.

"Lean on me," Kara said.

We're on Houl.

What did he know about Houl? It was a planet on the Outer Belt. The atmosphere was unforgiving, and discarded parts had developed AI. The surface itself was covered with eel-like creatures that produced electromagnetic fields. Terrifying. Basically the perfect place to put a prison if you didn't want anyone to escape. And he had a feeling it was Kalu's.

It was starting to come back now. Jeth had told him about a secret prison; Kara had told him about a place for experiments . . . He looked over her shoulder, at the door behind them, at the dead screens that had for hours been playing the same news. All those experts had said he was guilty. Was he guilty? The only thing that anchored him to any version of reality was Kara. But was *she* even real? Her eyes kept changing color. But she couldn't be a hologram—she was supporting his weight.

"Your eyes . . ." he said. But he was too afraid to say the rest. What was happening to him?

"Come on, Aly," Kara said. "We gotta move."

"Let's," her mom agreed. Aly noticed that Kara didn't look all that much like Lydia. Must take after her dad's side . . .

The hallway was a cylinder, not a right angle to be seen. It felt like they were inside a hard-boiled egg. It made walking almost impossible. Besides, he still felt numb and slow from whatever they'd given him, and he stumbled after almost every step.

Lydia pulled out a handheld, and a dimensional blueprint projected into the air. He understood, through the fog in his brain, that the shimmering hologram must be an image of the prison. It looked like a black cube of sliding, interconnected pieces. And they were inside of it.

Lydia nodded. "State of the art. Made on the backs of Houlis. The red marks show where the NX droids are stationed." She pointed at the moving dots. It meant the holo was somehow online. That Kara's mom's holo was somehow online. "This is our exit." Lydia brought her hand to the image and zoomed into the south quadrant, section 7E. Aly thought—no, he *knew*—that there were way too many red dots between here and there.

"Pavel's there, too," Kara said, pointing to section 7E. Aly felt something tight in his chest melt away. He'd known the soldiers took P when they got arrested on Rhesto, and Aly had been scared they'd strip the little guy down and sell the pieces for scrap.

Another tubular hallway intersected theirs, but they continued straight as Kara filled him in on the schematics of the prison—three columns and three rows made up of smaller cubes that moved separately, forever shifting, changing orientations. Each one ran on its own systems of plumbing, air, and artificial gravity.

Aly felt himself coming back to clarity, desperate to piece together the information, clawing at it like those crazy feral cats in the Wray.

"There have to be hundreds of configurations," Aly said slowly, sliding the toggle bar on the hologram back and forth to watch the way the prison rotated.

"It was designed that way, so that escape would be impossible," Lydia said.

"Is it?"

When Lydia didn't answer, Kara did. "We'll see," she said, with that same shrug she did—but it was less cynical, more hopeful than it was before. "It's not operating at full capacity. There are about thirty combinations."

Still: The odds weren't great.

They arrived at a hatch that Lydia opened with the keypad. This seemed wrong—why did Lydia know the combination? How had they even accessed his cell in the first place? Where had she gotten the holographic map?

Lydia disappeared, and they followed her through a transitional chamber between sections that worked like an air lock, with no climate control or gravity. He nearly froze his nipples off as he swam through the air toward the opposite door. Kara's long braid trailed behind her like a tail. Through the window he could see a hallway ahead, same as the one behind them—and when Lydia breached the hatch, they fell through and got sucked sideways to the right. But it wasn't sideways at all in this section. It was the floor. *That's* why the hallway was shaped as a cylinder.

Who'd designed this thing? He had to help Lydia up, following blindly. Aly noticed that she'd started limping after the last fall, but she was trying to play it off, power through it. Aly could tell, though. And by the way Kara kept reaching out to help her mom, he knew she could too.

Lydia glanced at the map, where three red dots were converging. "Right. As fast as you can. Now."

They all quickly skirted around a corner, just missing a droid. There was a trick to evading them, a start-and-stop motion, a rhythm that felt wrong until it didn't—same as the clutch on a pod. Except now they weren't just cruising from point A to point B. They were running for their lives.

Whatever Lydia had injected him with was finally kicking into high gear, and he started to realize that they were being

tracked by the deadliest machines the UniForce had ever produced. He was sobering up quick.

And *that's* when he started really paying attention.

"Are these *jail* cells?" Aly asked, pointing to the glass panes
that lined either side of the corridor. Each cell was transparent
from certain angles and completely dark from others, like the
lens of a solar glass. Inside one of them he saw the silhouette of a
woman—at least he thought it was a woman. She was hunched
over and looked as if she might be crying.

He wanted to shatter the glass, pull her up to her feet, and
tell her to run—but where? He didn't even know how *they* were
getting out.

"We have to keep moving, Aly," Kara said.

"We can't just leave them here." He felt anger simmering just
under his skin. He was furious at her, himself, at everyone.

"We can't stay, either," Lydia said. She turned around, and
Aly unconsciously backed up. "Do you have any idea what's at
stake? How important the two of you are? Better question—do
you know why they haven't killed you yet?"

He felt like his brain had been seared. A white-hot flash of
confusion and déjà vu.

"Why did they frame you?" Vin had asked. Challenged. "*I'm*
the spy. *I'm* the one who sent out the hail."

"They were prepping you, Aly," Lydia said now, answering
her own question. "They wanted to Ravage your cube. While
you were *alive*. Wanted all your memories so they could mount a
case against you. Prove without a shadow of a doubt that you did
it—that you killed the Princess."

Aly shook his head. He didn't believe it; he couldn't even think it. The Ravaging. He remembered all those people they'd found on the zeppelin . . . the woman drawing triangles she believed were her son's face . . .

Kara had said they were leaching memories, souls.

He suddenly felt like he might throw up.

Did that mean they had the technology, too, to twist his memories, to shape them into a story?

"Now take how horrified you feel and multiply it by infinity, and you'll know how I feel," Lydia said quietly. Her jaw was set. Her eyes burned into him, made him want to look away.

"Why?" Kara asked. Aly shook his head, afraid to know the answer. "What's it got to do with you?"

"It's got everything to do with me," Lydia said, looking back toward her daughter. "I'm the one who designed the technology. I'm the one who taught them how."

TWENTY-THREE

RHIANNON

AT last, she would come face-to-face with the real killer. *Nero.*

"I *know* I'm intimidating," Rhee said drily, "but are these escorts really necessary?" Her hands were cuffed behind her back as she walked alongside the man with the eye patch. Two NXs flanked her on either side, and the zipping noise of their joints grated on her nerves.

The man smirked in a way that lifted the scarred corner of his mouth. "Let's just say they're here to encourage your best behavior."

As if her life were a reward she'd have to earn through being quiet, obedient, good. The man clasped the back of her neck, the way her father would—but pinching it so that her muscles tightened involuntarily. The man wore Dahlen's ring on his pinky finger, which was curved around her neck toward her cube. Rhee didn't know where they were keeping Dahlen, and not knowing

279

made her feel like a balloon descending—all her logic, her perfectly constructed revenge fantasies, emptying out into the void.

"Where are we going?" They'd made so many turns that she couldn't keep count, until eventually they stood before a nondescript door.

It was an auditorium inside, stadium seating facing down into a dark pit that was the stage. Her skin crawled, recalling the moment Veyron had led her to the room of her ancestors' altars—the night he tried to kill her. Dahlen had saved her then. She only hoped she had time to save him now.

The droids split behind her and walked to either side of the room and halfway down the stairs, where they stood guard. Rhee walked down the center aisle, keenly aware that the scarred man had allowed her to do so. Whereas the auditorium on the *Eliedio* had been carpeted, with low lights and plush red velvet seats, this had a clinical quality to it. Shiny metal chairs. The antiseptic smell of bleach and lemon. A glass barrier, she realized once she descended all the way, that split the seats from whatever was on the dark stage. Rhee's hands had been cuffed behind her back.

She pressed her face up against the cool glass, watching her breath fog up, fearing what waited in the shadows.

The lights came on then, and Rhee swallowed a gasp. White tiles. Metal tables with wheels, covered in white sheets and sharp medical tools arrayed in delicate, almost beautiful arrangements—like an ancient mandala. Lining the wall of the round room were more tables, more vials, cranks for ancestors knew what.

Nero emerged. His wide shoulders cut a silhouette that Rhee

would've thought impressive before, but now she saw it for what it was: a man playing dress-up in his double-breasted blazer, desperate for power, full of hatred. "Princess," he said as he walked up to the empty center, bowing in Rhee's direction. His formality was a slap in the face. "How do you like my new facility?"

"You disgust me."

"I'm disappointed to hear that." His face hardened, its beauty smoothed away by something deeply sinister. "Because the truth is I admire you very much. Veyron did too."

Rhee felt sick at the mere mention of his name. She'd killed a man, and she would do it again. She would never be worthy of Julian or his forgiveness.

"How did you turn him?" she asked of Veyron.

"He begged to spare your life, said he loved you like a daughter . . ."

She banged her shoulder against the glass barrier in anger. "Answer me!"

"You know the answer, Rhiannon. In the end you *weren't* his daughter. And it was between you and Julian. I still haven't decided if I should spare the boy, seeing as Veyron didn't technically fulfill the contract."

"Julian will kill you first," she said, hoping it was true. He was strong, and fast. He had good instincts. But he also had a soft heart—he was too trusting. She should have stayed with him. Looked out for him, like she always had.

"I'm untouchable," Nero said, and Rhee feared he meant it. "Do you think I've acted rashly? That I seized my chance when I could?" He shook his head. "I own everything and everyone. I've been planning since I was your age, picking and choosing my allies, building a loyal army of followers."

"They're not followers, they're *viewers*, you fool. They're fickle. This isn't loyalty! You've preyed on their fear and—"

"And I got exactly the result I wanted," he said, cutting her off. "I have millions of Kalusians foaming at the mouth for war. We're going to invade Wraeta."

Rhee shook her head. Her mouth was dry. "Why?"

"You know the difference between you and me, Princess?" Nero asked, ignoring her and clearly relishing the moment. "I played the long game. But you—you want what you want, and you want it now. Do you have any idea how much time it actually takes to start a war? A successful one, at least . . ." He paused, and then brought his sleeve up to shine one of the brass buttons on the front of his blazer. "When one's plan fails, you have to have another in place, one you can enact immediately. And when Veyron failed, I found another Wraetan to blame for your death."

"How poetic," Rhee said through gritted teeth. But she fumed beneath the sarcasm. Veyron and the boy who'd been blamed for her death, both of them sacrificed at the altar of Nero's war lust.

"And meanwhile, you'd taken care of the hardest part: Seotra. So blinded by your own desires that you constructed a narrative, set up your father's best friend, and then had him burn. So you tell me: Who's the fool?"

Rhee felt suddenly hollow. Instead of blood and guts there was nothing inside except oxygen. Nero had lit a match and set her on fire from the inside out.

"At a loss for words, Princess? You? Ask me again—ask me

why I'm invading Wraeta." Nero's face lit up as he waited for her to respond. There was true happiness in the contours of his smile. But Rhee thought it was like watching skin peel away, exposing the rotten soul underneath.

Fine. She would play. "Why?"

"Because Wraeta has the overwriter."

Rhee would have laughed if she didn't know Nero was serious. The overwriter was another myth, a dangerous idea someone had claimed to invent at the last G-1K summit. A technology that could not only *read* a cube but *change* it, altering a person's memories and thoughts and feelings.

"You can't really believe the overwriter exists," Rhee scoffed, wishing she sounded more confident.

"I don't *believe* it does," Nero said. "I know it. Fame and adoration fall short. A face like this will age." Nero smiled again as he motioned to himself. "But power won't. Imagine being able to speak through any cube, to anyone at will, throughout the whole universe. Imagine being able to whisper to them, not through their ears but their minds . . ."

"You're sick." She shook her head. She felt numb. She didn't bother to ask why he thought the overwriter existed, or why he believed it was on Wraeta. He was obviously insane.

"And it seems you're cursed. Everyone you love dies." There were still glimpses of the man she thought she knew. The whole time he'd been plotting her death. It was beyond any kind of evil she could've imagined. She ached for her dagger. She imagined cleaving his heart into quarters, separating the arteries the way you might carve out the membranes in an orange.

"*You* killed them." Nero had taken everyone she loved away from her. Though Rhee remembered the Elder's words and felt a flicker of hope that her sister was still alive.

He shook his head. "That's not true. Not the Fontisian." He sighed. "I won't be the one to kill him. *You* will."

TWENTY-FOUR

ALYOSHA

ALY couldn't believe it. He was still unsteady on his feet—and Kara backed up, recoiling from her mom like she was diseased. Lydia had just told them she was responsible for all of this. When he tried to take Kara's arm, she yanked it away.

"You helped them Ravage those people?" she asked Lydia.

"I didn't know," her mom answered. "I was just a scientist. I was working on ways to speed up person-to-person transfers, to facilitate information flow. When I got invited to the G-1K summit I was thrilled. I never dreamed . . ." She trailed off. "Summits were just as much about philosophy as they were science. We were talking about existence and memory—and people came in with brilliant, crazy ideas. It's what made it so exciting. Dynamic. But when Diac Zofim claimed he'd found a way not just to extract memories but to change them . . . no one believed him at first."

"What are you saying?" Aly asked.

"Diac *invented* the overwriter before anyone knew it existed. But as soon as word got around, he ended up dead—and the tech disappeared. *That's* what Nero wants. He'll torture anyone with any answers until he finds it."

"That's why he's been Ravaging scientists who were invited to the G-1K," Kara whispered. "He's sorting through their memories, looking for clues about the overwriter."

Lydia nodded. "If they catch us we're worse than dead. We'd be *shells*. Every memory—every part of your mind that makes you *you*—ripped out, your humanity severed."

A part of Aly hadn't believed it was true until now. He looked over at Kara. "Those people on the zeppelin . . . You were right."

She nodded. Her face was stone-cold. "They'd had the procedure. All of them."

"Activists, scientists, prominent figures—they're disappearing, and being fed out into the world with no cube. There's no more time," Lydia said, edging closer. "Nero will put you up on that screen and make you say you murdered that little girl. And then he'll execute you to set an example."

Aly was *definitely* going to throw up.

Lydia took the device from Kara and held the projection of the prison layout, pointing out the safest route that had them evading any wandering Tasinn. "First right, sprint; third left, sprint; seventh left, normal pace . . ." She listed them as sequences of seven, and Aly barely thought as he took off, repeating the sequence in his head. It was the kind of distraction he needed, hustling on autopilot just like he'd done in boot camp. Follow orders, do them quick.

They sprinted some more, stop and go, kneeling, hiding, passing through more air locks, and figuring out which direction was up and which was down. And even though he'd gotten beat down by gravity, sore and bruised, falling every direction when they slipped between sections—he was getting into the groove, finding his feet again, and racing past both of them. Lydia was losing her breath, and at one point Aly and Kara had to put their arms together around her waist to hurry her along. She was limping. The last fall had been worse than it looked.

But they had weaved their way toward the south quadrant and were nearly there.

"Last door. Stay low," Lydia whispered as she touched the keypad and swiped them through.

"How did you get access?" Aly asked carefully.

"She hacked in," Kara said. He thought he'd noticed Lydia's face change, a flinch, almost—like an invisible insect had flown straight for her eyes. Vin had had that same look the day Aly left him behind on their ship.

They followed Lydia into a cold garage, fifty meters long maybe, all-terrain vehicles parked neatly in stalls. "There's the line of confiscated droids," she said pointing to the row along the wall. Aly found himself sprinting for them, calling Pavel's name—which was pointless since Pavel was powered down. Aly found him, eventually, compacted into his dome shape and hidden behind some boxier load-bearing models. He spun Pavel in a circle, looking for any external damage and feeling just like a little kid again, getting exactly what he wanted for his birthday. He thought about powering him up but was too scared;

they might've loaded him with some sort of tracking device or virus. They had to wait till they were somewhere safe so he could run the diagnostics and quash any added software. He squeezed Pavel, not caring if anyone was looking.

And that's when the alarm started to sound.

Everything flashed red. The noise was awful, like a crowbar cleaving open his brain, and he held P even tighter to his chest. Scrambling back, only the flashes of red to light his way, he got turned around and didn't know where he was. More important, he didn't know where Lydia and Kara were.

Then he heard the roar of a motor and was suddenly blinded by two headlights bearing down on him. An all-terrain rover skidded just past him to a stop, and reversed. The door popped open to show Kara leaning over the passenger seat.

"Get in!" she called over the screaming alarm. Of *course* she knew how to drive one of these things.

Aly hopped in, and when the door closed behind him he heard the air lock engage. He placed Pavel by his feet as Kara shifted gears, barreling two tons of metal death through the stalls of parked cars, zigzagging their way toward the exit. "Hang on!" she called behind her as she gunned it toward the garage door, a second layer of reinforced metal grates closing over the entrance. Red lights assaulted their eyes. They burst through both levels, the grates denting their roof. Once they'd cleared the exit, the rover bounced as it trod over the debris. It was dark, the sky scorched, the ground covered with millions of electromagnetic creatures that crawled and wormed over one another, crushed under their tread.

Lydia was slumped in the backseat, letting out shallow breaths. She'd lost her color; her skin looked gray. But they'd escaped. They'd done it.

"Thank you," Aly said, twisting in his seat to grab Lydia's hand. She did her best to squeeze his fingers, but it was as if all her strength had left her.

"You asked how?" she wheezed. "How I accessed all those doors? How I had the blueprints?"

"You said already." Kara looked at her mom through the rear-view mirror. "You hacked the system."

"*You* said that." Lydia licked her lips, but there was no water to give her. "I gave them what they wanted. Mind, body, cube— that trinity made this prison possible. Made it impregnable, or so they thought. But they created fail-safes, just in case."

"What are you saying, Mom?" Kara asked. Her voice was rising toward panic. Aly motioned for her to move over so he could drive, and she didn't argue. She crawled into the backseat with Lydia, and he slid over to grab the wheel.

The steering wheel vibrated in his hands, and he could feel how hard the car resisted the pressure of gravity bearing down on them. He did a two-step with the clutch and gas before he down-shifted. In the rearview he could see Kara slip her arm under her mom's head.

"He knows," Lydia said, locking eyes with Aly in the rear-view. "Don't you, Aly?"

"What is she talking about?" Kara demanded.

"Your mom wasn't a prisoner," Aly said, after a moment's hesitation. "She was a warden. Right?"

Lydia's eyes flickered, even as Kara shook her head.

"No," she said. "That's impossible. That's impossible. Right, Mom?"

Lydia didn't answer directly. "The Uniforce, they put something in me. A poison, right here, behind my heart." She brought her hand to her chest. "Once my coordinates get too far from the prison, it'll trigger. The whole thing will burst . . ."

"No."

"I haven't seen your real eye color in years, not since we first met." Lydia smiled, and brought her hand up to Kara's cheek. Aly felt a pulse of shock. So he hadn't been hallucinating earlier. Her eyes really were changing colors. "You stopped taking your meds?"

"Mom, don't worry about that right now. I had to lower my dosage because I was running out." Kara was clinging to Lydia, choking on sobs. "Please. What's going on? We'll slow down. We'll hide until we can figure out how to remove the poison . . . Aly, stop. *Stop.*"

But Lydia shook her head. "Don't, Alyosha. You both have to get far from here. You owe me. I risked everything so that you could escape. Do it!" she said hoarsely, and Aly kept his foot on the gas, wishing he could block out the sound of Kara weeping. He knew the feeling, pleading for more time, trying to reverse it, trying to make a different ending.

"It's too late, anyway. It was too late the moment we left the prison." Lydia coughed, and black liquid welled to her lips. For a long time, she said nothing, and Aly thought it was over, though he could still hear the wheezing of her breath whenever she exhaled. Kara was still crying, not even bothering to try to hide it. But finally, Lydia took a deep, rattling breath.

"You're not sick, Kara," she said. "Ancestors forgive me. There's nothing wrong with you."

"What do you mean?" Kara's voice wavered. Now her eyes were more than half green. What the hell? He'd never seen anything like it. Back in the Wray, some of the ladies used to take bleaching pills to lighten their skin and their eyes, but it always turned out blotchy and made everyone gossip. But this—this was different.

"Those nightmares you have? They're memories." Lydia was consumed by another coughing fit. Kara used her shirt to wipe away the blood.

"Memories? Whose memories?" Kara asked. "What are you talking about?"

"Yours. Before the accident. The overwriter—I was the one who invented it. I was the one who hid it, on Wraeta, not far from my first laboratory." Aly sucked in a breath as Lydia wheezed, struggling to continue. "Diac Zofim was my partner. We developed it together, but he ended up dead, and I had to hide it. I used it only once . . . on you. The medication helped keep the new memories from doing harm. It helped change your facial features, too, and your eye color . . ."

It all feels made up. Like I made it up, Kara had told him.

Lydia was slipping away. "But your blood—it's the key to everything." She fumbled for the coin Kara had shown Aly on the zeppelin, the one Kara had kept stashed in her pocket. "This binds you to your family. There's history in this coin . . ."

"What family? *You're* my family. You have to stay with me."

291

Kara was crying so hard, Aly could hear her gasping for breath between sobs. He felt his own heart breaking. He wanted to grab the both of them and sprint to safety, erase everything bad that had happened. "Please, Mom. I can't do this without you."

"You *can*," she said, even as she started to choke. "You *have* to. In Nau Fruma, the Lancer will—"

Suddenly Kara was screaming, as more and more blood bubbled out of Lydia's mouth.

"Clear her throat," Aly yelled, narrowly swerving to avoid a metal roadblock. "Clear her throat." He slammed the rover into park and lunged into the crowded backseat. Kara scooted aside to make room as they laid Lydia flat, working on getting her windpipe clear, telling her to hold on, to keep going, that it was going to be all right. They worked long after Aly knew there was nothing more they could do for her, and when finally, exhausted and shaking, he felt Kara's hand on his shoulder, he stopped. Lydia was gone.

Kara scooted back into the seat and eased her mom's head into her lap. "So she's comfortable when she wakes up," Kara said, her eyes now a vivid green, luminous and terrible, splintered with faint pieces of black.

"Yeah, of course," he said.

Kara ran her fingers through Lydia's hair and leaned her head against the window, crying quietly. Aly drove north, and tried not to look in the rearview mirror.

TWENTY-FIVE

RHIANNON

WITH a wave of Nero's hand, Dahlen was wheeled out, strapped to a rolling gurney. An NX pushed him into the center of the white-tiled pit and took a step back. Rhee felt raw and exposed. She urged her breath to slow. *Honor, bravery, loyalty* as she inhaled and exhaled, on the count of three, spacing them out so as not to feel faint. This was her fault. For all her talk of *ma'tan sarili*, she had abandoned Dahlen.

She was a fraud.

"What have you done to him?" Even from here, Rhee could see Dahlen's eyes were dilated. He took in the lights with a dazed expression that looked eerie on the boy she'd come to know. He was always so aware of every detail of his surroundings.

"We've prepped him." Nero walked over to Dahlen and picked up his limp hand, prying the Fontisian's index finger free so he could press it to Dahlen's cube. Dahlen's body stiffened, just barely, and Rhee knew it was from the jolt of electricity traveling to his brain as his cube was turned back on. He'd been offline for years. Nero had made him break his vow.

Nero pressed a panel on the wall, and a large holoscreen projected above them. It began to illuminate, and something took shape—an island against a dark sea. But as it started to sharpen and focus, Rhee understood.

"Get out of his head!"

Dahlen merely squinted up at it.

"Oh, we're not in his head yet. This is only the diagnostic makeup. Think of it like one of those paintings your mother loved to collect. It has an artist quality, doesn't it?" Nero said. "But we can scratch off the paint, unpeel the layers . . ."

"Leave him alone!" Rhee backed up and brought her knee up high, kicking down on the glass. It wobbled under the impact and immediately repaired itself.

Projected up on the light box were the peaks and valleys of Dahlen's brain. So many colors. The form of it was outlined in neon pink; jagged, yellow streaks looked like bolts of lightning scattered about. There were large swaths of green and blue, and they swirled into each other like a lush ocean. She wanted to tear it down so that no one would see.

"Let's access his playback, shall we?" An ornate metal crown, three feet tall and torturous looking, lowered from the center of the room.

Rhee looked at Nero. "What? No—" *There are things locked away in his mind.* "You want to . . . to *Ravage* him?"

He rolled his eyes as he circled Dahlen's body slowly. "Don't you want to know what specter haunted his childhood? What horrors produced the boy he is today?"

Rhee thought of the casual breathlessness with which Dahlen had killed. How he'd belittled her for mourning Veyron; cut away that Miseu's cube without so much as blinking; electrocuted Seotra, who moaned in agony until he turned to ash. Dahlen was psychotic, emotionless, cruel—Rhee had been certain at times. But his dedication, his loyalty—that was part of him too. And who was she, of all people, to judge his bloodlust?

Rhee shook her head. A small *no* was all she could manage to say.

"Then what of *that* memory?" Nero continued. "The one buried way deep down in this soup of consciousness—the one of your family? Maybe you can finally know the truth of how they died."

"You can't," she choked out. And yet, she *did* want to know. She'd obsessed over her family's deaths; she'd thought about their deaths even more than she had their lives. She had imagined the moment of impact, the fiery explosion, a thousand different ways. Filling in the gaps—however gruesome the details—had been like drinking salt water to quench a thirst.

If she could *see*, then she could *know*. She could stop obsessing. She could let it go.

"Or even," he continued, "where your sister is." He feigned surprise at the look on her face. "You hoped I hadn't known?"

She froze. He was one step ahead. He'd always been.

There are things he knows, and things he doesn't know that he knows, the Elder had said of Dahlen.

"Say the word, Princess. We can download his cube into yours. All his memories, his feelings, his knowledge—yours to experience. Even the moments he himself can't remember."

"What would—what would happen to him?" she asked. Rhee could hear the uncertainty in her own voice. Her *ma'tan sarili* corroding, just like her resolve. She was weak. She'd always been too weak.

"Does it matter?" he asked. "Agree to join me. Relinquish the throne and hand power over to your council, to *me*, and I'll let you live. You will be my top adviser. You never had what it takes to be empress. You were never meant to be empress, after all."

She opened her mouth to speak, but nothing came out.

"There's no shame, Rhiannon. Not all of us were meant to rule. Join me. I'll help you find your sister, and I'll let her live as well."

Rhee couldn't help the desire she felt, like all her atoms were rearranging at this moment, making room for the new knowledge she wanted so badly. For a way to find her sister, finally, after all these years. But at what cost? To make Dahlen a shell? To Ravage him, to reach in and steal his soul and wring it dry? It made her nauseated, then angry.

Honor. Loyalty. Bravery.

She wasn't capable of what Nero was asking. Killing was one thing. She couldn't ask someone to live after she'd taken away the very thing that made him human. The ancestors were watching, and perhaps Vodhan was too.

"No."

"You stupid girl! You'd die for a *Vodhead*?" Finally, Nero lost his temper. Spit gathered in the corners of his mouth. All his earlier composure had drained away, and what bubbled up in its place was his rage, his hatred, his petty ambitions. "I'd be doing your people a favor by killing you. A bleeding heart could not serve the throne. It certainly didn't serve your father."

"Don't speak about my father," Rhee said. She wanted to rip his tongue out of his mouth. "My father died with honor."

"How quaint." Nero grabbed the largest scalpel from the table next to him. The droids in the auditorium marched toward her, one coming in from either side. "I'll make sure you follow in his footsteps."

Rhee kicked at the glass once more as Nero moved slowly, methodically, lifting the scalpel to Dahlen's neck. Rhee saw the gleam of the razor-sharp edge from where she stood. It mocked her. She rammed the barrier with her right shoulder and felt the pain bloom in her joint.

Rhee heard it before she looked up—the crunch of metal, the hiss of air. Four prongs, each the size of her forearm, pierced through the ceiling of the auditorium. And then the walls clamped toward the center, closing like a fist. Something unbearable invaded her chest. The oxygen was vacuumed out, replaced by the poisonous compounds outside, filling up her lungs and lining her insides. Her face bloating, her body growing hot, strands of her hair burning away. The sound of an alarm, and red flashing lights . . .

The metal fist pulled, and the whole ceiling ripped away to reveal a gaping hole. The sound was swallowed up into a roaring, scorched black sky.

The droids that had run toward Rhee flew away mid-step,

their legs still pumping as they were sucked into the darkness and swatted toward the ground in the heavy gravity. She, too, was lifted into the air.

And the split second before her death, she saw Death.

Death was blue. Death was familiar . . .

It was the Fisherman she'd paid with Julian's telescope, the one who'd marked her. She couldn't understand what he was doing there, but it didn't matter. There was no time to think. He was fitted with a jetpack, a harpoon gun tucked under his arm. He bent backward, reeling in the giant slab of alloy wall as you would a giant fish. In his other hand, he held a short-barreled gun that he aimed straight at Rhee.

She hurtled toward him, forcing her eyelids to stay open despite the swelling. If she'd die, it would be with her eyes open. The Fisherman fired once. Twice.

Some sort of slime hit her square in the face. It hardened instantaneously into a soft plastic, and underneath the strange mask, suddenly she could breathe. The jellylike substance thinned out and spread all around her body, protecting her from the elements. She looked over and saw that the second shot had been aimed at Dahlen, and the same strange plastic encompassed him, too, gurney and all. Rhee nearly melted with relief.

The bully, the madman, and the empress—together once more.

Their protective shells thinned out into a ropelike plastic, tethering them to the Fisherman's belt. Through the cloudy plastic, Rhee could see little pockets of air bubbling up and circulating within the substance—all of it funneling toward her nostrils and mouth. It felt heavy on her eyelids, but she kept them open and managed to turn, somehow. The medical section of the prison had unspooled behind them. Debris was scattered across the metal ground, half-buried deep into the electromagnetic soil, so that it all looked like an organism that had withered on a vine. She searched for Nero, or the scarred man, but she could not see them.

Then the Fisherman fired up his jetpack and they thrust upward at launch speed, so that everything became a blur. Rhee and Dahlen sped behind him, tethered in their plastic cocoons.

TWENTY-SIX

ALYOSHA

ALY'S feet dangled out of the open tailgate. He turned his face up to the sun and thought of his ma, nagging him to cover up and get in the shade with her and Alina. "You'll get even darker," she'd say, like it was some sort of threat. Now Aly rolled up his sleeves so the sun could touch every last bit of skin.

Maybe he'd get darker. So what?

It was like the sun's warmth fueled him, activated his insides and made him even more pissed off. The whole goddamned thing was rigged, and everyone was losing. But at least there was something he could do about it, finally.

At least he could help Kara.

She was taking forever, and the only way Aly could measure how much time had passed was by the layer of grit that formed on his arms. In the weak gravity, the moondust floated up in a haze and landed lazily wherever it felt like. Wild, how much Nau

Fruma reminded him of Wraeta. It was the same kind of heat that made everything lag, even your brain. The kind of sunlight that made you squint or shade your eyes with the palm of your hand.

They'd come to Nau Fruma to find the Lancer, whoever that was, as Lydia had instructed them to do. Kara'd gotten them to this moon—talking her way into a trading post on Houl, bartering some simple repair work Aly did on a droid for their passage onto a freighter, scraping together spare credits to buy them clothes. All those languages she knew had helped them a lot.

It'd been less than a week since they'd escaped the prison on Houl, and since they'd buried Lydia's body. Kara had said she should've been cremated, it's what she would've wanted—but beyond that she didn't want to talk about it. Maybe she was processing it on her own? What could you say to someone who'd had her whole history overwritten? He felt like a *choirtoi*, the way he'd run around wanting to forget his past. Yeah, there were things that hurt to remember.

But his past was everything that made him *him*.

Kara didn't know who she was.

"Does this work?" Kara asked. He turned around to see her messing with a purple scarf around her head. When all her hair was tucked away, it brought out the shape of her face, like a heart. There were freckles across her cheeks he'd never noticed on her tan skin. He tried to memorize her, tried to soak in every detail, as if he could absorb the truth of her, of this moment, through the heat between them. "Do I blend in?"

What she didn't get was that she would never blend in. Not really. Plus she was wearing the *duhatj* too far back.

"Not exactly," Aly said. He stood up and brushed himself off. "You gotta kind of . . ."

He reached behind Kara to unravel the scarf, and her messy black hair fell everywhere. It smelled good—just a little bit sweet—and he brushed it out of her eyes for no good reason.

"Your eyes are still changing color," he said. Her right one had specks of green and yellow in it, like the first days of spring. And her left one was brown and deep and perfect for exactly those reasons. Aly cupped her face and she grabbed his arm; he thought she'd pull it away, but her hand stayed there, soft and warm.

"You don't have to help me," Kara said.

"I want to help," Aly said, taking in her face, the slight pout of her lip. His cube wasn't on. He'd have to remember every detail. It felt more important, precious somehow, knowing that once the moment passed it would be gone forever. "I'm not going anywhere, Kara."

She squeezed his arm, just a little. But a little was all he needed.

He ran his hand up the back of her head and felt her thick hair tangle in his fingers. She ran her palm up his chest, then grabbed a handful of his thin cotton shirt and pulled him in. Closing the distance between them was fast and slow at once, a desperate sprint to the finish line, where there was everything he'd ever wanted. Then, finally, his mouth was on hers—her lips soft and yielding and opening, a tiny gasp, a hot breath. The warmth of them finding each other in that dark spot, in that very center of their souls, was so perfect he thought he might lose his mind.

Aly wrapped his arms around Kara and felt the small of her back, right there where it dipped—and when she wrapped her arms around *him* he pressed his mouth in harder. She met him, and pushed back, and it felt like the only battle worth fighting. It didn't matter if he won or lost; he just hoped it would never end.

This was home, with Kara, with the girl who'd always believed he was innocent.

TWENTY-SEVEN

RHIANNON

ON board Dahlen's ship, they floated. Here on the outer edges of the Desuco Quadrant, massive rocks were adrift in the darkness, like giants curled up in a long slumber. The Fisherman often made catches here. Perfect conditions for the octoerces' feeding ground, Rhee had been told. And a perfect place for them to hide.

She pulled out Julian's telescope and sought out the octoerces in the darkness. There was enough radiant heat coming off the rocks to keep the temperatures warm, but there was no air, no atmosphere—and still somehow the creatures lived.

Before, she saw herself in them. Rhee, too, was resilient. She'd survive.

But now she thought differently. The octoerces were merely trying to feed. Swept up in the gravitational pull of any nearby bodies, their life was one of constant movement, from one food source to the next. Survival, it turned out, wasn't the same as living.

Dahlen balanced Rhee's coin across his knuckles, moving it back and forth between his pinky and index finger. It was the souvenir her dad had given her, the very coin that she'd snuck off the craft for—the one that saved her life. Rhee thought she'd lost it in the move to Nau Fruma, but Tai Reyanna had it this whole time. She'd planned to give it to Rhee on the day of her coronation.

"Focus," her Tai whispered as she snatched the coin from Dahlen's hand and shoved it into Rhee's palm. She'd made it clear—it annoyed her to no end that Dahlen was allowed to handle it as he did. The Fisherman shifted in irritation, passive-aggressively huffing in hopes they'd both be quiet. Despite his temperament, Rhee was thankful he was there.

After Rhee and Dahlen had rushed off Tinoppa in the wake of Seotra's death, it was Tai Reyanna who'd found the Fisherman. She'd reached out to a network of what she called "unsavory characters," seeking out the person capable of creating the mark on Rhee's face. Enough bribes had led her to the Fisherman, and a small fortune commissioned him for a new job: a jailbreak. Though Dahlen suspected, after all, that the Fisherman did have political leanings, and that perhaps he was a loyalist.

This was Rhee's trusted crew. She looked down at the coin in her hand. She didn't believe in lucky charms, but she hoped it would save her life once more.

"As I was saying," Tai Reyanna said, spinning back to face the holoprojection. They'd pieced together rumors from the Tais, known locations of safe houses from Dahlen's contacts, strange gravitational disturbances according to the Fisherman's research, and finally profiles on the people Nero had targeted for his horrific scheme to Ravage the scientists. Rhee knew there were answers and patterns, and that they would emerge, given time.

If they had the time. Nero's droids were equipped with a soft plastic similar to the Fisherman's. The droids had saved him, and Rhee thought bitterly that it was true—he always had a plan. His war effort had become even more aggressive. Attacks and retaliations had razed parts of both Kalu and Fontis, and deep-space combat was playing out between the two armadas just outside of Wraeta. Nero was angling to build an army, to make anyone with a cube his slave.

Tai Reyanna touched the holoscreen to enlarge a map of the universe. "I think we should follow the lead that puts Princess Josselyn on Derkatz," she said, zooming in. "An allied Fontisian territory, too far out for Kalu to attack directly."

"How many times have I told you?" the Fisherman insisted. With a flick of his hand he shifted the map to the other edge of the universe and zoomed in to nothing. "She's in hypersleep, stored in a black hole here."

"The intel isn't dependable either way," Dahlen said quickly. They'd been arguing for days. "What would you have us do, Princess?"

He turned to look at her with those cool gray eyes. He'd killed Seotra, for reasons that seemed perfectly justified and perfectly honorable to him. Rhee still mourned the former regent's loss, and all the opportunities she'd squandered to learn about her family and the political machinations pushing her father off his own planet. There was a part of her that could never forgive Dahlen, though he hadn't sought her forgiveness. And likewise, she'd never apologized for abandoning him in Navrum. The two of them were the same, relentlessly chasing down their vengeance. It was an understanding Rhee had with no one else.

And like her, Dahlen wished to be his highest self. But Rhee strove for honor because her ancestors looked on—whereas Dahlen did so because Vodhan saw his every move, knew of every intention in his heart, so he claimed. Which is why she wouldn't ask Dahlen to break his vow and turn on his cube, no matter how desperate she was to know what memories were hidden deep in the folds of his brain.

Say you're sorry. Rhee thought painfully of Joss, and how her mother had demanded they sit forehead to forehead and look one another in the eye until one of them was willing to apologize. And it was always Joss. It was never worth it to her to hold a grudge.

Say you're sorry.

"I'd have us reprioritize," Rhee said instead. The Fisherman and Tai Reyanna looked at her.

"What's that now? Reprioritize?" the Fisherman asked.

Rhee was scared. Scared she'd lose her sister forever, if she hadn't already. Scared what everyone would think of her, and what she'd think of herself. But there were choices to make.

As empress you must be fair, but decisive, her father had said. Not to her, but to Josselyn.

But Princess Josselyn was lost, and it could take weeks or months or years to find her. And the galaxy needed her now.

Dahlen nodded, very slightly.

"I have to come forward and take the throne," she said. *Get up*, she heard Josselyn say, an echo from all those years ago. *Get up*. "I'll find Josselyn. But first I have to stop the war."

EPILOGUE

KARA

IT was market day on Nau Fruma, but there were twice as many vendors as there were patrons. Kara scanned the monochromatic landscape of browns as far as the eye could see, wondering if they'd come to the right place. It didn't seem like a hotbed of secrets and intrigue.

"I imagined it differently," she admitted. But it was only a small town with a modest palace that looked more like a large house on a hill. Surrounding them were flat desert plains, and in the distance a sunken volcano crater. Crown's Rock, she thought it was called. Had she seen that on the holos once?

"I guess I thought it would be a little more lively, too," Aly said, wiping the sweat off his forehead just under the *duhatj*. He streaked pale dust across his brow like war paint.

They walked side by side. Kara could still feel the heat of his lips—how he'd cupped the back of her head and pulled her in, how the rest of her body followed and she'd felt the muscles of his chest against her own. They didn't hold hands. It felt too weird. But when his arm brushed hers, it was like electricity shooting up her skin. Pavel wheeled a few steps behind them like some old-timey chaperone.

"The region has been economically depressed for some time, as it has no major exports to speak of," the droid said. His tire treads left a trail in the dust behind him. "Rhodium mines were tapped several decades ago. The area was sustained mainly on tourism when Princess Rhiannon resided here, but in the last few weeks, the region has seen an all-time low."

"Well, at least people are minding their own business," Aly pointed out. "Not a bad place for some criminals on the run and a smart-ass droid," he added quietly.

Why here? Kara wanted to ask her mom. In fact, there were a lot of things she wanted to ask. *Who am I? Where do I come from? Why did you lie to me?*

But there was no time for dwelling on her past. She needed to focus and find the Lancer, whoever he was. Find out about this other family and about the nightmares.

Part of her was sure they couldn't be real. Especially the one that had always come back to her—whipping through the air wildly, clawing at nothing and afraid the rushing wind would tear off every limb. It wasn't real. Even if the *whoosh* in her ears and the scream caught in her throat felt like a memory, it couldn't have been real.

Whenever it started to feel like too much she remembered what Aly had said. *I'm not going anywhere.*

The most crowded part of the market was near the center, where dozens of people had gathered before a shrine to Princess Rhiannon. They'd left drawings of her and wrote letters—all on real paper. Flowers, berries, painted rocks, and knitted dolls too. Even sticky candies that had melted in the heat were scattered among the things.

"How's she going to eat those candies if she's dead?" a little boy asked his mom.

Kara looked away, her head foggy—like a migraine was coming on.

"You two want a tour?" a kid asked them. He looked a couple of years younger than her, and two oversized teeth crowded the front of his mouth. He led them from the market aisle and brought them around the back end of a row of tents. "A thousand credits each and I'll take you to see the Ta'an palace up by—"

He didn't finish his sentence.

Another boy lunged out of nowhere and tackled him to the ground. He rolled on top and got off a few punches as the first boy blocked his face and wailed. Dust rose up and surrounded them like a cloud.

"Hey!" Kara stomped in between them and pulled the second boy off. He had blue eyes and sandy hair. He flailed some more and even tried to throw a jab in her direction, but as soon as he got a look at Kara, he stopped and wiggled out of her grip.

"Take it easy," Aly said from the sidelines. "You did the job. He's down and he's bleeding."

The first boy, with the badger teeth, pushed himself up and ran. "Screw you, Julian," he called over his shoulder.

"Are you okay?" Kara asked.

He looked up at her for so long, Kara wondered if they knew each other. "The palace has been looted," he said, a quickness to his words. The Nau Fruman accent seemed familiar to her, like a song she knew the lyrics to once. "There's nothing left to see."

"Lancer!" a woman called in the distance. The boy briefly glanced behind him but didn't make a move to leave. He had the palest blue eyes Kara had ever seen.

"Lancer?" Kara asked. The mention of the name sent her pulse racing.

"Cool name," Aly said to the kid. His voice was casual, but Kara had felt him stiffen.

"It's all right. They named me after my dad. I used to hate it, but—" The kid stopped himself. *He's named after his dad.* "Anyway, I don't go by that name anymore."

Kara's head started to pound, a beat like a war drum. Suddenly she wanted to break this kid open and spread out all of his secrets. This was why her mom sent her here—to find this boy's father. It was uncanny. She believed in fate. She would pray to any and all ancestors, whoever they were. "Does he work far away?" Kara asked.

"He died," the kid answered. Kara thought to say sorry, but she didn't know if that would make it worse. "He was on the *Eliedio*."

The *Eliedio*. It was Princess Rhiannon's ship. Kara met Aly's eye, speechless. Not knowing what to say, she tried the truth. "I know how that feels. I lost my mom," she said. The boy wouldn't meet her eyes, but Kara knew he was listening. "It sucks. It sucks that she won't be there whenever I wake up from a nightmare. Or that I'll never hear her laugh again. And that she'll never, ever tell me what to do—even though I hated it when she told me what to do."

She could feel Aly's eyes on her, but there was no one else in the world apart from her and this other boy. His floppy hair and his sad blue eyes that finally—*finally*—looked back up at her. He wasn't much younger.

"And on top of her being gone, it's like I'm not allowed to be mad at her." Kara wanted to scream and cry, and she wanted to die sometimes too. She went on, this confession pouring out of her to a teenage kid who'd lost his hero, too, maybe. "But you keep it all bottled up, not for yourself, really, but so no one else has to deal with it. Until you get to fight someone. I bet it feels good for a second. But then that pain comes back bigger, sharper, like it's edging out all your organs."

The boy shoved his hands in his pockets, and looked even younger then. "Do I know you?" he asked.

"Maybe?" Kara said, genuinely wondering; they were connected somehow. "I feel like we might. We could. But let me ask you something . . ." She pulled her coin from her pocket. "Do you recognize this coin? Maybe your dad had one like it?"

The boy's mouth puckered. He glared at the coin—then at Kara. "What's your game?" he asked. "Is this some knockoff?"

"Knockoff?" Aly asked. "Hold up, do you recognize this thing?"

But the boy didn't answer. He just lunged for the coin, and Aly had to grab his bony body and swat him down onto the ground. He held him there as the boy thrashed, like he was possessed. But he had nothing on Aly's arm span. "You stole that from the Princess!" He spit out the word *Princess*.

"I didn't," Kara said. "I swear. My mom gave it to me." Of all the people in the world she didn't want to disappoint, it was this boy. They'd understood each other. Hadn't they?

"It's Rhee's!" he yelled. "It was made for her. One for her and one for her sister!"

One for her sister.

"Ancestors." Kara stumbled backward. Thudding in her skull. Was that the sound of her feet pounding, or the pulse of her headache? She was twirling and running, kicking up moondust.

A dream or a memory? She didn't know . . .

"Kara. We gotta go. What am I supposed to do?" Aly asked, but his voice was far away. So was the kid's.

She knew why she'd been sent here. Why everything felt so familiar.

Kara looked up to the palace. She remembered the two little girls, thick black braids down their backs. Playing tag. Laughing and yelling, the younger girl trying to outrun the older one.

The pain in her head crescendoed, and just when Kara thought she'd pass out, it broke like a fever. There was a cool, calm clarity that she hadn't felt in years. She blinked.

"What's happening to you?" Aly's voice said. "Kara, you're scaring me. I don't know what to do . . ."

She clutched the coin in her hand.

The girls were the princesses. This was their vacation home. They were sisters.

And the older one? Josselyn Karatana Ta'an. That was *her*.

ACKNOWLEDGMENTS

TIFFANY Liao, the most exceptional editor, who held my hand and/or called me out at every step along the way; I need you always. Jess Harriton, you godsend, for the smartest margin comments a girl could ask for. Ben Schrank, for taking a chance—thank you. Razorbill, you're incredible. Aurora Parlagreco for a cover beyond my wildest dreams. Thank you to Amanda Mustafic and all the amazing people on the Penguin sales, marketing, and publicity teams who worked on this book.

Lauren Oliver, for your expertise and tough love. Thank you for finding the story when I couldn't. Kamilla Benko and Alexa Wejko, my respective fantasy and sci-fi queens, I don't know how I lived a day before meeting you. Tara Sonin, for helping me remember the pure sweetness of fandom. Adam Silvera, who tirelessly advocates for me and so many others. Angela Velez, for your insight and fierce expectations. And to the rest of the Inkwell and Paper Lantern Lit teams: Stephen Barbara, Lexa Hillyer, and Diana Sousa, you are everything.

Beth Revis, Kiersten White, Kami Garcia—your support is immense. Thanks for your time and love.

My Macmillan family—Erin Stein, Nicole Otto, Natalie Sousa, Ellen Duda, and Ashley Woodfolk—for letting me read, edit, and chat endlessly about great books.

Dr. Christopher Gutiérrez, for your incomprehensible scientific genius. Kristina Pérez, for your incredibly dexterous mind. Pam Gruber and Mike Braff: your kind words saved me in the darkest of times while writing my umpteenth draft. Luis Martínez, you knew I had a book in me long before I did. To my honorary sister Marie Martínez, for your early read and your honest thoughts. And to Alana, for your boundless heart.

To my Ate, obviously. Jasy, for being the best person I know. Kuya, whose initial love of sci-fi sparked my own. Ellie, for being so open and kind and constantly amused. Juan and Julian, for making me laugh and bringing my sister so much joy. The boys, Mason and Logan, for your sense of humor and your strong sense of self. Dad, for your infinite patience as I crash landed through life—I love you. Mom, whose soul is spread across these thousand skies—I know you're giving me the side eye because this book is weird and maybe doesn't make sense. I miss you.

And finally to Kyle and your big, beautiful brain—this book wouldn't exist without you.

Honor. Bravery. Loyalty.

The three pillars of the Ta'an Dynasty will be tested in the
exhilarating sequel to *Empress of a Thousand Skies*.

Turn the page for a sneak peek at

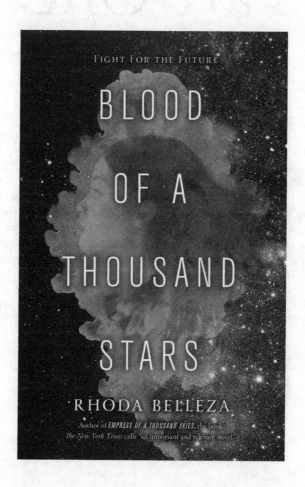

Coming February 2018.

Part One:

THE RETURNED

"An organic memory is an act of creation, of *re*-creation in fact—
and by definition an imperfect copy, corrupted by emotion and
an overload of sensory details. A memory recalled via the cube,
however, is the exact memory perfectly preserved. It's argued such
recollections are less visceral, or that something essential is lost. But
it seems little cost for the truth in returning to the same moment,
countless times, unchanged."

—G1-K Summit Appeal to the United Planets, the year 858

ONE

KARA

IF Kara was hot up here, it must've been hell down in the packed square. All of Nau Fruma was on a labor strike, and from her vantage point, the protesters looked like a single living organism—angry, undulating. For a historically neutral moon, Nau Fruma was not exactly peaceful these days.

Sweat stung Kara's eyes as she scanned the crowd below. She wiped it away with the back of her hand, smearing the moondust that had settled on her skin.

"Test," she said to Pavel, the small droid who sat beside her. The heat made everything shimmer in the distance. "Six o'clock."

A bright white light flashed across the terra-cotta brick building directly behind them. It was gone in a split second. Kara scratched at the surface of the rusty coin, the one she'd carried around always. It hadn't been anything more than a good-luck charm until Lydia told her otherwise.

This binds you to your family. There's history in this coin, she'd said with her dying breath.

Kara blinked away the memory. "Again, Pavel: nine o'clock."

Pavel swiveled west and used a small mirror attachment to reflect the sunlight.

"Again: two o'clock—"

"All right, all right, take it easy," Aly said as he climbed up the wire ladder that led to the roof. "You're more intense than half the souls I came up with in basic." He crouched down next to Kara, half hidden by the ledge.

"Just trying to prep," she said, pocketing the coin. He had no idea how militant Lydia had been. The woman Kara had thought was her mother had a consummate work ethic. Language testing. Survival training. Ways to smuggle credits, and how to get a good read on a person. Kara had thought it was absurd and paranoid, which showed how much she knew. It had paid off, in a way. Kara had survived, even if Lydia hadn't.

"You keep 'prepping' and someone down there might notice our little operation."

"They're too busy watching the picket line."

It had been two days since Kara and Aly had gotten to Nau Fruma, and just one day since Empress Rhiannon Ta'an had come forward to announce she was alive. Since Nau Fruma was a moon of Kalu, news of her return home was all over the holos. Kara would have been relieved about her sister's safe return, but the holos were also buzzing with the newest speculation: where Josselyn Ta'an was. Rhiannon's older sister.

If anyone in the universe knew the answer to that question, it was Kara.

Because Kara *was* Josselyn. Or she had been once, even if she didn't remember.

After informing the galaxy that she was alive, Rhee had outed Kara, offering a reward for her safe return.

Actually, she had offered a reward for *Josselyn*, the missing royal sister and rightful empress, the one whom everyone believed had died all those years ago in a spacecraft explosion, along with the rest of the Ta'an family.

Maybe Kara should've been moved by the gesture. She didn't have a single memory before the age of twelve. Lydia had told her it was a cube malfunction; Kara had believed it all those years, and filled in the big white blank space of her mind with made-up scenarios. And she'd gotten so good at it that soon, she was spinning entire tales, fabricating alternate lives on the spot while kids at parties nodded their heads, wide-eyed and amazed.

Underneath all the lies she'd told, the lies she'd *been* told, she had a true family and a real home—but what did blood really matter? Rhiannon was a stranger in every other sense of the word, and seeing her on the holos brought on a slew of feelings about a lot of people. Most of them dead and gone. Lydia, the scientist who had harbored her. Her *actual* parents, the late Emperor and Empress of Kalu, whom she hardly remembered. And Rhiannon, the girl who'd come back from the dead, who was in the process of assuming her crown . . . while Kara crouched on a hot roof hiding for her life.

Aly unscrewed a canteen and took a big gulp, his head tipped back, his mouth parted. Kara turned away and tried to focus. She squinted at the doorway across the way. Her bangs fell into her face, and she pawed at them, annoyed.

"These will help," Aly said. From his messenger bag he pulled out a bulky hunk of black metal that looked like two cups attached side by side. "They're called binoculars. Vintage military gear. They magnify your vision."

Apparently you could find anything on the black market. She took the binoculars and put them to her eyes. They were heavier than they looked, and everything came out blurry and small. "They don't work."

"You have them upside-down," he said, shaking his head and grinning in that way that made her forget her life was on fire.

"I knew that," she lied. She put the device to her face but immediately regretted it. The view was disorienting, claustrophobic, too narrow. She could only see a small cluster of people at a time. She ripped it away from her face and nearly dropped it.

"Whoa," Aly said, grabbing it from her hand. "Everything okay?"

She shook her head. "I feel kind of dizzy." She realized she had a headache, a light pulsing behind her eye. It wasn't the binoculars. The meds Lydia had given her were running low. Kara had been taking them for years; Lydia told her the pills were to help manage the severe headaches and nightmares from her cube malfunction. And even if they treated her symptoms just fine, Kara had discovered that the cause was a lie.

The pills did help with the headaches, but they were DNA suppressors too, meant to skew Josselyn's features—Lydia's own biological design, if Kara had to guess. For the last couple of weeks she'd been weaning herself off by taking half doses, then quarter doses, to fractions of a pill every other day. This morning she'd broken a pill apart without a knife, and most of it crumbled to dust.

Kara had almost cried. Not that she could tell you why. There was something about the end of one simple routine that tethered you to your past. Even if it was a lie.

"You take it," Kara said, handing the binoculars back. "Narrate for me."

"Well, you're not missing much," he said, staring into the binoculars. "Just a bunch of pissed-off Nauies." He rubbed the back of his neck like he always did when he was thinking. His shirt lifted up to reveal a strip of dark skin, his belly button a tiny outie, dimples on the inside of either hip.

"Are you well, Kara? I detect a sudden but minor change in your skin color." Pavel's eyelights went red. "The medical bible says this is a common physiological reaction to emotional stressors. Blood vessels open wide, flooding the skin with blood and reddening the face."

"It's called blushing," Aly said. He'd dropped the binoculars; the corners of his mouth had turned up just slightly.

"You're a rat." Kara nudged Pavel with the tip of her boot so that he rolled back with the force. She felt herself flushing more. "I'll open up that head of yours and rearrange all the inside bits," she threatened.

"Better watch out, little man."

"This is humor, correct?" Pavel's eyelights had gone red. "Because theoretically we're not too far off. There's new research to suggest that cube-to-cube transfers could be enhanced. Nearby neural pathways can give and receive the info without even being prepped, without even—"

Aly dropped the hand with the binoculars. "All right, P," he said, all the playfulness drained from his voice. "Chill out. She was just kidding."

"Have him try me," Kara tried to joke, but the mood had already shifted. Aly knew she didn't like talking about their cubes. The mere mention put her on edge, reminded her they had all turned theirs off in case Nero was trying to track them right now.

Aly closed the gap between them and slid his palm into hers. She tried to ignore the way it lit her skin on fire. "You okay?" he asked.

"I'm fine," she said, slipping her hand out of his grasp.

Aly gave her that look he made when he was trying to get a read on her—the slight pout in his full lips, his brown eyes opened wide so his thick lashes fanned out. He had a cut across his left eyebrow, the same spot where he'd nicked it when he was younger—but this time around, it had been the kid, Julian, who'd done it to Aly.

Julian hadn't exactly been thrilled when they landed on his doorstep looking for the Lancer. In fact, he got so intense that he'd caused a scene, calling them thieves and managing to get a jab in when Aly was trying to hold him down. But as soon as help came, all they did was scold Julian and apologize to Kara and Aly, who did their damnedest to keep their faces hidden. Apparently Julian had acted up after his dad had died, and his being known as a hothead worked in their favor.

Since then, Aly, Kara, and Pavel had been trailing him, but they kept their distance. Julian was their only connecting thread to the Lancer and the information he should have given her before his death. Kara was sure it had to do with the location of the overwriter—the same technology that Lydia had used to hack into Kara's cube and erase her memories of being Josselyn.

The same technology Lydia had told her about before she died. The one that Kara wanted to destroy.

But first she had to find it, and they didn't have a whole lot to go on. The three of them had combed all available information about the G-1K summits, where the galaxy's scientists got together to develop the cube—but nothing concrete turned up in any of the policies, ethical standards, reports, or updates. Kara even did a deep dive into the conspiracy theories about the overwriter, and some suggested a kind of prototype had been developed in the Outer Belt, which functioned by deleting simple memories stored on people's cubes via a giant shared network that rivaled UniForce's. But Kara already knew that, since it was *her* memories that had once been removed—and it didn't give her any new information. There had always been rumors. They needed something concrete. And their only lead was Julian.

Now, Kara waited for Julian to leave the dojo, like he did every afternoon. She squinted back down at the crowd. Today, she would finally get inside.

"If I could choose any superpower, I'd read your mind," Aly said.

"You don't want to be in there." She shook her head. "It's all messed up."

"I want to see all of it. Even the messed-up parts," Aly told her. He moved closer so that their shoulders were touching. "Especially the messed-up parts."

Kara fought the urge to look over at him but gave in anyway.

"Your eyes," he said softly, their lips a breath apart. She looked at that little spot at the center of his upper lip—where it dipped in just so. "They're changing color again."

Kara blinked. The rest of the world rushed back in; she felt like she'd woken up from a spell.

"Pavel!" she called back, and grabbed his mirror when he rolled close, bringing it to her face.

"I didn't mean anything . . ." Aly had started to say. But Kara shook her head. She saw it: the golden hue of her left iris, the tiny specs of green dotting the center.

"They haven't changed that much," Aly said, backtracking.

Kara's tongue felt thick. They *had* changed. She *was* different. The faint headache suddenly became an intense throbbing behind her right eye. She fished the eyedrops out of her pocket; they had quick-fix DNA-suppression properties to keep her eyes the same color. The liquid burned when she dropped it on her iris.

"Hey," Aly said, taking her hand again. "I don't know why I even said anything. I can barely tell."

She didn't pull away this time, but looked down at the way their fingers interlaced—and how his knuckles were red and raw from everything he'd been through in the last few weeks. It felt like a lifetime had passed since they met on the zeppelin. The world was at war. Everything had changed, including her face.

"You're a terrible liar," she said.

"Four o'clock!" Pavel announced.

Aly squeezed her hand. "We're done with the drills, P," he called behind them.

"Not a drill. Target at four o'clock."

Kara ripped the binoculars from Aly's hand and looked in the direction Pavel had called. There was Julian, exiting a structure, with his telltale slouch. Kara locked eyes for a fleeting moment with Aly before they gathered their things and each threw their *duhatj* on.

"You know what to do, Pavel," Aly called as he and Kara quickly made their way down the ladder. She was so nervous she was half sliding, half falling, and suddenly they had boots on the top floor and were flying down the steps to the street level. She burst out of the door, right into the crowded streets of the protest. Aly was by her side, pulling her back. "Slow it down," he said, adjusting the fabric of her *duhatj*.

But urgency coursed through her limbs. They were going to break into someone's spot. Julian was connected to the Lancer, their only lead—and he'd known Rhee, was friends with her even, judging by how defensive he'd gotten when he saw Kara's matching coin. But they were also in the middle of a protest, surrounded by a whole lot of guards eager to use their stunners if you gave them a reason.

A light flashed again at four o'clock from the lookout point— Pavel's signal of Julian's location. Julian was headed home.

Kara dove into the crowd. Aly was right behind her. The mass pushed forward, chanting and hollering about fair pay and lower export taxes for goods to the moon. She followed with a singular purpose, pushing her way through the crowd as the light hopped from building to building, all in a row, moving farther and farther away. Finally they reached the dome-shaped threshold, and Kara looked up to confirm one last time that the light was far away. She reached behind her to find Aly's hand.

But he was no longer there.

Kara got on the tips of her toes and looked for him, but he was nowhere—lost to the crowd. She'd been sure he was behind her. If she waited she might miss her window of opportunity: From her observations, she'd learned there were only fifteen minutes during the day when the temple was unused. That alone had been enough to convince her that whatever the Lancer had given his son was likely stored there, where it would be under near constant guard.

Looking toward the tower, she raised a hand to signal Pavel. She was going in.

Inside was a short hallway that led her through another threshold, and into a long room with high ceilings. Bamboo mats lined the floor, and a row of wooden pillars ran down the center. Material imported from Kalu, no doubt; there was no way a dusty moon like this had enough water to grow bamboo. Light flooded in through paneled windows all along the east and west walls. It was empty. Still, it vibrated with the intensity and violence she'd always associated with martial arts.

There was a small altar against the wall in the center of the room, with only one holo, one ancestor: Veyron. Otherwise known as the Lancer. Kara had practically memorized his face; she'd come across countless images of him during all the research she'd done in the last two days. In every available image he wore a stark expression: his mouth in a line so straight it was practically a grimace, the high brow and darker coloring of his Wraetan side, the intimidating stare of his ice-blue eyes.

But in this holo he had the hint of a smile, and it was taken outside—the sun's glow warm on his skin making it look tanner, more alive.

Scattered across the altar were simple offerings: a few pieces of fruit, a bowl of grain, and an old stick of incense burned down to its nub. One item stood out: a cylinder made up of small wooden pieces, of all different sizes and lengths, jigsawed together. The whole thing fit into the palm of Kara's hand.

When she lifted it, a beam emitted from its center and panned across her eyes. For a split second, she was blinded. The blue beam widened, and a holo of the galaxy appeared, a sprawling image that took up the length of the dojo and made Kara dizzy with its scope.

Kara heard a door slam behind her. She jumped back, dropping the cube. It clattered to the ground, and the holo disappeared into a sliver.

She turned and saw him. *Julian.* He looked even taller than he had a few days ago. He stood with his feet apart, his hands in fists.

"What are you doing here?"

"I was looking for you," Kara said smoothly. The lie came easy, even if her heart was racing and her head was throbbing. Of all days for Julian to come back . . . She couldn't help but notice he'd blocked the entrance she'd come through—and the exit she'd been intending to use.

His blue eyes fell on the cylinder. Its surfaces had reconfigured into an asymmetrical triangle. "How did you get it to unlock?"

"I didn't unlock it." Kara tried to keep her voice steady as he paced toward her. Could she get around him? There was a second door, on the far side of the room, but she didn't know where it led. "I just picked it up."

"You're lying." Then: "Tell me what it said."

So there was a message. Kara knew that this was what Lydia had intended her to find. That it was a message only Kara—not Julian, not anyone—could have opened.

Outside something slammed into the window. Kara could make out the figure from the inside, a dark form crouching low as it pressed itself against the window. Instinctively Kara and Julian both crouched.

The beating of her heart matched the pounding of her head. Right then and there, Kara made a decision.

When Julian's head was turned toward the window, Kara lunged past him, grabbing the wooden device in her hand.

"No!" He dove for her. His hand caught her foot and she flew forward, knees and elbows breaking her fall. The device tumbled forward, out of her hands—and Julian let her go to scramble for it, but Kara was faster getting to her feet.

Kara scooped up the device and hurtled out the door, relieved to see a staircase. The noise of chanting and shouting in the market was louder here—she was headed in the right direction.

"What did it say?" Julian's voice echoed back to her even as she pinballed up the steps, crashing around the twists and turns, making bruises she'd find only later.

She burst into the sunlight, and threw herself into the rioting crowd.

TWO

RHIANNON

RHEE no longer looked like a Marked child; the suction of the octoerces had faded, and her skin was once again the color of smooth sand. It had been just two days since Rhee announced her homecoming via a hijacked holovision channel. The Fisherman, who had helped Rhee and Dahlen escape from Nero's clutches after he'd found her on Fontis, had then reached out for help to a disparate network of anarchists—who didn't care one bit about restoring Rhee to her crown, but *did* care about the credits they received in return for their assistance. Shuttled in a series of unmarked crafts, flying under the radar of the very army Rhee should command, she arrived on Kalu under the cover of night.

Now, from the backseat of the ground vehicle, she looked out of the tinted glass and saw the streets of Sibu, lined on either side with thousands of Kalusians who'd come out to welcome her home. Colorful paper lanterns were hung all over the capital city, from balconies and over doorways.

Those are for us, Josselyn had said once, when they'd returned from an extended family trip.

You mean they're for me too? Rhee had asked.

That's what us *means,* Joss had said. She had always found a way to make Rhee feel silly and stupid and young. And just when the hope had started to deflate in Rhee's chest, Josselyn had nudged Rhee with her shoulder and smiled. It was then that Rhee knew: They were a team. She was the sidekick. She'd follow Joss anywhere.

She fished the coin out of her pocket. It was from the Bazorl Quadrant, from a time before they used credits. These pieces of metal had held value once, and her father had brought it home from a diplomatic mission. One for her and one for Joss.

Rhee had only recently learned Joss was still alive—that she'd managed to survive the accident that had tragically killed the rest of their family—but Rhee couldn't find her. Joss could be anywhere in the entire galaxy, and Rhee had to abandon her search before it had even started, coming home instead to claim the throne. Nero had forced her hand. He knew Josselyn was alive. The best Rhee could do was offer a reward for her sister's safe return, and hope she could get to her before Nero did. She had to end this war and stop his rise before he wrested control of her rule entirely.

In truth she wanted to kill him too. But she'd spilt enough blood, and she'd learned her revenge fantasies were just that: fantasies. Her trainer, Veyron, was dead. Andres Seotra, former regent to the Kalu crown, was dead. A trail of bodies, of destruction, lay in her wake. She should know better, cut off the thought of revenge at the root because it hadn't paid off, and it wouldn't this time, either. She needed to be smarter, more strategic.

Bloodshed wasn't the answer when she was trying to end a war between Kalu and Fontis. If anything, Nero's murder would only incite *more* violence.

The ground vehicle switched gears, jolting her out of her meditation.

"Don't concern yourself." Dahlen spoke up from the front seat. The Fontisian's eyes in the rearview mirror were gray; they shifted hues depending on the light. "I've scouted out the location, and the central district is where we're the most vulnerable. Extra archers have been placed there and there," he said as he pointed.

Rhee's eye wandered to the tattoos across his neck, detailed swirls that she imagined were beyond painful to receive. He must've mistaken her distant gaze for worry. It was the closest he had ever come to asking whether she was okay.

She searched for the right words, the ones to ground her in this moment, to explain every ounce of emotion that burdened her.

"Thank you for being so thorough."

He'd taken the security detail seriously. But for all his skill in combat, he'd misunderstood the enemy. Nero would never attempt a move against her with so many people watching. She wasn't afraid for her life. She was afraid of his mind—the vindictive ways he used people and pitted them against each other, as if they were all pieces on a chessboard.

Rhee looked down and realized her fists were clenched in the cloth of her dress. Last time she'd worn the ceremonial red dress, Rhee had been forced to kill Veyron, her trainer, the man she had loved like a second father—fought him off with everything she'd had, stabbed him in the heart, and sent him off into space. Because Nero had deemed it so.

Every thought, every memory of Veyron made her chest tighten—and led her back to Julian, his son. He'd been her best friend when there was nothing else good in the world, when her family had died and she'd been cast to Nau Fruma. If Julian discovered her betrayal, it would be one he'd never forgive. She'd finally summoned the courage to reach out to him. Since her cube was off, Rhee had been forced to use a radio telescope—a near-ancient piece of tech—at a safe-house pit stop along the way; she had to speak into a receiver to record her voice, and hope it made its way to the one radio telescope at an observatory on Nau Fruma.

There's so much to tell you.

And if that transmitted to him successfully, someone would have to be at the telescope at the moment it came in to receive it. It was a long shot, but the only one Rhee had.

She wasn't sure what he might have heard about his father's death, or what he might believe, but she'd needed to try—and if she failed to get through to him this time, she'd try again and again. If he was attempting to get hold of her, Rhee wouldn't know. If she finally succeeded, what *would* she say? Did she know about her part in Veyron's death? Would she tell him?

Honor. Bravery. Loyalty. It was her mantra, her *ma'tan sarili*, her highest self. Rhee focused on the spot between her eyes, and felt a touch of numbness that grew through her skull until everything was clear, dark, without context, and without pain.

When she'd centered herself, she opened her eyes to see Dahlen scowling out the windshield. She'd never seen him smile, and she wondered if she ever would. Especially not since what had happened on Houl, when Nero made Dahlen turn on his cube, forcing him to violate one of the sacred vows of the order.

Since then, Dahlen had become both more intense and more withdrawn, though she hadn't thought either possible.

"Are you okay?" Rhee wished she'd sat in the front, by his side, rather than have him up front alone as if he were hired help. Why hadn't she thought of it earlier? If he'd registered her question, she couldn't be sure—but she noticed the ends of his pointy ears went red.

"The Fisherman chose the snipers personally," Dahlen said. "You won't miss them, if you look closely."

Rhee decided not to press it. There would be time to talk later. Squinting out the window, she saw archers were placed strategically within each of the Twin Towers of the Long Now. The rounded white buildings had lush, green terraces spiraling up their length—a new addition to the city in the six years she'd been gone. These were the DroneVision headquarters, where Nero himself lived—and she didn't doubt he had his own snipers strategically placed.

She was glad for Dahlen, his command, his archers. Her Tasinn, the royal guard that had protected the Ta'an family for generations of rule, could no longer be trusted in the transition of power. As far as Rhee was concerned, they worked for Nero. It was a Tasinn who'd dragged her to Nero's little production, when he had lorded over Dahlen's body, prepared to extract his cube, to Ravage his memories on the spot. It was only weeks before, but so much had happened.

Maybe they believed the same silly fairy tale Nero spun over and over again: He was going to improve Kalu's standing in the galaxy. He'd focus on getting the crops back in order, bring all the farmers back, revive an industry long dead so they could find wealth once more. An exclusive, thriving world—just for them.

"Them" being the wealthy second-wavers who'd built their fortune on Kalu's agricultural industry. But they had squeezed it dry, demanding too great a yield from the planet's natural resources so they could sell it to the highest bidder on some far-flung planet. Now the second-wavers watched their fortunes dwindle, and blamed nearly anyone except themselves and their own terrible choices. Which is why they wanted all the immigrants and Wraetan refugees out.

Behind the confetti, the roses, the hopeful mood that had infused the city, an undercurrent of tension buzzed everywhere. Kalu was at war with Fontis. Even if you couldn't see it here, you could feel it. They'd passed people holding the Kalusian flag upside down, witnessed signs of poverty at the base of the lush, gleaming tower.

Rhee had anticipated her homecoming would infuriate Nero's supporters; she had come to displace him, after all, and reclaim the throne and leadership of all of Kalu. But Nero remained as slick as oil when it was announced she was returning home.

"Thank the ancestors," he'd said, citing those he did not pray to, and a religion he did not practice. The public ate it up. Never mind the fact he'd been publicly rallying to avenge her death by going to war with Fontis; he could hardly admit to having been the one to orchestrate her attempted assassination.

From what she could tell on the holos she'd watched during her flight here, dissenters were in the minority—a loud minority, however. It was nothing Rhee hadn't heard before: that she was too young, too beholden to her family's dynasty, too attached to the monarchy that had led the planet down the wrong path.

But now she saw their ranks had swelled. Or were there always this many people who welcomed the war with Fontis?

Humiliation started to sink down into her bones as they passed a burning effigy of a brown doll in a red dress and black yarn for hair. There were cheers. Then a woman snatched it away and threw it on the ground, stomping the limp figure; Rhee wasn't sure if she'd done it to put out the fire or to demonstrate what she thought of the Empress.

She looked away. Was it true? Was she as young and naïve as they accused her of being? It was clear now more than ever that the second-wavers were becoming a sort of ruling class. They led the charge on the anti-immigrant, anti-refugee—and now, the growing anti-native—sentiment here in Sibu. And if they were against native blood it meant they were against the Ta'an. Against her. They hadn't even given Rhee the chance to fail.

Instead they gravitated toward Nero—an evil, corrupt killer. The masses had already come to love watching him night after night on DroneVision for over a decade as the ambassador to the regent, and thus had come to trust him too. Earlier that morning, he had announced a territory-wide update to the cube operating system—the first in years—and a rollout was already in progress for those who opted in. The holos were broadcasting the news across the system. It gave Rhee a tight knot in her stomach, though an update seemed innocent enough. Everything Nero did was twisted at the root.

He may have tricked an entire solar system into thinking that he was their champion, but Rhee *would* help them. Her father had said being a ruler was difficult, sometimes thankless—and such a remark had puzzled her. Everywhere they'd gone he was showered with praise, with gifts, asked to dole out blessings, people longing to touch him with their outstretched hands.

Now she understood an inkling of that sentiment.

She'd end the war. Two wars, in fact: a war where soldiers were sent off to die, and the emotional war for the hearts and minds of her own people, here, in the very city she was born. Nero had been a heartbeat away from proclaiming himself regent. She'd temporarily snatched the position from him, but he would never cede power so easily—even if he had ostensibly agreed to step back.

She would do what her father had done, and unite everyone in peace. Even if the way she might achieve that peace was as thorny and thick in her mind as one of the dozen-armed cacti in the desert of Nau Fruma. The only certainty Rhee had was that she was a Ta'an. She could do it. She had to.

As she and Dahlen and the rest of her guards moved toward the center city, traffic narrowed to a slow crawl. The streets were packed with Kalusian citizens. UniForce soldiers struggled to keep them behind cordons. Rhee hoped that UniForce was still loyal to her, not Nero—she could replace the Tasinn, who were a small, elite force of personal guards to the crown. But she couldn't replace the entire UniForce army.

Daisies were everywhere—auto-cams on constant stream. They were technically called "day-sees" because of the light mounted on the bottom, but the word had been slurred over time into "daisies." They swarmed the windows of their vehicle, while Dahlen's handpicked guard of Fontisians rode madùcycles on either side and swatted them away.

"Rhiannon!" a voice screamed, loud enough to rise above the chorus.

She saw a man crawl over a barrier and make a gesture so obscene as their vehicle passed that Rhee almost looked away. The man was tackled by one of Dahlen's Fontisian guards, who'd gracefully launched himself off his madùcycle. He had the man's head to the ground within seconds. Rhee swiveled to look behind her as they sped past.

"Ancestors!" Rhee hissed. "Can't your men be more gentle?" She didn't want the Fontisian guard to give protesters more cause for unrest.

"Don't forget that they're *your* men," he said.

She didn't answer. It's not how the Kalusians would see it. The guards were all Fontisian, and like Dahlen they were part of the Order of the Light, a fundamentalist Fontisian religious group. The order was obsessed with maintaining peace, even if that meant working with Kalu and supporting Ta'an rule. They'd favored her father; he'd brokered peace between their two planets and ended the Great War all those years ago.

But that didn't mean the average Kalusian would be welcoming. To any Kalusian, a Fontisian was an outsider. Here was Rhee—their one true ruler, returned from the dead—flanked on all sides by security that, with their white-blond hair and sharp faces, looked a hell of a lot like the enemy. Judging by some of the sneers and looks of real fear in the eyes of the crowd, she wondered whether it had been a good idea for the order to take such a prominent role in protecting her.

But no one else had offered to.

"I don't want to get off on the wrong foot. The order already has a reputation of being . . ." She searched for the right word.

"Fanatical? Violent? Aggressive?" Dahlen reached down to shift gears roughly. The vehicle was self-driving, but as usual, Dahlen took no chances. He was worried, he said, that the tech would be hacked by Nero's cronies; there would be no accidents today.

"I'm trying to make friends of enemies," she said defensively.

"We will not apologize for our presence." He scanned the packed streets of Kalusians as they passed. Fontisians spoke in negatives; it made everything they said sound forceful and stubborn. Though perhaps it was because they *were* forceful and stubborn. "Such a stance isn't an adequate strategy when it comes to dissenters."

"Yes, because you have ruling a planet all figured out?"

He cocked his eyebrow as they stared at one another through the mirror. "Because *you* do, Empress?"

Rhee exhaled slowly but wouldn't respond—she was working on staying calmer, hiding her feelings better. That word, *Empress*, still felt wrong. She remembered when Julian had called her "Empress" in the Nau Fruma marketplace, as the meteors rained down above them the very last time she saw him, how the title had filled her with dread.

Her purpose, then, had at least felt clear, violent but uncomplicated. One life for many. Seotra's for her family's. But Seotra had been innocent. Her vengeance had been misguided, and she'd ended up killing one of her most powerful allies.

Her purpose was different now, though just as clear as before—to bring about peace.

They crested the hill, and for the first time in six years, Rhee caught sight, at last, of the palace. It took her breath away. It was the only thing from her childhood that had lived up to its memory—her organic memory. It was a feeling, different than the memories she had replayed on her cube, better than the crystalline perfection that made it seem smaller and quaint on her cube. In person, it was majestic. Red and gold, one thousand steps leading up to its entrance. The sun, as it set, looked as if it were slowly lowering itself on the southernmost spire—pierced open, and dripping fire on the orange, backlit sky.

As enormous, as beautiful, as vast as it was, what struck her the hardest was how strongly she sensed her father. She could see him pacing the marble corridors just hours before they'd leave for good because of the growing threat to their lives; her mother's sobs that same night bouncing between pillars in the fountain room. Only hours later, the craft that was supposed to take them to safety on Nau Fruma had exploded, killing them both. When she recalled a memory organically, like she did now, she experienced it with every sense, every facility she had. She was transported in time.

Cube memories weren't like that at all. The cube was precise; it rushed to the very moment you needed it to and then pulled away with the same cold efficiency. Not that it mattered—she'd temporarily turned off her cube so that they couldn't be tracked while they traveled.

But there was another reason she hadn't turned her cube back on. A deeper, unspoken fear she couldn't yet voice: Nero's ambition to find the overwriter. Rhee didn't think it existed. Not really. It was a technology without precedent, and anytime she'd heard of it, it was only in conjunction with the G1-K conspiracy theories. Only those on the fringes believed—or those, like Nero, who were prone to dramatics and flair, ready to chase down any mirage to secure his reign.

Imagine being able to speak through any cube, he'd said on Houl, *to anyone at will, throughout the whole universe. Imagine being able to whisper to them, not through their ears but their minds . . .*

Terror and revulsion snaked their way through her. But she didn't feel ready to tell Dahlen, not yet—not when the trauma of that night so obviously haunted him still.

Nero had unofficially taken up residence in the palace after Rhee's supposed death. But her return had forced him to retreat, physically in this case. Still, her adviser Tai Reyanna and her friend the Fisherman had been sent ahead to clear out the palace of any remaining Tasinn and install the Fontisian guard and private security that could be trusted. It had been a flurry of prep in just a week's time between vetting loyalists and transporting them in secret.

Dahlen nudged the vehicle forward through the tall iron gates, nodding at the two Fontisian guards as he passed. The guards closed the gate quickly behind them, against a surge in the crowd—some people crying, reaching out toward their pod, and others protesting, spitting as they passed. She vaguely made out the chant: "No more sharks!" but she couldn't be sure. The slur for Fontisians grated against her ears, making her ashamed of her own people.

As the gates closed, she saw a fight break out. A man had thrown another to the ground, and they'd been swallowed up in the center of the crowd. She sat up straighter to get a better look. Dahlen powered down the vehicle, and for a brief moment Rhee thought she heard the engine ticking off the last of its charge. But that was her heart: not a drumbeat, but a kind of wild crackling.

"There's a fight," she said to Dahlen.

"There are fights everywhere. We're not to exit until the guards on the stairs are in place and they've ensured—"

Before he could finish, she shouldered the door open and stood to face the crowd and look for the fight. The Fontisian guards rushed down the stairs toward her, but she held up both hands, demanding that they stay back. Dahlen had gotten out himself and walked calmly around the vehicle, like he was stalking his prey, but stopped at a fair distance—just a few feet behind her, nodding at his guards to follow her order.

Rhee's red dress flapped in the wind. She was close enough to the gate that the hem of her skirt pressed through the gaps in the iron rails. She put her hand to the metal, and the crowd grew silent. She'd say something now. Reassure them she was here, that the war would end, that peace would be restored. She felt their belief welling inside her, and for the first time, commanding the presence of her people, she felt a genuine ability to change the tide.

Her eyes latched onto a blonde girl in the front ranks a few paces away on the steps. She held a bow and arrow and her hair had been gathered in a thick braid that draped down her shoulder, practically alive, like a long white snake that she could charm. The girl's eyes were a hazel shade, yellows and oranges threaded through her irises like the color of a Nau Fruman sunset.

The girl opened her mouth, as if to call words of encouragement.

And then from the other side of the gate, an egg launched into the air. There was a vacuum of silence, as if the thousands of people clamoring forward had held their breath.

It landed with a crunch three meters short of where Rhee stood, and for a split second she was hyperaware, focused on nothing but the vivid yolk pooling sadly against the drive.

Then everything exploded. Whole pockets of the crowd seemed to collapse, tumbling people down beneath its weight. She flinched as protesters threw even more things. Trash. Rotten pulp of long-turned fruit. Glass bottles that shattered at her feet. Her supporters turned on them. She heard screaming.

Through the screams she heard a hoarse whisper, as someone from the crowd grabbed her through the rails. Iron pressed into her face. "Daddy's girl better watch her back."

"No one wants you here!"

"You took your sister's throne!"

Rhee yanked herself free. Something was spinning toward her, straight at her face. She dodged and nearly went down. Glass shattered with a high and hysterical noise. Gravel blasted her cheek. They were throwing bottles.

Dahlen grabbed her arm.

"Let go!" She struggled to regain her balance, stepping backward on her dress and feeling the hem rip. In a panic, she thought of the cameras watching, recording every second of this—everyone across the galaxy would see that she was afraid, that she had no idea what she was doing. Nero would make sure of it. And even worse, she realized, was that it was true. When other rulers might have spent years cultivating a relationship with the public, she'd been planning Seotra's death on another moon, in a foolish desire for vengeance. She'd been wrong. Now she felt like a fool. Naïve, like so many had said. "Let me go."

She managed to wrench free of Dahlen. She started to yell—she wasn't sure what, and couldn't have been heard over the crowd, anyway—when she heard it: a high-pitched squeal like a firework shooting up into the air.

Not a firework, though.

It struck the top of the nearby tower in silence. Rhee hoped it was a trick of the light. Then a massive blast of fire, and a deep rumble as pieces of the marble tower cracked away, sifted through the air, masses of stone as big as the vehicle that had carried them.

The crowd split. More screams. They dove for cover as the first stones hit with an impact that shook Rhee through her feet all the way to her teeth. Dahlen found her again, and didn't bother with her hand this time; he hauled her over his shoulder and ran.

They crashed through the double doors into the palace as more of the marble came shuddering down from the sky. Fontisian guards streamed in behind them before the doors closed with a resounding echo. From outside came the noise of splintering, screams as protesters crashed through the barriers, shouts and thuds as the guards drove them backward. The UniForce soldiers that had been present earlier had mysteriously disappeared, and left the riot to fester into this. More bottles exploded against the palace, and several eggs too. They shimmered on the window-panes, their yolks like suns dying in miniature.

Empress Rhiannon was home.